the Ministry of

DAWN

D0392964

"A good bet for steampunk fans." —*Library Journal*

"Ballantine and Morris's third entry in the Ministry of Peculiar Occurrences raises the bar for the entire series—and for urban fantasy as a genre. Extensive world-building, multi-faceted characters, fast-paced action, and an engaging plot all make for a thrilling, absorbing read . . . [An] expertly woven story." —*RT Book Reviews*

"*Dawn's Early Light* does not disappoint. It's full of action, explosions, and deceit." —*Seattle Geekly*

"Cute and charming, interspersed with sequences of dire peril and explosive action . . . You don't want to miss a delicious moment of the story." —*Kings River Life Magazine*

"Richly detailed, complex, and full of action . . . [Books and Braun] make an amazing team . . . Another great tale in the amazingly creative and entertaining Ministry of Peculiar Occurrences series." —*That's What I'm Talking About*

THE JANUS AFFAIR

"An amazing read, filled with wonderful characters, detailed world-building, and an intriguing plot . . . I cannot wait for the next installment." —*Badass Book Reviews*

"A fun romp through a London featuring housekeepers with mechanical legs, automated bartenders, hypersteam trains, and restaurants on airships." —*Steampunk Chronicle*

continued . . .

THE DIAMOND CONSPIRACY

**PIP BALLANTINE
& TEE MORRIS**

ACE BOOKS, NEW YORK

THE BERKLEY PUBLISHING GROUP
Published by the Penguin Group
Penguin Group (USA) LLC
375 Hudson Street, New York, New York 10014

USA • Canada • UK • Ireland • Australia • New Zealand • India • South Africa • China

penguin.com

A Penguin Random House Company

THE DIAMOND CONSPIRACY

An Ace Book / published by arrangement with the authors

Ace Books are published by The Berkley Publishing Group.
ACE and the "A" design are trademarks of Penguin Group (USA) LLC.

For information, address: The Berkley Publishing Group,
a division of Penguin Group (USA) LLC,
375 Hudson Street, New York, New York 10014.

ISBN: 978-0-425-26732-5

PUBLISHING HISTORY
Ace mass-market edition / April 2015

PRINTED IN THE UNITED STATES OF AMERICA

10 9 8 7 6 5 4 3 2 1

Cover art by Dominick Finelle.
Cover design by Lesley Worrell.
Interior text design by Kelly Lipovich.

To the talented authors we have worked with on Tales from the Archives and Ministry Protocol.

And to the equally talented curators and fact finders of the International Spy Museum in Washington, DC. This is our tip of the bowler hat to what you do.

ACKNOWLEDGEMENTS

Like Ministry agents, we rely on our backup team in the field, so it would be churlish not to mention the assistance we received for this book.

Thanks to Danielle Stockley and Susan Allison for guiding us on the path with the Ministry and keeping us free of the House of Usher.

Appreciation to our agent, Laurie McLean, and the talented team at Fuse Literary for providing logistical support in the field.

We thank Mildred Cady, Marie Bilodeau, and Marcus Gilman for help with languages beyond our reach, so we didn't put our foot in the cultural divide.

Our temporary intern of Awesome, K. T. Bryski earned our thanks for providing cover while we were under fire of deadlines and promotion.

And finally to all the fans and readers who have supported us with cosplay, fanart, comments, and hurrahs along the way, thank you for your support.

ONE

❧

Wherein Miss Braun and Mr. Books
Come to an Understanding

"Welly, would you please listen to me for just a moment?"
"Why is it that you just cannot admit that my mind
is much like my word in this—final!"

"There's no reason to snap at me!"

Wellington Thornhill Books, Esquire, knew he was still
exhausted, even after a brief rest he and his partner, Eliza D.
Braun, took upon their hurried departure from California. Considering the past thirty-six hours, an extension of the previous
eighty-four, their harrowing adventure had simply led straight
onto another assignment from their director at the Ministry of
Peculiar Occurrences. It was, indeed, hard to grasp that only
four days prior to their present altitude over the Atlantic, they
were in the Arizona Territories, held at gunpoint by a female
priest who apparently doubled as a bounty hunter. A gunfight
and shared deduction around his analytical engine later, they
were giving his masterpiece of engineering a field test of the
highest order. The motorcar, an unexpected boon from Doctor
Sound, who had apparently found the means to have it expe-
dited to Lakehurst, New Jersey, Eliza had dubbed the *Ares:
Mark I*. It was a designation he found a tad melodramatic . . .

. . . but now, after inspecting and servicing the mechanical wonder, Wellington considered it quite catchy.

So even though he was bone weary, and therefore slightly short-tempered, he could not understand why she was pressing the matter. "Miss Braun, let us agree that I have a far more intimate understanding of my motorca—"

"The *Ares*," she corrected him.

"All right, yes, very well, the *Ares*." Eliza crooked an eyebrow at him which took him a moment to interpret, but not as long as the previous one. He gave a heavy sigh, and added, "*Mark One*."

"By giving your motorcar a name and designation," she began, "you will have more of a bond with the weapon, a relationship, if you will. The better a relationship you have with your sidearms and weapon of choice, the more efficient and proficient you will become with them."

"Really?" Wellington gave a dry laugh. "As if you have given your own arsenal such personality."

"But I have," she insisted. "My *pounamu* pistols for example. Heinemoa and Tutanekai."

He blinked at her. "Are you telling me—" He shook his head. "You can't tell the two apart."

"Of course I can," Eliza said in a very sharp manner. "Heinemoa shoots better. Longer range, I tend to favour her over Tutanekai."

"Well now there's a surprise." He pursed his lips tight. "But when it comes to"—he glanced at Eliza—"*Ares*, I know its schematics and internal mechanics far better than you."

"And when it comes to weapons, I know some things better than you." Wellington went to counter, but she held up a hand between them. "I'm not saying I'm a better shot. I'm going to concede to that . . . for the time being." She approached him, standing well within kissing distance. "The Gatling guns in the headlights are impressive. Deliciously so, I would add. Your problem isn't firepower. It's weight."

"Weight?" Wellington asked, crossing his arms in what he knew was a defensive gesture. He had taken into consideration all aspects of wear and tear the field could muster.

At least, he *thought* he had.

"Yes. Weight. We were able to manoeuvre quite deftly against

Edison's motortrucks, but they were lumbering behemoths to begin with. What about the motorcar that came straight at us at the Montara Light? There was no way we could out-manoeuvre something like that. You did stop it with a rocket, yes. One of two. Wouldn't it have been ducky if you could have allowed for more of those little firecrackers?"

"No space was available," Wellington insisted. "I had two Gatling guns in the front and—"

"And one under the tumble seat." Eliza gave him a light slap on the forehead. "*Ares* needs to be a swift attack vehicle, not a bloody tank!"

Wellington opened his mouth to protest, but paused. Had he really been in the Archives for so long that he had never considered his motorcar as anything other than an armoured juggernaut?

Still, the forward guns needed stopping power. "So what do you propose for a replacement?"

"Swap them out for the new Maxims. More compact design."

The Maxim design was a tad more streamlined. *Dashitall,* he thought to himself. "The .303 calibre shells are a slight drop," he countered.

"Welly, you're shooting up to six hundred rounds per minute, and that is before you modify them. Which I know you will." And she was right. Again. "You're going to do damage either way, even going with a lower calibre bullet."

"But recommending a lower calibre?" He shook his head. This couldn't be happening. "You?"

Eliza sighed. "Instead of making some crass joke about size, I will simply say this—the Maxims are good enough for the Avro five-tens tethered on this magnificent transatlantic cruiser. They will be good enough for *Ares.*"

"Indeed."

Eliza grinned, and even with the grease smudges and grit in her skin, she looked positively stunning. "See? You're already losing arguments to me. You're getting the hang of this relationship. Well done!"

With a chuckle, Wellington stole a quick kiss from her lips. In the corridor, no less, where anyone could see them. He actually found the gesture quite liberating.

"Did I happen to mention," Eliza said, her voice lowering

into a most intimate tone, "I am so damn happy to be on this transatlantic flight with you and hours of nothing to do but to"—she leaned forwards to whisper in his ear—"stay in bed?"

The images that raced through his brain quite unhinged whatever witty comment he might have flung back. By the time Wellington had recovered, Eliza had turned a little to the long window that revealed the grand expanse that was the Atlantic Ocean, the sky around them clinging to sparse sunlight. Soon it would be night. Dinner, no doubt, with the stars providing atmosphere along with the *Atlantic Angel*'s in-flight musicians. With dusk quickly falling and their own airship driving into the night, they could both enjoy a leisurely meal. Tonight appeared to be shaping up as their first opportunity to take a breath and enjoy one another's company. All night long.

Finally.

"It was quite the jaunt, but I am ready to go home," Eliza said. When she faced him again, she slipped her hand under his arm and against his side. She clearly didn't care if they were improper between their appearance and public behaviour, because truthfully he was having rather improper thoughts. Why were they not having this conversation alone, in their quarters, while getting undressed? "But I do have one little question: are you still going to call me 'Miss Braun'?" Eliza gave a little shrug but this tiny detail rattled her without question. "Not that I don't find it charming and all, but there are limits."

The archivist looked into her eyes, and did his best to deal a smile that would pin her to the spot. This time he would not shy away, make an excuse, or say anything that would pull them apart. Instead, with his own grease-and-grime-stained fingers, he traced along her jawline with the back of his fingers—right there, in public. Between this and the quick kiss he had stolen from her earlier, she must have thought him very forward. Good.

"No," he said softly, "I shall only call you 'Miss Braun' when we are on the Ministry's time. In all else, I shall call you Eliza, Rose of the Southern Hemisphere, Athena of Aotearoa, Avenging Angel of Her Majesty's Empire . . ." He paused as her cheeks coloured from repressed laughter. ". . . and anything else that springs to mind."

On this journey, not the one home but this personal one with Eliza at his side, Wellington anticipated many moments like this. Moments of discovery, and he found himself wanting to discover even more. She leaned into his hand, even as her eyes darted around the viewing promenade. This was in earnest the first time they had a moment's tranquillity. The last airship out of Oakland followed the chaos and calamity that had befallen San Francisco so closely, the tension was palpable. For their own selves, this tension did little to prevent them from surrendering to fatigue. They lost most of the following day, as well, catching up on well-earned, desperately needed rest, awakening to their new orders, hurried travel arrangements, and—on catching at Station Lakehurst the connecting flight arranged by Doctor Sound—replenishing *Ares'* arsenal and carrying out a few in-flight modifications. With their own chariot of the heavens continuing into the night, the sudden peace and quiet they found unsettling.

Eliza smiled sideways at her partner, now the gesture meaning something more to him. "We have a few days to pass the time, and for once I think the Maestro, the Ministry, and even the director himself won't be popping up to spoil the damn moment."

As she leaned closer to him, he heard his own breath catch in his throat, and he could see that pleased her. This was such undiscovered country for him, but it was nice to know that he could make her smile so brightly with such a simple thing as being surprised. Eliza squeezed his hand. "I seem to recall that once you helped me out of my corset. Do you think you could do the same again?"

This time, when he wrapped his arms around her, pulling her against him, she gasped. It was a rather satisfying sound. "Eliza, last time I cut you loose from your corset, that was out of concern for a fellow agent. Right now, we are no longer serving at Her Majesty's behest. Therefore, I want to take my time."

They walked hand in hand back towards their stateroom. Wellington glanced at the temporary nameplate on the door. They were travelling under the names Mr. and Mrs. Lawrence, honeymooning in the United States and returning home to London. Once upon a time, Wellington considered, the cost for such luxury would have come out of his own pocket, even with the suite being the only room available at such short notice. However, as active agents, they were given appropriate lodging for their cover.

The bottle of champagne chilling in their stateroom, ordered while they were working on the *Ares*, was his offering, though. He could hardly be expected to have the Ministry director compensate such an extravagance.

Wellington had let her go in ahead of him; but after he shut the door, they collided like two objects hurled at each other. Her lips were strong and firm, and there was no single sign of hesitation. Hardly ladylike or of a fashion that the circles he grew up in would have approved of, but he hardly cared about such decorum now. That life was now a distant memory. From the way her hands roamed about his body, tore away at his coat and braces, she needed him as much as he needed her. Burying her hands in his hair, she pulled him against her as his own hands busied themselves pulling her clothing loose. Even her corset proved to be no hindrance.

Somehow they managed to pull themselves free of the wall and tumble back onto the bed, their lips and hands never losing contact. Quite the triumph.

Soon enough they found themselves taking full advantage of both the luxury of time with each other, and their stateroom's shower. He felt as if he were finally ridding himself of the dust, grime, and grit of his first sanctioned mission in the field as a Ministry agent, and at last able to show Eliza how much she truly meant to him. It had to be the longest shower Wellington had ever taken. Even when it came to the rare times he would indulge in a bath, he would never linger like he did presently. There was too much to do, too much to tend to.

Perhaps it was an illusion of the moment, not that he minded, but the water tasted sweeter off her skin. He could tell he was surprising Eliza, and could not help but smile when their lips locked. He not only needed to keep artefacts organised for the Ministry, it also fell upon him to keep the records, know the facts, understand the nuances of a case. That, coupled with his father's insistence on intimately knowing human physiology—presumably to make him a more efficient killer—offered him a rather sound foundation for intimacy.

The water, the soap, their hands exploring one another's bodies, it all became such a succulent medley of sensations that they allowed themselves surrender. If this was, in fact, what field agents did to unwind after a mission, Wellington could understand why Eliza was so desperate to return to it.

Eventually they abandoned the water, and tumbled into bed, giggling and breathless. The long line of her muscled back under his hands issued the most sensual ripples of lust throughout him, and he pulled her close, far closer than he had ever dared to possibly imagine. They traced each other's scrapes and bruises from this jaunt across the United States, lying tangled, warm, and cosy in the sheets.

"Quite the most dangerous woman I have known," he quipped, planting a series of little kisses across her ribs where the skin was purple and red.

"Considering your past with Sophia del Morte I will choose to take that as a compliment." She rolled over onto her front and traced her fingers down his chest.

Wellington tilted his head back. "Don't remind me. I am quite anxious enough sharing this bed with you. I would rather not be distracted by the thought she is somewhere out in the darkness, unattended." He rolled his eyes, giving a dry chortle as he added, "God be with any man to whom she has tethered herself."

"I don't think I like you talking about her while you are in bed with me," Eliza mused. She nipped at his neck. "And there is no need for you to be anxious, nervous, or even slightly unnerved in sharing a bed with me. I'm your partner. Your safety comes first."

"No need to hold back on my account." He twisted under her, pinning her to the bed in a nice bit of wrestling. "I assure you, my darling Eliza, I am most capable of—"

He suddenly felt something wrap around his waist and toss him to one side. By the time he had realised it was her leg that had slipped in the modest space between their torsos, hooked against his side, and then used his overconfidence as leverage—dear Lord, but Eliza was flexible!—he was flat on his back with this formidable agent now pinning him to the bed.

"—getting rather full of yourself?" she purred, her eyes dancing in the warm light of their suite.

His tactical mind wanted to know how she was managing to pin him so effectively to their bed, but the rest of him decided not to bother. This was a particularly lovely place to be at present.

"As we have nowhere else to be but here, Wellington Thornhill Books, let us enjoy tonight. No Italian assassins. No mechanised maniacs. Just us. How does that sound?"

"As my senior agent, I yield to your better judgement."

Her laugh was breathy. When she smiled at him, Wellington was hers. "Lesson One: The Art of Taking Your Time."

She took another kiss from him, merely the soft pressing of lips against each other. The hunger and lust were not there, but the want and passion were. He didn't need to ask her to know that for her—as it was for him—this was more than a mere tumble in the hay.

Looking into her eyes, Wellington shook his head, for once quite without words. Her long red-brown hair provided a curtain around their faces, sealing off the world—which was just as he wanted it.

As he fell deeper into her erotic embrace he could only wish their airship would encounter a headwind. *Yes,* he thought languidly to himself, *this is how it should be. For a moment, let the Empire and those within it fend for themselves.*

INTERLUDE

❦

Wherein the Arrogance of Youthful Friends Proves Costly

With Miss Eliza D. Braun currently out of the country, the Ministry Seven fell short of its lofty ideals and what Miss Eliza called "ethics." Christopher realised that, even as he held open the tiny kitchen window for Serena to crawl through. Liam was the one who had given her the boost, and slippery as an eel, the youngest of the gang was granted entry to these fashionable apartments. Miss Eliza may have accepted what he and the rest of the Ministry Seven did in order to survive, but there was a difference between acceptance and approval.

A little larceny Christopher justified here as a good way to keep their skills honed, as well as their reputation on the street intact. Much as it would disappoint her, it would not do to have Miss Eliza come back to find them accustomed to toasted muffins and clean clothes. Even with their misleading name, the Ministry Seven were her eyes and ears in the City, and this meant that all eight of them would need to dabble in the odd confidence game, a bit of tooling, or—as it was tonight—helping themselves to a toffken.

Just thinking of Miss Eliza and Mr. Harry—God rest his

soul—brought a smile to Christopher's face. Yet, lurking in the back of his mind was one rotten thought: even the ones with good intentions like Miss Eliza could go missing, especially with what her chosen profession demanded. This world devoured people, good and bad but usually it was the good ones first, leaving nothing except memories to remember them by. His own people had been mudlarks, and been lost to the Thames years before. Christopher hadn't been prepared for that.

Then there'd be Verity Fitzroy, their leader and guardian before Eliza. She'd taken care of them, and then she "grew up." That was when Christopher became their leader.

We have to be ready for the worst, Christopher thought. *Take whatever chances Miss Eliza gave them, but always be ready to go back to screwing and the jolly.*

"You coming or what?" Liam whispered, and Christopher spun around to see that Serena had already opened the door to the fancy doctor's house. He blushed red. Kidsmen shouldn't be caught daydreaming like right nitwits.

It was only five of them on this job. The twins were on another lark down in the West End, and Eric had a hacking cough that would have given the game away immediately. So he was back being nursed by Alice, which also turned out to be a nice way to keep her busy. Having spent time in the workhouse like the rest of them, she knew the game pretty well, and was actually harder to fool than Miss Eliza. She was a sharp one.

At least with one of them being sick, that appeared to soothe those crazy mothering instincts of hers. Alice could not have forced them to stay at Miss Eliza's apartments, but the maid would be mightily annoyed if she knew that they were taking the opportunity to rumble a doctor's house. No doubt hot baths and scrubbing brushes for all would have been a consequence. She did insist on far too many hot baths.

"See," Serena said, shutting the door silently behind her. "You come see if I ain't right—this gent is well-off."

Christopher raised his eyebrow, tucked his hands into his pockets and strolled into the quarters. "So you and Callum did a reconnoitre of the house then?" He liked using some of those fancy words Verity had taught him now and then. It made him look educated . . . which in these surroundings he felt he needed.

Serena followed on his heels. "Sure did. Today is the maid's day off, and master of the house hasn't been around."

"What d'ya mean he's not been around?"

"Normally, the good doctor's up at the palace like clockwork before a sparrow's fart, but past few days, we've not seen hide nor hair of him. Just been the maid."

He was impressed, though he didn't say so. Callum and Serena had been trying to show him despite being the youngest they were ready for jobs of their own. It was, he admitted to himself, not a bad wee score.

Liam and Colin were scoping out upstairs while Callum kept watch at the window, just in case the good doctor decided to stroll home early. Serena led Christopher into the front office, and he let out a long whistle. His gaze first alighted on a burnished oak desk and fancy green leather chair set in a grand room of scarlet and gold. He took it all in. The massive library. The fine couches. The grandest of grandfather clocks. And—

Why would a doctor have a map of the world, then? Seemed a little out of place for this plush study.

"So what's this doctor do exactly?" he asked, while following with his eyes the line of books out to the bay window overlooking a little garden in need of tending. Could that window serve as an entry point if they wanted to stage something grander than this quick haul?

Serena shrugged. "Not sure really. Something with the toffs. Think he has another office for taking their money on Harley Street, but he ain't never gone down to the East End, that's for sure."

She was a smart kid; Christopher had to give her marks for understanding what he was thinking. Though the Ministry Seven weren't much for doctors, he harboured a small respect for those rich doctoring folk that dared the industrial parts of London town, got their hands dirty, and risked catching God knows what. He had seen his own fair share of those bastards what gave the idea they cared about the Queen's lesser subjects, but it was nothing more than a toff's flam. The doctors of this district working in the rookery, though, all had a different look about them. Something in the eyes, which Christopher noticed. So it was right quick that Serena had sized up this mark as someone that didn't do that, otherwise it felt like stealing from their own.

The only childhood story he could still remember his mother telling him before he was on his own had been Robin Hood. Robbing from the rich and giving to the poor. That was the kind of larceny he felt was his gang's speciality. Stealing from their own kind felt too much like cannibalism.

"Fair mark then," he said, shooting Serena a quick smile. "Go check out the parlour for anything easy to fence. I'll turn the office over."

Once the girl scampered out, Christopher cast his practised eye over the library again, not really expecting to understand any of the titles butting against one another. The line of books was all leather-bound and luxurious, and if reading had been a better practise for Christopher, he might have answered his earlier question to Serena—what kind of doctor was this mark? First Verity and then Eliza had taught him the basics; because of that, he knew what he was looking for.

There were a few that had creases and marks on their spines, showing wear and tear in being pulled out and put back in on a regular basis. Then his eyes fell on a particular book that had what appeared to be a perfectly fine, unmarred spine, save for the cracking at the top—and only the top—of the binding.

Christopher flicked that one out, and immediately knew it was not all it claimed to be. Doctors took money from rich clients, and sometimes they tried to outsmart what they considered the ignorant folk. The weight was off, and sure enough, only its cover opened to reveal a hollowed-out centre holding a few precious gold coins and a small wad of notes—a treasure for the Seven. Quickly pocketing them to be divided up later, the young man returned the empty peter back to the shelves, and resumed his search through the books. If there was one, there had to be more.

On a shelf just above where he had found the bounty he saw another book and it seemed odd to be there shelved amongst words common for a toff.

"*Through the Looking-Glass*?" he whispered to himself as he reached up for it.

"Find anything?" a voice blurted from behind him.

Christopher practically leapt out of his coat, spinning on his feet to face Callum, the other mastermind behind this break-in.

"Cor' blimey, Callum!" Christopher swore. He took in a breath, shaking his head as if just yanking it free from a cold bucket of water. "That's the kind of fright what I don't need, ya prick!"

"Wot? You want me makin' noise like a great brass band then?" the lad snapped back at him. "We are wanting to rob the place without the crushers knowin', right?"

The boy had a point. They were supposed to be quiet, and the fact he hadn't heard Callum sneak up on him was a credit to his skill.

"Aren't you supposed to be the crow?" Christopher asked.

"Got bored. Besides, we've been watching. Not likely the doctor's coming home at this time o' night."

"Maybe, but we need to watch for all sorts of surprises here," he said, turning back to the oddly placed book. "Think we might have another peter or two in this libra—"

This time the book did not leave the shelf. He had only pulled it towards him by an inch or two before unseen latches clicked, clacked, and disengaged. This particular copy of *Through the Looking-Glass* was attached to something within the wall behind the bookcase. From across where they stood, another shelf of books lifted upward, disappearing into the low ceiling. Where the books had been was an opening leading deeper into the far wall.

Callum gave Christopher a rap against his chest with the back of the hand. "Pair of cracksmen we are, eh, Christopher?"

The older boy nodded, but he really didn't feel like celebrating.

Following Callum, each step going against his instincts, Christopher left the plush parlour of books for a slightly dimmer room. This chamber offered the same warmth and comfort of the larger office, but was more sparse in its decoration. Instead of a grand desk or a posh chair where a master would preside, a workbench served as the central piece of furniture here. Odd metallic clamps and magnifying lenses all fastened and suspended by jointed supports seemed to silently wait for something to study in detail. Christopher would have, at first, believed it to be a tinker's desk but instead of machinations of any sort, he saw bloody kerchiefs cradling syringes, a small burner still heating a suspended solution that bubbled steadily into glass tubes that worked in a small web over the desk to other glass containers of various sizes and shapes.

This laboratory was not without its comforts, though. There was a lovely, plush fainting couch, as well as a high-back leather chair that was even grander than the one in the main library. This secret room also had a single bookcase, and in the dim light Christopher could see these books had been read many times over, well-worn from the looks of them.

"Now will ya take a butcher's at this," Callum whispered, daring the far end of the lab. The shadows were thicker there, keeping Christopher close to the entrance.

Callum fed the lamp a hint more gas, revealing something like a jail cell, but more light exposed four arches all reaching a single, central point at the top. Giving a little chuckle, the boy walked into the middle of this structure, staring at the juncture which hummed and glowed with a strange blue light.

Something felt very, very wrong to Christopher. Not just with this job, but this place. That boiling potion for one thing meant that the master of the house would be returning soon, but they had been watching this place all night. No one had come or gone. Not even housekeepers.

That curiosity had now become something more like a powerful dread—far worse than peelers emerging from fog. "Get out from that thing, Callum. Now!"

That wasn't what he wanted to say. He wanted to say, *"We got to get out of here. Now!"*

"Wassa matter, Chrissy?" the boy mocked. "Something got ya knickers in a knot, ay?"

Normally, that sort of talk would send him into a fury, but Christopher just wanted to snatch whatever valuables he could see in the open and get the hell out of here. He could deal with Callum later at Miss Eliza's.

"Look, I'm just thinkin' this ain't right," he blurted out to the young boy. "The doctor's got something brewin' here an—"

"An' Serena and I kept a good watch on this place, I tolds ya. Good doctor's not been seen for a time, so we should be fine. Not a worry." Callum stepped out of the structure, moving deeper into the room. "Toff's got his fair share of trinkets," he muttered as he looked over a table of devices that Christopher couldn't quite make out.

His hand brushed the corner of an open book, causing him to tear his eyes away from Callum. With those basics of reading and writing Verity and Miss Eliza had taught him, Christopher knew something important when he saw it. What gave him an unnerving concern on turning the tome around to face him were words he did recognise: names. Lords and ladies of England, all high muckety-mucks, their names accompanied by strange symbols and squiggles he couldn't understand. They burned into his brain. Perhaps later he could decipher them with some help from that toff Books.

He turned the page, and suddenly his throat went dry. "We have to go."

Callum snorted. "Chrissy's all nervous at the sight of blood and pointy things?" he snickered, flicking his fingers against a rather menacing contraption. It looked like a gun, but with a large needle, similar to the bloody syringes on the tray next to the fainting couch.

"If'n I say we go," Christopher insisted, tucking the ledger under his arm, "I say we go!" He then stepped out of the secret chamber and chirped three shrill whistles.

The other boys and Serena came pounding down from upstairs, all in answer to Christopher's call.

As soon as the others reached the doorway of the parlour, Christopher took a quick head count. Save for Callum still doddering in the secret room, they were all accounted for.

"What's the game then, Christopher?" Serena asked, her face a mix of concern and frustration. This was, after all, her score.

"A bad feeling, is all," he spoke quickly. He looked over his shoulder. Whatever Callum found, it had better be the bleeding sword of King Arthur himself to ignore his call. "Callum, what is—"

Something invisible hit him, but it was unmistakeably solid. Christopher felt its breath, hot at first then cold like a winter's gale, as he was tossed back like a rag doll, striking one of the fine leather seats in the parlour. The smell of rotten eggs made him gag, and for some odd reason all of the hair on his body was standing at attention.

Serena's scream sobered him up rather quickly, and when Christopher looked up to the secret room, he understood why the girl's howl threatened to summon the blue bottles.

From the secret room, a bright white-blue light flickered and flared while tentacles of electricity seemed to dance about the strange, cage-like structure within. Occasionally a bolt would whip out and strike the wall or one of the metallic trays by the fainting couch.

Through the glare, on the other side of the room, was Callum, trapped by the table of odd contraptions. Christopher didn't want to tell the younger boy to make a run for it. From the looks and sounds of this electric beastie, one of those bolts could do some harm—harm beyond Miss Alice's repair.

Maybe it would die down. Maybe this thing—whatever it was—did this for a spell then stopped. If only Miss Eliza or Verity were here to let them know what was up. "Stay there," he bellowed to Callum over the sounds of the electric storm, though he could hear no noise from the boy. Something was drowning out his words on the other side of the device, but his mouth moved, and he waved frantically.

Luckily, Liam was a first-class lip-reader. "He says he's fine, and what the bloomin' hell is this thing?"

It was a terrifying moment, but somehow Callum's joke made the situation a little less.

Christopher handed Liam the ledger. "Right, I'm going to go get him. Whatever you do"—he pointed to the book in Liam's hands—"you get that back to Miss Alice. Miss Eliza and Mr. Books both needs to see it."

Just as he turned to run into the storm, the light flared once more, knocking him back only a step or two. The light flickered out just as quickly as it had exploded in front of them, only now inside the cage-like structure was a man. Simple as you please, as if he had ridden the lightning itself. The gent was tall, well built, a cane in one gloved hand whilst in the other he held a doctor's bag. Something about the cut of his jacket suggested massive muscles—the kind not usually found in the gentry.

If Christopher could not take the man alone, Callum was behind him. If Liam passed the book to Serena and joined in the fray, the man would be all but done. He was about to lead the charge of his companions, when the man made eye contact with him; and Christopher, try as he might, could not move. His instincts simply would not allow it.

It was like looking into an abyss. All of the children stood, their mouths agape, trapped in horror, at the thing posing as a gentleman. The creature wore the shape of a man, but his eyes contained no soul. Nothing. He sized them all up as they all sized up the day's cuts at the butcher's shop, its mouth peeling back into an inhuman smile.

This wasn't some demon conjured by a bad bottle of gin. It was every horror and nightmare Christopher remembered as a lad descending upon him, threatening to smother him completely. This was a monster right in front of them, and the children for once were mesmerised.

Then the doctor lurched forwards suddenly.

"Bugger me," came a voice from behind him.

Callum had apparently attempted to knock the man down, because he couldn't see him the way Christopher and the others could. Maybe if Miss Eliza were here, she could take him. Provided she had a stick of dynamite handy. Just to be certain.

The monster's hand dropped his doctor's bag and latched upon Callum, all in one swift, inhuman movement, and hoisted the boy up by that one hand in a curiously weightless way—as if he were a handkerchief.

"Naughty lad. Whatever shall we do with you?" it asked the boy who was now finally getting a good look at him. The gentleman-creature looked at the two trays of bloody syringes and instruments, then back to Callum. "I can think of several things." And that smile grew impossibly wider. It was no trick of the eyes. The corners of his mouth were nearly touching his ears.

Callum wet himself. Christopher could not blame him. Not for being so terrifyingly close to this monster. This monster that would serve as the death of them all unless they moved. Now.

"Nommus!" Christopher screamed. *"For fuck's sake, nommus!"*

On the street you learned the moment to run, and one look at that creature and Christopher knew they had no chance. The remaining Ministry Seven didn't need much urging. They bolted down the hallway and out of the back door as if the hounds of hell were on them. Christopher made sure to be at the rear, though his instincts were now screaming to go faster.

All but one. *The book!*

His eyes went to Liam, who was clutching that ledger tight to his breast. *Good lad.*

Christopher did not recall the struggle with a door or even a gate. He burst out into the streets, the memory of that smile that threatened to split the man's head in two driving him on. Looking at the others, he knew they felt the same. Christopher heard nothing behind him, save for the usual sounds of London town. The man, or whatever it had been, had not followed them.

That did not mean he was going to stop, or tell Serena, Liam, and Colin to follow suit.

"Jigsaw puzzle!" he shouted, clapping his hands at Liam. "Jigsaw puzzle!"

Liam tossed into the air the great ledger, which Christopher immediately caught and tucked under his arm, and then he ducked off to his right as the other three scattered like dandelion seeds in a strong breeze. To any bystander, Christopher's run would have seemed erratic, perhaps in a panic, but he was—as were his compatriots—gradually progressing to their designated place of safety.

When he saw the three children in front of Miss Eliza's apartments, it was the first time he felt as if he could take a proper breath. Together they climbed the stairs, pounded on the door, and were admitted by Alice. One look at their faces was all she needed to know something was wrong.

Christopher, for once, did not mind the maid's fussing over them. Much like in their flight from the doctor-monster's home, he had not noticed being led to any couch. Even the scones and tea before them seemed to appear in the same way as that thing had.

After a few fortifying sips, Alice turned to the children. "Now, please tell me what this is all about! Where is little Callum? Can I expect some bobbies to break down Miss Eliza's door?"

That was when the dam broke. Christopher didn't even try to stop them all telling the story. He sat still while Liam,

Colin, and Serena gabbled out what had happened. Their eyes
grew wide again in the telling.

When they were done, Alice looked to Christopher. "Is this
true?" she asked quietly.

He blinked. "You understood us?"

"I lived in a house with five brothers and sisters. It's a bit
of a skill."

The hard cough from the boy lingering by the door made
them all jump.

"Where's Callum?" Eric asked.

"We had to leave him," Christopher muttered.

It was as if the sickness slipped away from him like a veil,
an unexpected rush of colour coming to his face as he shouted,
"You did wot?!"

"Eric, you weren't there! You didn't see . . ." Christopher's
throat tightened. If he cried, he cried. He had earned their
scorn tonight. They had been *his* responsibility. He had promised Verity he would protect the Seven . . .

What would she think of him now?

"Christopher," Liam spoke, his voice almost unrecognisable. He spoke with some sort of wisdom Christopher never
heard within the boy's clever remarks. "You were on the fly,
and we were with you. If you hadn't gotten us out of there,
we'd all be in lavender."

The burning in Christopher's eyes raged. What would Verity think? "It happened just like what we all said," he insisted,
turning tear-filled eyes to Alice as a blurry semblance of Eric
took a seat next to the maid. Probably life with Miss Eliza had
prepared Alice more than most for such a wild tale, but he
appreciated that she didn't dismiss their story as childish fantasy. He then motioned to Liam. "I found something. Thought
Miss Eliza should have a look at it."

The maid opened the book and gave a slight gasp. "Bless
my soul. These are—"

"Turn the page, Miss Alice."

Her brow creased as she did so, and the small scream that
immediately followed was only just smothered by her hand.
She slammed the book shut with a hard *snap* and set it on an
end table as if it were suddenly too hot for her to hold on to.
"This demands the mistress' attention." She quickly turned

back to the children. "So he got a good look at you then, did he?"

"Yes," he replied, feeling like there was a stone lodged in his throat. He knew what she was getting at; there was no place in London that would be safe now.

"Right then!" Alice got up from the table. "First things first." She hoisted up her skirts so that her gleaming brass legs were visible. Christopher blushed, even though they were not the normal flesh-and-blood lady's legs. That much was obvious when a tiny jet of steam shot out of the right one, and it opened like a jewellery box. However, Miss Alice's idea of treasure was a well-oiled shotgun. Having taken it out, checked that it was loaded, and that she had a good stash of shells for it, Alice closed her leg.

"Good," she muttered to herself. "Now, Serena, Colin, and Liam, hurry into the kitchen and bundle up some food. For all of us. We'll pick up Jonathan and Jeremy on the way. Eric, I want you to finish up that chicken soup I fixed—*broth and all*—then dress yourself in those clean clothes I had set aside for you."

"But I don't really like the broth, Miss Alice," Eric protested.

"Not a word out of you," she snapped. Everyone gave a start, to which Alice closed her eyes and took a breath. "I'm sorry, Eric. Just trust me without question. We have quite the journey ahead of us."

"Journey?" Christopher asked. "I don't think there is anywhere in this whole world that . . ."

Alice's hand wrapped firmly around his shoulder. "Buck up, young man. Don't think this is the first time I've had to go into hiding while in the mistress' service. We have a plan, a place where we will be safe. All of us."

Her eyes were so alive that Christopher believed her. *Without question,* as she said to Eric. She wasn't that much older than he was, but she radiated the kind of belief that he was happy to hold on to. Like Verity and Eliza, he trusted her.

Christopher could only hope that Alice took more from the latter than the former.

"What about Callum?" Serena demanded, sticking her head around the corner of the kitchen.

He shot Alice a look, and her expression turned grim. "Don't worry, we'll get him back. Miss Eliza and Mr. Books will help us set things to rights."

Christopher nodded slowly. He had seen those two accomplish amazing things. They'd certainly give the man with the dead eyes a run for his money.

It was the other name in the ledger that gave him pause.

"But how will they know?" Serena persisted, her frown deepening. "She's all the way in America!"

Alice didn't seem at all worried. "Do you still have that scarf the mistress gave you?"

The little girl darted over to her coat, pulled it from one pocket. She looked suspiciously up at the maid. "Miss Eliza said I could have it, you know."

"No arguments!" Alice chided, threatening Serena with the same tone that had startled them all earlier.

Serena stared at her a moment, then her eyes lit up. "The magic button, you mean?"

"Bugger it, I'd forgotten about that fancy alarm of Miss Eliza's!" Christopher exclaimed, feeling like a right idiot. Miss Eliza had given it to Serena as a means of communication around the time Mr. Harry disappeared. He frowned. "But will it work across all that distance? America's a long way off . . ."

"It will if you do this," Alice said, as she plucked the button free of the scarf and laid it on the table. Before anyone else could move, Alice pulled the coal shovel from its place by the fire, and brought it down hard on the little piece of brass.

Serena let out a scream of outrage. She actually stamped her foot and glared up at the maid with blazing cheeks and eyes. "You broke it! It was a present, and you broke it!"

Alice pointed to the pieces. "It was always meant to be broken in case of an emergency, child. As a communicator it has a short range, but as a distress signal, it can cover half the globe, Miss Eliza said."

All of them peered down at the destroyed button, and they could see the remains of it gleaming faintly red.

"Wherever she is in the world, she'll come," Alice said with deep conviction. "She'll come and she'll set things to rights." She ran her eye over the children standing before her.

"She'll find the quickest way back, but we're not going to wait for her here. We better get moving before things get nasty."

As all the children trooped to the door, Alice laid her hand across Christopher's shoulders. "This is not your fault."

They were kindly meant words, but he couldn't simply forgive himself as quickly as the Seven did. He could not stop wondering what sort of dewskitch Callum was suffering under the thing they had encountered. He also wondered what he would do if they couldn't get Callum back.

Once Eric appeared, dressed in similar clothes as theirs—only far cleaner—Alice gave a quick nod. "Right then, are we all ready?"

Alice then motioned for the children to follow her . . . into Miss Eliza's bedroom.

"Um . . . Miss Alice?" Christopher stammered.

"Drastic situations call for drastic measures," Alice said and then beckoned for the five of them to follow. "From here on, quiet as the grave . . . lest we truly find ourselves there."

TWO

❧

Wherein Phantoms Take Flight

Eliza was trying to remember, when was the last time she was this sore and it pleased her this much?

Their fourth day in the air, their first over the Atlantic, the tension between them she was determined to break, tapping into every detail she knew from Burton's *Kama Sutra* masterpiece to consummate their relationship. They had a night and full day in nothing but their naked glory, only interrupted when a steward dropped off a food tray by the door. She had expected, following that *exquisite* first night together, their amorous adventures to get a bit tiresome.

What a terrible assumption. Good Lord, but that man was nimble.

Tempted as they were to enjoy their second transatlantic day lost in a few of the seven deadly sins, Wellington and Eliza dressed and then joined the company of their fellow passengers, and the breathtaking view of their transatlantic journey, with a splendid luncheon.

During the meal, Wellington leaned in and whispered, "There's another couple five tables away that appear to be glowering at us."

Eliza inclined her head and then reached into her handbag

for her compact. The reflection it afforded was a couple of what appeared to be impressive standing, and indeed they were shooting pointed, rather haughty looks in their direction. Each time the man or woman—who had to crane over her shoulder to look at them—did so, they muttered something just before shaking their heads.

They also looked as if they had not slept well.

"I think we just met our neighbours," Eliza quipped.

They both burst out laughing, not having a care what disparaging looks they earned.

The rest of the day, they agreed, belonged to the *Ares*. Wellington and Eliza needed something other than their own carnal delights to distract them as it felt they would never reach the shore. She was anxious to get back to headquarters, regroup with the others active in the City, and begin investigations into Peter Lawson, the Duke of Sussex. What they had seen did more than just threaten the integrity of the Ministry, but hinted to a possible threat against the Crown itself. Sussex was far too close to Her Majesty for comfort, but they would need to build their case and make it as strong and as airtight as it could be. The *Ares* gave them both a focus and a distraction that took less of a toll on their bodies.

Or so Eliza thought.

Once more, as they had been their first night together, they were stained with grime and grease, weary worn from their work on Wellington's motorcar. With materials that the Office of the Supernatural and Metaphysical had supplied to them just before launch, the Mark I was now outfitted with the lighter, slimmer Maxim guns behind the headlamps. It was a real surprise to see that the Americans, who prided themselves as being innovators of technology and industry, were so well stocked in products from Samson Fox and the Leeds Forge. Wellington seemed most excited to incorporate these flues into the engine array. She recalled how Wellington, a year ago, bored her to the core with his prattling on about the sciences and modern marvels. Now, listening to him talk about the importance of corrugated boiler flues and how it would increase efficiency and output from the *Ares*, was akin to reading a good book. She had seen what the Mark I had done in its initial test run, and provided Wellington's theories were correct—and she had this feeling that they would be—she could share in the thrill Wellington took from this addition.

Albeit, for probably different reasons.

The refitting of *Ares* was going smoothly. The only thing that could slow down their progess . . .

"I have been reconsidering the replacement of all the Gatlings, Eliza."

. . . would be if Welly questioned her judgement call concerning the ordnance.

"Strange, as I could swear we had shared this conversation yesterday."

"We did."

"So you've reconsidered after sleeping on the matter."

He pursed his lips, then said, "I wouldn't say I *slept* on the matter per se."

She paused, then felt a smile form on her lips. "Oh yes, how silly of me to forget that."

"I'm surprised you could." Wellington grimaced, working a kink in his neck. "I am tenderised enough that I'm ready for stew."

"We just need to build up your stamina, Books," Eliza said, rapping the back of her hand against his chest. She hoped he hadn't caught her flinching as she did so. Good Lord, that should not have hurt her as much as it did. "And with all the lifting and torqueing and refitting we have done today . . ."

"But the Gatling under the tumble seat . . ."

"Oh now, Welly . . ."

"No, just listen to me on this, and yes I know we have talked about this, but—"

Eliza stopped, turning to look at Wellington. He looked most perplexed.

"Welly?"

"This—" His mouth was open but no words came out. Then he cleared his throat and said, "This is how you feel when you talk to me, isn't it?"

Eliza grinned smugly. "How's it fit?"

"Not . . . not well." He shrugged, nodding in resignation, then continued. "The Gatling gun is heavier, yes, but it has stopping power that you would need, dare I say want, when you wish to dissuade those wishing to engage in pursuit, yes?"

She leaned in to counter his argument, just as she had done in the past concerning the retrofit of the headlamp cannons; but there was a sound reasoning—dammit—in his argument. Why couldn't her arguments have those too?

"I'm just considering where we would need the extra 'kick' as it were and I am thinking we would rather have it covering our escape."

There had to be a way she could get in a final say on this . . .

Oh, damn it all, he was right. "Explosive bolts as before," she insisted, resuming her walk to their stateroom. "If we have to take flight, we will not want that much weight."

"Agreed." He was quiet for a few footsteps, and then added, "I like this, Eliza."

"Like what?"

"Sharing this. With you." She turned to see him smiling, and her heart leapt. If there was a way for him to always look at her in this fashion, that would suit her just fine. "I thought I should—"

"Why are we standing out here, in the hallway?" she asked. "Shouldn't we be in our room, telling one another this?"

"Naked?"

"Preferably."

Wellington pushed past her, digging deep into his pockets for their room key. "You are quite right. Why are we having this conversation here?"

On reaching the door to their suite, Wellington hesitated, then looked over to her. "What is that?"

Eliza stretched out her arms as if to ask *"Whatever do you mean?"* but then heard the odd chirping sound coming from inside their suite. She went to reach inside the slit of her skirts to retrieve the '81 from her thigh when she paused.

That was her signature distress signal from the Ministry ETS.

"Wellington, open the door now," she insisted.

Once the door was open, it was Eliza's turn to push aside Wellington. Now she could hear the signal loud and clear. Eliza felt her heart leap into her throat again—but not in a good way. Dashing to the pile of discarded clothes from their first night, she rummaged through them, the sound of the alarm growing louder as she did so.

"Eliza?" Wellington said, locking the door behind him. "Whatever are you on about? What is that infernal noise?"

Finally, from the bottom of her discarded skirts, she located the tiny golden locket that was the source of the wailing. When Eliza flicked the hidden switch, the sound stopped, but there was no corresponding relief, at least not for her. Clenching the little device in her hand, she turned to Wellington. She would have loved to leap back into bed with him then and there, but the message the little locket had delivered had cooled her ardour like an Arctic plunge.

Wellington's face was now contorted with concern. "What is it?"

Eliza clambered to her feet, tossing the locket across to him. "It's the Seven," she said, feeling a sudden fear-fuelled alertness course through her. Only scant moments before, she had been exhausted and ready to settle in next to Wellington, perhaps for a hint of intimacy before drifting to sleep. Now, she only felt the thrumming of her heart, her mind racing with what she needed to do next. Something had to be done, even from where they were. "They're in trouble. Real trouble."

"I don't mean to sound flippant," Wellington began, his thumb tracing the edge of the tiny alarm, "but that is hardly out of charac—"

"No, Wellington," Eliza said, going to the dresser and opening it to fetch clothes. She had no clue what kind of clothes she had, needed, or wanted for whatever she was about to do. She was finding her mind quite flustered, if not muddled, by the signal. "The last time we received an alert like this was during our case with Kate and the disappearing suffragists. It was what I used to call the children to my apartments."

"Yes, I recall."

"That was in London," she said, rummaging through her clothes and fishing out denim jeans, a waistcoat, and a weapons harness. "We're over the Atlantic. The alert I have for the children has a safety feature wherein if it is destroyed, the Ministry ETS powers and delivers a strong sonic alert to me. It lasts for only twelve hours, but I should be able to pick it up wherever in the world I am." She shook her head. "Welly, only Alice knows of this safety feature."

"So Alice triggered this distress call," he said.

"Which means Alice has the children, and they are all on the run," Eliza said, trying not to think of the Seven's faces. The signal had been in Serena's keeping. Sweet, little Serena. "She knows what to do, what we have planned, but if the tracker has been compromised . . ." She could not panic—not bloody now. "We don't even know if this happened at my apartments, and Alice has been incapacitated."

Wellington seemed to appear from nowhere, making her jump ever so slightly. He took her face into his hands, keeping his soft and soothing gaze locked with hers. "Then we have to get to them." She went to ask him, but as if he were some kind of mind-reader, he shook his head. "The *Ares* lacks the range to get to London. There are, however, the *aeroflyers*."

"You would leave your motorcar?" she asked. "But that's your—"

"Sod the car, Eliza. These are the children we're speaking of. Bit higher in priority," he gently insisted. "We'll figure out how to collect the *Ares* later, yes?"

She wanted very badly to kiss him there and then, but instead she said, "Grab the essentials. Whatever you will need for, say, a day. Two at most." Eliza motioned with a nod of her head to the wardrobe. "Wear that herringbone coat. That should keep you warm, and bring your driving gloves."

"Our destination?"

"Eventually? Normandy. I've left instructions for Alice to reach a safe house there. Large enough for her and the children."

She grabbed up only the basics she would need for everyday wear. As for Wellington, his razor and cologne would suffice. Perhaps he could do without shaving cream until reaching a safe house. They should have something for him there. He might look a bit haggard after a few days, but considering his days in the bush, he would manage. The undercover nights of luxury they had enjoyed on board the *Atlantic Angel* were done. She and Wellington were about to make a mad dash for England, thousands of feet over the ocean and—hopefully—within range of Old Blighty's shore.

"This is a plot borne of insanity, you realise that, yes?" he asked, but there was a grin on his face. He had even taken the liberty of packing her things alongside his into their smallest of suitcases. If needed, she could jam the suitcase under one of the seats so it would not hinder them much.

"Perhaps." And she grabbed her own coat and gloves. "You will just have to trust me on this."

"I've made it this far," he said with a shrug. "I just hope we are not embarking on a fool's errand."

"If we are," Eliza said, "then I will make it up to you with the finest dinner in Paris that you have ever known. Did you pack your corset?"

"Right next to yours." Wellington motioned to the door. "After you, Madame Icarus."

Shooting him a look of warning, Eliza led the way from their suite, out of their luxurious stateroom, off the first-class deck. Lower and lower they descended into the airship's gondola, the thrumming of the *Angel*'s massive engines growing louder and louder in her ears. Occasionally, they would pause, waiting for the maintenance crew to pass by them. On reaching a massive iron door clearly marked "Authorised Personnel Only—No Passengers," Eliza slipped into her coat and encouraged Wellington to don his own. They found themselves moments later in a strange mix of hot and biting-cold air as the final deck of the vessel stretched out before them. Eliza turned back to Wellington and made two Ls with her right and left hands and rotated them in a circle around each other. *Hand signals from this point,* she was saying to him. With a nod, and shoving his bowler hat lower onto his head, Wellington motioned for her to continue to lead.

The cold bit and stung at Eliza's cheeks, and she secretly wished she had remembered a scarf of some kind, but the ruffs would have to do. The fact was, many creature comforts would have to be sacrificed from this point forwards. They pressed on through patches of thick darkness, through small pools of light coming from the tiny lamps intermittently placed in the bay. She held up a fist and stepped back between two towers of crates, waiting to see if any crew were passing. The clatter was coming from a Portoporter rumbling along the metal gangplank. Perhaps a request had been placed by someone in first class for a checked suitcase, or there was a crate that had slid out of place during their voyage. Whatever the case, Eliza chose to wait. If automated carts were tending to a command from either the bridge or the concierge, disrupting the Porto-porter could easily broadcast their own presence.

Once the *clickity-clickity-clack-clack-clack* of the Porto-porter faded to the thrumming of the airship's engines, Eliza looked over her shoulder and motioned for Wellington to fol-low. Judging from the vibrations in the grating underfoot and the undulating of sound around them, they should be closer to their means of escape.

From the floor of the bay, Eliza could just make out the emerald glare of two caged lightbulbs. Once she opened the domed hatch, perhaps as soon as she unlocked it, someone on the bridge would be notified. They would have to be, if not now then once they detached. Regardless of when the *Angel* would receive word, they would have to move quickly.

Eliza looked over at Wellington, who was casting glances to either side of them. He did not appear nervous or even slightly uncertain. It was more a matter of heightened alert, and of being resigned to Eliza's word.

She had to admit to herself—she preferred it like this.

She tapped two fingers against the back of her wrist. *Time's an issue.* She then pointed towards her own eyes. *Eyes open.* Wellington nodded in reply. Eliza reached out to him, placing a gloved hand on his cheek. *Thank you.* Not necessarily one of the approved silent signals used in the field, but Wellington understood.

Eliza spun the wheel faster and faster until underneath her feet she felt the sharp snap of the lock disengaging. Immedi-ately, the lights on either side of them switched from green to red, and just over the howl of air, alarms blared in an undulat-ing pattern.

Far underneath the access ladder rolled the Atlantic Ocean and thin wisps of clouds, both slipping into a fast-approaching night. Attached to the bottom of the small access ladder was the aeroflyer, shuddering ever so gently as their airship contin-ued forwards.

Eliza looked back at Wellington and made two fists. *Hang on tight.*

She stepped onto the first rung, and then slowly began her descent towards the small flying machine. Once free of the

Angel's hull, freezing air pushed Eliza into the ladder, far harder than she had anticipated. Her foot slipped, but she tightened her grip on the rungs and struggled to keep her balance. Eliza looked up at Wellington, who was threatening to scramble after her, but she kept him still with a single look. Her dangling foot found purchase once more, and she continued downwards until finally finding the cabin of the aeroflyer. Still gripping onto the access ladder with one hand, she reached out for the rung suspended over the pilot's seat, grabbed hold of it, and guided herself into place.

Wellington was slowly making his own way down the ladder, one hand sliding down the outer rung of the ladder while the other defiantly carried their small suitcase of clothes and necessities. *Always the gentleman,* Eliza thought as he made his way to the gunner's seat. *To the very last.*

Underneath her chair she found a pair of goggles and an aviator's cap. *Aviatrix for this flight,* she thought to herself. There was also a leather mask connected to an unseen section of their flyer. Perhaps this was a high-altitude breathing apparatus, or a communication device, or a combination of the two. Dangling from the mask, she noticed a small coil of cable that offered a connection. Checking the cap, a suitable outlet was apparent.

"Wellington," she spoke into the mask once she'd joined the two, "can you hear me?"

She glanced over her shoulder and could see Wellington adjusting the mask. Once he had made the link between mask and aviator's hat, his voice crackled in her ears. "You said the aeroflyers were the Avro five-tens. I do believe this is a five-ten *A*, an ingenious design that Westinghouse had a hand in developing. An electric engine that, once the charge depletes, immediately switches to a steam engine, but the steam engine actually recharges—"

"You can study it later," Eliza replied tartly, looking overhead at the release catch. She turned each valve one at a time, watching as bright white steam expelled then disappeared into the light of dusk. "Are you ready?"

"Just one moment," he said. Then came a loud *pop*, followed by another from behind her. Eliza looked over her shoulder to see Wellington hefting the Maxim off its housing to toss it overboard, out into the shadows of the coming night. "That should make us considerably lighter, granting us a little more range."

Discarding weapons would usually send Eliza into a right fit but not this time. "We should be able to make it to land, at the very least."

"So that's the plan?" Wellington said with a grunt. Another glance over her shoulder revealed Wellington was removing as much of the machine gun's mountings as was permitted. "Fly into London and—"

"Correction, Welly, we're aiming for shore. We don't have the range to make it to London, but to shore . . ." She checked the instruments, not that she fully understood what she was looking at, and lied. "Without a doubt."

She felt the small craft shudder, and caught a glimpse of some unidentified metallic apparatus tumbling into the darkness underneath them.

"Right then," Wellington said as he settled into his chair. He secured the belt across his lap and gave Eliza a sharp nod. "I am all set."

Fumbling underneath the control panel, she discovered a crank, similar to ones found in other motorcars, and after giving it a few hard, fast revolutions, the centre prop spun to life. A moment later the right and left props followed suit. She opened the throttle, just as she had been taught those years ago, and all three propellers disappeared in a blur of revolutions.

"Batteries are full," Wellington reported. "Boilers are as well. Ready for launch." She felt his head rub ever so gently against the back of hers. "Now, if you please. There is a delegation from the *Atlantic Angel* at the hatch wondering who the hell is about to nick off with one of their aeroflyers!"

With a cheery wave to the *Angel*'s security crew, Eliza reached up for the release. With a hard *kthunk* audible even with the rush of air around them, the aeroflyer dropped, but only a few feet before Eliza pulled back on the yoke, then made adjustments accordingly to how she handled the steering, how open the throttle was, and exactly how to manage the disruption of air currents. They banked dangerously close towards the gondola, only to level out. The passengers of both first and second class were obvious, pressing their faces against the observation windows to get a glimpse at this wild and unexpected display of derring-do. Eliza could still make out, in the deep violet of night, the smart white hats and blazers of the bridge crew. She gave a proper salute to the captain before banking away from the *Angel* and shooting ahead into the grand void.

Her fingertips now felt in the dark for what her eyes had caught a glimpse of, and there at the top of the dashboard Eliza found the solitary switch. It flipped up, and from behind the various gauges a soft light rose, illuminating the cockpit enough for her to plot their heading in the simplest, most base manner.

East. They needed to head east.

"Are you all right up there?" Wellington asked.

"As well as we will ever be," she returned, glancing over her shoulder. Now the only thing piercing through the absolute darkness were the *Angel*'s running lights, a considerable distance behind them. "If we follow an easterly course, we should hit . . . something."

She was expecting to hear that droll in his voice when things were at their worst, but instead he came back with "Indeed. Even if we reach Ireland, 'twill serve as a story for the ages."

"You seem resigned to whatever Fate has in store, Welly. Not sure if I like this."

"For what it is worth, darling," he said quite frankly, "the past two days have been sheer bliss. If we die on this madcap escape, I will be happy to perish with you."

Eliza let out a laugh. "I really don't want to die."

"Neither do I, so please focus on flying this bloody thing and returning us to *terra firma* with all speed, safely."

Her eyes went back to the instruments. She had plenty of altitude. Her course was steady. All that she needed was the pressure to remain constant, for the tailwind to continue, and to last through the night and into the morning. Finding solid ground was going to be the real trick.

Aside from landing safely, of course.

INTERLUDE

❧

Wherein the Hand of Her Majesty Is Felt

Gertrude "Galloping Gertie" Courtney was used to people trying to kill her. She was used to knowing their names, in many situations. She was not used to the assassins being her own colleagues.

The Webley-Maxim Mark I—or, as she and her mates back at the Dark Continent referred to it, "The Brass Knuckles"— cracked open under her grasp. Cradling the open weapon in her left arm, she slipped free the three empty casings there, replacing them with fresh ones. Gertie then checked the magazine and noted that she had at least half a clip. So, in all—five bullets, three high-velocity shells.

She bit her bottom lip as she jerked the weapon shut and hefted it with her right arm. It was a roll of the bones if she had enough ammunition on hand to see another sunrise over African skies.

As she crouched in the dark alleyway, her heart racing, her breath coming out in short white clouds before her, Gertie knew whatever she did, she could not flee to one of the Ministry of Peculiar Occurrences safe houses here, either in the city or country. They would assuredly know the network. Even minus the signet ring she had thrown away earlier, the Department was still able to track her. That was their speciality, their forte. Pubs preferred.

Favourite locations for dead drops. Even her frequented tea shops. The Department seemed to be able to track her scent, as if Old Man Quartermain himself had passed down the skill to them.

The back alleys of the East End were a labyrinth, though, and perhaps she could lose her pursuers in its shadows. Even with little changes over the years, Gertie still knew her way through these streets. She would have preferred to be back in Africa, back in what her countrymen and women referred to as the bush but she now called home.

Gertie adjusted her left arm, feeling the hot, sticky blood pooling in her gloves. It was fortunate she was right-handed, but her attacker managed to get in a lucky strike with the blade. For the first few city blocks, she was running through her mind which likely toxins anointed that blade. It had been a deep cut, meaning whatever poison employed could be swift, but then it dawned on Gertie that the Department wouldn't have made her termination so public. That was not their sworn duty. When she caught a whiff of her own blood and saw the few drops that managed to stand out even in the filth-strewn streets of London, she understood exactly what they were planning.

Slow down their kill.

Follow the trail.

Wait until she was far gone from the eyes of Her Majesty's subjects.

Her elbow shattered the windowpane beside her, granting easier access to the physician's office. Gertie started counting silently to herself as she ransacked the examination room, stuffing bandages, alcohol, and—as luck would have it— cocaine into her coat pockets. About the time she had reached "fifty" in her counting, she heard movement upstairs.

Time to leave.

With a cursory glance outside, Gertie slipped back into the alleyway and continued her escape into the darkness. Her eyes darted left and right as she kept moving forwards, deeper into a city she had once been familiar with, but not a place where she felt as safe as she did in Africa. It was supposed to have been a quick stay in the London office. Three more days, and she would have been on the first airship back to Cape Colony. She had enjoyed the extended stay at headquarters, but was more than ready to return home.

Tonight, it was her imperative to return to her corner of the Empire and disappear into the Serengeti.

Gertie paused in an alcove just before what she could only assume from the commotion was a pub, its patrons still enjoying the night's revels. She slowed her own breathing, straining to hear anything other than the bawdy lyrics of the drunkards and whores caterwauling from rented rooms above. She couldn't completely trust the summation of her current hiding place, though, as she was feeling a bit foggy from the loss of blood.

She slipped off her long coat and casual jacket underneath. Again with a quick look out from her hiding place, Gertie tugged and tore at her shirtsleeve, removing the blood-soaked fabric to look at the gash running down the length of her bicep. Even in the dim light of this alleyway, the wound looked as if it were a second mouth screaming in desperate need of a surgeon's skill. Gertie quietly removed the alcohol's cork with her teeth, took a deep breath, and bit hard into the bark tissue as she poured the solution over the cut. She then fished out the syringe and loaded it up with a healthy dose of cocaine. The right amount, she knew, would numb the pain and still keep her alert. Truly a wonder drug.

Provided the dosage was *just* right.

Once her wound was bandaged up, Gertie slipped back on the evening jacket. The night air on her face caressed her skin as would the fingertips of a lover. Details attempting to hide in the shadows, such as a couple enjoying a tryst in another alleyway, a poor sod unconscious and being picked clean by street urchins, and a priest seeming lost in a small book of scriptures, all now came into a hard focus. The dosage she had administered was spot-on, apparently. Using the remaining alcohol to clean her hands of the blood, she shoved her left hand into the pocket of her coat, and fixed her right's grip on the Brass Knuckles. Gertie's mind was already starting to clear as she slipped back into the dim light of East End.

Still no sign of her pursuers. Hardly a reason to celebrate. "Galloping Gertie" Courtney was a Department matter now.

Slinking through the back alleyways and sticking to shadows, she once again ran through her mind what few options remained. Safe houses? Absolutely not. Contacts? There were a few still active she could call upon using aliases, but would the Department have accessed her previous cases already?

Gertie lacked details as to exactly how much time elapsed between the Department's orders and her own receipt of the Phantom Protocol alert. Best assumption: they were well aware of her previous cases, her aliases, and her contacts.

Her *known* contacts. And that conclusion had brought her to this particular alleyway across from the Princess Alice.

No movement from the windows above the pub, as far as she could see. Gertie looked down at the Brass Knuckles. The damn thing was too big for a proper holster so if she wanted to appear inconspicuous, she would have to risk going in unarmed.

The clip ejected into her hand and disappeared into her right pocket with her spare ammunition. Setting the weapon aside, hidden between empty crates, Gertie suddenly felt as if she were naked against the elements. *Only for a few moments,* she assured herself. With another look at the Princess Alice, Gertie pulled her bowler hat down as far as it would fit over her head, shoved both hands into her pockets, and started a slow walk to the pub, adding a slight limp to her step for a final effect.

Patrons wandered in and out of the pub but Gertie, instead of accepting the warm invitation of the Princess Alice, veered across its entrance to follow Wentworth. Pausing at the first alleyway to look either side, her head still hung low and shoulders hunched, she took stock of her corner of East End. Passersby, the very subjects she had kept safe from villains and adversaries well beyond any sort of imagination they could nurture, paid no mind to her, although gentlemen would glance nervously in her direction. Hopefully in her current outfit, she appeared no more than a short bruiser, hunched within her own garments to mimic the effects of a heady night. This disregard allowed Gertie the opportunity to slip into the alleyway without concern or notice. Sparing one more glance over her shoulder, breathing the easiest she had all night, she paused at the bricks opposite Princess Alice's rear entrance.

"Five inside," Gertie whispered as she tapped on the lightest brick in the wall, progressing to the left. "Three down."

With a gentle push, the brick swivelled on a centre pivot point. She reached inside a second brick and swung it open. Inside the tiny compartment lay several small leather portfolios. She flipped through them to review legends—Donna Tenlen, Martha Rose, Clara Smithe—only she knew the full details behind. Inside each passport wallet was enough currency that could get her around the world undetected, and far from the reach of the Department and, if necessary, the Ministry.

She reached further into the nook and gave a little gasp of delight that materialized briefly as fog, only to disappear in the night's embrace. The British Bulldog, no enhancements or compressors, was a welcomed sight. A reliable sidearm, and far more practical than the Brass Knuckles or the Remington-Elliot '81, it cracked open to reveal itself more than ready for a firefight. The bullets should have been just fine, judging from the pistol's condition.

Bulldog and ammunition in her right pocket. New identities and money in her interior pocket. She gave her left hand a slow flexing of the fingers, and felt only a slight pressure where the cut had been bandaged. She could move, but the wound would need stitches. Ideally now would be the time to test her seam-stress skills, but she didn't think her pursuers would allow her a moment to pause for sewing. The bricks ground softly against one another to return her hiding place once again into the seemingly featureless static brickwork of the alley. Armed with identities, currency, and a second gun, Gertie lacked only one other essential: an escape from London.

Returning to Wentworth, the feigned limp once more add-ing character to her silent persona, Gertie shot quick glances to either side of her as she hobbled back to where she had stashed the Brass Knuckles. She was thankful, in this hour closing on midnight, that there were no signs of any Depart-ment agents. She knew them as true night dwellers, living for the dark and devious dealings that called for them to creep out of hiding to answer the Queen's every nuisance. If the Crown found anything or anyone tiresome, she would call upon them and they would answer without question and act with effi-ciency. Their loyalty to Queen Victoria bordered on fanati-cism. This was one reason Gertie found the Department detestable, a rather thankless job if there ever was one and hardly inspiring in her evaluation of the Empire.

Now, after what she had witnessed at the Tower, her loathing of the Department had transformed itself into a cold fear. If she could just get out of the City, her chances of survival would triple. While cities like Paris and London worked tirelessly to create gas and electrical wonders to chase away the shadows of night, the Dark Continent never failed to enthrall her with the night sky. African skies were unparalleled. The nocturnal vistas stretched high and distant, the twinkling canvas decorated with a breathtaking brushstroke of a brilliant multitude of stars.

Yes, Africa, Gertie pledged to herself. *I will come home soon.*

She suddenly felt her heart picking up in its pace, the Bull-dog weighing heavily in her coat pocket. Was that woman across the street staring at her?

With her affected walk, her own cherub-like profile concealed by the lapels of her long peacoat, Gertie narrowed her eyes on the woman, neither her wide stride nor her limp faltering as she did. She paused to cough, turning in her direction as she did in order to steal a prolonged look at the woman standing as still as a millpond in the dead of winter. The lady was wearing a tweed jacket one would normally wear when bicycling or riding, and she was doing neither at the moment.

The stranger's stoic expression turned into a mirthless grin. Whether it was directed to her, Gertie couldn't tell. Her parasol then opened and was placed gingerly on her right shoulder.

Gertie didn't bother to look behind her. She just ran, her escape now reduced to the final granules gathering in the top chamber of an hourglass, slipping faster now that she had been discovered. This was not going to be a simple egress from London any longer, not by any measure.

The world around her disappeared on ducking into an alleyway, continuing down identical alleyway after identical alleyway. This shortcut burst out into another street. Gertie's pace never slowed, which was why she stumbled on hearing the yell of the hansom driver, immediately followed by the scream of horses. She rolled away, feeling the spray of dirt and gravel as the horses' hooves stomped angrily against the road, before scrambling back to her feet.

In the brief glance she stole of the hansom driver, Gertie noticed him checking his pocket watch. He did so, but there was no fare in the cab. There were no fares to be seen anywhere around them. Even as the horses had stilled, the pocket watch remained open in his hand.

She had to keep running, had to put as much distance between her and the Princess Alice. Her impact with the man and—from the smell of her—paramour, sent a hard shock to her injured shoulder. She heard the gentleman's cane clatter to the ground, and was certain she landed on a top hat. Through the pain of the impact, Gertie managed to pull herself back on her feet, even under the prostitute swearing a true tempest of vulgarities that she would normally not leave unanswered, but she answered only to the "flight" instinct at present.

Run, she thought quickly, *run until you cannot anymore.*

Gertie had no idea how many alleyways or street corners she had put between herself and the pub before she came to an intersection and froze. The Amédée Bollée was much like the gentlemen still wandering at this hour through the quieting streets of London's East End—a diamond in the rough. Gertie clambered into the cabin of the motorcar and pressed the starter. Its rapid *click-click-click* resembled that of a time-piece, or perhaps a time bomb counting down to the moment when everything would disappear in a singularity of fire and force. Instead, she heard the rush of flame and felt the engine shudder in front. Underneath the motorcar, wisps of pearlescent smoke rose around her, standing out in stark contrast to the night. Gertie released the brake, fixed her grip on the steering wheel, and pushed the accelerator forwards.

The loathing that had become fear was now daring to manifest itself as panic. Through the thick veil of the Amédée Bollée's boiler steam, Gertie could see the woman in tweed appear in the street ahead of her, her parasol still open.

She slammed the accelerator forwards into the car's floor-board, but instead of launching forwards, chains leapt out of the dash to bind Gertie's wrists to the motorcar's steering wheel. The metal looked deceptively fragile; but the more Gertie struggled against them, the tighter the coils grew, digging deep into the agent's flesh. The accelerator could go no further, but her motorcar did not budge. The engine merely thrummed smoothly in reply, its idle never changing even as she thrust the pedal forwards again and again.

Then her eyes went to her left. Stepping into the light were the man and his paramour she had careened into during her mad flight from Wentworth Street. Both were wearing the same tweed jackets, just as the woman with the parasol. Her gaze jumped to the right where a hansom cab came to a halt on the other side of the street. The driver climbed down from his perch, revealing from underneath his black cloak a similar tweed pattern. Gertie didn't know why she felt the need to do so—it seemed to be a futile, desperate act—but she gave another tug against her bindings while giving the accelerator another hard push. Neither made a difference, apart from drawing blood from her wrists.

This intersection was miraculously deserted, the windows of the surrounding houses dark, and vacant, so there would be no other witnesses except Gertie's Department companions.

The woman who had dogged her heels collapsed her parasol before taking a few steps closer to the motorcar. Gertie could just make out in the fine curved handle three buttons, and it was an emerald one her gloved finger pressed.

Steam from underneath the Amédée Bollée thickened again, but this time rotors and gears within the motorcar's engine began to run, the soft, steady idle becoming more of a snarl as the motorcar trembled, but still went nowhere. Faster and faster the inner workings of the motorcar cycled, the snarl ascending higher and higher to a whine. The entire car was shuddering violently now, and all Gertie could do was tighten her own grip on the steering wheel to keep the chains from cutting any deeper. The parasol woman in tweed then started to grow taller. Gertie blinked at this oddity, eventually realising it was her own changing perspective that was causing this illusion. She craned her neck over her shoulder to watch as the Amédée Bollée's passenger section collapsed on itself while the steering wheel shifted forwards within her grip. She turned back around to see the front of her motorcar reaching into the night sky, beginning its own folding pattern as well. She could only assume that this sequence would continue until she and the motorcar were of a more practical size, to be easily transported and disposed of.

Gertie watched the parasol lady disappear from her sight as both the front and rear of the motorcar began another folding sequence. She swallowed through the hard, irritating tension growing in her throat. This death under the Department's supervision would be just as she imagined. It would be efficient. It would go unseen. It would remain secret.

It would not be quick.

INTERLUDE

◆◆◆

Wherein Miss del Morte Finds She Does Indeed Have Limits

This was not what Sophia del Morte had expected when she joined the Maestro on his mission. Watching over the doctor that ministered to him was something she'd have thought was more appropriate for someone less skilled and with more patience than she had. The Maestro had insisted that the good doctor was one of the most important people in all of the Empire, and that she was the only one he trusted to keep him safe.

Unfortunately, as Sophia had just discovered, the term "good" was not a term that could be applied to Doctor Henry Jekyll, and he was apparently unhappy to have someone watching his every move. He had slipped away from her and returned to his old apartments, against the strict instructions of the Maestro. This reflected poorly on her, and she did not appreciate the slight.

The control room had reported a sudden power spike from the doctor's laboratory. Twice. She recognised that power signature. Following the second instance, Sophia stormed across the compound to the laboratory the Maestro had constructed for him. For a facility that had once served as a slaughterhouse, the doctor's laboratory was clean, bright, and well organised.

It also terrified Sophia to her core whenever she had to step within it.

She pushed open the double doors, her temper burning brightly in her eyes, her hands ready to at least slap the disobedient doctor. The reek of the laboratory, however, struck her dumb for a moment. Last time she had visited the doctor's domain, the air smelled unnaturally clean. If "sterility" had an odour, it would have been this chemical smell. She did not care for the scent. Now, she longed for that unnerving smell. What hit her on entering the lab was rank, a combination of death and decay that nearly choked her where she stood.

Throwing the sleeve of her jacket over her nose, she blinked through suddenly watering eyes and saw Henry at the far end of the laboratory. His back was to her, and he was bending over something that she couldn't quite see.

With bile welling in her mouth, Sophia gasped out what she had meant to be a stern reproach. "You used the Culpepper device, Doctor! You made me look extremely foolish in the eyes of the Maestro . . ."

He didn't look up, merely waved his hand at her. "I needed something from my apartments. No need to concern yourself, my dear. I had taken precautions not to be apprehended." He turned and grinned over his shoulder at her. "Called in an old friend for protection. I was perfectly fine."

Sophia's nausea subsided. The doctor had used the serum on himself, and let the monster roam free?

"As it turned out it was most fortuitous," he said, beckoning to her. "Come look for yourself . . ."

The cheerful tone in his voice and the merry look in his eye did not make her feel anything but dread. She most certainly did not want to go closer, did not want to see what the smiling doctor was doing, or to whom. If Sophia did not look, then she would be ignorant, and ignorance "was the path to disaster," so her mother had taught her. Slowly she walked the few feet needed to stand at Henry's side by the long table.

It was a boy. The doctor had snatched a child, and brought him back to his lab.

Sophia pressed her lips together. That was another thing her mother had instilled in her: *No children*. They were not "innocent" so much as "blank slates" upon which impressions could be made. Children could be influenced, trained, and refined. There was always potential in them. Good or evil? That depended on the guardian. Therefore, children were never targets. As she looked down into the eyes of the lad who lay on Henry's table, she remembered what she had been taught. Anyone can be a mindless killer, anyone can have no scruples, but it is the person who holds on to just one that remains in control. It had been her mother's rule and Sophia's too. She would not kill or injure a child unless one attacked her.

This boy with his wide frightened eyes tried desperately to cry out, but no sound—not even a whisper—came. He could not be more than twelve, and the pleading in his eyes was directed solely at her.

"He's quite secure." That was when Sophia noticed there were no bindings holding the child. "Paralytic agent I've been working on. Quite effective. He may look tense, ready to bolt, but his muscles are completely relaxed. So relaxed, his vocal chords are incapable of working." He gave one of his syringes a flick of his finger, making it ring lightly. "Very happy with this little cocktail."

For a moment Sophia contemplated snatching up one of the doctor's many sharp instruments and plunging it into his eye, but she knew that impulse carried consequences. There was nowhere in the world, no hole she could crawl into, that would be deep enough for her to hide.

From either of them.

"Who is this?" Sophia asked, her voice flat and devoid of any emotion. Her skills of deception held her in good stead in such moments.

"Some gutter rat. I stumbled on a horde of them breaking into my house. The little girl was particularly endearing. A scream that could shatter glass. Oh, how they scampered when we appeared." The doctor's laughter sent a chill through Sophia's body. "We managed to get this one. I would have loved to grab another, but sadly it was not to be." His grin was genuinely delighted. "Fate brought this little cherub to me. I needed a new test animal." He made a flourish with his hands over the boy. *"Et voilà!"*

The boy shuddered, the sweat on his forehead indication of how hard he fought against the toxin Henry Jekyll had administered. The urchin was skinny and dirty, but he was still a child. Sophia tried to harden herself against what she knew she was bound to see, by thinking how many boys just like this died every day on the streets of London, how perhaps the next winter might have killed this one anyway.

Yet, Sophia could not help but think of her brother, and for an awful moment she saw him on the table before the doctor. What would she have done if that were true?

"What will happen to him?" she asked in a disinterested tone.

Henry, who had turned to his long bench of shining medical devices, replied in a slightly more excited manner. "Oh, don't worry, I won't be wasting him. Our plan needs good soldiers, especially after the grand unveiling. This young man and I will accomplish a great deal together." He shot her a chilling yet completely affable grin. "After all, this is what we are accomplishing here, yes? Progress?"

Sophia could not bear to think what this experiment might become. "I am sorry, Doctor, but the sciences are not my expertise."

"This is more than just the sciences, my dear signorina," he said, his eyes sparkling in the light of the burners that created his concoctions. "This is about progress. Control and command of the human mind. Unlock its mysteries, and progress occurs. You know this. You've *lived* this. All that the 'Maestro' has taught you, and you answered to that so readily, only to discover—"

"Yes, I know," she said quickly.

The disdain in Jekyll's voice whenever he spoke the Maestro's name served as a reminder of who held the true power. Sophia had allowed herself to desire more than just employment from the Maestro. She had fallen under the spell of the Duke of Sussex, Peter Lawson's curious dual personality. She knew that Lawson's alter ego, the Maestro, was the true power, the dominant personality of the two; and she was determined to win his approval and, perhaps, manipulate him to her will, as she had done with so many men of power. Yet she had been disappointed to find out the person she had thought so special was nothing more than a broken experiment.

That was when she discovered Jekyll. The puppeteer. He was far more dangerous than a stranger to her. Jekyll was a wolf, dressed in the trappings of a lamb.

"Progress," she repeated, looking at the boy on the table. "I have no doubt you will fulfil the Maestro's wish and, in turn, achieve your own accomplishments." She gave a slight shrug. "We must maintain illusions as well, mustn't we? Allowing the Maestro to believe he is in control."

"Of course." He glanced at the clock. "Speaking of the master of the house, he's about to drop in 'unexpectedly' right about . . . now."

The creak of the laboratory doors opening changed the moment. Sophia watched in the instant as Jekyll slipped from the master manipulator to humble servant.

When the Maestro entered the room he somehow brought shadows with him, even into the stark brightness of Jekyll's domain. He was flanked by soldiers as well. Soldiers he believed to be his—when these "Grey Ghosts" were actually in the service of Jekyll. The Maestro's mechanical arms, breathing apparatus, and brass helmet were today cobbled together with an evening suit that still managed to look smart on Sussex, even in his mechanical chair that glided towards them as if he were ice-skating. The elegance he exuded against the technology he wore only served to make him more terrifying. Behind the helmet's slightly grimy brass fixtures there was nothing of the man within to be seen. He was impregnable, a tower of modern power.

Yet the collection of machinery threatening to devour him, supposedly granting him life and superhuman power, was merely part of the grand illusion. None of these apparatuses assisted him in staying alive, but they did perpetuate the illusion. Even though she knew the Maestro to be nothing more than a lie, he still possessed a power, a power that, if Jekyll lost control of it, would carry heavy costs. What she had heard on the *Titan* after her harrowing flight from San Francisco assured her of that.

And Jekyll was hardly a trustworthy sort. Glancing at the soldiers flanking the Maestro and Jekyll's examination table, she shuddered at the doctor's intentions for them.

Accompanied by a small, savage outpouring of steam from the breathing apparatus on his back—something Sophia now regarded as nothing more than cheap theatrics—his raspy voice was accentuated with mechanised amplification as he spoke. "I see you have caught a little rat for your experiments."

Jekyll turned away from the Maestro and winked at Sophia as he prepared a syringe of a serum she did not recognise. "I was just telling your lapdog here that very thing."

Sophia clenched her teeth, and only the presence of the Maestro stayed her hand from slitting the doctor's throat then and there. In her brief time with him, she had noticed a certain attitude towards women from the doctor, just one of many traits he possessed that made her skin crawl. She would have liked to impart on this *bastardo* some manners . . .

. . . but then, who would control the Maestro?

"I trust this means that you will be able to stabilise Victoria." One brass hand with its articulated fingers rested lightly on the laboratory bench. The boy's eyes now welled up with tears.

Sophia forced herself to look away from the young wretch.

"Yes, yes," Henry said, pulling the serum bottle free of the syringe. He remained ridiculously certain that the Maestro would not simply turn and smash him into the ground. "The Queen is merely a means to an end, bear that in mind."

Sophia could not help herself. The idea that this doctor would brush away control of the British Empire as a stepping stone to some kind of greater achievement was insulting. This was the end that the Maestro had envisioned all along. She knew that.

"So what would the end be then?" she broke in, while stealing a glance up at Jekyll.

The doctor's stare was a warning. When he tapped the stopper to squirt a small measure from the tip, he smiled at her as though she were a bug he was ready to squash. "Progress has always been the goal. If I may?"

"You may," the Maestro said, watching Jekyll and the boy with keen interest.

Jekyll leaned closer to the paralysed boy and spoke gently into his ear. "Lad, I know you are scared. And you should be." He held the syringe in front of them both. "You and I are about to take great steps into the unknown. Like those grand explorers who traverse the poles, and those daring aviators talking of travel to the moon, we are about to test the limits of human knowledge and existence. Together, we will accomplish amazing things."

When the needle pierced the boy's skin, its viscous liquid slowly entering his neck, the urchin finally made a sound: a strained, breathy moan. It was soft but just audible to the three of them.

Jekyll tapped a small timer by the examination table, completely unmoved by the child's pathetic wail. "What is power, control of Empire and Crown, compared to the betterment of the human race?"

Sophia only barely held back her desire to clench her hands into fists, as the subject of the experiment foamed at the mouth. Jekyll's only response to the lad's distress manifested itself as furious scribbles in a nearby notebook.

"What are your plans for this one?" the Maestro asked, leaning over the boy. The sound of his ocular focusing on the boy's torments underscored the whimpering.

"Make him compliant. At first." Henry glanced up from his notes as he watched the child begin to settle into his serum's euphoric side effects. His eyes jumped to the timer, then back to his notebook. "This batch is still experimental, more so than Victoria's present formula, so it remains uncertain what effects it will have on him. The question I have to answer for myself is, will the results appear in other subjects."

"Victoria is still too valuable to risk." The Maestro's ocular focused on Sophia, but she doubted he really saw her. "Yet it would be pleasant to be able to control all of the aspects of her personality. Her anger in particular."

"I'm not interested in temperament control so much as I am interested in tapping into muscle stimulation. The human body is quite a machine, capable of astounding things, if we know how to tap into its possibilities."

Sophia remained silent, the best policy at present. The two of them were imparting valuable information that could be useful to her later.

"Consider the unexpected side effect with Her Majesty," Jekyll said as he placed two fingers against the boy's forehead. "Her particular cocktail was supposed to restore vitality and vigour, but it actually repaired skin cells and restored muscle tissue, which returned her to her youth. I have to now build on that unforeseen discovery, and see if I can reproduce those results here."

"In order to share with others?" the Maestro asked.

"Cure your ailments, for example, or unlock amazing potential in others," Henry said. His eyes then flicked over to

Sophia. "Provided I find other willing test subjects." His grin faded as he returned to his notebook. "Building on the success of Her Majesty's treatment, I believe this batch, which could lead to an army of supremely strong and supremely compliant soldiers, will help your cause."

The Maestro straightened, the steam engine on his back singing an eerie note, and gestured to Sophia.

"You will continue to help Henry, my dear, in whatever he needs. If he needs more test subjects such as this one, then do not hesitate to drain the city of its guttersnipes."

"Children, in the beginning," Henry interrupted. "Much easier to control. As my experiments progress, I will need men." His eyes returned to Sophia's, this time the look not sly or covert. He wanted the Maestro to see this. "You can lure men for us, can't you?"

The Maestro's ocular, brandishing a sapphire glow today, remained fixed on her. Sophia had the horrible sensation that he could see inside her. In there, he would find cracks in her faith, and that would make him terribly angry.

Through her dry lips she managed to grate out, "Yes, Maestro. Whatever is needed."

Jets of steam escaped from the back of his suit—a malevolent hiss. "Then I suggest you begin immediately."

A change in her perception of the Maestro and Jekyll reducing her to nothing more than his concierge had helped her find a fresh anger and outrage, dangerous bedfellows to the terror she felt being caught between both men. She had always been a woman in control. Even on feeling herself surrender to the charisma of the Maestro, Sophia maintained a model of decorum.

Now, she was a toy in a child's hand, quickly abandoned if deemed dull or uninteresting.

"As you wish, Maestro," she stated with a quick bow.

As she turned to go, her hand flickered out, and hidden by the fullness of her sleeve she scooped up two of the vials on Jekyll's desk. As she slipped her prize into a pocket inside her jacket, she had no idea what to do with Jekyll's serum, but at least for a moment it felt as though she had taken a little bit of herself back.

Yet it was cold comfort as the boy behind her began to scream once again.

THREE

❧

In Which Our Amorous
Duo Invade France

The landing in Cornwall, while utterly dreadful, had been most fortuitous for agents Books and Braun. As the area's infamous Prussia Cove was a favourite haven for smugglers, it did not take them long, with what funds they had between them, to secure passage to Normandy. The journey—hosted by whom Wellington and Eliza discovered were the infamous Carcaise Family—was neither comfortable nor arduous; but with what uncertainty awaited Eliza at the agreed-upon emergency rendezvous point, this crossing of the English Channel might as well have been a slow boat bound for China.

This particular stretch of beach, where Eliza and Wellington now stood, led to their final destination: a Ministry of Peculiar Occurrences safe house Eliza knew intimately. It was her familiarity with its location and security that made it a perfect hiding place for Alice and the Seven in light of a worst-case scenario, although looking at it would give one pause. On its best days, this structure had probably stood when Elizabeth sat on the throne of England. It was small and inglorious enough to be far from the tourist trails—so perfect for her needs.

Eliza scanned the area one more time, wishing they had

helped themselves to a pair of functional binoculars in their flight from the *Atlantic Angel*.

As they made their way more inland, Wellington let out a relieved sigh as he brushed sand off his sadly battered bowler hat. "I can't wait to have a proper cup of tea at the manor house, and get the smell of that smugglers' boat out of my nostrils."

She glanced in the direction he was looking ever so hopefully. Off to the left, less than a mile from the Ministry's tumbledown château, was the manor house Wellington anticipated as their final stop: a decidedly modern building with decidedly more chances of modern comforts.

A smile flickered over her lips, even in this bleak situation. "I hate to be the carrier of bad news, Wellington, but we are not going there." She turned and pointed to the far more ancient ruin above them on the hill.

"Oh," was the only reply he gave, but she could guess what he was thinking. Much as they might make their living in the bowels of the Ministry Archives, Wellington preferred the conveniences of the day: analytical engines to make his tea, cars to fly him where he needed to go, and intricate listening devices. Eliza liked those sorts of things too, but she also enjoyed safety and security. This safe house was just that.

"How can you be absolutely sure that they are there?" Even though Wellington had seen her maid in the full throes of battle, he would persist in thinking of her as a simple servant. "Alice is not only resourceful, she is loyal to a fault," Eliza replied with a frown. "I have utmost confidence in her."

"Very well then," Wellington said, glancing her way. "We should proceed with caution, though. We still don't know what caused Alice and the Seven to flee London."

Neither of them said the name of Lord Sussex or even his shadowy alter ego, the Maestro; nor did either of them dare utter that of Sophia del Morte.

Eliza nodded. "Still, it wouldn't do to get killed at this point. Especially after that rather sickening Channel voyage."

"Quite." The archivist placed his hands on his hips as he looked around them. "Low scrub down here, right up to the front door, forest to the rear of the château. Sharpshooters could easily be settled in either area."

The tone of his voice reminded Eliza that many things had

changed since she'd first been banished to the Archives of the Ministry of Peculiar Occurrences. Back then her impression of Wellington had been quite different. Now that "rather pompous stuffed shirt" was her partner and fellow field agent. Sometimes the inner workings of his mind—particularly the instincts of a coolheaded marksman—frightened her.

However, spending this eventful year together, she had learned to trust him; and though she dare not say it, perhaps more than that . . .

"Well," Wellington said, making her jump just a fraction, "there's nothing for it. We're just going to have to go up there."

Eliza reached out and lightly stroked the line of his chin. It had only been a few months before that she would never have dared such an intimacy. "I wish we had a few more guns, agents, and even some of Blackwell's madcap devices right now. It feels like we are hanging out here by ourselves—"

"Because we are," he interjected. Wellington's hand found hers, and he squeezed it lightly. "Backup on this would be wonderful, but this is not so much a Ministry, as it is our, affair."

Eliza pressed her lips together. She had to find out if the children were there—and Lord help anyone who got in her way. Her ragged in-drawn breath must have given her away.

"As you said, Eliza," Wellington said softly, "Alice is quite capable of defending herself, and come to think of it so are the children."

"You're right," she replied, pressing a quick kiss on his mouth. "I am sure we will find them eating some of her scones, drinking ginger beer, and having a fine old time."

That was the image she kept firmly in her mind as she took the right-hand path up the slope towards the château. Wordlessly, Wellington crept his way through the low scrub. Luckily, she was dressed in her usual, slightly scandalous, trousers that suited her lifestyle more than skirts and bustles. It would have been hell through this sort of prickly terrain. Eliza kept herself low against the horizon, and stopped every now and then to listen for anyone nearby. It was impossible to be completely sure, but she remained confident the safe house had not been compromised—at least in the exterior. She worked her way around the crumbling building and abandoned gardens, towards the rear door, where Wellington was waiting, a Remmington-Elliot at his side.

Only a few of the blank windows within the château's stern face still had shutters. The main structure was still intact, but the place gave off an air of melancholy that suggested it was on its way to nothingness. Drawing Tutanekai out of his holster—seeing as this would be close quarters, this was the preferred pounamu this time—Eliza reached out with her free hand and rapped on the door. It was the very new and solid door she had requested installed. No use trying to protect those that needed protecting with only a rotten piece of wood to hold invaders off. She now realised it had been the right choice.

She gave two knocks in close succession, a pause, two quick knocks again, another pause, and then one solitary knock. It was the knock of identification she used for her apartments back in London, but also a secret knock used only between Ministry operatives.

The sound of the bolt being withdrawn might not necessarily be a good omen. Eliza glanced at Wellington and gave an abrupt nod. They raised their weapons.

"Come in, miss!" The familiar voice from inside unlocked a little tension in Eliza's stomach. Still, Wellington stepped back while Eliza pushed the door open with her foot.

Alice was sitting in a rocking chair facing the door, a large barrelled shotgun aimed directly at it. The look on her face was as fierce as a mother lion, and for an instant Eliza feared for her life.

Then the moment passed like a cloud blowing away from the sun. Only then did she notice the lanky form of Christopher standing in the corner by the door. It was he who had drawn the bolt, but his face was stern. A Bulldog was in his hand. Eliza had seen the oldest member of the Ministry Seven in many situations, but never like this. That realisation tempered her relief.

"Miss Eliza!" Alice cried, leaping up and running towards her. The maid's legs hissed and clanked as she came, and when she collided with her employer it was with a bone-shaking thump. Alice had worked very hard to overcome her workhouse beginnings, so this display was delightfully unusual.

Eliza did not correct her, but instead hugged her tight.

Wellington let out an uncomfortable noise when the maid embraced him tightly too. "It is good to see you, Alice," he muttered.

Sometimes that "stuffed shirt" aspect of the archivist still reared its head. It would be something she would need to remedy.

"Christopher?" Eliza called to the young man by the door; but he did not come forwards, instead moving to peer cautiously out of a side window. He said nothing to either of the agents, and though Eliza admired his dedication to duty, it worried her.

Alice let go of him, and seemed to regain her composure. She hitched up her skirts, displaying the brass and gears of her prosthetic legs. A compartment slid open where she stowed the weapon; and then the thigh hissed shut, keeping the trusted sidearm within her reach. Alice was the kind of maid that was proficient in a variety of fields, and very handy to have around when things got tricky.

"The rest of the children, Alice . . ." Eliza started, but didn't get any further.

A door at the end of the hallway burst open and the remaining Ministry Seven tumbled out of one of the back rooms, squealing her name. Eliza was knocked back on her heels as all six of them hit her.

As she reached out to touch each of them or pull them close, that was when she noticed. Seven. Not eight. One of the quirks of the Ministry Seven was it was not strictly true—a relic of a little trick they had pulled on her.

After two head counts confirming the unpleasant truth, Eliza's gaze shot back to Alice. "Where is Callum?"

The maid looked as though she had been kicked. "Callum's been taken."

"Arrested?" she asked hopefully. That, at least, could be easily remedied.

"No," Alice replied, her voice low and suddenly serious. "Callum was *taken*."

Eliza had been through death and disaster in many forms working with the Ministry, but she hadn't felt as imperilled as she did in that moment. She had truly never imagined having children of her own, and had taken the Seven under her wing without thinking about it. Now, hearing Alice's words hit her, she realised that her love for them ran deeper than she'd thought. For a moment all tactical and logistical considerations dropped away. Cold terror consumed her.

Wellington was at her side, putting an arm around her

shoulders, but she noticed his face was as bereft of blood as hers felt. "Tell us the whole story."

Alice gestured them into the kitchen, with the children, now quiet and grim, following behind them. Only Liam remained, watching the window in Christopher's place, his face just as grim.

In the kitchen the fire was lit and the smell of warm baking filled the air. In the manner of all Ministry safe houses, the chimney was a concealed one, with the smoke funnelled underground so as not to give away their location. Eliza took a seat next to the fire, and Serena wriggled her way onto her knee. Wellington sat opposite, the rest of the children clustering around him. The way Alice shifted from foot to foot showed her inner turmoil.

Eliza held out her hand to her. "Alice, we need to hear what happened. I am sure you did your best . . ."

"It wasn't her fault," Christopher said from his place by the door. "It was mine. He got taken right in front of me."

Eliza knew that look in the young man's eyes—she'd worn it herself, many times. She'd lost agents in the field before, and in every instance felt the responsibility of it. That it now lived in Christopher was almost unbearable.

"What happened, Christopher?" Wellington asked, his voice low and calm.

The boy looked down at his feet and spoke only to them. "It was a fancy doctor's place. We went to check it out first, knew when he was out. It was easy to break into. It was just the five of us: me, Callum, Serena, Liam, and Colin."

"I got us in," Serena piped up, sounding rather proud, but immediately was silenced when Christopher shot her a sharp look.

"Go on," Eliza urged.

The eldest boy cleared his throat. "It all looked nice as pie. We were just collecting some goodies, and we found this weird room downstairs. Then this man appeared, he had all these needles an' things . . . then . . . then we had to run."

"He was dead," Serena said, her fists tight on her dress, "in the eyes."

"I swear," Christopher said, a tremor in his voice as he continued, "the man was not natural, not one of God's creations is what I mean. Bloody monster, he was."

They'd certainly seen their share of those. Particularly in the Americas. "And where did this monster come from?" Her eyes ran over the children, demanding utter honesty.

"It was the door of hell, Miss Eliza," Christopher answered.

"Come off it," Colin barked. "There was this cage. Odd looking, it was, and it was spitting lightning bolts in all directions. That's why we couldn't get to Callum."

Eliza and Wellington shared a solemn look. The Culpeppers might be dead, but their inventions lived on.

"I told everyone to run, and we did," Christopher said, his gaze staring in the fire as he recalled. "We last saw Callum in that monster's hold. We ran to your home, Miss Eliza. No one else would believe us."

"That's when I reckoned we had to come here," Alice said, her eyes gleaming with almost tears. "Callum wouldn't be able to stop from telling whoever has him about you, miss."

Eliza leaned across and squeezed Alice's hand, just once. "You did the right thing—*very much* the right thing. The rest of the children are safe because of you. Well done."

Her maid suddenly let out a sharp cry and crossed the kitchen to a wall where rucksacks hung. She grabbed one and opened it on the centre table. "The children snatched this from that doctor's place. It is something you must . . ."

A rapid knocking made everyone in the kitchen jump.

"Miss, there's people outside, comin' this way!" Liam shouted even as he kept banging.

Eliza and Wellington darted to the window and carefully nudged aside one of the shutters.

Five men were immediately obvious, making their way to the door of the château. Eliza's right hand dropped to her pistol.

Wellington stayed her hand. "Look at the tweed they are wearing . . ."

Her eye was not used to taking in fashion details in such situations; but Eliza, on recognising the pattern, let out a long sigh. A sigh that turned into a soft groan.

"Who else wears such a dreadful tweed with such cheap bowler hats?" Wellington slowly shook his head. "The boys from the Department."

"The Department." She was so mad she could spit. "This is the last thing we need right now."

The Department of Imperial Inconveniences—formed in the last few years and fancying themselves as dreadfully important—were, in Eliza's mind, best qualified in cleaning up after the Ministry. Hardly what she would deem "reliable" when it came to support or competency of any kind in the field. If they cocked up their cover, as these pillocks were prone to do, Eliza was going to have someone's guts for garters.

As she turned away from the window to go deal with them, her face flushed with annoyance, Wellington laid a hand on her arm.

"You don't have the best history with the Department," he said softly. "Mind if I go out and share a quick word with them?"

Eliza let out an angry grumble, but saw the sense of it. She'd never been an agent known for her diplomacy, especially inter-departmentally. "Fine," she said, flicking her hand in the direction of the door. "But those fools owe us a drink when all this is sorted out!"

"I'll see what I can do," Wellington said with a shrug.

She followed him to the door, grabbing a Remington-Elliot, and allowing it to spin on her finger before presenting it to Wellington handle first. "Take this."

"Tosh, Eliza," he scoffed. "Perhaps Doctor Sound also picked up your distress signal. They are probably our extraction team."

She heard him reassure Liam of the same thing, probably trying to calm him down too, just before he stepped outside to disappear into the sunshine.

This extraction had better lead to the fastest of debriefings. The sooner they returned to London, the sooner they could be on their way to finding Callum.

"Miss Eliza," she heard Liam—still by the door—ask, "are these fine gents taking us back to Old Blighty?"

"Certainly, and once we're done at the Department," Eliza grumbled as she walked over to a counter, "we are going to get Callum."

She remembered that in one of these cabinets . . .

"There you are," she whispered on finding the bottle of scotch.

While she poured herself several fingers' worth of the spirit, her eyes strayed to a modest stack of newspapers on the counter top. Just as she had trained the maid for this situation, Alice purchased local newspapers, staying apprised of what was going on wherever she managed to stop for any given time. The agent let out a sigh, and thumbed back, following Alice and the children's journey in reverse. The newspaper at the bottom, a rag she recognised from London, was devoted entirely to the rumoured plans for the Diamond Jubilee celebration next year. The Queen had just recovered from a bout of ill health, and everyone was worried the old dear was going to pop her clogs before hitting the actual event—though no one wanted to say it.

As Eliza flicked through the pages, her eyes found a headline on the second page. It was a black-bordered column of a sensational nature, this one reading in bold letters:

THE TERRORS OF TECHNOLOGY:
Another Motorcar Accident Only Impresses the Dangers of Automated Travel Machines

Usually her attention would wander onwards to the latest news from the outskirts of the Empire, but she had to know why this journalist would instil a fear of science into the paper's readers. Maybe this was Welly's influence. Something was nagging in the back of her head about the newspapers, but her eyes had already taken in a name that washed away any chance of figuring out what that was.

It only took a moment to process the words.

She immediately flipped the newspapers to the one dated on their arrival in the country. She quickly scanned the columns . . .

. . . and found another familiar name staring back at her.

Eliza called out, feeling her heart pound a pace, "Alice, I'm going to need something from you. *Now!*"

INTERLUDE

❦

Wherein a Man's Past Catches Up
with Him, Much to His Relief

I t was damn hot in Queensland. Not much surprising there. It was one of the true consistencies of the world after all.

Luckily for Bruce Campbell, formerly of Her Majesty's Ministry of Peculiar Occurrences, it was a good excuse for a beer—not that he really needed one. Still, finding a pub in Rockhampton was about as easy as throwing a stone and hitting dirt.

Bruce decided that today the Royal Fitzroy Hotel would get his business. He'd been too long under a noon sun chasing the weasely sod who had bushwhacked his client's train, and now it was time for a break. He was sweating under his hat, and it was running down his back. It didn't matter if you were born to it, there was something about Queensland heat a body couldn't get used to.

Like most things in life, Bruce thought, *you just have to learn to cope*—and it just so happened that beer was his favoured mechanism. His grey stallion, Eureka, was ready for a rest too. They'd both reached the end of haring around the bush for one day. When Bruce slid his long, lean form down out of the saddle, Eureka let out a long grateful breath, and shook himself. The tall stallion didn't need to be hitched, and it was the former agent's policy not to anyway; it was sure as eggs that as soon as he did there would be the need for a quick getaway.

Bruce patted the steed's sweating flank, rewarding the faithful horse with shade, a well-deserved rest, and some water. He left Eureka swatting flies with his dark tail as he strode into the hotel, knocking dirt off his boots while taking stock of the pub. It was the usual round of ne'er-do-wells with nothing better to do in the middle of the day. A collection of broken-down miners, old men . . . and him.

He'd only been in town for three days, but the barman knew him by now. He nodded, and a shot of rotgut whiskey and a beer appeared. It was the kind of magic that Bruce appreciated. After he knocked back the shot, he proceeded to the beer with relish. The barman filled the shot glass a second time without comment or having to ask.

It bothered Bruce that his target was appearing more and more elusive. Without the Ministry's resources, tracking someone down was much harder than he'd expected. Still, it was this or stay home with the wife, and sell insurance.

A fate worse than death as far as Bruce was concerned.

He'd much rather stay out in the wilds of the outback than go home to Emily. She had a lady's name, but carried the disposition of a ship's angry quartermaster. She was not so terrible the first week he was home. In fact, she was quite pleased to have her beau back in the same hemisphere. The pleasantries faded rather quickly in the second, and by the month's end, he was reminded of why he had not hesitated when assigned to the home office. So what was a man with his particular set of skills to do after an agency had dismissed him?

What he did best—catch those that would do ill. No, he would stick it out in Rockhampton and eventually get his man . . .

. . . after he'd drunk a few more beers.

When someone jostled his elbow causing him to spill his beer, Bruce felt his temper flare. It was a double offence. For one, he was reminded that his reflexes were not what they had once been. He had always been underestimated as a bit of a lumbering lummox, but when he needed to remain alert he could avoid brushing up against complete strangers. Complete strangers could easily turn unfriendly, and he knew one agent too many who never made it home on account of that. Every day away from the Ministry's service meant his reflexes would grow dull. Such laxity could end up costing him his life, considering the colourful types he crossed back in his cloak-and-dagger days. He hated that feeling.

The second offence, of course, was the wasting of perfectly good beer. No, it certainly wasn't *good* beer, but it was cold and it was his. Now part of it was on the floor.

He slammed his mug on the bar and was about to deliver an elbow of his own when the smell of roses reached his nose. A woman. *No,* Bruce corrected himself, *a lady*. A smile stretched on his face before his eyes had properly focused on her, a face currently concealed by a large hat that was tilted towards him. Hopefully the face was as pleasing as the figure, an ample bosom just visible. The lady was also prettily dressed—too pretty for this particular pub in this particular town.

Bruce cleared his throat. "Now usually I'm the one buying drinks, but I believe in women's rights and all that. Seeing as you made me spill a bit, I believe—"

But his clever jape abruptly ceased when the woman finally turned to him with a greeting. "Hello, sweetie."

There were many women from Bruce's past. Many. Perhaps numbering into triple numbers, but there were some that he would prefer never to cross paths with again for a number of reasons. Topping this long list of ladies best left unseen was Beatrice Muldoon, the fair lady in front of him. It was hard to tell with her sitting down just how tall she was, but he recalled very well her towering over him last time they'd parted. He also recalled what a splendid right hook she carried as she had punched him several times in the face. From recollection, he'd gotten blood over her pretty dress and that had made her quite cross. That night had been the last straw with her when it came to their occasional trysts.

The news of his marital status had also not impressed the tall blonde woman from the Department of Imperial Inconveniences one bit. He presumed that was what had finally severed ties between them.

Maybe there had been a change of opinion. Perhaps she'd spent some long lonely nights thinking on their times together. He was pleased to see that she was still the vision he remembered her to be.

Bruce leaned back slightly on his bar stool. "G'day, Beatrice. Bloody hot, isn't it?"

"Nothing I can't handle," she said, picking up a beer mug of her own and taking a swig. *Yeah,* Bruce thought as he watched her drink, *that always kept me comin' back. Refined and posh, like a proper lady, but a hard drinker and stout brawler.* Beatrice set down her drink and asked, "I wondered if you'd come home after that nasty piece of business with the 'Spooks' and your cock-up."

Thinking on his failure to the Ministry and that particular parting Bruce still found painful, and the Australian had learned the drink also helped him avoid thinking about that pain.

"Well, I had made my bed, now hadn't I?" He shrugged as he took a good swig of his own beer. "Perhaps it was time for me to come back to Australia. When a man loses all that he has known and all that he has come to believe in, what better to do than go back to the beginning, wonder what you hath wrought, and find out if you can make it right?"

"How poetic of you, Bruce," she said, allowing her eyes to wander up and down him. "I think excommunication has released the philosopher in you."

He snorted. "Coming home after the things I have seen and done has given me a perspective. I'm trying to appreciate it." He then pointed a finger at her and warned, "And while you may think you and your Department types are clever with the nicknames, they aren't welcome by me."

"Oh, how cute for a Spook," Beatrice teased, "getting your dander up for an agency that wouldn't give you the time of day."

He gave her a wry grin. "They were good to me. I could have been better to them. Mea culpa."

"So this is how you are spending your penance?" Beatrice asked, taking in the colourful assortment of outcasts. "Bounty-hunting train robbers? A far cry from what goes bump in the night, isn't it?"

Bruce noticed he was pounding down his beer rather

quickly, and this concerned him as those instincts he knew were softening up the longer he was away from the Ministry were now kicking up a bit in his noggin. It could just be a coincidence that Beatrice Muldoon, agent of the Department of Imperial Inconveniences, was in Rockhampton, at the same pub as him, at the time he happened to ride into town on a bounty that only he knew the details of . . .

Bruce had never been very fond of coincidences, and in his line of work they were suspicious.

Behind the bar, in the dingy reflection of its mirror, the former Ministry agent let his eyes skip around the room a little. He knew exactly what to look for, particularly as this was the Department he was dealing with. There was no telltale sign of that signature tweed immediately apparent, but considering the amount of dust covering everyone, and not to mention the dim lighting in here, Bruce took cold comfort in not seeing any other Department agents. He gestured for another beer just to appear calm, but when it arrived he wrapped his fingers around it and waited for her to speak. She didn't.

Because it was Beatrice, because the two of them enjoyed a past together, he decided to play along. "So, Beatrice, exactly what—or who—brings you all the way down under to the backside of Her Majesty's royal bum?"

Beatrice folded her hands in front of her. "You know how I hate the cold." Her voice was surprisingly light for such a tall woman, and marked with the stain of the upper class. "I thought a change of scenery was in order. Somewhere warmer."

He couldn't help laughing at that. "Darlin', you've come to the right place. We only have two seasons down here: bloody hot, and bloody hot and wet. But I don't think either of those are the reason for your little visit to Rocky." He leaned forwards a bit. "You aren't getting lonely, are you?"

The Department agent stiffened, and a flicker of anger over her features told him she was only barely keeping herself in check. That temperament was yet another reason he'd enjoyed her company so much. Beatrice had always been a very passionate person.

"Not at all," she finally replied silkily. "In fact, I am far too busy to get lonely. The Department is keeping me on my toes."

"Really?" Bruce tilted his head. "Now that's quite a turn as only a few months ago, I heard—oh, what was that bloke's name?—Bernard Wilson, that's it. I heard Wilson say the Department was coming up a bit short when it came to case-work and funding for projects."

"Oh, we're getting the funding now," she replied, and now there was a hint of a smile around her lips. "The higher ups finally came round."

He didn't let it show on his face, but that didn't settle well with Bruce. The Department had always been the poor sister of the Ministry, either taking the leftover cases that were the most ridiculous or cleaning up after the Ministry when things got messy. A good example was that whole Phoenix Society hullabaloo. Tidying up after that affair, and trying to quell the two neighbouring towns that the Havelock Manor employed, stretched their resources thin. Truthfully, investigating strange lights in the sky and tracking down fairy folk made the Department the butt of many a joke back at the Ministry. Well, the butt of *his* jokes when he was at the Ministry, anyway.

Hearing that the Department now had received favours from those closer to the Crown made his skin crawl.

Bruce pushed his beer back and forth a little. "Did you using any of your amazing charms have anything to do with that? I bet lots of those lords would love a—"

Beatrice cut him off before he could say anything more. "That has nothing to do with it. Things have changed." Her ice-chip blue eyes locked with his. "And that uncanny perception of yours is exactly the reason why I happen to be here in charming Rockhampton. We are in need of talent."

That look was so sharp, Bruce felt pinned to the bar stool for a moment. He knew when a lady wanted him; it was a special ability of his, honed from years of experience, and the look Beatrice was giving him now was familiar. He covered his surprise and the twitch in his trousers by taking a small sip of his beer.

She must have recognised the look on his face, because her jaw tightened again. "Not that kind of talent, you git! I meant, for the Department. We have a vacancy."

Bruce snorted as one of his jokes, specifically the one about how those not good enough for the Ministry went to work for the Department, sprang to mind. "I don't know if you can afford me, darlin'."

Beatrice leaned in close. From this angle he had quite a delightful view of her impressive cleavage. "We need you, love . . . and we have the money to allow you that kind of life you enjoy. Excitement. Danger." She gave Bruce a wry smile as she reached for the shot of whiskey he'd forgotten about, and toasted to him. "Maybe, even me."

The mention of money did intrigue him, since he did prefer wine, women, and song to beer, whores, and accordion music. The offer from Beatrice, as well as the sight of her kicking back that whiskey, made this development even more tempting. However, he was not going to slide into bed with the Department without knowing exactly what they wanted. And they must have wanted something badly from him to have come all the way to Australia.

"I'm afraid my skills have gotten a bit rusty," he said mildly. It wasn't that hard to be convincing as she had snuck up on him. "More to the point, why would the Department hire one excommunicated from the game? I am damaged goods, especially when it comes to being a fella you can trust."

"My recommendation."

If someone would have brushed Bruce with a feather, he would have fallen off his bar stool.

"This would be more of a permanent placement." Her hand dropped over the top of his and held it tight, along with his attention. "We need you, Bruce."

This was starting to get interesting. "And why exactly is that?"

Beatrice's fingers clenched around his ever so slightly. "Your knowledge of the Ministry."

Bruce leaned back. Those instincts were now screaming at him to punch her as hard as he could and run. "My knowledge of—"

"Dead drop locations. Safe houses. Protocols," she continued. "We need your help mopping up our current mess."

He tilted his head again. "Mopping up? I hope that is a simple way of saying bringing in agents out of hostile territories?"

Beatrice pursed her lips, appearing to size him up. He

suddenly felt like a wallaby being measured for the pot. "The Ministry of Peculiar Occurrences has been deemed an inconvenience by the Queen. We have a few loose ends to secure. I told my superiors if there was any man capable of leading this undertaking, it was the Thunder from Down Under himself, Bruce Campbell."

He didn't blink or move a muscle as they stared at each other.

"I would have thought," she said in a soft undertone, "after what they did to you, that wouldn't be a problem."

Despite everything that had happened between him—the betrayal against Doctor Sound, the heartbreak he brought to his best mate, Brandon Hill, and his breaking of trust with the Ministry—this news hit Bruce like a kangaroo kick to the stomach. Perhaps he'd hoped someday to be forgiven, return to the comforts and friendships he'd made there. No, the Ministry had its faults as did any agency that served at the behest of the Queen, but they had been good people, the lot of them. Good people who would have opened their arms to him again, once they had seen him a reformed man.

And yet, here was Beatrice casually telling him that was all impossible.

He was certainly not the smartest agent. He was the Ministry's muscle, without question. Bruce was quick enough to know when Beatrice referred to loose ends, she was talking about his fellow agents. Brandon, Eliza, and Maulik, if he was in from India. Regardless of their desire to sock him on the chin, those agents were still his mates. They were his mates . . . now deemed an inconvenience in Queen Vic's eyes.

Suddenly the train bushwhacker faded to insignificance. Why the hell would the Queen get rid of her Ministry?

It had to be the fault of that plonker, Lord Sussex.

While Bruce took a long draft of his beer, he thought about where the agents would go, how they would react to this. If he knew any of them—which he did—he knew they wouldn't go easy. Then he thought about the Department of Imperial Inconveniences and how thorough they were when given an assignment. They might have been nitwits, but they were well-trained nitwits, and they did excel in a few skills. Tracking, for one.

Then he thought on the unfortunate fact that he had never trusted Beatrice. He'd bedded her several times, certainly, but did a roll in the hay equal trust? Hardly. There was something shifty about the tall woman. He'd never be able to turn his back on her, and he'd always been too lazy to keep much of an eye out behind him.

This afternoon, however, he did. And on catching the inside lining of the bloke sitting behind her, noting the signature tweed that Beatrice herself was wearing proudly in her hat and riding coat, he knew a great deal rested on his next few carefully chosen words.

There was one more uncomfortable fact he recalled about Miss Beatrice Muldoon: she didn't take rejection at all well. Bruce slipped himself out of her grasp and patted her gloved hand, trying to think of a way to avoid any nastiness. "Now, Beatrice . . ."

Her eyes narrowed as she sat back, slipping out of reach. "Last time you used that tone on me Bruce, you rather hurt my feelings . . . and then I rather hurt something of yours . . ."

It was definitely time to switch from beer to whiskey. Then again, the glass mug in his hand could make for a better weapon than a shot glass. He took in a deep breath, and shook his head. "I don't want to get back into the game, Bea. Sorry, but somewhere I lost my way . . . and it cost lives. Like I told ya, I need perspective, and hunting down my mates just ain't the perspective I need at present."

Beatrice let out a long sigh and adjusted her hat, pressing back one of the jet hatpins that held it in place. "They told me this was going to be a waste of time, but I insisted. I thought I knew you better." Her smile was crooked. Bruce recognised that particular smile as being the very same one just before she'd knocked him down with that vicious hook of hers.

His eyes flicked back over to the man behind her. He suddenly had to get up from his place at the bar. He glanced at the mirror again, and simultaneously four more patrons—one of them wearing the tweed in his pants, two showing it in their coats, and the last one in the kerchief tied around his neck—also got up from their tables. All at the same time.

Yeah, Bruce thought to himself, *this kind of blunder is* exactly *why the Department is a right joke.*

"So," he said with a laugh, "what did they tell you to do if'n I said no?"

Beatrice's eyes narrowed on him as her smile turned decidedly bitter. "I think we're past the point where I tell you what's going on. I think we're at the really pointy end of the conversation."

He caught the flash of metal at her wrist which revealed some kind of armguard, as he slid away from a strike she'd aimed at his hand. Bruce knew his dismount off the stool was not exactly smooth, but he found his feet quickly enough and brought his mug around. The glass was of a good, solid stock as it dislocated the jaw of the bloke trying to flank him. Didn't that idiot realise there was this giant *mirror* behind the bar where they sat?

He took a few steps back, easing into a pugilistic stance. Beatrice's blue eyes flashed, and she gestured behind her to those other four agents at the other end of the saloon. He could see their dingy reflections not closing in on him, but barring any exits. They all had clean sight lines, but Miss Bea—obviously the senior officer—right at this moment was buggering proper Department procedure. This wasn't going to be a simple, elegant cleanup. She wanted to get into it with him.

Fair enough.

Beatrice slid off her stool and took up a similar stance. Bruce had forgotten that she was a good foot taller than him, and the delicate sleeves of her dress, stretched tight over impressive musculature, also reminded him of how physical she got in bed—and in mêlées such as this. The inhabitants of the pub, who had undoubtedly seen their fair share of fights, picked up their drinks and relocated to the edges of the room. When the piano player was on a break, this was the only entertainment to be had.

"Bea," he warned, "I'm gonna give ya—"

The right hook, Bruce realised, he had been worrying about too much, as it was a *left* hook to the cheek that connected soundly, knocking him back into a table where a pair of miners were too settled into their drinks to notice what was coming. They looked at Bruce, then turned their eyes to Beatrice. Lady or not, she had spilt their beers and would pay. Or so these poor sods thought.

This was hardly an even match as she was a trained agent, and her return strike was much quicker. Still, everyone has the ability to land a lucky punch, and that was exactly what the shorter of the two men did. Bea toppled into three miners standing off to the side. One of them cushioned her fall, while the other two entered the fray.

Bruce, now back on his feet, braced himself against the bar as Beatrice started bearing down on him. Once she drew close enough, he brought the empty mug by his hand around. The glass shattered against the armguard just before her other fist came around, clocking him hard enough to make his head ring. He had taken more than his fair share of blows to the face, so the blood was totally expected, but the surge of numbness and the watering of his eyes caught him by surprise. Was he really that soft after only a month out of the game?

A hard *click* sobered him up in a moment, and his vision snapped into focus. Beatrice was pointing the girded arm at him. He had to move and move now.

Something dug into the wood planks where he had once lain, but he continued to roll until he was up on his feet. Bruce reached behind him and slipped out the forearm-length rod sheathed in his belt. With a quick flick of his wrist and the flip of a switch, the rod snapped with a sharp hiss to its full length. It sliced through the air and struck hard against that concealed armguard of Beatrice's. He managed to get two more strikes before she wised up to what his plan had been. The backhand against his immense, square jaw knocked him back, but it did not knock away his smile. Knowing what damage his baton could do, Bruce knew whatever device she had under that blouse was rightly buggered.

"Goddammit!" she swore.

And there was his confirmation.

Bruce had just taken one step towards an exit when a fist—not Beatrice's—knocked him back. He shook his head to try and find the Department agents within the fray. Apparently blokes and sheilas were all joining in now, not for the honour of a lady nor to defend a man when he was clearly bush-whacked. No, people were now joining the brawl for the hell of it.

However, this kind of chaos could make the Department's

job far easier. Bruce decided to adhere to one method: swing at anything that moved.

This tactic proved to be a good one for him as on several occasions he caught a glimpse of tweed. Whether it was the Department's tweed or just some poor sod with terrible fashion sense, it was hard to say. Bruce was still standing, and so far no one had—

The cupped hand did not slap, strike, or even bop his most sensitive and sacred of muscles. No, the cupped hand grabbed, crushed, and—yes—twisted his balls. Twisted just enough to keep his attention.

"Bring him in for reorientation, they said," Beatrice shouted over the brawl. She was leading him back to the bar as she continued, her breath pushing back strands of hair that were now tousled and wild. "Resolve this matter quickly and efficiently, they said." Bruce gave a little groan—a touch of pleasure in that, he hated to admit—when she squeezed just a fraction more. "No, sweetie. I'm going to *enjoy* this! For as long—as—*possible*!"

With that proclamation, Beatrice picked him off his feet and threw him onto the bar, the wind rushing out of him as he pounded, chest first, into its sturdy wood. Whoever had called her sex the gentler one, had never met a bruiser like Miss Beatrice Octavia Muldoon.

Bruce had hold of the bar. The publican had retreated to a place of safety, but unfortunately a collection of empty bottles, glass mugs in various states of quantity, shot glasses, and a few coffee mugs had not. He could feel Beatrice switch her hold from his balls to the waistband of his trousers, and then forward momentum. He continued down along the far-too-long length of this bar, his sharp connection against broken bottles and heavy glass tumblers reminding him why bar brawls were a losing deal, but wildly entertaining to bystanders. He would much rather have been the one doing the sweeping instead of Beatrice. Even the empty glasses hurt, but not as much as knowing his sweep along the bar was also resulting in wasted spirits. It was enough to make a man cry. A whack to the bollocks and then this!

Suddenly, he felt open air. End of the line. Once clear of the bar, Beatrice flung him off with a little cry of victory. He landed against the wall in a heap, giving him a second to look on Bea. Even looking like a well-dressed but completely mad woman, she was still a thing of beauty. In a brawler sort of fashion.

"What are you smiling at, Campbell?" Beatrice roared.

He guffawed as he stood, brushed himself off, and shrugged. "Just remembering what a goer you always were."

She charged at him, but this time Bruce brush-blocked the incoming hook, sweeping the arm under his and locking it against his side. He then grabbed the other arm and pinned it behind her as he twisted, bending her back into a dip. Her mouth tasted salty. Either her lip was cut or a tooth was loose, but she was still a lovely woman to taste. She kissed like she fought. To win. And that was what her tongue was now doing—tasting every part of his mouth and savouring him as he did her. For a Pom, she kissed better than some frontier girls he had known.

Their lips parted with a gasp, and Beatrice was trying very hard to keep focus. That kiss had obviously caught her off guard.

So did Bruce's forehead which connected hard with hers, knocking her back into a small knot of men who were still enjoying report with one another's fists.

With Beatrice occupied, Bruce kicked two bottles, one for each hand, up from the floor. One he used as he would have used his baton, had he not lost it in the fight. The other he lobbed to his left at a Department boy daring to raise a pistol. It had been a long time since Bruce had fielded for the Queensland cricket team, but he had apparently lost none of his skill, for the bottle hit the agent, even shattered on impact.

That one must have been green as the manor's lawn. The Department's rule was no mess, no fuss. Guns rarely played into their schemes.

Returning to the heart of this drunken storm, an empty bottle his only weapon against trained Department agents and pub patrons, Bruce ducked and weaved through scuffles until he found a clear path to the saloon's window, which he propelled himself through, rolling then running through the clearing he had made for himself outside. Eureka, being the horse that he was and knowing his master all too well, had already turned himself around. Bruce had just leapt up into the saddle when he heard a scream, a passionate if not primal scream that he knew belonged to Beatrice. He snapped the reins and thundered down the main street, his head down and low. It wasn't Department policy to make for public executions but he would not leave anything to chance. Ride fast, ride hard.

The dusty remains of Rockhampton soon behind him Bruce Campbell was now wrestling with what he had never dreamed of doing again. There were a few connections he could contact but the next few days he wouldn't call luxurious. He had to get out of Australia, do a quick drop by in South America, and then get back to Pommyland.

It was time to come to the Ministry's rescue.

FOUR

❧

In Which Wellington Books Is Asked to Descend into Maelstrom's Flames

Wellington stepped out of the cottage and tried not to cast his eyes longingly at the manor house looming in the distance. It still looked just as warm and inviting as it had moments ago. His eyes looked around their safe house, noting barrels of fuel for the internal heating system close by the rear entrance, perhaps the *only* convenience this shack offered. If the approaching Department operatives were the extraction team, then thankfully they would not need to "make do" as they had been doing since their escape from the *Atlantic Angel.*

Over the sound of the pounding surf, he could just hear his own feet sliding through the thick, emerald-green grass underfoot. Perhaps while waiting for travel details to be sorted and—with the inclusion of the Ministry Seven—clearance granted, Eliza might enjoy the moment's rest, even enjoy this lovely vista with him.

Behind the Department agents, the English Channel stretched wide and open. They must have a transport of some kind over the rise, ready to take them back home. As details in the man's suit became more prevalent, Wellington made certain that his hands were visible to the approaching Department operatives. These were allies, that much was certain; but, there was no reason why both he and Eliza shouldn't be careful. Field meetings like this one were always tense.

"A lovely day," Wellington announced, as protocol dictated. "Bit windy for my taste."

"Perhaps," the man in the signature tweed of the Department of Imperial Inconveniences replied, "but excellent weather if you want to fly a kite."

Wellington halted and slowly lowered his hands. With confirmation made, he looked behind the contact to see five others, all wearing the signature Department fashion, following a healthy distance behind him. They were positioned at least two hundred paces apart, as if covering as much ground as five people could. Wellington forced his smile wider as he saw the two women and three men come to a halt while their leader continued to approach. *It's the tweed,* Wellington assured himself as the man tipped a black bowler in his direction. *I've always been unsettled by the Department's choice of tweed pattern.*

"The Ministry was expecting you in London, and when you all were nowhere to be found and the *Angel* was missing one of their aeroflyers, we were called in. We've been visiting every safe house in the network. Good thing we lot enjoy travel," the agent said, a jovial lilt in his voice. "How are you holding up, old man?"

Wellington felt his smile tighten. He particularly didn't care for the "old man" moniker, but chose to continue the pleasantries. "Considering the scenery and the conditions we find ourselves in, none the worse for wear."

He nodded in approval. "Excellent choice, Normandy. Lovely time to come. Name's Cavenaugh. Samuel Cavenaugh."

"Wellington Books, Chief Archivist."

The main raised an eyebrow at that. "Really?" He took a step back from Wellington as he said over his shoulder, "It's the archivist."

The Department agents now slowly crept back, widening their spread across the open field. Wellington kept his focus on Cavenaugh, the earlier tingle in the back of his brain kicking harder now.

"What happened up there, old man?" he asked.

"An emergency of a personal nature," Wellington replied. "We will need to get back to London quickly."

"How many in your party?"

"Enough that we are going to need more than a small boat to get us back to Her Majesty's shores."

"Blimey!" Cavenaugh laughed. Wellington did not feel inspired to join in. "Travelling with a small entourage, are you?"

"No need to fret. In light of this emergency, we all had to be light on our feet." Wellington motioned to Cavenaugh. "Much like you all, I'm sure, when you received the call about us?"

"Light on our feet?" he chuckled. "That we were, old man. That we were."

He really wished Cavenaugh would stop calling him that.

"So you were about to tell me," the Department agent continued, pulling out a pad, flipping it open as he touched the tip of his pen to his tongue, "how many are coming back with us?"

His mind was ready with the answer, a full account of who was awaiting for safe and secure passage from Normandy. That answer never was given voice. He suddenly felt very vulnerable. "Well, there is just myself, Agent Braun . . . and her maid. We were returning from the Americas when we received an alarm from her."

"Just you, the colonial, and the maid," he muttered. "No one else?"

Wellington knotted his brow. "Should there be?"

Seconds ticked away between them in the quiet, save for the odd call of seagulls and the waves breaking on shore.

"All seems to be in order then," he said, returning the pad into his pocket. "Time to come in from the cold then, Books?"

Cavenaugh held out his hand. Wellington knew he should take it, but the tingle in the back of his skull was now something akin to a migraine.

Oh, this is silly, he thought to himself. "Thank you, sir," Wellington finally replied as he willed his hand to reach up.

The bullet split Cavenaugh's forehead in a blink, sending tiny rivulets of blood in every direction from the point of impact. Wellington turned to see Eliza holding the Webley-Maxim Mark II in one hand while cradling in her other arm a

Samson-Enfield Mark III. She fired off a second shot, and
Wellington saw one of the remaining five Department agents
fall. The other four were scattering, producing what he could
only assume were sidearms.

"Eliza, what in the bloody hell—?"

"Stuff it, Books," Eliza said, tossing him the Mark III. "If
it moves"—she jammed into his coat pocket what he knew
were spare shells—"make it stop."

Wellington hefted the weight of the Mark III, Alice's
unmistakably, as Eliza fired off another round, downing
another Department agent. He looked back at the house, then
looked at the rolling valley overlooking their position.

On this side of caution, he thought as he shouldered the
weapon and fired both barrels on the fuel by the cottage.

The explosion wrapped itself around that corner of the château, creating a wall of thick, heavy smoke that cast a dark
shadow in the direction of the valley. If he had the best of
conditions, the smoke would have drifted straight across to
hide the field from sight. A wall of smoke heading into the
valley, however, could make even the most seasoned of snipers
uncomfortable.

"We have three making a run for it," Eliza called over to
him. She then dropped to one knee and fired. "As I said, we
have *two* making a run for it."

"Just to remind you," he said, taking a defensive position at
her side, "gunning down the field auxiliary does not reflect
well on agent evaluations, you know this, yes?"

"Duly noted, Agent Books." She looked back in the direction of the accompanying brush and trees further inland.
She adjusted the settings on her pistol's scope and added, "We
can't let any of them leave these shores. Are you with me,
Books?"

Wellington cracked open the Mark III and replaced the
spent shells with fresh ones. "Without fail, Miss Braun."

He had just snapped shut his sidearm when Eliza yanked
him down. Something cut the air above him, followed only
scant seconds later by the crack of a gunshot. Eliza looked at
him and signalled silently, *Two, ahead, bearing to the left.*
Wellington nodded, fixed his grip on the Mark III, and joined
Eliza in a slow belly crawl through the grass. Only a few feet

later, Eliza tapped Wellington on the shoulder and motioned for him to break off and flank their intended target.

He kept himself as low as possible, suddenly becoming aware of just how out of practice he had become in stealth tactics. He paused, and shifted himself onto his back. A new tactic was needed.

His shoulder slipped back and forth in his jacket; and once that arm was free, Wellington shimmied the rest of himself out of the garment. Quietly, carefully, Wellington cracked open the Mark III, draped the dark coat over the exposed barrels, and then rose the coat upwards. He paused, then lifted the coat up a hint more.

The gunshot shattered the surrounding serenity, but the intended kill shot was immediately matched by another. Wellington sat up to see Eliza holding out her Webley-Maxim as her target fell.

He had just removed his coat from the shotgun when he heard something snap behind him.

Wellington immediately rolled to his left, flicking the Mark III shut with a quick movement of his wrist. "Down!" No sooner had he finished the solitary word than he was on his knees, firing the first of the shotgun's barrels. The Department agent spun on one foot and fell hard to the ground.

He slinked over to where the agent had landed and trained his weapon on her. "If you please, discard your sidearm, thank you very much."

The woman's eyes narrowed on him. "You've cocked this one up, mate. You have no idea."

"No, perhaps I do not, but I do know how the Department works, so let's talk about that. Snipers?"

The woman winced, glancing at her shoulder wound. "One. On the rise." She gave a dry laugh. "Nice tactic with the smoke screen."

"We have our moments, Miss Braun and I."

Her name must have worked as a means of summoning, as a rustling from behind him grew. Eliza emerged from between the tall grass. She looked between the two of them. "So what do you know?"

"I suppose I should be asking you that, shouldn't I?"

"Later, Welly," she replied.

"We have a sniper in the rise. Probably has eyes on the cottage, and our smoke screen is on its last."

"We're not going to make it back to the cottage. Not at present."

"Surrendering," the Department agent chimed in. "Have you considered that?"

Eliza answered with a quick jab from her pistol's butt into the woman's injured shoulder. "I suggest you keep your mouth shut. I don't take too kindly to being double-crossed by my own government."

"This is not a betrayal of government," she hissed through clenched teeth. "This is our job."

"We are fully aware of your Department's job," Wellington interjected. He looked at the Webley-Maxim in Eliza's hand. "How are the compressors?"

She glanced down at the gun, adjusted one of its dials, and said, "It's still in the green."

Wellington glanced through the tall grass at the rise looking over the cottage, then back to the wounded Department agent. He tossed her his kerchief. "That's for the shoulder. Apply pressure as best you can. Now then, off you go. Start walking."

"Start walking?" the Department agent asked.

"To the rise. Call off your sniper."

Eliza grabbed his arm. "Wellington?"

"Up," Wellington ordered. "Now."

The woman groaned slightly as she pulled herself up to her feet. She looked over into the direction of the few modest trees in the distance, grimaced as she attempted to support her injured shoulder, and then started to slowly walk towards the grove.

"Wellington," Eliza seethed, "I swear, if you believe—"

"Reroute your pressure to Barrel Three," he whispered to Eliza, motioning to the gun. "Push it to critical. It should give your bullet a good amount of extra range."

"That's going to completely burn out the internal compressors, making this Webley-Maxim Mark II just a Webley with a lot of fancy decorations."

"I know," he bit back. "So you will have one shot. Don't be at home to Mr. Cock-up, all right then?"

Eliza went to retort but then froze. Her bright blue eyes gleamed for a moment, just before she turned her attention to her sidearm. As she continued to flip switches and turn dials, the pistol's lights flickered from green to yellow while its top barrel indicator switched to a blinking red. Once Eliza gave him a nod, they began following the Department agent from a distance.

"Leighter?" the agent called out. "Leighter? Come on out. I think we're—"

Her head exploded, the impact of the bullet resembling a dull thud accented by a crack of a whip. On the sound of the actual gunshot, Eliza rose up on one knee, bracing for the recoil. The Department agent had not even hit the ground before Eliza took her one shot. White smoke devoured her, only to spit her out seconds later from the incredible pressure built up inside the gun. Sparks were now flying from the various wires and piping on the outside of her Mark II while steam slinked out from the top barrel as a serpent of pearlescent smoke.

Eliza hoisted herself up. "Target down," she stated, her eyes still looking in the direction of the rise.

Wellington, still low to the ground, did not quite share in his partner's confidence. "And your confirmation of this is . . . ?"

"I'm still alive." Eliza looked down at Wellington. "The Department isn't going to issue a musket for their agents, now are they?"

Her logic never ceased to amaze or educate him. "Fair enough."

The heavy smoke from the burning barrels was now nothing more than a haze marring the pristine beauty of the French coast. It had served its purpose, but the smoke could attract attention. As this was a matter involving the Department, they were now counting the seconds. It was borrowed time with an extremely deadly interest rate they now spent. Wellington took the lead with Alice's shotgun shouldered and at the ready. Eliza cast away the ruined Mark II, filling each of her hands with her pounamu pistols.

"Leighter," as the female sniper had been called by her fellow, was slumped against the rise where she had taken lookout.

Her scope was still open, its wind gauge still spinning in the light French breeze. Eliza's one shot had entered the girl's neck.

"I couldn't duplicate that shot if I tried," Eliza muttered.

"I doubt if I would ask you to," Wellington returned. "Muzzle flash?"

"No, I caught the smoke from the shot along with the sunlight reflection off the scope. That was my target. Even adjusting for windage I was hoping for, at best, taking out the rifle." Eliza went silent for a moment, staring at the dead woman. "She was on our side, Wellington. On *our* side."

"And they just eliminated one of their own," Wellington said, kneeling by the dead agent and relieving her of her coat. "Have we been deemed an inconvenience?"

"Not us," Eliza said, her eyes still on the corpse. "The Ministry."

"The *entire* Ministry roster?"

"Alice had a paper from England, probably Portsmouth or Southampton. The story was a column on the perils of technology. A motorcar had apparently exploded, claiming its driver."

"Yes, and?"

"The driver was Simon R. Boswell."

Wellington blinked. "Agent Boswell?"

"Welly, he doesn't even own a car! He's scared to death of them!" She raised a finger to keep him quiet and added, "There was a local paper in the stack, as well. The headline mentioned a contact I had worked with when here with Harry. Her name is"—Eliza paused and shook her head—"*was* Anne-Marie Bouvier. According to the reports, *Boulangerie Lavande* exploded in the early morning hours. The entire building just went up in flames."

"Hardly the signature of the Department."

"So I thought, until I read through the column. Bouvier's body had been found stuffed in one of her ovens."

"Stuffed? In an oven?" Wellington stammered.

"According to the journalist it was quite the macabre scene. When the blaze was put out, investigators reported the till had been untouched. The money in there had been reduced to ash."

He shook his head. "Why would the Queen suddenly deem the Ministry an inconvenience?"

"No idea. Unless . . ." Her thought faded as a wind bent

aside the tall grass, creating emerald waves along the valley. Eliza looked over the field reaching to the château. "Could all this be an elaborate ruse? What confirmation do we really have, apart from the tweed, that these are Department agents? They could be Usher."

"This would be something very much their style." He cradled the sniper rifle and Alice's shotgun in one arm while holding the woman's bowler and coat. "I suggest we move. Whether they are the Department or Usher, we won't have much time. Once this lot fails to report in, reinforcements will come."

Eliza holstered her pistols and stretched her hand out for the sniper rifle. "Just a moment."

Shouldering the weapon, she pointed it in the direction of the main house. Before Wellington could even speculate what held her interest there, Eliza returned the rifle to him. "Get back to the château," she ordered before turning towards the main house. "We make for Paris within thirty minutes."

"And you are . . . ?" Wellington asked.

"Fetching the mail," she said. "I'll be fine. Just be ready to move."

With time slipping away, Eliza felt the need to get the mail?

"Wellington, you yourself said it," she called over her shoulder. "Not much time. Do not dally."

There had to be a reason—a very good reason—for Eliza to check the mail at the main house. Yes, a very good reason.

Perhaps by the time Wellington reached the safe house, he would have it.

INTERLUDE

❦

In Which Old Friends Reunite
and Settle Scores

The machete blade would hardly ever be described as elegant, but to Agent Brandon Hill that only meant it was misunderstood. Yes, perhaps by design the machete was designed for one purpose and one alone, but even with manual deforestation there was a skill. You could easily whack away at a patch of flora all day and exhaust yourself after only a few feet into the jungle, or you could set a pace, know where to strike, and at what angle to strike vegetation in order to remove it with one stroke. Brandon understood this discipline, having watched and learned under Aztec guides that knew this jungle intimately. He understood the machete was not just some brute of the bladed world, but an underestimated advantage when deep in the heart of darkness.

That underestimation dearly cost Agent Dirk Dandridge of the Department of Imperial Inconveniences. When Brandon's machete sliced cleanly into his neck, he must have at that moment truly appreciated what that tool could do in the hands of a skilled master.

South America had always held a special place for Brandon Hill. His Canadian lineage considered, one would have expected his aversion to the heat as being ingrained, but Brandon felt right at home here in this tropic region. The Department fellows were still acclimating to the climate change, and their sluggishness was one more advantage he held over them. Considering how many Department agents were on his heels, Brandon needed every advantage he could get his hands on.

Presently, another advantage he held was that he was ducking through the streets of Colombia with all the dexterity and knowledge of a street urchin. All his years of foot chases and eluding enemy agents were offering a windfall. He had to keep moving, and most importantly avoid getting cornered.

When Brandon came around the row of buildings to find himself at a dead end, he knew this evening's entertainment was now reaching its Fourth Act. The finale was under way and near its climax.

His eyes darted from house to house on either side of him, and when he brought his foot up to kick in the worst of the two doors he was offered between them, he hoped he had chosen wisely. The door frame splintered at the lock and swung open revealing a dingy hovel of some fashion. He needed stairs, and those were at the far end of the modest dwelling. If there were any locals harboured within he did not hear their screams or shouts of protest that a white man was intruding. He needed to climb and he needed to run.

He had just cleared the second landing when he heard feet behind him. Brandon paused at the third landing only for a moment to try and assess how many were in pursuit. From the looks of the shadows and the thundering underfoot, at least five were on him. He needed to clear two more landings before he took the chase to the rooftops above.

Sunset was just about to begin, and that would be his fixed point. Before Brandon stretched modest stone buildings close enough to one another for him to jump between them as if they were stones across a brook. The further he would move from the centre of town, though, the more perilous the jump from rooftop to rooftop. He set in the direction of the sunset, knowing the aeroport would be closer at the end of his run.

The first two jumps were simple enough but on the third he felt himself landing a bit harder. His mind told him he would need to keep moving, but his body was imploring him to rest.

His fifth rooftop landing caused him to wince in pain. Just a minute to rest. That was all he needed.

He looked back and could make out three shapes in pursuit now. They were well within sight, but his lead was considerable. That, Brandon took comfort in. He sheathed the machete, lifted his knees one at a time up to his chest, just to give them a bit more of a stretch, and then returned to his flight across Colombian rooftops. Just a bit further and then he would return to ground.

His feet skidded to a halt as he looked at the next building before him. The gap looked to be a good ten feet, which, if he gave himself enough of a lead, he could make. The problem was the drop down to it, which was closer to fifteen feet, although it appeared more like twenty-five. If he did not get the landing just right, he risked breaking an ankle or worse on impact. He had to time the jump precisely, otherwise this merry dash would end badly.

"For the Ministry," he muttered as he walked back to the far edge of the rooftop.

One chance would be all he had. One. Sodding. Chance.

Was his mind playing tricks with him as he sprinted towards the edge? It seemed with each step into the rooftop gravel, with each pound of his foot against the roof, he was actually losing speed. He knew he needed to rest. He knew he needed water. What he truly needed was a bit of luck. He needed to soar as a hawk between the two buildings, and then surrender himself to the sciences of nature so that his body would bend and move as it was designed to do. The medical practice was always on about how the human body possessed so much potential but it never went utilised. It was wasted on idle lifestyles and lazy pursuits wherein the human race chose to observe rather than participate. When Brandon launched himself into the space between dwellings, the coolness of dusk enveloping him in a loving embrace, he hoped to tap into that potential and reap its benefits right there and then, as he needed them straightaway.

First, there was a sinking feeling he had not pushed off hard enough, that he would fall short. Then he felt that odd, queer sensation of gravity, its invisible maw sucking at him and bringing the lower rooftop at him at a dizzying pace. He had to time this perfectly. Brandon dared to reach forwards with his right foot, his favoured side, and reminded himself in this strange, macabre state of existence between rooftops to give in to the forces of nature. Let his body do what came naturally.

He felt something solid touch his toe. He allowed his leg to bend. *Yes!* He allowed his hand to touch the ground. *Yes!*

His shoulder did not fare so well. *Oh bloody hell . . .*

There was an audible snap that ushered in a silent wave of pain emanating from that point. He gave out a hard, guttural moan as his body rolled, several times, his dislocated limb striking the rooftop. He was going to have to snap it back into place when he had a moment.

His body stopped at a pair of feet. Even in the dying light of day he could see the tweed in the man's suit trousers.

"Agent Brandon D. Hill," the gentleman said, pushing him on his back, "you, sir, are quite mad."

"Oh right you are, mad as a hatter," he quipped, "but not so mad that I couldn't give your lads a good foot chase, eh?" That's right. There had been five of them. He only saw three continuing across the rooftops. "So what's it to be then?"

"It is my duty to make certain there is no trace of you remaining, Agent Hill," the Department man said, drawing what Brandon recognised straightaway as an exciter of Axelrod and Blackwell's design. "According to our new weapons designers, this ought to do the trick."

"Oh dashitall, man, are you serious?" Brandon swore. He winced as he pulled himself upright. That injury to his arm was right smart, it was. "I was expecting some finesse like a tranquiliser followed by a bath in sulphuric acid, or perhaps something more diabolical such as being wrapped in cloth as a living mummy and then trapped in a sarcophagus with flesh-eating scarabs." With his good arm he waved in the direction of the Axelrod-Blackwell exciter. "You're going to kill me with a *clankerton's* ray gun, are you?"

"It's called the Jack Frost," the Department man said, turning the dial on the exciter's side to its highest setting. "It's supposed to freeze you solid so that you turn into an ice statue. Under this sun, by noon, you will be nothing more than mist. Not a trace of you left behind."

Cremation through cold. "Oh, that's ripping," Brandon said, most impressed. "Quite some style shown there. Nice one there, chap."

The agent nodded. "We thought so." He barked over his shoulder. "Neville?"

"Yeah, Terrance?"

"Go an' collect the other lads. I think they might want to see this contraption do its work."

"Rather," the other one—Neville, Brandon gathered—said eagerly as he made for the exit. "We'll still be able to make that last airship out."

He was still turning for the door when the door opened seemingly of its own volition. It knocked Neville out of the way, and shortly thereafter a figure emerged from the thick shadows of the stairwell. The "Crackshot," a favourite of Brandon's from the Wilkinson-Webley line, dispatched without fail the three agents watching from the rooftop overhead. Brandon held his breath at the fact he had just witnessed three head shots within quick succession of each other, a feat that even by his fellow agent Eliza D. Braun's standards was not to be dismissed. The fourth and final bullet in the Crackshot drove itself through Neville's heart as his saviour placed the weapon square on the man's chest and fired. Now spent, the Crackshot clattered to the ground as did Neville.

Gaslight was now mingling with dusk, giving just enough light to the man now closing on them, a steam baton hissing to its full length with an ominous striking of metal on metal.

Sweet Mary Mother of God, Brandon Hill thought quickly as his rescuer stepped closer, the rugged man's dark gaze narrowing on Terrance. *Of all people . . .*

What cheek! "Terrance, why don't you pull that trigger now?" Brandon asked bitterly. "I would rather not owe this man a damn thing."

"Brandon, hope you don't mind this but shut ya' hole, I'm rescuin' you," Bruce Campbell spat.

"I don't know who you are," Terrance began, splaying his fingers around the Jack Frost, "but I will fire if you so much as take one more step."

"Go on, do it!" Brandon screamed, his pain now dislocated much like his actual arm. He felt himself falling into a

wild fury and he did nothing to stop himself in his descent. *"I would rather have fuck all then be indebted to this bastard!"*

Bruce halted. He couldn't disarm the Department man, but Bruce wasn't about to drop the baton either. "I had that coming, Brandon. I'll admit to that."

"You," Terrance said, stepping back from Brandon, "have chosen the wrong time to look out for a friend. Stand next to him," he said, motioning with the Jack Frost.

Bruce nodded, looking at Brandon. "Do you mind?"

"He's the man with the exciter. I'm the one with a dislocated shoulder." Brandon shook his head, frustrated. "Why would I be the one in charge?"

Bruce stood next to him, close enough for Brandon to bite him in the calf, which was tempting. Of all the people to die alongside, why was God engineering such a terrible, horrible jibe such as this?

"According to the clankertons, this setting should work for two as well." He pointed the Jack Frost at them and then gave a slight nod to Bruce. "Agent Hill here doesn't seem to appreciate the sacrifice you made, friend. Rather sad, that is."

"Nah, it ain't," Bruce said, dropping the baton. For him to do that, it really was over. "I knew the odds. I rolled the bones. It was worth it, mate."

Brandon looked up at the square-jawed Australian. By Jove, he was sincere.

Well, blimey.

The blue-white light devoured the surrounding shadows, blinding them both for a moment. The cold felt so very, very strange, as Brandon knew that while dusk was far cooler than day, it was not the kind of "chill" that should make his teeth chatter, which this did. He saw his breath for a moment, then saw it again. He could feel Bruce flinch beside him as the air grew colder and colder . . .

Then it was done.

"Crikey," Bruce whispered. "I would call him a 'poor bastard' if'n he hadn't meant this for us."

"Rather," Brandon agreed.

Agent Terrance Sorry-I-didn't-catch-your-last-name of the Department of Imperial Inconveniences was now encased in a large pincushion—for that is what it looked like—of solid ice. His hands were the only part of his body that seemed to be flesh, but from his forearms an eerie sheen of ice began, blossoming outward and then forming as thick, bone-white spider legs that reached out for purchase but could find none.

"Did this bloody thing—" began Bruce.

But Brandon finished the thought. Something they did often when working together in the field. "—backfire? It does appear so." He hissed on shifting where he sat. "Good thing Axelrod and Blackwell are mad as members of Parliament."

Bruce looked him over as he picked up his steam baton. "Did I hear right? Dislocated shoulder?"

Brandon nodded. "Hurts like the right devil, it does."

He looked at the baton in his hand, then back to Brandon. "D'ya want me to set it for ya?"

The man towering above him was not the man he expected—or *wanted*—to see; but this was hardly a strange situation for either one of them. The Americas. Prussia. Hong Kong. Egypt. How often had they set one another's limbs in order to reach safety. It was practically part of their job requirements for the Ministry. Certainly, he could risk managing his way to one of the local doctors and they could set his shoulder, and probably do enough damage to it that it would permanently never be proper again. Bruce had, however, set his shoulder at least twice while on assignment. This was nothing new.

"Go on, old friend," Brandon said. "You know wh—"

The baton sliced through the air and struck hard into Brandon's shoulder blade. That would be the second time Brandon heard another sickening snap within a single evening. Not pleasant, at all.

His intended scream was instead a choked yelp, followed by a growl that turned into words. "You could have let me finish, you daft prick, so that I could prepare myself."

"Really?" Bruce leaned closer to him. "How's the shoulder?"

Brandon slowly rotated it back, wincing still but not as sharply as he had earlier. "Tender, but it works."

"Then you were ready," Bruce stated. He then regarded the steam baton in his hand. "Had to pick this up before leaving Queensland. Thanks for letting me break it in properly."

"You're welcome." The pain of dislocating his shoulder

was now taking its toll, but that wasn't all. As he got to his feet, he found out how much all of the rest of his body ached.

"So you feel up for telling me what's the score?" Bruce asked, retracting the weapon to a smaller size.

"Certainly, but first," and Brandon cocked back and struck Bruce's jaw. Had he not been so sore, he would have knocked him on his ass. Instead, Bruce merely stumbled a bit. "That was for Ihita."

Bruce worked his mandible left and right, rubbing it gently and then moving it up and down. "Fair enough. Now, what—"

Brandon gathered up enough strength to bring his foot right into Bruce's crotch. Chances are he hadn't felt anything like that since his last mission in the field, before he set his sights, for whatever ridiculous reason, on working in administration.

"That was for me. Now, we're even." As Bruce remained on one knee, Brandon took a deep breath and motioned around him. "It all started when this chap, Dandridge, stopped me in a brothel."

"A brothel?" Bruce wheezed.

"I was in need of comfort, seeing as something a bit more tangible had been torn away from me. Please," Brandon warned, "do not interrupt me again as I may be reminded of certain things and may find myself in a need to vent pent-up frustrations."

Bruce gave a nod as he motioned with a free hand for Brandon to carry on.

"He introduces himself as a member of the Department, come to bring me in for an emergency extraction. That was when I asked him, 'You mean the Phantom Protocol where I am supposed to go underground or otherwise be a target for your lot?' and that's when things got sticky."

"Six on one?" Bruce raised himself to his feet, shaking his head. "Hardly fair."

"Good thing you were there to even up the odds." Brandon glanced over to Neville, but really had nothing to say about the dead Department agent, or his compatriots. "Good to see you, mate."

"It's good to be seen aboveground, mate," Bruce replied. "Had a bit of a scrape in Rockhampton. Thought I'd head to South America, see if you could use a hand."

"So, now what?"

"Phantom Protocol, eh?" he asked. Of course Bruce wouldn't know. He wouldn't have received the signal as his ring didn't leave with him. "We keep moving. It's all we can do."

"But where, Bruce?" Brandon asked. "This is the Department."

"The world's a big place. Two people can disappear in the Empire, you know that."

A voice that crackled, *"Salutations, my fellow Ministry agents!"* made them both jump.

The all-too-familiar voice was coming from the Jack Frost. *"I can make the bold conclusion that if you are hearing this, you are Ministry agents, as these cads from the Department of Imperial Inconveniences have commissioned our exciters. We have delivered our order, yes, but we would hardly turn on those whom we swore to protect with our works of science. That is why Doctor Blackwell and I have rigged all our weapons to fail. Catastrophically.*

"Now if you have been caught off guard by the appearance of the Department, allow me to explain. Doctor Sound has enacted Phantom Protocol. We are now, officially, dark. If you are wondering exactly what you need to do at this point, I recommend you make certain on the twenty-second of April to rendezvous with your fellow agents at the beginning. The beginning, as we all know, is the best place to start, yes? See you very soon. Remain vigilant."

The Jack Frost sparked and sizzled, and then smoke slipped out of its top vent. Night had now fallen over Colombia. Brandon remembered the Department agents talking about the final airship leaving later that night.

"Did any of that make sense to you?" Bruce asked.

Brandon motioned to the rooftop where Bruce had felled the three Department agents. The building he had made his daring jump from now looked far taller than before. Brandon was exhausted, but better passage awaited him once he and Bruce found those tickets. "We'll need to grab some airship tickets from those lads up there."

"And then what?"

"You heard Axelrod," Brandon said, shrugging his still-tender shoulder with a wince. "It's back to the beginning."

FIVE

❦

Wherein a Science of Ages
Past Reveals the Truth

On opening the door, Wellington was greeted by the sound of a simple shotgun's hammers pulling back to a firing position.

"Stand down, Alice," Wellington assured the maid, and the weapon she shouldered dropped, but only by a few inches. "All's well."

"Where's Miss Braun?" she asked, the children slowly emerging from the shadows to huddle behind her.

"She's . . ." It sounded even more ridiculous when he said it aloud. ". . . fetching the mail."

"She's *what*?!"

Wellington emptied the contents of his arms out onto the large table in the centre of the kitchen. "You know the lady's mind as well as I do," he said, handing Alice her Mark III back. "She insisted, and I would not question it for we know that way lies madness. Thank you very much for your side-arm, by the by." He flipped open the jacket and pulled from the inner pocket the sniper's identity. Her name had been Esmeralda Helen Leighter, or at least that was the identity she was travelling under on this assignment. He flipped through her passport, quietly marvelling at the amount of visas decorating its pages. Travel, it appeared, had been second nature for Esmeralda. "Come along," he muttered, oblivious to those gathering around him. "You must be in here somewhere."

On the back flap of the identification, adhered with a small dollop of beeswax, was a single page document, folded several times over. This, if protocol was being followed, should have been her travel papers. Once free of the passport, the paper opened of its own accord, revealing quite an itinerary. Esmeralda had set foot on France's shores on the same day as Wellington and Eliza. After a few days in Normandy, her next destination was to be Malta, then Egypt, Sudan, and Kenya. The transportation plans ended there. All of her stays were brief. Only a matter of days.

A knot formed in his throat as he saw the telltale stamp in the travel order's lower-left corner. It was the crest of the Department of Imperial Inconveniences. This was no ruse. This was, in fact, their own government.

The door opening caused him to jump. Eliza entered to a jubilation of concern and relief. She waved her hand, blushing a bit as she spoke. "Please, no fuss. We have mere minutes before someone comes looking for their own or the *Sûreté* are called in to investigate. Alice, get the children ready. We have a difficult and complicated road ahead of us."

"Yes, miss." She motioned to the children, gathering them around as a mother hen would with her chicks. "Come along, Mr. Books and Miss Braun are on the job now."

"I managed to get the coat off that Department bloke you were chatting it up with," Eliza grumbled, tossing it on the centre of the table. "Bastard was wearing a Stinger on his forearm. From the looks of the trigger, it would have gone off the moment you shook hands."

"Charming," Wellington sneered.

"I also managed to find a few identifications and—"

"Are we going to die?" cut Serena's voice through the hubbub.

No one moved. Eliza stared for a moment at the cream-coloured envelope in her hand, appearing to be at a loss for words.

Wellington tossed the Department agent's passport onto the table before him and walked over to the child clinging on the skirts of the formidable Alice. Sinking to one knee, Wellington looked into the little girl's eyes. "Are you afraid, Serena?"

"Yes, Mr. Books," she said in an unexpected tone of purest honesty. "We've been in some scrapes, to be certain, but nothing like this, being chased to Froggyland and all."

"Well then"—he paused, looking at them all before continuing—"good. I'm glad you're scared. You all should be. This is not the time to posture and pretend you are greater than the sum of your parts. We are facing our own government, and these agents are not to be underestimated. I did, and it was nearly the death of me. The Department of Imperial Inconveniences is unlike any foe you have ever stood against. They will make Diamond Dottie and her lot look like the St. Johns. You follow?"

One by one, including the eldest, Christopher, they nodded.

"Do not let that fear inhibit you, though," Wellington continued, giving Serena's arm a gentle squeeze. "You must channel it. Allow it to heighten your senses, quicken your reflexes, and that will come with time. Time that Miss Eliza and I intend to earn for you all." He turned back to Serena and smiled warmly. "No, little Serena, you will not die. Not while Eliza and I draw breath." Wellington then motioned to the other Ministry Seven and nodded. "We will need to travel light and as covertly as a party of ten can."

Arms suddenly wrapped around his neck as Serena hugged him. It was a gesture that he would not have anticipated from the street urchin, but one he returned with equal genuineness. He heard Alice whisper, "Come along, everyone," and Serena broke the embrace.

How far he had come. Once upon a time, Wellington would have felt the need to check for his wallet. Now, he felt robbed of additional affection from the youngest of the Seven.

"So you know for sure it's the Department?" Eliza asked.

"Their seal is on the travel orders. This Esmeralda Leighter was quite the world traveller, and a few of her passport stamps I recognise from case files." He shook his head, poking at the passport. "While they might be able to make the documents, I doubt they have access to the Department seal."

"Agreed, we'd have even more trouble if that was the case." It was obviously an uncomfortable thought, because she quickly changed the subject. "I think you've got a champion there with little Serena."

The chill that swept over him threatened to knock him over. He suddenly felt the need to hug that child once more.

"Whatever—" Wellington chided himself as he felt a tear in his eye. Now was not the time for emotion. "Whatever do you mean?"

"The way you rescued Serena during that Diamond Dottie con. A child of the street wouldn't forget such a gesture. Serena, more so." Eliza tore open the envelope with her finger. "And thank you. I think you reached them all. We're going to need some faith to get us to tomorrow, or wherever this takes us."

Wellington motioned to the envelope. "What exactly is that?"

The card Eliza pulled from the envelope was a bright red colour with sections—squares and rectangles of varying length—appearing to be randomly cut from it. He could not decipher any real pattern to the holes in the card, except that on a glance the sections were all the same height.

"Orders." She flipped the card over. "Page twenty-one. Come with me, Wellington."

He followed her to the adjoining room, a modest parlour that offered a gaming table, a small couch and chair for pleasant conversation over tea, and another pair located by a single shelf of books. Eliza immediately went to it and ran her finger along the spines one by one.

"And there you are," she whispered, pulling from the collection a single volume.

Wellington looked at the title of the book and sniffed. "*Countless Hues of Crimson*? Oh, Eliza, I would not even allow Archimedes to urinate on such drivel. This author, H. J. Rodwell, mocks English grammar on so many levels. I believe this book could encourage the Empire to remain illiterate! And his characters—*Oh, don't get me started!*"

"Are you quite finished with your book review?" Eliza asked, her eyebrow crooked sharply. "Because these are our orders."

His brow furrowed. "An erotic novel of dubious merit?"

She held up the card, and Wellington could just make out printed in its corner *Page 21*. "Watch and learn, Welly. Watch and learn."

Over her shoulder, Wellington observed as Eliza flipped through the pages to the designated spot. His eyes scanned the words there, and his heart sank at the horrible prose staring back at him:

> And when her minuscule offer for creating nocturnal chemistry was regarded as nothing more than a disrespect, a vow mocked by her, a crowning insult to her love, she was immediately afraid he would destroy her.
>
> "Oh but this rings true of your deviant desires," he scolded, just as the time they did first meet at the Hellfire Club. "But as per our own circle's laws, I should spank your bottom red, shouldn't I? I am the lion king amongst our pride. Trust me on this—I will punish you, my little Anastasia, and you will know in the pleasure of your pain I am the only one for you."

Wellington let out a groan. "I think a small part of me just died."

"Not the most elegant of prose." Eliza gave a chuckle as she added, "And not particularly erotic either."

"And yet, ladies of society could not snatch this novel up any faster."

"Indeed," she chortled. "Imagine Axelrod and Blackwell's surprise."

He went to agree, but his words drowned in the bile that this clunky prose had already evoked. "I—beg your pardon?"

Eliza flipped the book to the cover. "H. J. Rodwell is actually Axelrod and Blackwell. This," she said, flipping back to page twenty-one, "was what you missed being in the Archives. A new contingency plan for field operatives, cooked up by R&D and approved by the Old Man. The idea was to publish a series of encoded messages in a book no one in their right mind would read. This way, we could get the orders safely to secure hideouts by merely purchasing them from a bookshop as opposed to using a secure courier." Eliza shook her head. "However, no one expected *Countless Hues of Crimson* by first-time author H. J. Rodwell to become the next literary sensation."

"Don't remind me."

She held up the red card. "Ready?"

The card fit the width of the page perfectly, and on lining up the top right corner of the book with the card, Wellington's breath caught in his throat. The perforated card, which he now recognised as a Cardan Grille, revealed only segments of words and parts of prose. Its original awkwardness was now replaced with a direct message from headquarters:

>   min
>   istry   dis-
>   a vow   ed by   crown
>   immediately
> destroy
>   rings
>   meet at the
>   circle's
>   red
> lion   Trust
>   no
>   one

There it was—the death warrant. Not only was the Ministry disavowed by the Crown, but the Department of Imperial Inconveniences was now hunting them.

And possibly, from their reaction to you, his father whispered in his ear, *they know what you are.*

Perhaps, Wellington replied to his ghost, *but so does she. And I love her. Eliza and I will rise beyond this.*

"Doctor Sound must have sent these orders after informing the Queen that the prince and his valet were killed," Eliza said, her eyes reviewing the revealed message again and again while working her ring free. "And this is page twenty-one."

"I'm afraid I don't follow."

"This is Phantom Protocol. We are dark. From the postmark and the number on the Grille, we have twenty-one days to carry out these orders. Less than that as we met with Alice and the Seven."

"To get back to England?"

"To reach the rendezvous point, which is this Circle's Red Lion, whatever that may be."

Wellington grinned. "And this is why you could consider yourself fortunate to be smitten with a walking, breathing, analytical engine like me."

Her lips pinched and twisted into a smirk. "Explain yourself, Welly."

"The Red Lion, a quaint pub located just inside Avebury Circle," he offered, his head bobbing back and forth jauntily, "and where the Ministry itself was founded in 1839."

Eliza blinked. "Really?"

"Brilliant spot of planning, that is."

Eliza looked at the message, her smile fading slightly. "Provided Her Majesty also does not wax nostalgic as Doctor Sound does and deduces his fall-back position."

"Fortune favours the brave, does it not?"

"It certainly favours you," Eliza said, pecking him quickly on the cheek. "To think it all started with a kiss in the Archives . . ."

"Later, my sweet, later," Wellington chided, taking a look at his pocket watch. "We are on borrowed time."

"That we are. Children?" Eliza called. "Are we ready?"

A moment later, the Ministry Seven and Alice appeared. Eliza slipped on the coat and bowler of the Department which, as fate would have it, fit her quite neatly. Alice and Wellington made their own checks of shotgun and sniper rifle, respectively, as Eliza crossed the kitchens to the hearth. She reached up for where the poker hung, but she tugged the poker downwards and the hook shifted forwards and down. The stone floor before the hearth sank deeper into the ground.

"Christopher, come with me. We need to arm ourselves."

"Yes, Miss Eliza," Christopher said with a nod.

"Make this a quick arming, if you please," Wellington said, glancing at his watch and then outside. "Time waits upon no man."

"Luckily I *am* no man," she quipped before descending with Christopher into what Wellington could only assume was the safe house's armoury.

"What be the plan, sir?" Alice asked.

"We are returning to England. All of us."

"Pardon me, Mr. Books," Colin spoke up, "but no offence intended towards you or Miss Eliza, wouldn't it be smarter if'n we did do what's we do's best and take to the streets? Even in Froggyland, streets are wot we know best."

Wellington admired the boy's fortitude. However, Colin needed to trust him on the matter. *"Dis-moi, comment vas-tu se déplacer autour de Paris, même à la campagne?"*

"What are you on about, Mr. Books, speaking all Frog-like?" the boy snapped.

"I think that was the point Mr. Books wanted to make, Colin," Eric said, a light snicker peppering his words.

"I would never doubt your inherent talents on survival in the streets," Wellington started, placing a gentle hand on the deflated child's shoulder, "but if you were to be caught by the authorities, it would only complicate matters if they discover you are English children loose in Paris. In the case of the Ministry Seven, particularly as you are truly seven now, we must practice safety in numbers." Wellington called down to where Eliza and Christopher disappeared. "How's it coming along down there?"

"Nearly done," Eliza returned.

"Make sure to bring up a map, if you please."

"Already done, Mr. Books." Christopher popped back up with a large folio in his hands. "Shall I remove Old Blighty from here?"

"Bring the whole collection up with you, Christopher, there's a good lad."

The eldest of the Ministry Seven returned back to the kitchen, only this time he had upon him a small rifle resembling Alice's and two belts of ammunition and sidearms across one shoulder. Liam and Colin both let out delighted gasps but were quickly silenced by a look from both Christopher and Wellington. In his opposite hand, Christopher carried a large book of maps.

"No chance of any walking sticks down there?" he called down to Eliza.

"Concealed sword, single-shot rifle, or reinforced titanium?" she asked.

"A sword would be lovely, thank you," Wellington replied,

as he opened the book of maps and began flipping through various regions of England and Europe.

"Beg a pardon, sir," Christopher began, relieving himself of the small arsenal he was carrying, "but you passed by the England map."

Looking up from the atlas, Wellington adjusted his spectacles and grinned. "Well done for knowing your geography, lad. And yes, I did pass by it." He returned his eyes back to the maps. "We need to map a course back to England's shores, but," he said before pausing at a map of the eastern coast of France, "we are going to have to enjoy a more scenic route."

"How's that, Welly?" Eliza's voice echoed from the connecting chamber of the armoury and the kitchens.

"We have to assume that if the Department know our safe houses, then the Ministry network has been compromised completely."

"Agreed," Eliza said, piling into the centre of the table more sidearms and weapons, along with a fine dark-wood cane with a lovely brass handle.

"Then it would not also be a far cry to speculate they are watching all ports at present. Airship, sea ferry, smuggling boats, or otherwise."

Her face darkened at his theory. This was sure to be another one of those times where she hated him to be right. "So what's your suggestion?"

"We head east, not west."

She looked as if she were about to protest, but then gave a slow, steady nod. "Head further away from the safety of Britannia?" Eliza stepped closer to him as they both examined the map. "So how deep are we delving into the belly of the beast?"

"I was hoping you could give us an idea of where to go," he replied, sweeping his hand across the map of Europe. "Since you have all your field experience to call on."

"We could try Barcelona or Madrid, but again we might have the same problem." Eliza tapped her finger on the map. "Even though we have operatives and offices in so many locations, we really do not have many havens to choose from—not if the whole network is compromised."

Wellington felt the need to brace himself against the thick, wooden table. He had only been activated two months prior to this, and now he found himself disavowed and a target of Her Majesty's Department of Imperial Inconveniences. A cramping pressure worked across his back and shoulders, no doubt a manifestation of the responsibility he and Eliza were undertaking.

"Welly, are you all right?"

He looked up at Eliza. Why didn't he have an answer for her?

"Stop," she said softly. "This is our responsibility, and we will see it through. We just have to consider our options."

"Yes," he uttered, his voice dry and strained. "I'm just concerned about the distance we will need to cover." He then looked up at Alice and the Seven. "All of us."

"Are you certain, Miss—" Alice started.

Eliza immediately cut her off. "I will not have you all leaving my side. Not until we are all safe. The Department, as you all saw today, has a long reach. They could attempt to use you against us."

"We kept clear of them peelers once before," Serena stated.

"That as may be, but I'd rather not take that chance again." Eliza made eye contact with them all, even Alice, before adding, "We stay together."

"Coo, mum," Eric said, taking his hat off, "we feel as if we're being a right trouble. If we has just stayed in London town, them Department blokes would have forgotten about us, seein' as how big the city is and all."

"No, Eric, you don't know these people as I—" Eliza then stopped in her words, and Wellington was not certain if he should be thrilled or slightly concerned at the light that danced in those brilliant sapphire eyes of her. "That's it," she whispered. She was looking out into space, and it was obvious she was planning their trip.

"Eliza, what's it?"

"As far as we can conclude," she began, flipping back pages of the atlas as she spoke, "the Department is focusing their efforts on our network of safe houses and active Ministry theatres, yes?"

"It would make the most sense," Wellington replied.

"Then what if we were to lose ourselves in one of the

grandest theatres of them all?" Her hand turned the page and she straightened to her full height, presenting it to Wellington with a bright smile and breathless satisfaction.

Wellington looked over the map from end to end. Alice and the children leaned in together, then looked back to their ward with a collected movement that Wellington could swear had been choreographed for the ballet.

"Pardon me, miss," Alice spoke, much to Wellington's surprise, "but that's a mad thought, that is."

Christopher wasted no time in having his own thoughts heard. "Miss Alice is right, mum. We have done some daft things before, but this is—"

"Bloody brilliant, this is!" Wellington said, placing his hand on the map. "The journey will not be easy by any stretch, but once within the borders we could easily disappear."

"All of us?" Christopher insisted.

It was Christopher's authority that caught Wellington off guard. The boy was on the cusp of manhood, but it was his age that had made him the "leader" of the Ministry Seven, not necessarily the lad's confidence or savvy. However, Wellington recognised the tone in his voice. He himself had used such a tone with officers above him when orders would be issued that put his men in harm's way.

The Ministry Seven had lost one of their own, and Christopher would not let that happen again.

"Christopher," Wellington said, giving Eliza a quick glance before addressing him, "I know this may appear reckless, but I understand Eliza's strategy. We need to go where the Department will not expect us to go, and the further we get from the Empire, the safer we will be."

"But they could still be there, yes?" asked Christopher.

"It's a possibility," Eliza said. "But we will be safe there. I have a reliable contact."

Wellington blinked. "You do?"

"I do." She crooked an eyebrow at him. "Don't look surprised, Welly. I've not blown up *all* my friends in my missions abroad."

"So, what about us?" Christopher asked, motioning to the rest of the Seven and Alice. "How are we going to get out of this together?"

Eliza nodded. "A fair question." She started flipping back through the atlas to the map corresponding with their hideout. "Once we divvy up weapons, food, and gear, we will have one more stop to make."

Wellington glanced at the pile of supplies in the middle of the table. Wasn't everything they needed there already?

"There," Eliza answered him, her finger pointing at their next stop within French borders.

Very clever. "Well played, Miss Braun. Well played."

SIX

❦

Wherein Two Gentlemen Take a Journey

If there were anything more magnificent than a hypersteam train, Wellington Thornhill Books had not seen it. Until now.

Standing on the platform of the Gard de Norde, waiting for Eliza to appear, though, he found himself in awe of the *Stahlblitz*. This was the Franco-Germanic hypersteam express that continued to break all records for travel across Europe. Wellington couldn't help letting his eye trail rather lasciviously over the technological marvel that dared with each voyage to break what hypersteam enthusiasts called the hundredfold. The train gleamed in the gaslight of the platform lamps like a slim, polished-brass bullet, literally humming with excitement on the tracks.

His hands itched to examine the refinements German engineers—and perhaps the more gifted clankertons—had made to the original design. Eliza had disappeared into the hustle and bustle of Paris, with vague instructions to meet her at the station at midday. Could she possibly have known that he would be so close to the magnificent *Stahlblitz*? It seemed like a punishment indeed if she had.

He was lurched out of his reverie when a hand landed on

his arm. His grip tightened on his walking stick, ready to deal a blow to whomever had taken such a liberty with his person.

One look at the familiar face and the oddity of it all made him stop.

The sparkling blue eyes of Miss Eliza D. Braun never ceased to give his heart a start, but the light-brown handlebar moustache perched on top of her lip muted that usual moment's elation. She made for a very dapper, short man, with a dark bowler jammed down over her head, and a suit of strangely familiar tweed on. She had also done a very convincing job of, once more, tying down her rather impressive bosom, so much so that he wondered where it had all gone.

"Hello, my love," she said in a voice pitched only a few octaves below her usual voice.

"Miss . . ." Wellington stammered, feeling his temperature rise a little as he tried to brush off her hand. "I mean . . ."

"Mr. Elton Bellington," she cut him off, waving a pair of tickets beneath his nose, while at the same time drawing him away from the press of people passing through the entrance. "You, my darling, are Samuel Cavenaugh, and we are off to Hamburg." She looked him over, and after a quick glance to either side of her, remarked, "Looking rather spry for a dead man."

"What cheek, Elton. Our fellows back at the Department will talk." He took the tickets from her and examined them. He glanced around them and leaned in closer. "Eliza, these are for a *shared* single berth, we cannot . . . that is . . ."

"The Department is looking for a man and a woman, so we not only disguise ourselves as their own but pose as two men travelling together." Her smile under the all too convincing facial hair was still the same one he loved. She gave one of the moustache's curls a tiny stroke with the back of her index finger. "I hope you can accept my little turn with facial hair. It's all the rage in Berlin, you know?"

"But you don't think sharing a berth will attract attention? Two men, one cabin, and a cross-country excursion?"

The bemusement in Eliza's eyes faded, replaced by a strange concoction of pity and frustration.

"Think of where we are going," she said, taking the hand in which he held their travel arrangements and placing a gentle kiss against it, jamming Wellington's breath in his throat. "Handlebar moustaches aren't the only rage in Berlin."

Now he knew he was flushing red, perhaps because she had hit a sore spot. Aside from his military service, and the odd holiday or archival business, he was nowhere near as well travelled as Eliza. His education and childhood had not been very conclusive to learning or experiencing anything outside what his father had wanted him to learn.

It didn't mean he didn't want to, though.

"You really should get out more," she sighed.

"Your disguise is rather masterful," he conceded.

She winked at him. "I do make a rather handsome young man, if I do say so myself." She tucked her hand into his elbow, leaning her smaller suited frame against his. "Let's try and find our carriage. We might have to get a little more . . . relaxed when we get there."

The wicked look she gave him sent a frisson of anticipation up his spine. Still, there were other things to consider. "What about Alice and the children?"

"Oh, I do believe *Sister* Alice and her children are managing quite well," Eliza said, craning her neck in the direction of what sounded like a right scolding.

Wellington followed her gaze to a nun wagging a finger in Liam's face. He would have come to the boy's rescue had he not known the nun was, in fact, Alice. The stop Eliza had suggested at the priory had been so they could help themselves to the Seven's present disguises. The school uniforms and all the children bathed and cleaned to nearly military standards made the Ministry Seven almost unrecognisable. Christopher, Wellington could not help but be impressed, remained in character as a quiet priest, keeping a Bible pressed close to his chest. Alice, donning the habit, was ordering the blushing Liam to return the pinched wallet back to the man. With all attention on the lad caught in the act, the world was oblivious to Serena deftly relieving another two ladies of their coin purses.

Eliza merely shrugged and whispered, "They are probably thinking of the journey ahead. One of many reasons why they make such wonderful operatives for the Ministry: their survival instincts."

They continued along the platform, with occasional jets of

heavy steam lingering around their ankles, the thick conden-
sation parting to their steps. "They are in second class. I didn't
think it would do to make our entourage obvious," she said
cheerfully, tipping her hat back to examine the numbers on the
carriages they passed. "Alice and the Seven are all comfortably ensconced separately from us. Elton and Samuel can have
some quality time."

He didn't quite know what to say to that, especially since
she pressed her body up against his. It didn't matter the situation, he was all too aware of her impressive attributes hidden
beneath her disguise, and a yearning built in his own body to
pull her loose of those bindings. That particular image burned
suddenly very brightly in his mind, and he had to jerk away
from her a fraction in embarrassment.

"Oh, Wellington," she said with a slight purr in her voice,
"you have the very same idea as I do." Before he could object,
she wheeled him around and placed a kiss full on his lips.

While the sensation of her fake moustache tickling his lips
was at first a little distracting, her firm yet soft mouth on his
soon overwhelmed his surprise. He clutched her closer, and
suddenly realised that the men's outfit suited her rather well,
and that the very idea that her feminine curves were concealed
beneath it was actually rather exciting.

With some sadness he released her, and set her back on the
platform. Wellington adjusted his suit a little, but couldn't help
looking at Eliza with a slight smile. He hoped her blood was
pumping as hard as he knew his was.

Her hat and facial hair were a little askew, and it took her a
moment to adjust them. "Perhaps you have been to Berlin."
Eliza locked her fingers in his and pulled him to the door of
the first-class car. "This one is ours, and I do believe our cabin
is a sleeper by chance too."

"As long as it has a lock on the door," he said, already tugging at his cravat.

The hypersteam was quite full, and they had to push past
their fellow travellers to find their accommodation, but find it
they did. Luckily, it did indeed have both a bed and a sturdy
lock. Eliza tugged the door open, and they fell into the rather
close quarters. Wellington could only feel her warmth on him,
and craved to touch her skin.

"The Ministry is going down like a punctured airship." Eliza yanked the rest of his cravat off him. "We're being chased by the whole damn Department." Her lips traced along the line of his neck, while his fingers had real trouble with the buttons of her jacket and vest. "And Lord knows how many of our fellow agents have been killed."

"All ample reasons," Wellington said, circling her waist and staring into her eyes, "for us to make the most of the time we have."

The quarters were close, and the train was starting to pick up speed exiting the station. With one hand Wellington managed to yank down the blinds on the door, while cupping her body against his. The binding on her curves was going to present a challenge, but part of him thrilled to it.

She smelled different in the Department tweed, but underneath, the faint whiff of her perfume reached him.

"Wellington," she said into his ear, "we are both entirely overdressed."

He pulled her hair loose, wrapping his fingers in its dark ruddy curls. "That moustache will have to go." His voice did not sound like his own, but he rather enjoyed hearing it so primal.

A loud bang at the door made both of them jump. Eliza leapt backwards, giving both of them room to draw the Remington-Elliots from their holsters, even with their clothes hanging slightly askew. With a nod in his direction, Eliza leaned towards the door.

"Ja?" she asked. *"Kann ich ihnen helfen?"*

"Miss Eliza?" whispered Alice in reply.

Eliza opened the door to see Alice the nun staring back at her, a large leather-bound ledger clutched tight in her arms.

"I made sure I was not followed," she assured them both, "just as you taught me."

"Come in, quickly," Eliza insisted, waving her in with the small pistol, "before you are seen."

Once the door shut, Alice gave a long sigh. "Once the children situated themselves, they were asleep within minutes. Poor things were tuckered right out."

"Alice," Eliza warned. Wellington afforded a grin at how Eliza, even in this mad dash across Europe, insisted that her maid practice a polished approach to communication.

"Sorry, miss. They were exhausted so I insisted they have a rest. There was little protest." Alice then presented them both with the large book. "With all the excitement at the château, I did forget to bring this to your attention again. Christopher and the children had this with them, and while I hardly understand the letters as you and Mr. Books here would, I understood enough to know you both needed to see this."

Eliza opened the leather-bound journal and scanned the names. "What do you make of these notes?"

He adjusted his spectacles as he read over her shoulder. "These notations look like formulas of some sort. A chemical breakdown." Wellington pointed lower down the page. "And there, same formula. And there."

"Welly," Eliza began, following the notes from where he pointed to the names associated with them. "That's Arthur Pembrose, the Duke of Manchester. And that's Margaret Bent, the governor of the Bank of England."

"Her husband is on this list as well, few rows up," he said, narrowing his eyes on the chemical formulas. He looked up to Alice. "Did the Seven find this ledger at the house they had broken into?"

"Yes, Mr. Books. Christopher said the house belonged to a man in the medical profession."

Saving her place in the book with one hand, Eliza flipped back to the first page. Her eyes scanned the page, coming to stop on the name in a corner of the first page. "H. Jekyll."

"Seems that 'Doctor H. Jekyll' enjoys a very exclusive clientele," he said as Eliza turned the page.

"Wellington!" Eliza hissed.

The book was across her lap, open flat to reveal both pages. Across the top of the left page in a brilliant flourish script read a single name:

Peter Lawson, the Duke of Sussex

Opposite it was written another name:

The Maestro

For the Duke's page, there were chemical notations far

more complicated than the previous pages. Wellington's own understanding of the chemical and medical sciences were limited, but he could tell there were many variations from the original formula at the top of the page. Lower down, the same formula appeared, only with other elements bonded to it, a few adjustments to hydrochlorides and sulphates here and there.

The notes on the opposite page—the Maestro's page—Wellington understood perfectly.

"These must be the schematics for that odd chair the Duke of Sussex was sitting in when we saw him in California," Eliza said as her hand ran down the page's length.

"Yes, but these designs make no sense." His fingertips followed a section of the piping from the large tanks in the back of the chair. "If this were a life support system, as it has been designed to appear, then these tubes would connect with the chair's occupant. Look here." He traced one pipe to a metallic gauntlet. "This vents pressurised blasts to the glove."

"What would that do?"

Wellington chuckled. "It would flex the fingers."

"That's it?"

He shrugged. "That's it."

Eliza seemed to catch on to the patterns quickly. "There's a connection between this tube and the Gatling. We all know what that does. Another that goes to the ocular."

"I would gather that controls brightness and intensity. Maybe colour, if so desired."

Her finger tapped on a small box that was connected near the bottom of the chair's array. There were callout notes, showing what appeared to be power output computations and temperature limits. "This looks like a control point."

"And according to the doctor's notes, this is controlled wirelessly."

"This isn't a life support system," she said, furrowing her brow. "This is a gigantic puppet."

"Who doesn't love a touch of *grand guignol*?"

"So Sussex is completely off his nut, as he thinks he's this Maestro character," Eliza said, her eyes going from page to page, "but the getup is being controlled by this doctor? Why?"

"Doctor Jekyll is not trying to cure him." Wellington turned the page. "He's manipulating him."

"Mr. Books." And both their heads snapped up from the book. Wellington was actually startled at hearing Alice's voice. "I'm scared. I've never been more scared in my entire life."

"We all have good cause to be, Alice," Eliza said.

"No, miss, you will understand my mind"—Alice motioned to the book—"once you turn the page."

Wellington returned his attention to the open book in Eliza's lap as Eliza followed Alice's suggestion, and the name across the top of the page threatened to steal his last breath:

Alexandrina Victoria, Queen of the British Empire

They stared at the name of their ruling monarch for a long time. Wellington didn't need to consult the notes. If the Duke of Sussex and the Maestro were an indication of the doctor's work, it was up to his extremely vivid imagination to envision what Jekyll had in store for the Queen.

"We need to get this to the director immediately," Eliza said, finally closing the book and placing a single hand on it.

"Posthaste I would say." Wellington went to the door, peered down either side of the corridor, and then turned back to Alice. "Return to the children, and follow the plan we discussed."

"Yes, sir," she said with a light curtsey. Wellington checked outside the door once again, and gave a nod to Alice. With a quick look at her reflection in the window, she slipped out and headed back to second class.

Eliza's eyes drifted to the window; though because darkness was falling quickly, the only view was an occasional light racing past. The moment's passion seeming to have been left behind in Paris, the subtle rattle of the hypersteam lulled Eliza into a moment's relaxation, perhaps the first time since their madcap flight from the Americas. The rocking started working its hypnotic effect on Wellington as well. As a soldier he knew very well the value of catching sleep whenever possible, but part of him didn't want to close his eyes, even when Eliza drifted off.

He still wanted her desperately, moustache and all; but

these revelations were the final straw. It was enough to surrender to the fatigue.

He watched her in the soft light of their cabin, and felt torn between keeping a dutiful watch over his partner in the field, or following suit and getting some well-earned sleep as well.

His eyes shifted to the door. Their compartment was locked—for whatever worth that held.

His eyes jumped to the book still in Eliza's loose grasp. The Duke of Sussex under the control of this Doctor Jekyll terrified him enough, but this madman had access to the Queen; and they had been performing experiments on Her Majesty. They had irrefutable proof.

They also had the Department of Imperial Inconveniences on their trail, but hopefully masquerading as their compatriots in tweed would be enough to buy them some time.

By God, he was tired. Just a few minutes' sleep, perhaps.

Wellington reached inside his jacket and checked the Remington-Elliot. Compressors were all in the green. Three bullets, at the ready. He concealed it under the blanket at his side, pointing at the door. The rest of the cover he draped over his lap. Wellington let his eyes drift shut, knowing that his training—both military and his father's—would snap him awake if that lock so much as rattled. He would protect this compartment and its valuable contents with his last breath.

He could only hope it would not come to that.

SEVEN

❧

Wherein Our Daring Agents
Travel Old Paths

When Wellington and Eliza stepped down off the hyper-steam at the Cologne station, their disguises were still intact. Much as she would have relished a hypersteam tryst, they had instead taken some absolutely necessary rest. They had the children, and Wellington was with Eliza, so somehow everything would be sorted out.

The children and Alice however disembarked further down the length of the platform. The Seven were looking around them with wide eyes; and while the gawking suited the younger children, it did little to perpetuate Christopher's current guise as a young priest. Once again the former urchins of London streets were in a new country. The Cologne railway station was quite similar to many of the ones in London, but everyone bustling around them was speaking German. It was hardly surprising they were so shocked; they had only just recovered from French after all.

Alice only briefly met Eliza's gaze, before hustling the children towards the street. They would take a carriage to the agreed-upon hotel, which by sheer coincidence would be just across from where Eliza would meet her contact. Or so she hoped.

Eliza slipped her hand into the crook of Wellington's arm. He didn't flinch, and the two "gentlemen" made their way to the exit.

"Do you know Cologne?" Wellington asked Eliza, in a conversational tone.

Memories flashed, some of them entirely too improper to share with her new lover. "A little. I was for a time working in conjunction with the *Reichsamt für besondere Aufgaben* or Section P as they tend to get called."

"The Ministry equivalent in Germany?" Wellington said, as they rounded a corner and hailed a cab. "I didn't think that we had much interaction with them."

"You'd be surprised what doesn't end up down in the Archives." She fixed him with a wicked grin. "Some things Director Sound likes to keep off the books . . . even if they are yours." She could tell that the mere idea of his Archives being incomplete was a terrifying one, just by the slight twitch in the corner of his mouth. "Section P is even more secretive than we are. While we were holding a joint investigation, they kept Harry and me at a distance. It's not like I've been inside their headquarters or anything."

A cab pulled up in short order, and once safely ensconced in it, she placed another kiss on him. It was undoubtedly an inappropriate gesture in the field, but she didn't know when the opportunity would strike again.

For once, Wellington Thornhill Books did not complain about protocol. He kissed her back, cupping her face in his hands, until they were quite breathless. When he pulled back, he was smiling. "Perhaps I am getting a little too used to that moustache."

Eliza smoothed it against her face, then twirled its tips in a playful manner. "I'll make sure not to throw it away."

As Cologne rattled past them, though, pulling them back once more into the fray, her mind turned away from sensual pursuits to the real problem at hand. The Department would risk international incidents if deciding to operate in Germany without permission from Section P. Their pursuit across the

Channel to France was a clear indication of exactly how driven the Department was at present.

However, Eliza knew for certain one of Section P would not be amused by the Department's appearance within the Prussian Empire. He had been burned by them, and given the time of day, she knew exactly where he would be contemplating that very fact.

How was it best to brief Wellington on all the details first though? It was the manner of this agent's downfall that still hung around her neck.

She stared out the window for a moment, before broaching the subject. "So, Wellington, I hope I can count on you to be professional . . ."

Eliza heard the archivist shift slightly in his seat, but she still didn't look at him. "I would hope my professionalism is still intact despite our new"—he cleared his throat, before lowering his voice a fraction—"affections."

"Good then, because I need you to let me handle this. Stay out of this conversation, absolutely silent." She leaned up and rapped on the roof. *"Halten Sie bitte hier."*

The carriage lumbered to a stop well before their destination. Paying the fare and disembarking, Eliza pulled Wellington into a nearby alley. He watched curiously as she shed her overly masculine image, stripping her lip of the moustache and shaking free her dark red hair from its high bun. She even went so far as to take off her ascot, and unbutton her shirt just a little.

"How do I look?" Eliza asked him, replacing her bowler back on her head.

Wellington's eyes gleamed, and she suddenly learned something more about the archivist: women in men's suits were rather attractive to him. Her wearing of men's trousers was one thing, but it was plain the tailored attire had quite an effect on him.

How delightful, she thought, filing it away for later use.

He went to kiss her again, but Eliza slipped free of his grasp. She had unleashed a tiger for sure.

"Now, Welly," she said, putting her fingers against his lips, "I didn't pull you in here to take advantage."

He looked a little crestfallen, but he jerked the edges of his jacket straight. "I'm sorry, Eliza, not quite befitting of a gentleman, I know."

She squeezed his hand. "Oh, I think we both know you're not a gentleman all the way through."

It was lovely to know she could still make him blush. "So, what's the plan then?" he asked.

"You go around the corner and take a seat at the Café Mechanisch. Order something, but make sure when I get there not to even look my way."

"So I am your muscle then?" he asked with a twinkle in his eye. "How charming." Then he raised her hand to his mouth, kissed the back of it, and strode off to do as asked.

Eliza let out a sigh and girded herself. How long had it been since she'd seen Marius? Admittedly, the last time had been rather spectacular. With a final flick of her hair, Eliza walked boldly out onto the street and round to the Café Mechanisch.

She spotted Wellington and saw that he'd taken her advice seriously. He already had a tea in front of him and was busy ordering some breakfast from the waiter. Not once did his eyes flick in her direction. Sitting out in front of the cafe, Marius von Hoff was smoking a cigarette and scanning the newspaper lying in front of him.

For most agents, being in the same place at the same time every day would have been beyond foolish. However this was Marius' job. He had once been in charge of protecting the industrial heart of Cologne. The Ministry became involved when a small brood of *Rübezahl* had descended from the mountains and started sabotaging factories. Section P was in need of assistance and a young Eliza D. Braun—following her own experiences with *taniwha* in the South Island—had been loaned to Germany as a specialist. It was the beginning of a productive and promising partnership.

Then, four years ago, when Section P discovered the Rübezahl targeting a facility specializing in airship construction, the German empress had decided to reach out to her mother for help. What should have been a routine operation meant to deter the Rübezahl quickly spiraled out of control as Queen Vic, unbeknownst to Section P or the Ministry, sent in the Department. The cock-up that ensued ended with von Hoff's demotion. While not completely disavowed or blacklisted,

Marius' duties now kept him on watch over the mess he had made. The fact this permanent assignment made him somewhat of a target was really only a bonus to his superiors.

They had not spoken since her quick flight from Germany, but over the years, she had managed to keep tabs on the fallen agent, always relieved to hear of his safe returns from diplomatic assignments and shuttling messages between Section P and informants.

So it was with some trepidation that Eliza took a seat opposite him, and plastered on a smile that she hoped gave the appearance of confidence, and not self-satisfaction. To be sure, there was no satisfaction in her sudden extraction back then, leaving him to carry the can for the whole mess.

Marius looked up, and not one ounce of surprise flickered on his face. He leaned his wiry frame back into the cafe chair, and stroked idly at his moustache, which had only become thicker and more magnificent since the last time she'd seen him. Admittedly, back then it had also been on fire. Just a little.

"Fräulein Eliza D. Braun," Marius said, "I would say this is a surprise, but . . ." He shrugged and tried to show how indifferent he was by taking a sip of his coffee.

Unfortunately for him, Eliza knew how he operated, and his studied disdain didn't fool her. "It is good to see you, Marius. It's been, what, four ye—?"

He held up his hand to forestall her. "I know all about the Ministry's status. Sightings of Department agents in German territories are already stirring up a bit of trouble. We have intercepted communiqués on hunting down disavowed and retired Ministry agents, one or two more aggressive wires from the Department demanding our intelligence on your safe houses. Overall, these *Arschlochs* are making my and my colleagues' lives miserable." His eyebrow arched as he looked at her. "Judging from your current fashion choice, you have already survived a debriefing and have been reassigned. It is as I have always believed: Government agencies come and go, but spies will always survive. Valued assets, regardless of what politicians and field directors may believe," he spat bitterly.

Eliza sighed, glancing at her Department tweed. "If only it

were that simple, old friend. If I had done as you believe, my debriefing would have been more of a defenestration." She fluttered the lapel of her coat. "It was either this agent or me."

Marius sat up fractionally in his chair. Now finding himself at the centre of information like a very-well-dressed spider, he revealed that true nature Eliza always knew him to be: a terrible gossip. Marius enjoyed scandals and secrets as much as her mum had when she got them down by the fence line, chatting with Mrs. Lainson who ran the butcher shop.

"That sounds uncomfortable," Marius said in a measured tone. "We were not informed that the disbandment of the Ministry was quite so . . . final." A flicker of the man she'd once known darted across his face. "I'm sorry about that, Eliza."

It was impossible to tell if that was a sincere lament or not.

She waited for a moment, letting him sit in silence while she ordered a cup of coffee from a passing waiter. Once her drink arrived, she stirred in a touch of cream, the favour she was about to ask of Marius seeming to swell in her throat. Playing off his disgust with the Department, a tactic he would have recognised, felt cheap; but Wellington, Alice, and the Seven were relying on her.

Eliza could feel Wellington's presence to her right, like a warmth. She might not have the resources of the Ministry at her disposal, but she was not without support.

First though, she had to clear the air. She locked eyes with Marius. "I'm sorry about what happened. I had to leave with the ambassador. I had to . . ."

"I understand, Eliza." He stared at her a moment, his dark eyes completely unreadable. "When the Department blundered into the operation, I knew there were far too many cooks involved, and when the stew bubbled over . . ." He stroked his moustache again as if remembering the flames that had once touched it. "It was, how you say in New Zealand—a *Hundefrühstück*." He gave a grin and took up his coffee for a sip. "A dog's breakfast.

"I never felt ill will towards you. We were an efficient, effective team. The Department was out of our control, and I remained silent to protect my partner." He took a sip of his coffee, then set it on his saucer. "That silence was not easy. When you were wrongfully exiled from New Zealand after your work there, I wanted to reach out. Instead, my heart went out to you."

Eliza had underestimated this man. Terribly. He had been a brilliant field agent to work alongside. Whatever she believed to be unresolved matters was nothing but ancient history.

She cleared her throat. "Well, now that's out of the way, I think you know why I am here."

"I believe I do, but why are we having this conversation"— he jerked his head towards where Wellington was earnestly scanning his newspaper—"without including your partner?"

"Observant as ever," she commented.

"It was the smell of his tea," he shot back. "I would have suspected he was a tourist had I not seen him wearing the same dreadful tweed as you."

Eliza gestured to Wellington, and the archivist, after glancing around the street a little bit, came over and sat with them. Mercifully he did not introduce himself, or make a sound. For once he was taking her advice.

"To be fair we are all working with a little less these days," she said. Marius and she stared at each other across the table for an extended moment.

"So you journey deeper into Europe, putting more distance between you and your organisation, whatever remains of it, and then double back undetected. *Sehr gut.*" His dark eyes eventually darted away from hers. "Why would you want to go back to the country that has nothing but a death sentence for you both?"

Eliza glanced over to Wellington, before leaning forwards and revealing in a hushed voice, "The Ministry enacted Phantom Protocol. We are still in operation as we have uncovered a plot to remove Queen Victoria from power and put a madman named the Maestro in her place."

Disclosing the Phantom Protocol order to a member of Section P not only put their operation in danger, but any surviving agents of the Ministry as well. They were supposed to be dark. Now Marius knew. Eliza could only speculate what was running through his mind presently. It was a high risk recruiting Marius, intentionally or not, into their circle; but what Eliza knew of the kaiser, he was Queen Victoria's favourite grandson. He was also the most loyal. He would not want to see her disposed of for some commoner to take her place. If that were to happen, there would be a greater commitment of the Prussian Empire in retribution for Queen Victoria's fall.

Wellington kept silent, his gaze flicking between the two of them.

"Phantom Protocol?" Marius frowned. "I suppose that means whatever resources I provide, this is off the books as the Department has already been in contact with Section P?"

"Of course."

The German agent sat still for a moment. A carriage rattled past the cafe, children rolled a hoop down the street, and a woman began an argument with another on the corner. Normal everyday life carried on around them, but important decisions were being turned over in the brain of Agent Marius von Hoff. While Section P barely trusted him with anything more than low-level clearance orders and requests from diplomats, Eliza offered to him the fate of the British Empire.

He probably knew that.

"I do not have much to lose," he said finally, and Eliza realised that she had been, all unknowingly, holding her breath. "If you are right and succeed, Section P is put in good standing with your agency, and perhaps a favour or two will come our way. A good word from your director may even restore my credibility. If we are caught either by the Department or my people"—he tilted his head—"I will be put out of my misery. So what to do with the two of you?"

"The ten of us."

Marius nearly choked on his coffee. "Ten?"

"Wellington and myself." Eliza gnawed on her bottom lip softly. "My maid, and seven children, ages seventeen to eight."

He pinched the bridge of his nose and let out a long, slow breath. "Ten people. Yes. Of course. This is you, after all." His eyes flicked open and fixed themselves on Eliza. "My contacts may be able to wheedle your way into the delegation . . ."

"Delegation?" Wellington could no longer keep himself quiet. "To what?"

Marius shifted in his seat and then continued. "With your queen's Diamond Jubilee coming up next year, preparations are already under way. We have a large delegation heading to London by airship. Businessmen, diplomats, security advisors,

quite a crowd are heading there with their families. Luckily—
or not, depending on your perspective—I am in charge of shep-
herding these wayward lambs safely from Berlin to London on
Monday morning."

"They are still planning on celebrating the Jubilee?" Eliza
asked, a frown forming in between her eyebrows.

"Why wouldn't they?" he asked.

She knew how her queen did love grief. Sound's lie to the
world would no doubt have plunged Victoria into deeper
mourning—if that was possible. "With news of the prince?"

An expression of utter bafflement crossed Marius' face.
"You mean of Prince Edward setting off on a world tour for
his mother?"

"Yes," Wellington blurted out suddenly. After an awkward
pause, he added, "We were assuming the Queen would want
the entire family in attendance, so having the Jubilee without
Prince Edward there seems a bit surprising."

Eliza shared a look with Wellington. They had heard
Sound reassure Bertie that he would tell his royal mother that
he was dead. She felt Wellington tap her knee, and she got his
point. This was not something to be revealed to a foreign
agent, even one who was a friend. If they ever saw the director
again, he would have some explaining to do.

"So tell me about this delegation," Eliza said, inclining her
head to Marius. "It sounds like quite a handful, but easy for a
few more people to slip in among them, yes?"

Marius' own lips lifted slightly as they ventured back onto
more stable ground. "As long as they remain inconspicuous.
Do you think by any chance *all ten of you* could manage that?"

Eliza and Wellington nodded, but the German agent's eyes
took on a merry twinkle. He knew her too well, Eliza realised.
So she leaned forwards and lightly placed her hand on his
gloved one. "I promise you, Marius, I will do nothing to
endanger your delegation. No explosions, no weapons at inappropriate moments, and no crass talk."

Now a real smile broke out on his lips. "Sounds very unlike
you, *meine Freundin*." Marius pulled out a business card, and
scribbled something on the back of it. "The airship is a government charter, and everyone is cleared before they set foot
on it." He slid the card to her. "Cologne station, Sunday night,

along with all the other guests. Until you are given travel papers, pretend you don't know me."

She took the note as calmly as she could. On the back was written some kind of code, *der alte Löwe*. She took it and slipped it into her pocket. "Hardly any time to enjoy Cologne then? A shame."

"Remember, if you are caught," Marius said, leaning back in his chair, "the Section and I will deny all knowledge. And do not expect help from us once you are in England again. The kaiser would not look kindly on any help we give the enemies of his grandmother—even if they turn out to be helping her."

"Understood," she said, downing the last dregs of her very strong coffee. "If we can get the Ministry reinstated, it'll be good to work together again."

He gave her a slight tip of his bowler, and then looked at both of them. "I will also talk to my man about better disguises. We have got to rid you of that dreadful tweed." He took up his newspaper once more as if they no longer existed.

As she and Wellington walked away from Café Mechanisch, she had to stop herself from giving a little skip. They were going back to England, and on their way to quite possibly giving the Department a bloody nose. Things—in her estimation at least—were looking up.

EIGHT

❦

Wherein Mr. Books and Miss Braun
Are Once More Interrupted

Trusting Eliza's friend was not an easy thing for Wellington to do. Even though he was more than confident he had her affections and her attention, he could not quite chase away the green-eyed monster when she was around men with whom she might have shared intimacy. She'd never really given him any reason to doubt her—which only served to make him feel worse about his base and primitive masculine instincts. If there was anyone who he could trust in the world it was Eliza D. Braun.

A pleasant stay in a foreign country would have been welcome if it were not for the collection of children, an eagle-eyed Alice, and the constant threat of discovery by the Department. Instead of touring the sights of Cologne, their first and only night was spent working on plans for their escape.

At midnight, Wellington and Eliza slipped out of their hotel room to meet with Alice and the anxious children. He was left bemused how large families made it through winter, with children nearly bouncing off the walls like rubber balls. Games of quoits and hangman really didn't cut the mustard for the extended stay. Two hours later, contingencies in place and timetables agreed upon, they returned to their room, locked the door, and kept watch in shifts.

The relief on arriving at the railway station Sunday night to catch the designated train for the Prussian delegation was indescribable. Eliza's friend, Marius, was there, though working hard to contain and organise the rather large deputation of prominent families and their servants gathered about him.

"We are supposed to meet with his contact," whispered Eliza. "He's going to be far too busy to talk to us."

"So," he grumbled, "a nun, a priest, six children, and two people wearing similar tweed just need to blend in until a contact appears." He forced a smile. "What could possibly go wrong?"

"Stillgestanden," a voice spoke from behind them.

"There is that," he said, not turning around just yet.

"Just act normal, but not innocent." She smoothed out the front of her jacket. "If you try to appear wrongfully accused, that serves as a tell worse than over-anxious. Just act normal."

"Such a subjective term, that is."

"Ready?" she asked. A moment later, Eliza turned towards the voice. *"Verzeihen sie mir?"*

The police officer stepped well within striking distance of Wellington's walking stick. He fought the urge to look to either side of them. Could they make the train if they struck him down? If it were the two of them, they could easily move and conceal themselves in seconds.

All ten of them? They would be captured within seconds.

The officer looked at Eliza first. Then to Wellington.

"Ist das jetzt in Mode?" the officer asked, motioning to the tweed pattern they shared.

Eliza smiled pleasantly and replied, *"Passende Muster-kombinationen sind der letzte Schrei in Paris."*

It was driving Wellington mad not knowing what they were saying to one another.

The police officer narrowed his eyes on Wellington, then on Eliza, and clicked his tongue. Wellington felt his grip on the walking stick tighten.

"Der alte Löwe braucht einen besseren Schneider," the man said with a wry smile.

Wellington felt his shoulders drop. *Thank God. A friend.*

"Fräulein Eliza D. Braun?" he asked, his hard features now easing as he presented them with a thick envelope. "Agent Rutger Kaufmann. I would normally follow this with 'Section P' but my old friend Marius tells me we are having a bit of fun without the kaiser's knowing."

Wellington suddenly felt a sense of dread slip under his skin. The smile he was wearing was one he had seen before—on Eliza's face.

"Agent Kaufmann," Eliza said in a hushed tone. "This is my partner, Wellington Books. We thank you for your help."

"Those are your travel papers and legends." He then presented them with a thinner envelope. "The maid and children are in second class. I managed to procure a single compartment for the two of you." He shrugged. "My apologies, but all the suites have been taken by the delegation."

"Believe me," Wellington said, "our priority is safe passage, not comfort."

"When next you see me, I'll be dressed as a porter. New clothes are in your compartment. Marius believes the children and maid should be fine in their own disguises, and then we will find something more appropriate for them in Berlin."

"Excellent," Eliza said. "Will we rendezvous with Marius at any time?"

"In Berlin, yes, but not until then." Rutger tipped his hat to them both. "Now, off you go. I will see you once we are under way."

Eliza gave Wellington a quick wink and wandered further down the platform to where she could effectively slip tickets to Alice and the children. His eyes roamed over the various travellers, eventually stopping on the only collection of people that had their own line of security keeping journalists at a considerable distance. Aristocrats were, Wellington had already observed, rather self-involved at the best of times. Put a group of them together like this, and soon enough there was the inevitable clash of personalities and arrogance. He caught sight of Marius standing on the platform, clipboard in hand, and a fleet of Portoporters at his back. It seemed very little against the ranks of German aristocrats who massed before him, though, complaining at the top of their lungs, or getting their servants to do it.

"So far so good," Eliza whispered into Wellington's ear on

her return. "Between what we have planned on reaching Berlin's Travel Centre, we should easily slip into the entourage without fail."

"The Travel Centre?"

"Yes," Eliza said, leading him towards the second-class compartments. "On account of its central location, the Germans constructed an aeroport around their largest railway station. It is now a major hub, and should be busy enough for us to easily make ourselves part of the group without much bother."

He slipped his hand around hers and gave it a squeeze. "Excellent."

Her grin was off-kilter. "Now all we need is to make it to Berlin."

Once in the cabin, Eliza shut the door and let the blinds down while Wellington pulled down the suitcase in the above luggage rack. He heard a tearing of paper, and Eliza was unfolding their travel papers.

The train gave an abrupt jerk and started off, sending Eliza into his arms.

"Thank the stars for those quick reflexes of yours, Wellington Books," she murmured softly. "Or should I refer to you as Your Baronship?"

Wellington blinked. "I beg your pardon?"

She returned to her feet and handed him his legend. "Baron Viktor Bommburst, and I am your darling wife, Willomina. We owe our fortunes in life to munitions and military defence." Eliza chuckled. "Bit of a ribbing from Marius, methinks. The children are travelling as a class of gifted youngsters, and Alice is our maid."

"Darling," Wellington blurted, "I know absolutely no German!"

"Don't worry," she assured him, "I will teach you a few key phrases if we find ourselves cornered."

When a knock came at the door, Eliza pulled out one of her pistols quick as a flash. Wellington peeked out the corner of the blind, before giving Eliza a nod, then opening the door.

"Your Grace," Rutger said with a smile as he entered their tight compartment brandishing a bucket of ice, a bottle of Riesling, and two glasses. "You seem to have been fortunate not to have any other passengers join you."

Now under the guise of a porter, Rutger slipped the bucket into a large ring by one of the windows. He then handed Wellington and Eliza empty glasses as he proceeded to open the bottle of wine.

Eliza raised a single eyebrow. "Dare I ask?"

"Presently, delegates are enjoying a delightful soirée on the observation deck. I thought Marius should not be the only agent enjoying the odd glass or two of wine, so I decided to liberate a bit of the bounty of our fine country for you and your partner here." Easing the cork out of the bottle, he poured them each a glass. "I can vouch for the label."

"Have you tried it before?" Wellington asked.

"This is my family's vineyard," he replied with a grin. As he filled Eliza's glass, he added, "However, whatever vines I attempted to cultivate and grow withered and died. My father suggested service to His Majesty, and that is how I found myself in Section P."

Once Wellington's glass was full, Rutger replaced the bottle back into the bucket. "Now, if you will excuse me, I have to tend to the other passengers. Easiest way to get up front, check on the children."

Wellington took a sip of the wine as he locked the door. Rutger had every right to be proud of his family's vintage.

He looked outside his window, seeing the countryside passing by in a blur. They just needed to stay alive for five hours. "Your friend Marius has pulled off a miracle," he said, adjusting his cravat and feeling just a little less tension in his shoulders.

Eliza let out a sigh, taking a long sip before resting her wineglass on a small pullout table. "I will agree with you once we see the Cliffs of Dover and are on the ground in England safely. We will be cutting it close, but should make the rendezvous." She shot him a sad smile. "It is going to be hard to avoid going to Miggins."

Wellington suddenly realised he was pining for his Archives again, and couldn't help but break out into a cold sweat when he thought of the Department fools rifling through it—or worse, attempting to dismantle what remained of his analytical engine. His valise, hopefully within the *Ares* at the London Aeroport, contained the heart and soul of his computation device, but what was still hidden beneath Miggins Antiquities remained the true treasure trove of the Ministry.

"We will manage," she said gently, snapping him out of his worry.

Eliza took his hand and squeezed it, and despite all the troubles around him, he couldn't stop himself. Setting down his own glass of wine, he leaned over and kissed her, the smell of her skin and the taste of her lips overcoming him like fine brandy. Every moment that could have offered them a touch of the delicious intimacy he enjoyed on the *Angel* had been sacrificed out of fatigue and stress, and they still had very little at present, yet as their kiss deepened he was very glad that the door had a lock on it.

The swaying of the train and the closeness of the cabin made it just more erotic, and before Wellington knew it, he was sitting on the cushioned bench with Eliza straddling him. He became suddenly aware of the curves that were underneath her jacket and shirt.

"I knew, while the tweed is dire, you liked this look on me," she managed to gasp before kissing him again, working free the ascot around her neck. How he had missed this side of Eliza. "I hope you don't mind my allowing you to enjoy me in it fully."

She tore open her waistcoat, revealing her Ministry-issue corset. With the disappearance of the ascot, the curves of her breasts were in full display.

"I intend," he said, placing light kisses on both of them, eliciting soft moans from her, "to enjoy you fully out of this dangerously appealing look, as well."

Eliza pulled him closer, her legs tightening around his hips. They had been on the run for what seemed like a lifetime, and it had been so long since they had enjoyed one another, since he had felt her fingers against his skin.

The train was suddenly moving slower, the rocking becoming more and more subtle. Three hard thumps made her jump a little, but Wellington growled out. "It's just the changing of tracks. We're heading onto a spur line, to get to the aeroport—"

"Travel Centre," she panted.

"Whatever the bloody thing is called," he hissed before

pulling her neck closer to graze his teeth and tongue against it. Wellington assured her, "Chances are this route is rarely used so they have to stop to switch tracks manually. We're perfectly fine. We will be under way in just a moment." He tugged at her Department jacket. "Now please, for the love of God, let me ravish you!"

Her coat was proving difficult in removing as her whole body was tense. He wondered how relaxed she would feel if they were ever closer, skin on skin. It was amazing how one simple touch of her hand could lead him to such rash thoughts so quickly. She was quite as dangerous as the weapons she preferred.

Then came a loud knocking at the door.

They both froze and looked at each other, their raw, blind desire lifting as the three knocks sounded again.

"Bloody hell," Wellington seethed.

"Yes, this is hell," Eliza returned as she sprang away, picking up her jacket from the floor. "A train compartment with no water basin in sight. Maybe I should use some of the ice in that bucket, drop a few cubes down my cleavage." She laughed drily. "So much for this," she said, discarding the ruined vest. "Have you seen my cravat?"

He held it up as the knocking occurred yet again.

"I can only imagine what Alice and the children are up to," Wellington said, feeling a hot flush on his cheeks as he went to the door.

He pulled the blind to one side to catch a glimpse of Rutger. He appeared to be alone.

"I think we're about to find out," he said, opening the door. "Rutger's returned." He turned to the Section P agent, apparently short of breath.

"We seem to have a problem . . ." he panted.

"Has Liam stolen another wallet?" Wellington asked.

Rutger never answered as he slumped, then pitched forwards. When Wellington caught him, the long knife sticking out of his back revealed itself.

"Now let's jus' take things nice and slow," came a voice from above him.

Wellington looked up to see two men pointing Remmington-Elliots at him. Compressors were all in the green. One man appeared as someone's bad attempt to squeeze a gorilla into a suit while the second looked as if he could be knocked aside with a thought.

"I know you, Miss Eliza D. Braun," the larger agent remarked. "It's been—what?"

"Four years."

Wellington looked over his shoulder at Eliza, as he had never before heard such venom in her voice. Her eyes had never seemed more cold and hard as they did in that moment.

"Yeah. Nasty business, that." He gave a shrug. "Then again, this is our speciality, ain't it? Nasty business."

"You dolt!" snapped Wellington. "You just killed a German national! What in God's name—"

"Listen up, mate," the hulk said, pointing his pistol into Wellington's face. "I got orders to bring you in and sod the rest, but I can jus' as easily tell the toffs upstairs that you put up a right fight."

"Easy there, Malcolm," the smaller Department agent warned. "We got orders."

"I don' like the way this prick's talking to me, Georgie."

"You'll like what I have to say even less," Eliza suddenly piped up.

"Go on, bitch." And now Malcolm's gun was on Eliza. Wellington felt a heat rise under his skin. "Give me a reason to defend myself. Please."

"Let's all just keep our wits about us, yes?" Georgie asked. "We'll just get ourselves all cosy for a train trip to Berlin, see a bit of the countryside, yes?"

That was when Wellington realised the train was still not moving.

"Now why don't you just get up slowly?" Georgie motioned for Wellington to stand. "No need to do anything heroic."

The train suddenly lurched forwards, sending Georgie into Malcolm, and Eliza into Wellington. Unlike the tweed-wearing gorilla, Wellington managed to prevent himself from toppling over. His foot braced against the passenger seat, keeping him upright as he caught Eliza. As the Department agents fell over each other, Eliza grabbed Malcolm's thick wrist, the one connected to the hand holding the gun, and drove her forearm up into his elbow. The man's arm bent in a most unnatural way with a sickening crunch. A heartbeat later, the man's yell filled both compartment and corridor. Georgie was scrambling to get back on his feet, his pistol drawing a bead on Eliza. Wellington pushed off the bench, launching himself as he did when making a try on the rugby pitch. He collided into the diminutive Department agent, knocking him out of their compartment and into the corridor. Wellington forced Georgie's wrist into the corridor's window-sill, then a second time; on the third time, something fell in between them. Attempting to cover the dropped pistol with his body while keeping hold of the agent seemed simple enough in his mind. In the waking world, the archivist apparently needed to be a part-time circus performer—preferably, a contortionist—for this to work.

Something snapped from behind him, and Malcolm's screaming muffled slightly. He smiled at Eliza's strike, but the smile disappeared on feeling a blow from Georgie's elbow against his skull, rattling his senses soundly. The Department agent began wriggling out of his grasp. Another punch to his head caused Wellington to release him.

Dammit.

He took in a gasp of air and glanced over at Eliza, who was bringing the wine bottle about for what looked like a backhand blow to Malcolm. When the bottle came around, it remained intact. Wellington did not think Malcolm's jaw could say the same.

"Eliza!"

Her eyes wild, Eliza looked up to Wellington then caught a glance of Georgie heading towards the rear of the train. First class.

"He doesn't leave this train unless it's moving!" she said, her grasp still tight on the blood-stained bottle.

The train, now travelling at its top speed, rattled under-neath Eliza and Wellington as they made their way through the remainder of second class. On the gangway between the final second-class car and the initial first-class car, Wellington could see the Department agent fighting to keep his balance as they rattled along.

Eliza chucked the bottle into the night. "Welly, hang on to my belt," she said, opening the gangway's small gate.

"What in God's name—"

"I need to send a message to Marius!" she shouted over her shoulder, drawing one of her pistols. "Now hold on to my damn belt!"

They were not travelling at the blinding speed of a hypersteam, but there was hardly any comfort to be found as the night folded around Eliza. He could see her pounamu pistol drawing aim on something at the rear of the train. The shot sounded like a bullwhip's crack and then Wellington caught the glare of something small exploding. She pulled her arm in and then gave Wellington a nod.

Back on the iron landing, Eliza nodded. "Right then, let's go get Georgie."

First class was quiet. No one outside their cabins, perhaps on account of the gathering Rutger had mentioned. Wellington and Eliza had made it to a division between first-class accommodations and a dining car before catching up with the Department agent.

"Eliza," Wellington said, "he's too far ahead. At this rate, he'll reach the delegation and—" His imagination filled in the rest. "Oh, dear Lord . . ."

"That won't happen," Eliza chuckled as light from the door ahead of Georgie made the Department agent stop in his tracks. "Marius got my message."

Georgie looked back at Wellington and Eliza, then back to Marius. His hands suddenly shot upward as he was saying something. Perhaps he was identifying himself as Department and, on pointing frantically back at the two of them, warning Marius of rogue agents out to do harm to the imperial delegation.

Marius' sudden punch must have come totally unexpected.

Georgie stumbled back into one of the tables, and then scrambled back behind the dining furniture as Marius advanced on him. From Marius' vantage point, he had Georgie cornered.

From Marius' vantage however, he could not see the knife that Georgie drew from an ankle sheath.

Damn.

Wellington burst through the doors at the moment Georgie attacked. Marius caught the man's wrist on descent, but the ferocity of the lunge sent both men stumbling back through the doors from where Marius came. They both hit the next car, remaining locked in the struggle for the knife. The train lurched, giving Georgie a moment's advantage, and he pushed. The blade now quivered just over Marius' throat as the Section P agent found himself bent backwards over the gangway's iron railing.

"Get down," a voice commanded behind him.

Wellington did not question Eliza, but simply did as told.

A gunshot roared in the empty dining car, and Eliza's bullet pierced the glass window between her and Georgie, knocking him off balance and sending him down to the gangway. Marius pulled himself upright and winced. That must have been hell on the man's back.

"Excellent shot, Eliza," Wellington said, pulling himself up.

Eliza holstered her pistol and shook her head. "I'm growing fond of shooting Department agents. This will not serve well for future inter-departmental operations."

"I would say," Wellington agreed.

Turning back to Marius, still on the gangway, Eliza said, "Four, von Hoff! You owe me—"

The jest ceased abruptly as Georgie leapt, only this time the attack's momentum sent both men over the junction.

"Marius!" Eliza screamed, pushing Wellington aside and running to the gangway.

Wellington ran to the window of the dining car, trying to peer out behind them. He ran for the junction between cars, joining Eliza at the rail. Her eyes were frantically searching in the darkness. For what, Wellington didn't know, but he looked into the inky black, interrupted only by the soft lights of the train.

"He's gone," Eliza finally whispered. "Marius is gone."

INTERLUDE

❧

In Which an Illusion Falters

The woman stood in the Duke of Sussex's parlour, taking in its opulence, the details of the artwork surrounding them, and trinkets from his travels abroad. A beautiful woman would hardly be unwelcome in his home, yet every instinct in his body screamed to get her out of there. It was the same woman who had so impertinently summoned him to an audience with the Maestro. She had dressed differently then, but just as wantonly, perhaps wishing to tempt him.

As if she could.

Her creamy long neck was in evidence as she had her dark hair pinned up, and a vast expanse of matching soft curves, since she was wearing a grey shirt over the top of her corset. Captivating as she was, the fashion for undergarments being on show with a certain set of society had never sat well with Sussex. Still, even unfaltering in his devotion to his family, the Duke was still a man. Her wicked, immodest dress undoubtedly made his pulse race and distracted him from important thoughts. Her slim legs encased in a pair of highly inappropriate riding breeches hardly calmed his nerves.

He cleared his throat. "What did you say again?"

Her voice was soft, traced with the exotic beauty of Tuscany, and yet with all her allure, she somehow still managed to warn him of what she was capable. The thunder from outside preluding her words should have been melodramatic, but Sussex found the moment rather ominous. "My master is here. He demands an audience with you about our plans for the celebration."

Adjusting his cravat, Sussex did not meet the beautiful intruder's eyes. "How did he get in? This is my house, my sanctuary. I never—"

"There is nowhere closed to my master," she replied smoothly. "He goes where he wills, and today he wills that in your house you welcome him."

Sussex's thoughts immediately turned to Ivy. Fenning had told him she was entertaining some of her lady friends downstairs. Certainly there was nothing to be done about the Maestro being here, but he could only hope that Ivy kept the tea flowing and the gossip along with it.

It was most fortunate his sons were both away at boarding school.

Sussex got to his feet and, though his stomach was rolling with fear, said to the woman, "Where is he?"

"In the library." She tilted her head and examined him with her bright eyes. "You look ill, my lord. Do you need a glass of fortification before this?"

Last time she had shown no concern for his well-being— quite the contrary in fact. This change in attitude made him feel, rather strangely, better.

"No, I am quite well. It was just the oysters I ate last night."

She nodded, though did not smile or make further comment. Instead, she turned and led him to his own library, as if somehow she was the footman to the Maestro, and now it was Sussex who was a stranger in his own house. She opened the door to the room that had once been a sanctuary, and following him in, shut it behind her.

Sussex glanced around the library, and at first all he saw was familiar: the warm scarlet drapes, the polished wood, the rows of leather-bound books. Then a figure turned to face him, but it was an entirely human one. Henry Jekyll, his old friend and doctor, was here.

Sussex felt his throat seize. Why was Henry here? Was he also bound in servitude to the masked and terrifying man in the brass suit? The doctor had the protection of the Queen of the British Empire now. What could the Maestro possibly hold over this brilliant man of science to make him betray his loyalties to the Crown?

He opened his mouth to ask that very thing, when the hiss of steam venting caught his attention.

Spinning around, the duke caught a glimpse in the flicker of lightning of the Maestro, standing within the thick shadows it supplied. He was frighteningly silent in his approach considering all the metal that was strapped on him. Or perhaps he'd been standing there the whole time watching Sussex enter the room? Either possibility was not worth contemplating.

He glanced at the woman and Henry as if they could supply answers. The Italian whore crossed her arms in front of her chest, her face settling into a vaguely disappointed cast. The doctor's expression however remained calm, in fact with a slight smile on it.

"Peter," he said, moving forwards to shake the duke's hand, "wonderful to see you again. You look"—he peered into the woman's eyes—"well enough."

"I am not," Peter snapped, only to hold his breath again. As he slowly exhaled, he motioned with his head in the direction of the Maestro. "Not when such company calls upon my house like this."

Henry shared a strange glance at his female companion, but swivelled quickly back. "You remember the Maestro, though, don't you? From the airship when you were on holiday?"

Sussex frowned. Memories were tricky things, almost as elusive as eels. He pressed a hand to his head. "We were on the continent, doing the grand tour by airship . . . I remember that . . . and then . . . then there was an accident . . ."

"I was there. You saw me." The Maestro's voice came out twisted by the brass and steam. "I saved your whole family, and on the return voyage to England, I began conversations with Henry here."

The recollection was fuzzy. Sussex recalled the airship well enough, with its delightful panorama. "I was sick," he said slowly, his gaze never leaving the metallic monster's brass helmet. "My valet had to care for me most of the time, but then . . . yes there was an accident . . ."

He remembered the screaming, and the terrible sensation of the airship losing altitude. People had been running about and he'd been unable to find his wife or his valet. "Was . . . was there a shooting?" he asked, taking a seat while he struggled with his twisting memories.

"There was." The Maestro did not move from his spot near the dark window, but his glowing ocular seemed to brighten. It was blue this time, seeming to reflect his mood. Was there compassion in the Maestro's words? "I took damage in your defence. I would at least hope you remember that."

Sussex looked towards Henry, but the doctor merely grinned at him as thunder rumbled softly outside.

"Something amusing, Henry?" Sussex snapped.

Henry's face grew suddenly still. "I am merely observing two very good friends of mine finding common ground."

The question sounded choked. "Good friends?"

The Italian shifted slightly at that, and Sussex was almost sure she had let out a very restrained gasp. The duke felt as though he were trapped in some terrible nightmare where everything familiar was suddenly not.

"I don't know why you are involved, Henry." He put his head in his hands, just for a moment and closed his eyes. "We agree that change is needed, that the Empire is crumbling around us and we must treat that which slowly kills us from the inside. I know Victoria, under your care, is ready. She agrees a purge is needed." His gaze switched to the Maestro. "But this . . . this monster . . . is he really necessary?"

"Oh, I find monsters are usually very necessary in matters of violence—even if it is for the betterment of the world." Jekyll took a step forwards and placed a hand on the duke's arm. "You and I are men of reasoning, logic, and science, my dear fellow. The Maestro here is the instrument that is capable of the acts we both know are necessary, and he has, upon his call, resources that are key to success." The doctor patted him as if he were a beloved pet. "We need you to sign the order placing the Maestro's Grey Ghosts in charge of the Queen's safety. Government bodies are so . . . particular about memorandums, following orders and all that bureaucracy."

Sussex swayed on his feet, his gaze darting around the room for an escape. If he ran fast enough, perhaps he could outdistance the assassin and the hulking brass monstrosity. Certainly, the rain outside would slow the Maestro down.

But abandon Henry? His saviour?

The duke's hands clenched in and out on themselves. The doctor was everything to him—in truth possibly more so than Ivy and his boys. Without sanity he was nothing at all, and Henry was his doorway to great things.

The doctor was standing stock still, looking at him as calmly as he ever did. For his own part Sussex felt as though the carpet had been literally pulled out from under him. He'd trusted the doctor all this time, placed his sanity, his position in society, and his very dukedom in his hands. When there had been no one else that could help him, Henry had appeared from nowhere to offer him hope. Now that same champion was asking him to put pen to paper and place the Queen's well-being under the care of the Maestro.

"We have skilled men. Soldiers dedicated to our sovereign, ready to lay their lives selflessly for her." Sussex wiped away a stream of sweat that was now coursing down his forehead. "I know nothing about these Grey Ghosts other than they answer to him." As Sussex pointed to the Maestro, another flash of lightning caught the sheen of his armour.

He had been bold to do so, but the Maestro remained motionless, the sapphire glow of his ocular steady and constant.

"As a doctor I know there is a time and use for every instrument." Jekyll tightened his hold on the duke's arm. "The Maestro's personal army is an instrument we will need during the celebration. Without the Grey Ghosts, the purge cannot occur."

"Perhaps you have simply lost your edge." The angry words came out in a hiss of steam that made Sussex jump. "Typical."

Sussex refused to be put in his place by a creation that might or might not be human. Who knew if there was a man of any kind in that twisted brass façade, and if there was, if he was even an Englishman at all?

Tugging down on his jacket, gathering the remaining tatters of his pride about himself, Sussex crossed the library and from a side table by his grand desk took out a cigarette from a silver case emblazoned with his family crest. The sight of it granted him a fresh courage.

"Lost my edge, have I? Says the machine hiding in the

shadows." Sussex knew he was scrambling for ideas, some way to hold off the inevitable. He struck a match and lit the cigarette between his lips. "If you are the instrument Henry believes you to be, you appear to be a rather blunt one. I assume in your fashion you would be more useful as a hammer."

It was a rather lovely insult at his costume. Even the Italian strumpet seemed amused, catching a glimpse of her covering her bow-shaped mouth.

He took a long deep puff of his cigarette, and blew the smoke in the Maestro's direction. From his distance, it made no difference to the creation's breathing, but Sussex hoped the symbolism was apparent.

"How do I know you will follow our plan?" he sneered, daring to step closer to the Maestro. "How would I know your mind, your intentions, for the Empire? I am a gentleman of the House of Lords. You?" Closer still. He would have never dared to advance on the Maestro like this in the past. However, that was on his terms. Peter was still master of this manor. "You're a beast trapped in brass. We share *nothing* in common."

He stared into the blue ocular that was presumably the brass man's way of viewing the world, and tried to imagine the face that was buried in there behind the layers of technology. He was an abomination, but still mesmerising. He could see himself reflected in the grimy, battered surface, like a twisted distortion in a puddle of water. He observed the lines of bolts that held the man inside.

A single flip of a latch, and he would unlock the Maestro's mask just enough to see what hideous deformity lay beneath it.

He heard the door open from behind him, but the velvet, familiar voice took his gaze away from the Maestro. "Peter, don't."

The cigarette tumbled from his mouth as a clap of thunder sent a tremor through the library. Everything was falling apart around him. There was no stopping it now.

Ivy did not look surprised. She stood there, her hand resting lightly on the door handle, while her gaze roamed over the rest of the people in the room. Words stuck in Sussex's mouth as she gave a slight nod, entered the room, and shut the door behind her—all with no comment. She was wearing a tea gown to receive her innumerable ladies that she entertained for the betterment of London's urchins. Ivy always had a cause. Her dark hair was pinned up, and she looked every inch the high society, respectable matron, yet when the words came out of her mouth, Sussex feared he might never let any out of his again.

"So, Peter has found his courage, has he?" She shot a look at the Italian, a flicker of disdain passing over her face, before she took a seat in the chair between them.

"Yes, Ivy." Henry's smile threatened to light up the library, outshining the gas lamps around them. "We thought you were occupied for the night."

She waved her hand dismissively. "The ladies have all been fed and watered, emptied of the contents of their pockets, and sent on their way."

The world dipped and swayed, so much so that Sussex thought he might pass out altogether. Ivy had no questions for him, no concerns for the thing in their house. And she knew the assassin. She *knew* her.

"Ivy?" The pounding rain outside sounded stronger than his own voice, weak and trembling as it was.

The brass mechanical man let out a dismissive snort of steam, causing Sussex to step back as he was acutely aware of how much within the Maestro's reach he was.

Ivy smoothed the lines of her beautiful dress, inclined her head and looked at him with the coolness she usually only reserved for servants. She had always been warmth and comfort to him, but now he saw none of that.

"Yes, Peter?"

"Did . . ." God, his throat was dry. He tried again. "Did you know about all this?" He waved his hand to encompass the massive joining of human and brass that threatened to take over his room, the still doctor, and the slightly smirking Italian woman.

Ivy nodded, her eyes boring into Sussex. "I was one of the first people Henry here approached." She leaned forwards a little, motioning to the chair before her. "Sit down, my love, before you fall down."

His hand gripped the seat's high back, and he cast one final glance at the Maestro, who watched everything from the shadows. Turning his back on the Maestro, he found, did not fill him with as much dread as facing his wife.

Once he had settled into the chair, his wife's features

softened as she took his hands into hers and confessed, "I was so worried for you, Peter. You were never the same after the war. You just became worse by the month, and it fell upon me to consider our family. I confided in Henry, and he seemed to think you would make an excellent subject for his trials." Her bottom lip began to quiver as tears welled in her once-cold gaze. "Look at all the good he has done with you. You have come so far."

"I have?" he asked, a sob of his own escaping into the dimness of the room.

"She loves you with such devotion . . ." hissed the brass man from the darkened corner, "though God knows why."

Now the foreign woman offered advice. "If you share this devotion, and trust her, you will listen to what she has to say."

His head pounded, threatening to split and spill his brains all over Ivy's immaculate dress. Then, on Henry's gentle nod to him, Sussex realised these were his only friends, his only loves in the entire world. Henry had kept him from madness while Ivy had been his steadfast supporter for many years. She was, after all, the mother of his children. And even the assassin. She had kept his secret.

He licked his lips and asked Ivy, "What should I do?"

"You need to sign the order, just as Henry has instructed." Her voice was a low croon. "Give over control of the Queen's protection to the Maestro, and let the Maestro do whatever monstrous deeds he needs to."

It sounded like such a simple thing to do. "The Queen. She relies on me. This is my sworn duty—"

Ivy's grip tightened suddenly on Sussex's, causing him to cry out. If his hand had been trembling, the vice-like hold she had on him remedied that straightaway. He had no inkling Ivy possessed such strength.

"Stuff duty," she snapped, her tone so sharp he was afraid it would cut his throat. "You've had a butcher's at the orders, now do wot the good doctor here done told ya to do! Sign the bleeding paper and be done wi' it!"

His wife's voice had never sounded like that to him. If he wasn't so certain of her breeding, Sussex might have believed Ivy was spawned from the East End or some other terrible district.

"Ivy," came Henry's gentle, comforting voice, "no need to excite yourself."

Whatever horrifying humour had overcome her now slipped away from her, lifting as would a morning fog. The darkness disappeared from her eyes. Her touch was gentle again. She ran her fingertips along his cheek and tittered lightly.

"My dear Peter, I love you and have never been more proud of you."

On her proclamation, Sussex slipped out of the chair to fall on his knees before her, allowing himself to collapse into her lap, sobbing in the folds of her dress. She smelled so sweet: warm roses, and exquisite tea. He felt secure there, and not even the aggravating hisses of the brass monster haunting him could destroy that peace.

Her hand began to slowly stroke over his hair, as calming as his own mother's—or rather the nurse who had raised him. Sussex felt a pen slip between his fingers. Raising his head, he saw Henry leaning down towards him with the instrument, his smile kindly and reassuring. With a silent acknowledgement, Peter Lawson, Duke of Sussex, understood. It was perfectly all right to sign orders charging the Maestro with the Queen's protection. Perhaps the Maestro's intentions remained a mystery, but Henry believed in Sussex's vision of the Empire's future. Henry was convinced the Grey Ghosts played an essential role in bringing this vision to a reality . . . and Sussex trusted Henry.

With no other thought entering his brain, the duke scribbled the required signature onto the parchment. Then with a sigh of contentment, he let the pen drop from his fingers and roll away. As Sussex put his head once more in his wife's lap, he felt so much lighter, both spiritually and emotionally, knowing that he had done the right thing.

Ivy whispered as she stroked his hair, "I'm so very proud of you, my darling." And with that, nothing much else mattered.

Let the summer storm outside rage all it liked. He was safe at home. At last.

NINE

❧

In Which Our Heroes Take
Stock of Their Resources

I t was a typical summer storm, sudden and uncalled for.

The country bus puffed and rumbled over the road from Salisbury with the passengers stoically silent within. Under her cloak, Eliza was holding Wellington's hand with her left, while her right held the sleeping Serena against her shoulder. Just a mile or two more, and their journey would hopefully be done.

The Travel Centre had proven a far greater challenge than originally anticipated. Their flight to London had been delayed as the delegation's liaison was nowhere to be found. His disappearance sent the collected nobility into a chaotic uproar. While that meant the Bommbursts and their party of gifted school children could easily mingle into the Prussian contingent, the contingent's inability to operate without a Section P agent overseeing every last detail detained the airship. The safety buffer of time Wellington and Eliza believed they had dwindled to a deficit. If they could not pick up a bus straight after their arriving in London, it would be dangerously close to rendezvous hour.

Directly opposite, Alice and the children swayed in time with the bus. Some were asleep, but Alice and Christopher were not. The maid was cloaked and Eliza knew that her hand had to be resting on her knee, close by the rifle concealed in her Ministry-created leg. Christopher, who Eliza had reluctantly armed somewhere over the Channel, had his head turned looking out into the growing gloom.

His face was already that of a man, but the loss of Callum was still plain to read on it. She knew better than to tell him it was not his fault, but she hoped that when they tracked down the missing boy he'd at least forgive himself a little.

Since they were not the only passengers crowded and packed into the public bus, conversation was impossible, but Eliza shared a look with Alice. The young woman had ceased to be a maid, and her face was that of a real warrior. The New Zealander could only hope that Alice would not have to release any of her formidable talents with that shotgun tonight. Tonight they would, if all went well, be at least among friends.

The rain had just begun pounding on the roof when the bus pulled to a stop outside the Red Lion public house. Wellington gave Eliza's hand a squeeze before taking Serena from her, and stepping out. With a nod to Alice, the children were now awake, alert, and stepping into the heavy English rain. They all scampered towards the low white building with its thick layer of thatch, and Eliza just prayed they were not being observed, because the heavy rain coupled with the final hours of their flight had become so harried it was impossible for her to tell otherwise if they were safe or not.

Serena rubbed her eyes sleepily and slipped out of Wellington's arms. She always wanted to be treated like a grownup, and any sign that she wasn't made her rather upset. Her eyes widened at the little pub they all gathered in. It was warm. It was familiar.

But was it safe? Did they make it in time?

"Where are we, Mummy?" she asked, taking hold of Eliza's hand in a way guaranteed to make the agent's heart melt.

"The Red Lion Inn," she told her. "This is the only public house in all of England within a stone circle."

"Avebury is incredibly ancient," Wellington broke in, but Eliza stopped his history lesson with a well-placed look. She knew the Seven had been through enough without being lectured on a past they had no interest in.

"I'll book us rooms," Alice said, gathering the children

around her. A broad-faced woman wearing a rather worn apron was already hustling in their direction. "You go find our friends."

Christopher did not look impressed that he was being syphoned off with the children, but he nudged Eliza. "I'll look after 'em," he said in a low voice.

"I know you will," she replied with all sincerity.

Wellington was already ahead of her, walking deeper into the pub. A fire was crackling in the hearth, making the room welcoming. With the hour and the weather as it was, there were no locals nursing pints at tables or along the bar. There was only one person present, apart from their own persons and the publican.

Director Sound, a sturdy mug in his hand, stood with his back to the door. For a moment that was all she could see. Her heart surged. While the good doctor remained alive, so did the Ministry.

"Have you seen the circle?" she asked gently. Please, God, if he responded with the passcode, this ridiculous chase would come to a close.

"Far more impressive than Stonehenge." He turned to look at them both. The smile he gave them both brought tears to her eyes. She had to cover her mouth to smother the sob she knew would escape. "It's magnificent!"

Doctor Sound was lucky that neither she nor Wellington rushed over to him. Instead they ordered their drinks—a beer for her, a cider for him—and wandered over to join the director at a table. The twinkle in his eyes said all that she needed to know: he was just as glad to see them as they were to see him.

He then said in an overly loud voice, "Can you just imagine all the pagan men and women worshipping their gods here? I bet there were blood sacrifices and lots and lots of carrying on. Some of these rituals celebrated *naked* I dare say!"

Wellington afforded a laugh. Eliza could not help herself in joining him. Throughout all this, the director still carried his endearing oddities.

"Very good to see you, agents Books and Braun, very good indeed," he chortled. "How was your trip from Germany?"

Wellington raised an eyebrow. "Sir, how could you have possibly known we were . . . ?"

"I have my sources," the director assured them, though his confidence sounded a little hollow. "Even in such dark times as these, I still have my sources."

"It was a comfortable enough trip," Eliza said, taking a sip of her beer. "But we were all worried about what we would find once we got here." Her eyes darted around the empty room.

"You find us alive," Sound said gravely. "At least some of us."

As if on cue the door to the Red Lion banged open and two men burst into the room, both with rainwater pouring off their hats, which they promptly removed.

Eliza's mouth opened ever so slightly. "Barry Ferguson?"

The young man—who had chiselled features with auburn hair that was neatly trimmed, save for the top which seemed to flop about a bit—straightened up and tugged at the bow tie around his neck. When his eyes fell on Eliza, he seemed to glow with happiness much like a boy on Christmas morning.

"Eliza Doolittle Braun!" he trumpeted, his pitch far too high and his voice far too loud. "Heavens to Betsy I never did think I would see you again!" Then his voice dropped an instant later, his eyes slowly casing the room which would have made no logical sense as he had already identified her boldly and brashly as it were. "Mind you, I didn't think this would be the place our paths would cross again. Perhaps a lovely pie shop." And then he pointed at her, his words a manic stream of consciousness. "A *proper* pie company where one could get a decent pork and apple pie, or perhaps a pub somewhere in Auckland—your dad's maybe?" He clapped his hands. "Right, neveryoumind, we are here, we are reunited, and it's bloody good to see you again, Eliza Doo!" He turned away as if to say, *Right then, we're done*, but he held up his finger and waved it in the air as he added, "One more thing—tell your uncle Roger I borrowed his tractor. Hope he doesn't need it back."

"You see what I have to work with, Basil?" a gravelly voice replied behind them all.

The man shaking rain free of his cloak had a head of wild white hair. His expression was stern, hardened it would seem over years of service to Her Majesty. Between him and the director, there was a certain familiarity. Their hands clapped together in a firm greeting that softened the agent's expression.

"Still, I can't complain about the young upstart. He did get us here after all."

"Rough journey from the North Isle?" Sound asked.

"South," the agent corrected with a curt nod. "We were following up on a case in Dunedin."

"Managed to catch a rugby game while we were there," the younger man added. "Blimey, those Frogs do know how to keep that ball moving."

The director gave a little chuckle, then beckoned Wellington and Eliza over. "Lachlan King, I'd like you to meet Agent Wellington Books. Agent Braun, I'm certain you are familiar with."

"Oh, quite," he said with a charming smile. Eliza felt her skin prickle at the man's greeting. She remembered first meeting him in the Wellington office when she enlisted into the Ministry's service. Old as he was, King was quite charming, especially when sitting opposite a young recruit at a candlelit dinner. "Glad to see that you are still thriving in the field as I imagined you would. And Books, is it?" His brow furrowed and then he turned back to Sound. "Any relation to that rather odd archivist you have back at headquarters?"

"I am that rather odd archivist from headquarters," Wellington offered before Sound could speak.

"Really?" King straightened slightly, adjusting his cravat, and then looked Wellington from head to toe. "And you're out in the field now? A rather lofty jump, is it not?"

"Believe me, Lachlan," Eliza said, placing a gentle hand on Wellington's arm, "he is more than fitting for the job."

"Well then"—he rapped a pair of leather gloves against Wellington's chest—"if you have won the approval of Braun here, that will suffice."

Sound then motioned to the younger man. "And this is his partner, Barry Ferguson."

Barry was exactly as Eliza remembered him back when they grew up together in Auckland. Same bright eyes of wonder, same wide smile, same enthusiastic demeanour that, much like a small incendiary, could explode at any moment. She watched him shake Wellington's hand, so hard that Wellington nearly lost his balance.

"Pleasure to meet you, sir," he said to Wellington, his excitement still apparent as he continued to catch his breath.

"Cannot tell you what a pleasure this is. I mean, you and Eliza Doo here, working together, eh? That's just brilliant, that is." Again, his voice dropped in its volume but the intensity was still present as he said, "Big fan of that analytical engine you have in the Archives as well. Tried to make one based on the descriptions we have on record. Almost got it. Couldn't get it to make a proper cup of tea, though."

"Perhaps I can help you with a new design once this brouhaha settles down?" Wellington asked the young man.

Barry's eyebrows rose slightly. "Oh! That would be grand!"

"Barry," Eliza said, snapping the two men out of their reverie. "When did you join the Ministry?"

"Oh, shortly after you left," he said, turning back to Eliza. "Seemed like a good job. Good pay, nice people, exciting life traversing the world." He took a breath, and then his expression of elation slipped away. He now looked a bit embarrassed. It was as if his honesty compelled him even when it was better not to say anything. "It was also a nice way to, well, keep tabs on you, as it were. You know, let your mum and da' know you were safe."

"Gentlemen," Sound interjected quickly as Barry was taking another breath, "if I could debrief with you over here. So far, you are our only representatives of the Antipodeans. I would like to hear the condition of our Australia and New Zealand operatives."

The three of them adjourned to the fireplace as Wellington and Eliza countered to a small table by the window. Raindrops large and heavy pounded against the panes of glass, occasional claps of thunder making their frames rattle ever so slightly. Eliza took in a deep breath of her own now and smiled. It was good to see Lachlan and Barry again. Delightful reminders of home.

Well, perhaps not *entirely* delightful as Wellington asked the inevitable. "Doolittle?"

"It's a family name, I will have you know." She then grumbled, "You have no idea how close I came to be called Philippena, another family name I was quite happy to avoid."

"Doolittle?" Wellington asked again.

The second time asking crooked her eyebrow. "Drop the query, Books, if you wish to *enjoy* my company tonight. Or ever, for that matter."

On the door opening again, Eliza felt her own smile widen, a rush of both euphoria and relief on the agent shaking the rain free of his own cloak. It was impossible not to recognise the enigmatic agent of the Ministry straightaway, but then again it was impossible to mistake the man for anyone else considering the ebony hood completely encasing his entire head, a pair of dark lenses set where eyes would be.

It was also impossible to mistake Agent Maulik Smith for any other when his synthesised voice tickled your ears. "Oh my goodness, Agent Braun is present. And here I thought I was in a place of safety."

"Stuff it, Maulik, and give me a hug!" Eliza pulled the bulky man close. "I've been wondering about our comrades abroad."

"Indeed, and far be it an easy task for me to simply 'blend in' with the locals," he chuckled, his laughter crackling through the tiny set of speakers in his throat. "Still, I managed to escape Kolkata. Once out of India's borders, it was nearly smooth going."

"Nearly?"

"Bit of a dust-up in Egypt, but I managed to get free with our man, Rateb, here."

The dark-skinned Egyptian was even more dishevelled than he had been when they had first met in Cairo only six months ago, but when they had seen one another he had been tearing through the streets of Cairo in search of Field Director Marcus Donohue. Now Khaled had the Department of Imperial Inconveniences chasing him to the lush green moors of Salisbury. Quite the change for anyone coming from a land of sand and heat.

"Agent Rateb," Wellington said, extending him a hand. "I mean this wholeheartedly when I say it is a pleasure to see you again."

"Likewise," the Egyptian said, clasping hands with Wellington, "which was made possible with Agent Smith here watching over me."

"Dammitall, man, how many times do I have to remind you?" the concealed agent quipped playfully. "As we are now fugitives, I insist that you call me Maulik!"

"So are you all of the Egyptian office?"

"No. Many of us have 'gone to ground,' as you English would say." He then motioned with a hand to Maulik. "I was pinned down by the Department when Agen—when *Maulik* found me."

"What about Donohue?" Wellington asked. "Being as English as he is, I doubt if he will simply blend in."

Khaled looked quickly between Wellington and Eliza, his skin growing suddenly pale.

"Oh dear," Maulik interjected, "I'm afraid returning to the field has isolated you a bit, now hasn't it, old chap? Field Director Donohue is dead."

"Dead?" Wellington and Eliza asked in unison.

"Yes, poor sod," he said, his hood bowing ever so slightly. "I suppose the heat got the better of his sensibilities and judgement. Khaled here discovered he was selling artefacts from the Egyptian Archives to those immortality-seeking madmen, Methusulah's Order. Small, easy-to-conceal items, but ones that pack a rather nasty punch."

Eliza felt a tightness around her throat. Was this why the entire organisation had been deemed an inconvenience?

"When Khaled had gotten wind of his transgressions, Donohue chose a coward's death. A Remington under the chin, bullet to the brain."

"How long had he been doing this?" Wellington managed.

"That's what we were trying to ascertain when we received the Phantom Protocol order," Khaled said, a haunted look lingering behind his eyes. "As I was the ranking officer, I remained behind to see to our Archives, meagre as they were after only six months. We still don't know exactly how much damage Donohue left in his wake."

Eliza shook her head. "Bugger."

"A tragedy," Khaled muttered.

For the next few minutes, more agents were filtering in from the outside. Lady Caroline Sidman was a bit of a surprise as Eliza assumed she would have taken refuge within her family. Once free of her own cloak, Lady Caroline smoothed out her skirts and joined the growing contingent surrounding Doctor Sound. Another pair of gentlemen came in from outside, both of them waving to Eliza cheerily before greeting one another, and now the room began to take on a heavy warmth. Her eyes looked from either side of the small gathering of Ministry brothers and sisters, searching for any other familiar faces that had been at the back of her mind during their flight from Germany.

Miss Shillingworth appeared in the room, her sharp eyes darting from each agent before she turned, locked the door, and then powered up the Lee-Metford-Tesla Mark IV, once she gave the director a nod. From the looks of how she checked the weapon, Eliza knew the lady was more than adequate with the rifle.

"Thank you, Cassandra," Doctor Sound said. He then made a circular motion with his hand as he took the centre of the room. The small crush of people gathered around him, and he stuck his thumbs in his waistcoat and slowly turned in place, taking them all in. "How many?"

"Seventeen, sir," Cassandra replied, her eyes looking out the small window set in the door.

"Seventeen," he repeated sombrely. "From all corners of the globe and Her Majesty's Empire, seventeen managed to find safe passage." His smile only added to the heaviness in the room. "Cold comfort, I suppose."

"Considering the Department is taking us to hunt as would a hound to the fox," Lady Caroline ventured, "I would say that we have fared quite well."

"I would echo that sentiment," Lachlan chimed in. "We only just made it from Dunedin, but then again, we had more of an opportunity to elude capture. The South Pacific is, after all, quite a big place."

"Any ideas who we have lost?" Maulik asked.

"Confirmed deaths have been difficult, considering Phantom Protocol, but according to the newspapers, we lost Dominick Locklear off of Madagascar. He was on assignment there. Pirates, according to the journalists. Considering the waters that claimed him had been clear of such activity for months, I find that rather convenient.

"These are the deaths that I have deemed dubious in manner. Upon first glance, they seem feasible, but only a few questions raise suspicions. Then we have other manners of death far too conspicuous, but most assuredly from the hands of the Department. There was our operative in Paris. Ran a bakery as part of her cover. She was found stuffed in one of her ovens." A gasp from Lady Caroline and soft sounds of shock punctu-

ated the silence. "Miss Shillingworth and I happened to inter-
cept a missive concerning the whereabouts of Agent Courtney."
Whispers of *"Galloping Gertie"* and *"The Department's in for
it now"* filtered in the air before Sound continued. "It was a
self-collapsing Amédée Bollée. Quite ingenious, if not so
dastardly."

More gasps, this time accompanied by the odd swear or
three. Eliza felt her heart sink. How many more would be
simply erased from existence?

"I don't doubt some of our number have gone completely
dark, and perhaps—if time and resources allow—we will be
able to send word to those unable to reach this rendezvous. We
will simply have to watch, wait, and pray."

"Doctor Sound," Barry called over the current of hushed
speculation between agents, "I don't suppose now would be a
good time to do that? I could rummage about this place, see if
I ca—"

"No, it most certainly is not," the director stated firmly.
"While yes, this place is secret, it is still a gamble all of us
convening here. For a number of reasons. In particular, concerning those who are familiar with the founding of the
Ministry."

"And exactly how many is that?" Khaled asked.

"Two," he replied.

Eliza had always been impressed with how Doctor Sound
was able to mask his own emotions, making it absolutely
impossible to understand where the man stood on situations
and scenarios. However, with that simple reply, Sound conveyed deep concern, if not fear, of the other person who might
be able to gather where the Ministry would retreat if ever a
worst case like this would arise.

"I believe we are safe but I also believe that safety is tenu-
ous at best." Sound tapped his fingertips together as he followed the ranks of agents. "Once we are in a secure location,
I will share with you what I know, but here? Now?" He
stopped, looked around him, and shook his head quickly. "No,
out of the question. Best to wait."

"So how long do we tempt fate?" Eliza recognised the
voice as Whittaker. Edinburgh branch.

"Protocol dictates that we are to give operatives exactly

one hour before and after the time dictated in the orders. Beyond that, we are dancing with the devil."

The murmurs of concern were working on Eliza's final nerve. They were an elite among the ranks of Her Majesty's servants, regardless of budgets tightening at the various offices. They adapted and they succeeded. This was a new and terrifying spot to find themselves in, to be certain, but Eliza would not stand to simply surrender to panic or dubiety.

And most certainly she was not going to surrender to any of those cloth-eared gits in the Department!

"What are your orders, sir?" Eliza asked, silencing the room.

The last time a man of Sound's age looked at her that way, it was her father. He had been so proud of her rising to the rank of field agent for the Ministry; and while he could not trumpet that pride around Auckland, it was more than evident in the way he looked at her. Seeing that in Sound's eyes created a strange lump in her throat.

"Thank you, Agent Braun." Sound took in a great breath and looked at all assembled. "Under Phantom Protocol, we were all to meet here. There are provisions and resources stockpiled that allow us to run operations for a time; but even I did not see our current scenario. The longer we stay at the Red Lion, the greater the risk we take in being discovered.

"What we need is a secure location, somewhere we can work in secret and be assured of privacy, even from the Crown. I have a few ideas where we can regroup, but I am not certain we can completely rely on these supposed safe havens. Every query I make threatens our already uncertain anonymity."

"Sir . . ." came a voice from beside Eliza. "I believe I have a solution."

Wellington? How did he believe that he, the recently promoted field agent, held a viable, secure option for the Ministry in his hands?

The door leading to the inside of the pub burst open again, causing Cassandra to shoulder her rifle and prime it in one smooth, clean manoeuvre. Other agents, Wellington included, all drew a variety of concealed pistols. Where Lady Caroline had been hiding her rather impressive sidearm, Eliza had no clue. The two men were shaking off the rain as well, both their coats showing hard wear. Their journey had not been an easy one, perhaps harder than anyone in that room.

Eliza drew both her pistols, however, when Bruce Campbell revealed himself from underneath the tattered and soaked Stetson. As if this situation could not get any worse.

"Oh my!" Brandon exclaimed on looking up at the variety of firearms pointed at him. "Agent Brandon D. Hill. Canadian Victoria Branch. Cheers, all."

No one lowered their weapons.

"Don't take it personally, mate," Bruce said, patting Brandon's shoulder. "I think this is my welcome home, not yours."

Some of the weapons returned to their hiding places as Bruce crossed the length of the room to Doctor Sound. Cassandra Shillingworth, however, countered behind him, keeping her aim on the back of Bruce's head. Both of them had been properly identified as allies, and yet Shillingworth was still ready to take a shot. And she was not the only agent doing so. Those present on Bruce's admission to spying on the Ministry were all waiting for the word.

Why Brandon of all people was keeping company with him completely befuddled Eliza.

"Doctor Sound," Bruce said, removing his hat, "I'm sure I'm the last person you expected."

"You are quite right. The last I would have expected," the director stated, "or needed."

The Australian nodded. "All right then, Fat Man, have it your way." Bruce took stock of everyone in the room and gave a huff. "You lot seem to be in a right spot of trouble." His mouth bent back into a grin as his eyes stopped on Eliza. He gave her a wink and announced, "Well, you can all relax. The Thunder from Down Under is here to save the day."

Eliza glanced around the room. Not one pistol lowered.

This long night just became longer.

TEN

❧

Wherein a Wolf in Sheep's Clothing
Is Let Loose in the Henhouse

"You've got some cheek!"

Hearing those words from Eliza would have come as no shock to Wellington. It was, however, unsettling, hearing those words uttered from his own lips. Eliza was, most assuredly, rubbing off on him.

As the Australian turned to face him, Wellington swore he was growing by inches. *Never mind,* he thought quickly as he holstered his weapon. *I've held my ground with him once before. It would be a pleasure to do so again.*

"Are you sure you want to address me in that tone, Books?" Bruce asked as he cracked the knuckles of his right hand against the palm of his left.

"Just stating what is on most agents' minds right now." Wellington motioned to the gun barrels still trained on the Australian. "Or did you fail to notice the silent opposing vote to your presence here?"

"Once they remember why I'm good to have around—"

"Or remember what a complete and utter prat you are," Eliza bit out from behind Wellington.

"Well, it ain't like you can be particular with who you can

trust, now can you?" Bruce turned in place much like Sound had done earlier, but instead of taking stock of the agents around him, Bruce was merely looking for how many were present. "I'm guessing you lot don't even number to twenty. From where I'm standing, it looks to me that you might welcome an extra hand, now wouldn't you?"

"Agents," Doctor Sound finally spoke, and Eliza had never heard his voice so completely and utterly cold. Whatever was the undercurrent in his demeanour, Eliza was certain it would not bode well for Campbell. "Stand down. I want to hear what *Mr.* Campbell has to say." His eyes still fixed on Bruce, Sound motioned with a single finger to Miss Shillingworth. "Not you, Cassandra. Keep your rifle primed and ready. Just in case he refers to me as 'Fat Man' again."

Wellington glanced over to the bespectacled assistant who hefted the Mark IV quite aptly. He could tell she had no intention of missing.

"You may no longer serve in the ranks of the elite, Mr. Campbell, but that is certainly no license for you to not show respect where it is due."

"The *elite*? You lot?" Bruce motioned around him again and barked, "And exactly how is the elite faring up against the Department of Imperial Inconveniences? Hmmm, let's take a head count and see who is still alive, shall we?" Bruce tossed his wide-brimmed hat onto a table and removed the tattered duster. "Just goes to show you the fate of the *elite* once you ousted me. Fell like a house of cards, now didn't you?"

"And we were so secure with you around," Eliza hissed. "I'm sure Ihita felt safe with you in our ranks."

"Eliza," Brandon said, stepping in the line of fire between Bruce and Cassandra, "Bruce and I have come to an accord with that. I think you should too."

Her gaze switched to Brandon, her focused bitterness suddenly scattered by the man's unexpected compassion. "Ihita was a friend of mine, and you—"

"Will consider myself most fortunate if I see her again in the hereafter, but making Bruce suffer for that which he has already paid penance for will not bring Ihita back, and believe me, if that could have done so I would have made him suffer all the way from Colombia to here." Brandon looked at the agents around him and said sombrely, "And for those of you who still hold Bruce responsible for Ihita's death or for the dereliction of his sworn duty, Bruce is most assuredly correct in one respect—we are hardly in a position to be particular in the company we keep."

There were murmurs of consent, but neither Eliza nor Wellington echoed any such acknowledgement. Much as it was in the standoff, they were hardly alone.

Apparently, Doctor Sound agreed with them. "Kind words, Agent Hill, but forgive me if I take an opposing view to your own. I was duped once by Mr. Campbell here, and it cost me an agent of the highest calibre and the lives of several innocents. I will most certainly not be beguiled by such an individual ever again." Sound slowly approached Campbell who, much to his credit, stood defiantly as would have the Rock of Gibraltar against a sailing frigate. "Explain yourself, man."

Bruce looked him over for a moment. It struck Eliza as curious how he was assessing the director. After all he had done against the Ministry. Yes, Doctor Sound was right: it was very sweet for Brandon to forgive him, but that did not mean to simply put past transgressions behind and carry on.

"There was an attempt to recruit me in Rockhampton," Bruce began, his gaze locked with Sound's. "The Department must have figured I turned on you once before so I'd probably go off and do it again. I chose instead to voice my displeasure."

"Your displeasure?"

"In underestimating me." Bruce then motioned to Brandon. "Once I found out what I needed to know, I set off for South America, fastest flight I could manage. I had a notion where I could find Brandon."

"If it hadn't been for Bruce here, I'd be in a right state," Brandon offered. "In getting here, Bruce and I came to an understanding. I wouldn't say it's like old times in the field betwixt us, but I will say that Bruce is a good bloke to have at your side in a firefight. Our flight from Colombia was most exhilarating."

"I see. Thank you, Agent Hill." Sound tipped his head back, considering the Australian with deep scrutiny. "So, Mr. Campbell, you wish to come in from the rain, as it were?"

"Yes, sir," he replied, the man's confidence never wavering even as he added, "because it's the right thing to do for me mates in the Ministry."

"And what better place to seek shelter, as well, but in the last place the Department would come looking for you—the very agency you betrayed," Sound stated, one eyebrow raising ever so slightly.

Bruce went to retort, but closed his mouth as his gaze went from Sound to the agents assembled. Eliza always had regarded Campbell as being more of a brawler, less of a strategist. In her own partnerships with the Aussie, he preferred to let the bullets or his fists do the thinking when facing the opposition.

A brilliant deduction on Sound's part, and spot-on from the look of Campbell's reaction.

That didn't mean Bruce was finished. "Doctor Sound, you have no reason to take me back in. You just don't. Hell, if I were still assistant director of the Ministry, I would advise you not to do so, on account of how compromised I am. That being said, I do have insight on those who might have influenced ol' Queen Vic to deem us—I mean, the Ministry—as an inconvenience. If I wanted to disappear in Australia, I could have without a worry. Pick up the ol' bird and the kids, disappear in the outback, sure as Aunt Fanny's your Uncle Bob." He looked then directly at Eliza, then to just behind her where she knew Wellington was standing, his hand holding on to hers. "Some of you have no reason to trust me. Fair enough. Guess that means I'll have to work a touch harder for you lot." He returned to Doctor Sound. "I want to make this right. As my fellow Southerners can attest, that's how we prefer to handle things when plans go pear-shaped."

Before anyone could respond, the door leading out to the pub flew open again. This time, Bruce and Brandon joined in the collection of firearms that just seemed to appear. By the time Cassandra whirled about with the Mark IV shouldered, the couple entering had come to a full stop, their arms reaching high into the air. The lady was apparently attempting to adjust her spectacles by repeatedly scrunching her nose. The gentleman seemed hardly as distraught or as nervous as his partner. He simply looked at all the pistols at first with an ire of *"How typical."* His expression fell after a few moments. Eliza glanced at Wellington, who rolled his eyes. He knew what the look meant as well.

Their shared thought was now given voice as the newly arrived gentleman spoke with bottomless disappointment. "Pistols? We are on the verge of the twentieth century. I would expect at least half of you to be brandishing Experimentals, especially in our current pickle." He then dropped his hands and rapped the woman on her arm. "Told you, Josepha. We should have accepted the Department's offer. At least they *appreciated* our work."

"You really believe the Department would have been honourable considering what they were asking of us?" Now Doctor Blackwell turned to face Professor Axelrod, dropping her own arms and placing fists on her hips. "Just a moment—it was *your* idea to work from the inside!"

"Well, yes, because of your deductive reasoning, Josepha—" And on that, Doctor Blackwell gave a high-pitched squeak and motioned with her head to the collected agents. "I mean, *my esteemed colleague, Doctor Blackwell*—it was your deduction that swayed me to a more level head concerning our Ministry compatriots and the situation at hand."

"Which is why we had to take matters into our own hands, survive by our wits and intellect as it were."

"Hallo, Josepha! Hallo, Hephaestus!" chimed Barry from the back of the room, only his arm waving madly, visible over the crowd of agents. "Good to know you're all safe and sound!"

"Barry," they replied in unison, nodding.

"They were supplying weapons to the Department!" claimed Maulik, still refusing to lower his sidearm. "Well, weapons of a sort."

Axelrod gave a heavy sigh and corrected, *"Exciters.* We were supplying the Department with *exciters.* If you are to present evidence of our treasonous intentions, please do so with the facts as they are, not wild conjecture."

Sound blinked. "Is this true?"

"Of a fashion, yes," Blackwell replied.

"Of a fashion?" Sound asked incredulously. He appeared quite torn between curious and outraged.

"Yes, sir," interjected Bruce. "Seems that these clankertons here—"

"I beg your pardon," Axelrod and Blackwell snapped.

"—were supplying Experimentals, but they were more flawed than usual." Eliza looked back at Blackwell and Axelrod. Both were fit to burst. "The bloke that had Brandon and me dead to rights turned himself into a bloody Italian ice."

"Oooh, he was attempting to use the Jack Frost, was he?" Pistols were lowering as Axelrod fished out a pad and pencil from inside his jacket. "Details. I need details on exactly what happened, particularly after discharge."

"You see, since Doctor Sound forbade testing upon willing human test subjects"—she shot the director a glare, which drove Sound to pinch the bridge of his nose and screw his eyes shut—"we sabotaged the exciters by designing them all to misfire, once pressure inside the exciter's manifold could find no escape valve and reached critical failure."

"Come again?" Khaled asked.

"They made a gun with a sealed muzzle," Wellington stated.

"Very *good*, Books," Axelrod said, pointing at him with his pencil. "I knew getting out into the field would improve your comprehension of my work."

Beside her, Eliza felt Wellington flinch.

"Wait, just a moment," stammered Bruce. "Out in the field? *Books?!*"

Doctor Sound cleared his throat, returning attention to him. "We don't really have the time for this witty repartee as somewhere out there the Department is still following their own orders. Now then, I assure you we will debrief once we have a secure location in which to do so." He turned back to Wellington. "Agent Books, I believe you were to present us with an option?"

"Yes, sir," he said. Giving a quick glance to Eliza, Wellington drew himself up, and started again. "I would like to propose—"

"Forgive me, Agent Books," interrupted Sound. He craned his neck to make eye contact with Miss Shillingworth. "Cassandra?"

"Yes, Director?"

"I honestly don't care if it's the bloody Duke of Edinburgh, if that door opens within the next two minutes, shoot."

Her face came aglow with excitement. "Gladly, sir."

Sound returned his attention to Wellington. "You now have approximately one minute and fifty-three seconds, Books. Make it count."

"Yes, sir." The grating in his throat as he swallowed nearly knocked him back a step. He suddenly craved a drink. Perhaps the journey was catching up with him. "We need a location secure, remote, and unknown to the Crown. I know such a place."

Don't you dare, boy, a voice from the past warned in his mind.

It is no longer yours to rule over, Wellington seethed inwardly. *You saw to that.*

"Go on," the director urged.

Wellington blinked, feeling Eliza nudge him gently. "Yes, this location I would prefer to reveal only to you, Director, before we can be assured of security within our own ranks."

"Are you suggesting," came Agent King's voice, "that perhaps we are not secure?"

"I am suggesting"—he held a hand up towards Bruce, but didn't turn to look at him—"all present company aside, that we cannot afford to grow comfortable. The Department tried to recruit Bruce. We have no clue what agents we rendezvous with from here on, or if any in this room, have been compromised."

"And when do you suggest we can begin trusting one another, Books?" Maulik's mechanical voice asked. Even in its nature, Wellington could detect its hint of disdain.

"That, I leave to the director's discretion." Wellington felt the need for a drink again. Something harder than cider. "Tomorrow night, I will provide you with the coordinates there, sir."

"And you're certain of this location's secrecy?" he asked.

"Quite," Wellington assured him. "But there is a condition attached."

"Is it too much to ask for things like this to be simple?" grumbled Bruce.

Sound glanced over at the Australian and then his gaze flicked backed to Wellington. "And that condition is?"

"A head start." Wellington pulled Eliza a step closer to him and said, "I will need some time to prepare the location for your arrival. It will be myself; Agent Braun; her maid, Alice; and the Ministry Seven overseeing this."

"The Ministry who?" Brandon asked.

"Eliza's network of children," Shillingworth said, pushing a strand of white-blonde hair from her eyes. "They're in just as much danger as we all are."

Sound looked around the collected agents, all of whom were boring into Wellington and his superior. Wellington could feel the clutches of fatigue tightening around him, but he would not surrender to them just yet. He speculated that if he were feeling this tired from his own journey through Europe and back, his fellow agents coming from all points of the Empire also felt the same. They needed to just stay out of the Department's clutches a little longer.

"I know what I am asking of you, Director." Wellington tightened his grip on Eliza's hand as he cast his glance around the other agents. "I know what I am asking of you all, but I have to make certain the location is secure. It's . . ." He took a deep breath. "It's been a while since I've seen the property."

The silence seemed to press upon him, threatening to squeeze out the precious life remaining within his already-fragile shell.

"You shall have the time. No more than eight hours, but you will have it." Sound motioned for Miss Shillingworth, whispered something in her ear as he relieved her of the Mark IV, and sent her back into the great room of the Red Lion with a final nod. "We can hold up here for a little time, provided you are away immediately," Sound began, but then he looked around him and gave a sigh. "As we all are here and still draw breath, we are safe for the time being. The publican here is an old friend to us. Has been for some time, and his loyalty is unfaltering. This is where the Ministry began, and only two people know that. Provided that secret remains as such . . ."

His gaze turned to the solitary window of the room they all occupied. He seemed to be peering into the past. Whether it was long ago or only recent events, Wellington could not ascertain, but whatever Sound could see through the warped glass haunted him—that much was easy to tell.

"Right then," he said, his full attention now for the motley crew assembled around him. "We will have to make do with whatever rooms they have available here."

"We can assure you," interjected Eliza, "at least two rooms will be open."

Sound looked at her askance, then recognition popped across his face. "Oh that, right, yes, quite. Well, let us see if we can procure a few more then . . ."

As Sound moved off, the agents began to mingle once again, their eyes glancing over in their direction, accompanied by either dismissive shrugs or disgusted shakes of the head.

"Or," Wellington grumbled, "I can just let you all rot, while Eliza, Alice, and seven children find safe passage back to somewhere safe and secure."

"Oh, come off it, Welly," Eliza said, playfully rapping him on his arm. He furrowed his brow as he rubbed the spot she'd just struck. She did not have a clue as to how strong she was. "You're brand spanking new—*officially*—in the field. There's an amount of trust that needs to be—"

"Eliza, I have been working in the Ministry for close on seven years now. I rebuilt that archive from the madman's folly it had been left in. Each of these agents, at least once in their careers, save for the far-flung remote corners of the world, have exchanged correspondences with me. I'm not some poor recruit straight out of basic training armed with a rifle and my solemn vow to Her Majesty."

Eliza looked over the agents again, and her mouth twisted into a scowl. "Well, sod 'em if they don't like it, you're the one saving their collected arses, now aren't you?"

He tugged on his lapels and nodded. "That, I most certainly am."

Bursting from the crowd, came the lanky agent Eliza had recognized from New Zealand. Ferguson. "Eliza Doo, good, wanted to catch you and Books here before your leaving." He spun on his heel to Books and said, "And if nobody has ever said it or says it tonight, thank you for your sterling work in the Archives. Bang up job you did there, and I have no doubt you will excel in the field."

Wellington noted the break in conversation. He must have been waiting for a response. "Thank you. Much appreciated."

"Don't mention it," Barry said, waving his hand quickly as he turned to Eliza. "I was wondering if you, Eliza Doo, needed my assistance?"

She tipped her head to one side. "With?"

"Preparations," he said, clapping his hands together, rubbing them together with glee. "Ol' Lachlan can probably do with a tick or two without me at his side, so I thought you'd fancy the company."

"I would, *normally*, Barry, but"—she motioned over to Wellington—"this is Welly's dance. I am simply following his lead."

"Oh right, right, right," Barry replied, nodding. "Mind if I tag along then, mate?"

"We need to move fast," Wellington said, glancing over the lanky man. "And we will be travelling with children. I don't know if you—"

"I *love* children, and children"—he pointed to himself—"they *love* me!"

"He is rather gifted with mechanical devices," Eliza offered.

It was still a grand estate. An extra hand would be needed.

"Very well then," Wellington said, shrugging, "grab what you need. We leave in ten minutes."

"Brilliant!" he shouted, catching a few glances from the other agents. "I'll just let Lachlan know where I've gone off to then, shall I?"

And then he disappeared into the room once more.

"Looks like you have a fan there, Welly."

He raised his eyebrows. "Yes, charming. In that odd sort of way."

"That odd sort of way, mate?" she asked, her words rising ever so slightly in tenor.

"Well, you know what I refer to." Wellington felt the grin on his face. It had been some time since he afforded himself such a luxury. "It's a behaviour indicative to colonialists."

"I will smack you here in front of all these agents, I swear."

"I would be disappointed if you didn't, Eliza," he chuckled back.

"Shall we proceed then?"

"Let's," he said, motioning to the door.

They had only gone a few steps before Eliza stopped and

asked, "So this secret location of yours—when were you going to let me in on it?"

That was to be expected. "Yes, about that . . ."

"I thought we had sorted out that whole 'partnership trust' matter while we were in the United States."

That was to be expected, as well. "Old habits. I did not want to lay any foundations for irrational fears, nor did I want to instil any false hope. It was a final option, for many reasons. However, considering the circumstances, I'm finding that keeping this secret to heart was more of a benefit than a burden."

"So where are we headed tonight?"

Wellington grew acutely aware of the temperature in the room. While he knew it was warm, mostly in part to the fire in the small hearth and the collection of agents around him, the archivist shivered. This was a chill that, no matter how hard he would try with either fire, drink, or the company of this beautiful woman looking up at him, he would never be able to remedy.

"Home." The word itself sounded hollow, empty. No comfort whatsoever. "I am taking you home, Eliza Doolittle Braun."

INTERLUDE

❧

Wherein the Honour Amongst
Thieves Is Sorely Lacking

I t was a London particular, and that was a particularly good
thing for Sophia del Morte.

The Maestro, after battling with himself in the duke's
library, had retreated from sight, withdrawing deep into his
own personal Bedlam. According to the mad doctor, the Maestro needed to consider his next move in this dangerous game
for the Empire. Sophia was no longer concerned. This marked
the end of her tether. The end of playing with the madness.
The end of pretending the doctor's experiments on the child
did not disgust her.

It was time to leave. *Long past time,* her mother would
have said.

After the Maestro had disappeared into his own solitude,
Sophia told Jekyll she would be taking dinner in town. He did
not appear to approve of this, to which she responded with a
choice insult in her native tongue and left him to his own
maniacal devices. Yes, the insubordination would call down
the Maestro's wrath, but she no longer cared. The Maestro, in
her eyes, was no more substantial than a morning's mist.
Tonight, Sophia del Morte took back her control.

Tonight, she would secure her way out.

During dinner, when the rather handsome waiter presented her with a drink, compliments of the establishment, she saw through the base of her wineglass, typewritten on a paper cocktail napkin, her way out:

```
BLACKFRIARS BRIDGE
30 MINUTES
```

Dabbing her mouth with the message, Sophia stuffed the napkin in her handbag, left sufficient payment at her table, and excused herself from the premises, her eyes flitting to either side of the establishment to see if anyone else appeared to be finishing up their meal with her.

What had finally brought her to this point? Possibly the look in the boy's terrified eyes? Perhaps when she witnessed the macabre display of the Duke of Sussex conversing with himself? He quivered and shook before an empty armoured suit, given the illusion of life from a quaint control in the doctor's pocket. Perhaps it was the private army of radicals and disillusioned soldiers Jekyll was building, individuals believing themselves an instrument for building a better world when they were no better than the Maestro?

Or could it have been the doctor? She had caught several moments where he was watching her intently. Men desired her—that was no shock. She knew it, and exploited it. What was in the *medico matto's* eyes was not wanton lust. He was *studying* her.

It could have been any or all of these things, or simply accepting what she had been denying since San Francisco—the Maestro was a lie. An elaborate ruse. What terrified her more than the feeling of being deceived was the madman who possessed the control over the duke, and the Queen of England.

Yes, she had to break free. The ally she sent her message to was more than familiar with her services and skills, and could easily provide her shelter and secrecy from the Maestro. Accepting that, she knew not to grow over-confident in any allegiance struck. This "safe harbour" from the oncoming tempest was nothing less than a nest of vipers, and she would not simply trade one servitude for another.

The fact remained: this ally was her only option.

As she walked quickly through the fog-soaked streets of the city of London, she wrapped a scarf around her face in an attempt to keep the smell out. The odour of sulphur was overwhelming and apparently keen on choking her with its presence. It seemed apropos given the situation. The stench did clear her mind. She could not afford wandering thoughts to distract her, not with this meeting, on the possibility things went awry tonight. When people appeared suddenly out of the clouds of fog, all of them looked like potential killers from the Maestro, but all turned out to be merely citizens of London trying to escape to their homes. They would never know how close they came to being stabbed and gutted by an assassin walking a razor's edge.

Finally, she reached the embankment, and without a pause Sophia slipped over the edge, and dropped down onto the riverside sand. They must have selected this place and this current time on account of low tide. Looking to either side of her, she speculated if the deadly waters of the Thames at high tide posed a lesser risk than this meeting.

A scuttling of feet caused her to freeze where she stood. The handle of a knife concealed under her jacket still felt warm in her grasp. Something she detested about London—its propensity for sudden fog. It was hell on casing an environment. She watched miniature creatures scurry through pearlescent wisps. "Mudlarks" they called these children, scraping something resembling a living from what the Thames would leave in its tidal wake.

Blackfriars Bridge loomed before her out of the fog, its gilding gleaming only slightly. Sophia stood there and took in a long, deep breath, tasting the bitterness of the Thames in her mouth. Her fears, she ascertained as minute waves lapped against the viaduct's foundation, were unfounded, merely omnipresent to test her nerves. She was once a woman to be feared, not the one cowering as would a hound beaten to heel. Once far and away from the Maestro, Sophia would discover that woman again. Once her commitments were met—for this arrangement would undoubtedly carry a cost—Sophia would return home. Perhaps time in her beloved Italy, in familiar villas, would be exactly what she needed.

Another emerged from the pitch black underneath Blackfriars. His face was concealed by the shadow of his bowler's brim, but there were just enough touches of silver—a lapel pin, the head of his walking stick, and the cravat just visible between the lapels of his long, black coat—that Sophia recognised straightaway as her saviour's signature fashion. Straightening to her full height, she widened her stride and devoured the distance between them.

"*Buonasera, signorina,*" he said. His voice was velvet against such hard, terrible surroundings, but even her language could not quell the hint of his American accent.

Upon emerging into the dim light from lamps of the streets overhead, Sophia felt the air around her chill ever so slightly. It reminded her of the hollow dread on seeing the Maestro in his dishevelled, manic state, his mind warring between the real, the engineered, and the perceived. She still did not care for that memory. It made her feel vulnerable.

She received the same feeling from this man.

Unlike the Maestro, though, her contact appeared quite normal in every outward respect. He was well groomed, sporting fine carriage and confidence. Boundless confidence in his demeanour, a quality that usually Sophia found appealing in certain respects.

Not in this one. Something in this stranger's eyes urged her to flee.

"It has been too long," he said in a pleasant tone.

Her brow creased. "Have we met before, signor?"

"No, I'm speaking figuratively on behalf of the House of Usher. It has been nearly a year since we last heard word from you, and we did accomplish so much together."

That much was true. How many smaller governments had she thrown into turmoil with her talents. She had a nearly perfect record of service with the House. *Nearly* perfect. "A shame our relationship had gone as stale as it did."

He motioned behind him to the stone bridge and chuckled. "Should I state the obvious pun?"

Her mouth twisted. "Please do not."

He held his arms out in a wide "Very well, if you insist" gesture. He then seemed to catch himself as he opened his lapel. His hand suddenly stopped in mid-air as he said, "Oh my stars, but how foolish of me to be making such quick movements when our trust has been compromised."

"Most considerate of you, signor," Sophia said, her eyes still trained on him. "It would have been a shame to dispatch you so soon after our initial greeting."

He tipped his head into her direction and slowly—moving as languidly as his body allowed—reached into his coat pocket. After a few seconds, he produced a calling card.

Sophia motioned to the ground in front of him. "If you don't mind, and then five paces back."

The grin on his face did disarm her slightly. He seemed to understand her without fault. The contact stuck a corner of the card into the muddy ground, making the introduction stand upright. Easier for her to pick up. With his hands raised slightly, he took five generous paces back and waited.

Sophia still kept her eyes on the charming man as she stepped forwards to the card. Brushing it with her fingertips while keeping the contact well in sight, she stepped back to her original place and glanced down at the card.

Doctor Henry Howard Holmes

"A doctor, are you?"

"In a manner of speaking," he said, his voice suddenly clear as he stood next to her, reading over her shoulder, "yes."

The blade was out and resting against his neck. He could have touched her, placed a gentle touch on her shoulder, stroked the back of her hand with a finger, but she had not heard a hint of his approach.

She was beginning to develop a strong distaste for doctors.

"Back away. Hands out, palms away from me," she said, trying to keep her voice flat and unimpressed.

He smiled again and Sophia felt her breath catch in her throat. This Holmes would be quite dashing, were he not so unsettling. How had he been able to sneak up on her, completely undetected?

Another ripple of fear tore through her veins and she watched him back away, his smile brighter and brighter with each step. He knew she could have killed him, but what point would that have driven? She would still be in a desperate state.

Holmes now knew she was armed. She had also shown him in one simple gesture exactly how fast she was.

This wasn't intimidation. This was assessment.

"You are quite bold"—Sophia chastised him as best she could—"sneaking up on me like that."

"Terrible habit," he chuckled. "I suppose women such as yourself are my Achilles' heel. Perhaps, once our business concludes, I can win your trust properly. Instead of having notes delivered in secret across a dinner table, I can simply ask you for your company from across it."

She glanced at the announcement card again. The name suddenly triggered a memory. "Just a moment," she said. "Henry Howard? H. H. Holmes?"

He tipped his hat to her, a slight blush rising in his cheeks. "Guilty as charged."

"Interesting choice of words," she scoffed. "Aren't you supposed to be in a Philadelphia prison, awaiting the hangman's noose?"

"The House of Usher was impressed by my body of work, recruited me last year."

"So the gentleman in Philadelphia?"

"An astounding body double." He waved his hand dismissively. "And with the right contradictory evidence and quick recant, he will soon return to our ranks. Have no fear."

Sophia bent her hand back and the stiletto returned to its hiding place. "The House is in accordance then with my request?"

"Why wouldn't we be, signorina? You have given us sterling service in previous assignments. We would eagerly welcome you back to the fold."

"Even in light of previous events at my hotel?"

Holmes slipped his hands in his pockets, bowing his head slightly. His eyes fixed on a point just by Sophia's feet as he shook his head slowly. "Yes, most unfortunate business, that. There were some in the brotherhood that took umbrage with what you did, signorina. Most unfortunate, indeed." His eyebrows rose as he continued talking. "I did explain to those in opposition that we invited your wrath. My opinion was rebuked. Openly, in a rather brusque tone."

His brow then sank into a deep furrow. It was as if he was

conversing with the ground. Holmes was lost in a memory, and she was invisible to him.

"Rather brusque," he muttered, his features darkening. His head then snapped up, his eyes bright, even in the darkness around them, and he was back to a more congenial carriage. "But we came to an understanding. Our needs outweighed the desire for retribution against our brotherhood. We need you back in our midst, my dear, and I do hope you can find it in your heart to forgive us."

This was hardly the discussion Sophia first imagined. "I? Forgive you?"

"We were trying to tame you as if you were some dog failing to heel, and that was a terrible misjudgement on the part of the House. You most certainly do not slap a cobra against its hood and then expect it to answer your every bidding and whim. We should have shown more diplomacy in the handling of the Books affair, and for that we are truly sorry."

Sophia had planned to present a case for her return to employment with the House. She had been ready to make her argument compelling, an argument that could not simply be shrugged off. There were numerous deaths of Usher agents on her hands, and she would have to stand accountable for that.

But absolution from the House? Sophia's strategy was crumbling before her much like a child's sandcastle against a tide creeping closer and closer to shore.

"So far," Sophia ventured, "you seem to be showing a generosity that is not customary of the House of Usher. How do you benefit from this arrangement?"

"Our benefit?" Holmes gave a dry laugh as he softly clapped his hands together. "Your talents under retainer, of course. I would think that was obvious."

Yes, of course. "Excellent. Then shall we meet again—"

"Ah, yes, signorina," Holmes interrupted, "while I know your current employer may have an agenda under way, our own is rather sensitive at present. We have several projects currently under way, and I already feel myself spread thin. I believe we will need to move quickly." He produced from his waistcoat a fine silver pocket watch. He gave a tiny nod, closed the fob's cover, and stated, "Quickly meaning tonight."

"You mean, leave now. With you. Just like that?"

"Yes, you must make your decision now." He held out his hand to her.

Sophia felt the acknowledgement on her lips, wanted to reach out and take his hand; but there was something about actually making tactile contact with Holmes that kept her stock-still.

Run, a tiny voice in her head implored. *Run now.*

But it was merely the two of them. Only them. Meeting in secret.

She could not stop herself. "That is unacceptable."

"Really?" It could have been an illusion—a simple trick of the mind—but the shadows seemed to creep around his face as he retracted his hand, Holmes' expression appearing more sallow. "This, coming from the woman who sought help from us?"

"I did."

"And you thought it would all be on your terms?" Holmes drew in a deep breath, his eyes now boring deep into Sophia. "Excuse my candour, signorina, but you are hardly in a position to bargain the terms of this arrangement. You leave with me, now, or we part company."

Yes, Sophia did have to leave. Just not with him.

"You are underestimating this man I am currently entrenched with."

"The Maestro, you mean?"

"Not the puppet, Doctor Holmes, but the puppeteer. He is a physician such as yourself."

The shadows receded, but not by much. "Go on."

"It is the physician who is manipulating both the Maestro and the Queen of England. It is quite stunning to witness"—she tugged at the lapels of her jacket, feeling a sudden chill as she conjured a memory—"and rather unsettling."

"I see."

"I am under the scrutiny of not one but several influences, and I would prefer not to find myself under the good doctor's care."

Holmes nodded. "Does this sinister doctor have a name?"

"Jekyll. Doctor Henry Jekyll."

"Jekyll," he repeated in a soft whisper. His curious demeanour melted away and his tone turned quite brusque. "I believe I may have heard of his work in Paris." He tilted his head. "So you are suggesting I should wait here until you are ready to take flight?"

The sarcasm was not lost on Sophia. She could feel the brace under her jacket sleeve, knew a knife could be in her grasp in a moment. Something stayed her hand, and this annoyance was working under her skin.

Run, the tiny voice spoke again. *Just run.*

His hand extended once again. "Time to choose."

There was something ominous about the darkness around them suddenly. She knew they were still alone. She heard nothing out of the ordinary, could see no real threat lurking in the shadows. There were no tells of any sort. It was only the two of them, and that terrified her. From what he had revealed to her, he knew her abilities, was more than aware of her reputation, and yet he was meeting with her without attendants of any sort. The man held no fear of her, and yet was making small talk over her boundless talents, those same talents that were warning her to run. Run as she did in the streets of San Francisco. Run as she did when the Havelock estate collapsed around her. Run as if her life depended on it.

"No." And her reply seemed to hang in the air between them because, yes, her life—she suddenly realised—did depend on it. "I think not."

The gentleman nodded sombrely. "I seem to have misjudged you, signorina. How disappointing."

Sophia's senses had never felt more heightened. It was still the two of them and only them. Why did this bother her so? "I have no doubt. It is disappointing for me as well. I now have nowhere to go, but back to the Maestro."

"Oh, there are always options, although they may not be so delightful for you, signorina," he said, his mouth bending into a thin smile.

It was time to leave.

He wasn't moving.

Sophia took a step backwards. Then another. Then another.

"Dear Lord, woman, what are you doing?" Holmes chortled.

She paused, looking him over while taking stock of the distance between them. "I am taking my leave of you."

"While impersonating a crab, it would appear." He clicked his tongue. "Dear lady, you may go. I speak for the House of

Usher this evening, and if you have turned down shelter with us, then that is your decision to make. We will honour it without fault or fail."

"And what of you?" she felt compelled to ask him. "Will you honour my decision?"

"I suppose I am still of two minds about that."

They certainly could not stand there all night, and she certainly would not get very far walking backwards.

But he refused to move.

Another step back, one more . . .

Sophia spun on the balls of her feet and ran. She knew he was fast and silent. She would most certainly not hear him if he did make for her. There was no other option beyond this mad dash for the stairs. They were just in front of her, but they seemed as if they were being pulled away from her the harder she ran. When she suddenly felt stone underfoot, she thrust her other arm outward, catching the small pistol in her hand. She raised the gun up and threw her back against the wall, sucking in the foul air as she drew her aim.

Holmes was still standing by the bridge. He had not moved. There was very little light on him, but she knew—some primal urge in her had never been more certain before now—that he was elated, if not utterly euphoric. Holmes was dining on her terror as if it were a lavish seven-course dinner.

He tipped his hat to her as her gun fell to her side, her own whimpering now turning into sobs. She continued to cry as he turned and disappeared under the bridge, the shadows there welcoming him back, welcoming him home. He had returned from whence he had come, and now she could not keep him within her sight. Sophia could no longer see Holmes, but that did not mean she could not feel him. Her instincts knew he was watching her from the shadows.

"Oh, there are always options . . ." he had said to her.

Taking in another deep breath, Sophia pulled herself back to her feet, seized control of her faculties, and then took stock of the dark world around her. Still alone, still lost in the darkness of London.

ELEVEN

❦

Wherein It Is Proven One
Can Go Home Again

His fingers traced over the stone slab bearing the weathered letters carved into it. He would have replaced the name-plate had he cared. Now it would appear conspicuous. This close to the marker, the name was still legible.

Whiterock.

Welcome home, my son, the ghost whispered. *It was only a matter of time.*

This was no small thing for Wellington Thornhill Books to be heading back to his childhood home, just outside of Hebden Bridge, Yorkshire. Once he was back in the driver's seat, the motorised cart carrying himself, Eliza, Alice, and the children continued to chug up the abandoned tree-lined avenue, and though it was a warm May morning, a shiver danced up his spine. The oaks that lined the avenue were old friends, perhaps the only ones he had ever had in this place. He'd spent as much time as he could climbing their boughs, hiding from his father's valets and clockwork footmen. More than a few of the green sentinels probably still bore marks where he had cut his name, while reading his mother's novels in among their branches.

"Charming," Eliza murmured at his side. She tucked her

hand in the crook of his elbow, perhaps feeling the stress vibrating in his body.

Glancing over his shoulder to check on the younger passengers, Wellington was slightly startled at the sight of Ministry Agent Barry Ferguson, thankfully busy fiddling with some little gadget on his lap he had apparently constructed from a pair of garden shears, a broken tap handle, and a lady's compact. Wellington had completely forgotten extending the invitation to Eliza's childhood friend. He could only hope he remained inconspicuous.

"It was, once"—Wellington swallowed a tightness in his throat—"when my mother was alive." He shot her a look. "You two would have got along rather too well I think."

She pressed her lips together, though the corners of her mouth twitched slightly. She was pleased he was sharing this with her. It felt good to let her into his own little world of pain. *A problem shared is a problem halved,* his mother had often said, and once again she proved to be wise.

He smiled. It was so rare when he recalled his mother's voice. He wished it were her voice that haunted him.

"So how old were you when she died?" Eliza asked.

Wellington shrugged as he replied softly, "I was ten when my father had my mother killed."

He said it simply, but Eliza's hand dropped over his and squeezed. Coincidentally they had just crested the rise that concealed the estate from the prying eyes of the public; they had a fine view down at the big house itself. It was a Gothic monstrosity, thoroughly suiting his father's nature and only lightened by his mother's presence.

"Pull over, Wellington," Eliza insisted. When he reluctantly did, he motioned for everyone to stay where they were as he engaged the hand brake and dismounted from the driver's seat. Alice pulled Serena and Colin closer together while the rest of the Seven whispered to one other. As for Barry, he was muttering to himself now, something about ratios, and still utterly consumed by the project taking shape before him, so Wellington was sure there was a God above to be thankful to.

Eliza turned Wellington's gaze to hers by pressing her fingers gently against his cheek. "You don't mean that do you?"

"My mother was an excellent horsewoman," he said evenly.

"I do not think it is coincidence that she died immediately after having a raging argument with my father about my education. She wanted me to go to boarding school to be away from him, while he wanted me near so he could train me." It felt strange to say it out loud, but also very cathartic.

She let out a breath in a long steady stream. "Oh my, makes my tense family Christmas dinners seem rather trivial. Aunt Barbara's hatred for my mum has never run to homicide." Eliza immediately clapped her hand to her mouth. "I'm sorry, Wellington. That sounded awful . . . I didn't mean . . ."

He looked her in the eye, and couldn't help smiling. He hated being here, but somehow being here with her made it bearable. That, and knowing his using Whiterock for Ministry business would have incensed his father.

Leaning across, he cupped her face and kissed her soundly. When he let her go she was gasping rather satisfactorily. "You, Miss Eliza D. Braun, are the breath of fresh air this place needs. Since my mother's death, this place has been . . . hollow."

She grinned back at him. "I've been called many things, Welly, but I think that is quite the nicest of them all. Said in the nicest possible way."

"Got it!" Barry utterly broke the moment as he bounced almost out of the cart, clutching the fist-sized device and a tiny screwdriver. His attention now torn away from it, he stuck his head between them and stared down at the manor. "That's quite a house, Eliza Doo! Come up a bit in the world. *Noice!*"

Eliza's face went from beatific to stormy in a small instant. "Sit down, Barry, that's Wellington's estate not mine, as I told you three times already." Her finger was suddenly waved in Barry's face. "And what did I tell you about calling me by that nasty nickname?"

"Oh, I don't know," Wellington said, a wry grin crossing his lips. "I find it rather endearing."

"Don't encourage him, Welly," she warned.

"Would never dream of it, Eliza Doo," he returned.

Her fellow New Zealander went to say something but snapped shut his mouth, while Eliza turned to Wellington and growled out, "Let's go!"

While Barry's nature was overtly playful, the two nursed some sort of tension that Wellington could not quite ascertain.

He was completely sure, though, it was not romantic. From the look on Eliza's face it might well break into something that involved bloodletting.

Wellington hastily disengaged the brake and guided the motorcar back on the road to the manor before a fight could break out across the seats. The wind kicked up, as if in response to their respective moods. Eliza's dire frown threatened to be a rather unpleasant beginning to the re-establishment of the Ministry of Peculiar Occurrences.

"Don't mean to be rude . . ." Barry leaned forwards, his head popping in between them, and pointed to the manor. "But it looks a little . . . well . . . deserted?"

"We could hardly do what we need to do if it wasn't." Eliza placed her finger on the young man's forehead and pushed him back into the cart. "Do be a love, Barry, there's a good lad."

From his vantage point Wellington couldn't see all of Barry's expression, but at least the eccentric man went silent. He probably had experience with Eliza Braun's short temper before.

"This is very nice, Mr. Books," Liam spoke up suddenly. "A look at being to the manor born, eh wot?"

They pulled up to the front of the house, and Wellington turned to face Liam. The boy wore a smug look of contempt but it faded once he locked eyes with the boy.

"If you believe I lived a life of privilege, I did. On the surface. I assure you, Liam, what happened within these walls was not worth all the riches of the world."

Alice tightened her grip on Serena. He must have looked a tad frightening. That was fine. He wanted them to be frightened of Whiterock.

"Wellington?" he heard Eliza say.

He engaged the cart's brake and took a deep breath. The Ministry was depending on him. He needed to take control of Whiterock, not the opposite.

To break the icy silence, Wellington gestured out towards the estate. "It wasn't always this oppressive. Mother rode horses here, and she made sure to take particular care of the tenants too. In the summer she held wonderful parties out on the back terrace, and at Christmas she'd host a beautiful dinner." For a moment he was whisked back to those magical times, when his father had only been a distant cloud on the horizon, and his whole world was his warm and lovely mother. He smiled. "I'd sometimes sneak down from the nursery and peer through the bannisters at all the immaculately dressed people."

Eliza's eyes sparkled as she leaned against him. "I can just imagine you doing that. Curious as always."

Wellington knew Eliza would have loved those parties. The thought brought a smile to his face, even as his eyes wandered over the long grey face of Whiterock Manor, with its church-like windows, and looming gargoyles on every corner. His grandfather had the building remodelled back when Queen Victoria was a girl. Gothic had been all the rage so it wasn't really a surprise he'd chosen that style, though somehow Grandfather Henry had kept all of the gloominess, but yet managed to avoid the charm most others worked to instil in the architecture. It looked as if it had grown from the surrounding dour hills, like an iron frown.

Eliza shifted in her seat, and he knew her imagination was struggling to see the house as a place of beauty. "You did tell me your father is dead, didn't you?" she ventured.

Wellington ground his teeth before he answered. "Yes, I made absolutely sure the evil bastard was cold in the grave myself. I only left Whiterock when he was walled in the mausoleum, and after I was able to scour the house for any . . . infernal devices of his design. Believe me—this is the safest place we could ask for in all of England."

Wellington caught Barry's eyes huge with shock and curiosity, but before the conversation could turn completely morbid he went to one of the lion statues at the base of the steps. He pressed the brick he remembered slid back to offer him keys. The hiss from the front door's pneumatic locks made the chill silence of Whiterock Manor all the more unsettling. However, he would not be intimidated by a house—no matter how grand or full of memories it might be. He had his love at his side, and he was no longer that terrified, lonely boy. Eliza wrapped her fingers around his as Wellington disengaged the final lock.

"It might be rather grim"—she tilted her head up to look at the three-storey structure, long and low against the landscape—"but at least it isn't a ruin."

Barry stood there twisting his fingers on each other, as if

even in contemplation he needed to be moving. "Looks like a good solid roof. The rest doesn't really matter I suppose."

Eliza slapped his shoulder with a lightning-fast movement of the back of her hand, which made him leap in place. "We need a few more things than that, Barry. It's headquarters until we can return to how things were."

Her countryman looked completely unperturbed. He opened his mouth to reply, but Wellington, fearing more delay than they could afford, spoke up. "I retained an old army friend, Ralph Turenne, to act as caretaker, make sure water, sheep, or indeed people don't get in. I think it will suit our needs admirably."

"Will we expect his company sometime?" Eliza asked. "You said this house was secure."

"It is. I've been working through a solicitor. The solicitor in turn works through an anonymous member of the estate"—Wellington motioned to himself—"and the estate, upon my father's death was transferred to another. My mother, actually, under her maiden name." He chuckled. "Thank you, Parliament, for the Married Women's Property Act of 1882. Between that and a few skills I learned while in the Ministry, Lillian Morton was as Lazarus; and Whiterock remained standing, but in secret."

The final lock disengaged with a sharp hiss. He stepped back and took it all in. The stone gargoyles on the roof, the marble snarling lions on either side of the steps and grand doors, and the rows of windows, all vacant. He could not believe he was here again. The last place . . .

"So," Barry chimed in softly, "are we going to stand out here all day?"

"Ladies and gentlemen," Wellington replied with a grunt as he shouldered the large oak door open, "welcome to White-rock."

As Wellington walked into the foyer, the archivist was flooded with a thousand images, most of them unhappy, but a few like the sound of his mother's laughter, gave him the strength to do what was needed. The smell of camphor and dust sifting around him, he walked deeper into his ancestral manor with what he hoped was at least an outwards show of bravado. His only concession was never releasing Eliza's hand as they walked together into the main hallway. The marble floors echoed their footsteps, and then for a brief moment all was silent.

Until Barry Ferguson was able to get his bearings, that was. He spun around in the hallway, arms spread, head tilted upwards, and gazed at all the ancient stonework. Though there was not a gear in sight, he seemed to be experiencing some kind of epiphany.

"Nothing this old in New Zealand, is there Eliza Doo?" His voice bounced through the main hall, and probably woke a few pigeons in the distant bedrooms.

Her grumble managed to bring a smile to Wellington's face.

The furniture was all covered by white sheets, and the light filtered through the dirty windows in strange patterns. The only thing that was clean was his mother's portrait hanging right above the first landing on the stairs. It was apparent that Ralph had faithfully obeyed Wellington's wishes in this regard too.

"She's so beautiful," Eliza said, forgetting Barry for a moment, and stepping towards the painting. "I remember the one in your house, Wellington, but this one is even more spectacular."

He came up next to her. It showed his mother at the age of perhaps eighteen, just before she'd been married. "She was Lillian Morton then, youngest daughter of an aristocratic family with a lot of famous ancestors, but very little money. My father saw her at a garden party and apparently had to have her."

"So she didn't marry for love?"

"It was a match made in a Gentleman's Club. My father wanted the prestige of her family. His money saved hers. I don't suppose she had a choice."

"At least she felt she didn't." Eliza let out a soft sigh. "But she had you." She kissed his cheek and wandered away to examine the rest of the rooms.

Barry trailed after her, which was exceptionally foolhardy of him, but Wellington was not going to get between the two of them.

"Alice," Wellington said, turning back to the maid and children. "There are rooms upstairs . . . plenty of rooms. Pick out one that suits you."

"Very good, Mr. Books," Alice said in a tone he had forgotten. She was speaking to him as if he were lord of the manor which, regrettably, he was. "And what about servant's quarters?"

"Alice," he said, taking the maid's hands gently into his own, "after this little adventure across continents, I would not dare insult you in such a fashion." He motioned with his head up the staircase. "Find a room for the children, then find a room for yourself."

The maid went to protest, but Wellington shook his head and continued deeper into the mansion, the eerie silence interrupted briefly by the thunder of the Seven's footsteps up to the second floor.

Once again Wellington was reminded how his love had impeccable instincts. She might have never gone to Oxford or Cambridge, but she was smarter than any man he'd ever met there. By letting him have a moment to himself she was allowing him to gather his thoughts, deal with ghosts, and move on to the task at hand.

As Wellington watched Eliza he thought for a moment what a totally impossible lady of the manor she would make. Although she was gingerly removing dust sheets, and admiring the architecture of the place, he knew within weeks she'd be quite mad with boredom here. His mother at least had found ways to pass the time. Eliza, left to the same devices, would undoubtedly blow something up at a dinner party.

Or, at the rate he appeared to be working under her skin, Barry Ferguson. "Good Lord, Books, why on earth would you leave *this* lifestyle for a career in the Ministry?" he blurted out.

"Oh, for God's sake," she finally yelled, spinning around. "We are supposed to be securing and preparing this place as our new headquarters. You're supposed to be an agent, Barry. Start acting like one!"

Hurt filled the young man's eyes, and Wellington saw Eliza wince immediately. Apparently Barry could go from completely oblivious to intensely vulnerable in an instant. "Sorry, Eliza Doo, I just want to help is all . . ."

Wellington could see Eliza's jaw work, and then her shoulders slumped. "The name, Barry . . . just work on not calling me that . . . please!"

"Perhaps you could go up and check the attics, old chap?" Wellington stepped between them. "I had some idea of setting up a watch station from there. It's a good place to spot any unwanted arrivals."

Barry's face brightened as quickly as it had fallen. "Cracking good idea there, Books!"

When Wellington showed him the back stairs, he scampered off up them with apparently not a thought more of his hurt feelings.

"Thank you," Eliza gasped out, closing her eyes for a long second. "I do love that Ferguson boy, but he also happens to work on my last nerve."

"Don't be too hard on him." And this time, Wellington gave her a slight nudge. "Eliza Doo. It really is charming."

Shaking her head in playful frustration, Eliza set about once more examining what was beneath the dust sheets, and Wellington, tucking his hands behind his back, mentally ran over the penultimate time he had been here, to rub his father's nose in the fact he'd taken up a Ministry job. A lowly Ministry job. Wellington had no plans to return to Whiterock as its master. His father's money would keep things ticking over, and eventually the estate might be for his children, should he ever have any. Otherwise it would eventually belong to the people who farmed it.

"Now that's brilliant!" came an all-too-familiar voice from the kitchens.

"Bugger me," muttered Wellington as he grabbed Eliza's hand and tugged her over to the kitchen. "They cracked it!"

The two of them sprinted in the direction of three very excited voices. Once in the kitchen, Wellington pulled apart the dumbwaiter doors with a clatter, revealing what they had once kept secret.

"Oh, Wellington," she cooed from behind him, "how on earth do you always know the ways to my heart?"

With Colin and twins Jonathan and Jeremy frozen in the midst of their own celebrations, the hidden armoury truly was worthy of Eliza's approval. Rifles, pistols, and even a few experimental weapons, a small ballista, and lots and lots of ammunition, all of which had not seen any kind of attention since his father's death. "I could not crack the combination. Well done, boys."

Jeremy whispered something to Jonathan (or perhaps, it

was the other way around?) and Jonathan replied with, "Colin's rather good with puzzles, Mr. Books."

Eliza tapped at the small light fixture, and the gas flame brightened ever so slightly. She ran her fingers over the collection as Wellington motioned to the dumbwaiter. "You see, making use of the lift which goes up to all the floors, you will never be without access to what you need."

She nodded as she spoke over her shoulder. "Every house should have one."

"But, Mr. Books," Colin began, "these guns have not been cleaned in a right while."

"Very observant, young Colin," Wellington said. "Perhaps you three under the watchful eye of Miss Braun here could inspect these weapons, return them to good service?"

"Can we?" the boy asked, Jonathan and Jeremy mirroring their friend's expression.

"Perhaps," Eliza murmured. "We will see how we fare after lunch, very good?"

"Yes, Mum," they replied.

"Now, go on," she said, shooing them in the direction of the dumbwaiter. "I would like for you all to let Alice know we will need supplies for lunch."

"Perhaps Mr. Ferguson could go into town to help you all with supplies?" Wellington asked.

Jonathan whispered something to Jeremy. The twin thought for a moment, then whispered something back to Jonathan. With a quick nod to Jeremy, Jonathan asked, "Can Mr. Ferguson take us to the hardwa—"

"Absolutely! Not!" Eliza said, fixing the twins with a dagger-laden look. "Remember, we are supposed to be travelling incognito."

"Go on and find out what Alice needs," Wellington chuckled. He looked over to Eliza and winked. "I'll fetch Barry, Eliza Doo."

"You do that, Welly," she returned, her dagger eyes appearing a hint sharper.

An hour from the discovery of the hidden armoury, Wellington and Eliza were waving to Barry, Alice, and the children as they headed into town.

"Remember, Barry!" Eliza called out as the wagon rumbled down the causeway.

"Mum's the golden word!" he called back, then mimed sealing his lips shut.

"I understand the need to keep Barry out of a hardware store," began Wellington, "but the twins?"

"Future clankertons, they are," she said. Eliza then turned to Wellington. "So, where are we tonight?"

The idea unsettled him for some reason. "The master bedroom."

"Very good," she said. "Shall we?"

The double doors that opened to where Wellington always considered to be forbidden swung open. Eliza immediately went to the grand windows overlooking the impressive grounds of Whiterock and opened them up. It took only a few seconds for the staleness of the room to lift.

"Wellington," Eliza said, coming over to him. "This is *your* house now. Make it your own. Fill it with your memories."

"Easier said than done, Eliza," Wellington said, looking uneasily to every corner of the room.

"Opening Whiterock to the Ministry?" she asked as she walked around the bed. "I believe that is quite the start."

A betrayal is more like it, seethed Wellington's father in his mind.

"Perhaps," he said, walking over to the window. Could he truly reclaim Whiterock? Finally silence the ghost that haunted him?

"What on earth is this?" Eliza asked.

She was somewhere out of sight, so it took a moment for Wellington to find her in an antechamber that would have served as a changing room. Later in Arthur Books' life—or what he believed was as such—it had been converted into a private library. She was standing in a block of sun holding the corner of a sheet in one hand. With a quick jerk of her arm and the flutter of fabric, curtains of dust filled the air but failed to mask what Wellington had already guessed lay beneath it. Seeing it so abruptly revealed, though, made his stomach lurch.

"Father's chair," he said, though it felt as though the words were being extruded from him.

"This is quite amazing," she said before dropping the sheet.

Eliza bent down and examined it, running her fingers over the bellows that had once forced air into Arthur Books' lungs, and working dials where his voice had once issued forth.

"Was it some kind of accident," she asked, "that put him into this thing?"

"No," Wellington replied, still not able to bring himself to go any closer to it. "Excess. Too much drink, too much smoking, too much of . . ." He walked over to the window and opened it. He needed fresh air. ". . . everything."

"Well, he certainly knew his armaments." Eliza gestured to two small holes in the front of the armrests of the chair, and then to a small, dull-red button on the top surface, right where his father's fingers would have rested. "This looks like some kind of propellant device." She pulled out a Swiss Army knife, selected the horse pick and before he could stop her, poked the side of the chair.

Wellington reminded himself the chair's generator had been dead since his father's passing. It was no more dangerous than the man who once sat in it. He'd identified the body. He'd seen the mausoleum sealed. Arthur Books was dead and could no longer hurt him or the people he loved. He felt his shoulders slump.

"How ingenious," she said. "It looks like this shoots out a set of wires which delivers an electric shock. Blackwell and Axelrod would love to take this apart, no doubt." A frown settled over her face. "I've only ever seen this on one other occasion; a rather nasty House of Usher agent I tangled with in Cape Town. How on earth did he get this?"

"Father was never out of this house." His words came out sharp and defensive somehow. "At least, after his infliction," he added in a softer tone.

Eliza glanced up and raised an eyebrow. "I'm just saying I've never seen this anywhere else. Did he ever mention Usher?"

Wellington clenched his jaw and shook his head. "Never. I was his life's ambition, a living legacy that turned out to be a grave disappointment to him." He stared down at the chair, rapping his knuckles against its dark wood. "He spent a great deal of time, resources, and effort training me to be the soldier that would lead the Empire to great victories abroad. In the end I was able to break away from him. I joined the Ministry, just to spite him."

He knew he couldn't be the only person that had run towards a life in the government to get away from the path planned for them by their parents. There were plenty of stories in his own regiment that told as much.

"She won then," Eliza murmured. "He may have outlived her, but your mother won."

Crouched down by the chair, she stared up at him and smiled. Wellington recognised that smile. It was one of victory, the one of survival that they had shared many times on their previous adventures. It was something special between the two of them.

He coughed and adjusted his cravat. "You know, you're correct, Eliza. I never really thought of it that way." Somehow the atmosphere in the library lightened. "Let's see if we can finish getting the manor ready for our colleagues' arrival. I am sure that would also have annoyed Father. In so many ways."

"Sounds a grand idea," she said, levering herself up, her hand on the arm of the chair.

Click.

They both froze immediately. The sound hidden doors and compartments, and concealed locks, made was awfully similar to the noise bomb triggers made as well. For a moment they shared a look, but it was Wellington, despite his hatred of the chair, who moved closer to examine what she had accidentally triggered.

Eliza's hand remained where she had leveraged herself. Just in case it was some kind of weapon, no doubt. Wellington narrowed his gaze on the panel under her touch, and then he let his breath out slowly.

"It's all right," he said, wrapping his fingers around hers and lifting them away from the chair. He placed a gentle kiss on her fingertips and nodded. "It's not a trap."

"Bloody exciting childhood you must have endured!" she quipped through a quivering voice.

"One way to look at it." Both their eyes turned to the wicked chair, and Wellington's head inclined to one side. "It's some kind of secret compartment."

Given his knowledge of Arthur Books, this was quite

surprising. What could possibly be important enough for his father to conceal so close to his person? He knew for certain it would not be a love letter or anything so romantic.

Eliza pried her knife under the panel and levered open the concealed compartment, but she took a step back, giving Wellington the time and space to examine what they had found.

He, for one, was done with his father's secrets interfering with his life. "No, thank you," Wellington spat. Then, in a more gentle tone, "If you are curious, however . . ." He motioned to the chair.

Her eyes locked with his for a moment, but she nodded. When Eliza's fingers withdrew the telltale ring, the moment seemed to condense. It was unmistakably the silver signet ring surmounted by the embossed form of ravens that was worn by only one group. The House of Usher.

"That bastard," he whispered. His fist tightened around the ring until the metal raven dug into his palm. "He's been dead for nearly a decade, and still he will not grant me peace . . ."

"Wellington?" Eliza's soft voice somehow managed to reach him even through the rage. "Wellington, you're more than that."

Mother? Did you know? Wellington closed his eyes. *Is that why you fought? Is that why he killed you?*

"*Wellington!*"

Arms were around him now and he was down on the floor. He felt sore, an aching that threatened to smother him, but he also felt a tight embrace, and the harder he trembled, the tighter the embrace became. A burning sensation came from his hand. He didn't have to look. He knew the Usher insignia was cutting into his skin.

"Wellington, it's all right," Eliza whispered. "You are an agent of the Ministry of Peculiar Occurrences, an agency dedicated to stand against the House of Usher. You won." She stroked his hair as she held him. "You beat him. It's over."

Wellington wanted to believe that, but something instinctual told him this would not be over until Usher collected their prize.

TWELVE

❧

Wherein Our Agents Settle into Their
New Accommodations and Brandon Hill
Displays Astounding Culinary Skills

"Now is certainly not the right time to mention the ring to the director," Eliza reminded Wellington, even as they watched the convoy of motorcars and horse-drawn carts coming up the drive. They had discussed away most of their remaining hours, but come to no real conclusion, except for this one. She pressed her hand on the door, preventing him from opening it. Wellington could have moments of blind and unfortunate honour. "This couldn't have come at a worse moment in the Ministry's history, my darling archivist, and you know it."

He pressed his lips together and would not meet her eyes.

"Welly," she said, her voice rising sharply, "I mean it. What is the point of bringing this up now? Your father is dead, you are an honest and true member of the Ministry—you've proven that over *and over* again. We need to stick together, and people need to trust you."

It was a blunt blow, and it was designed to be that way. Still, Wellington looked up in utter shock. He immediately saw what she meant; he could imagine how some of the other agents, hurt, angry, and grieving, might look at him differently if they found out his father's connections. If the words "House of Usher" ever came out, it might mean the end of the Ministry entirely. People who had just been attacked by their own government were not likely to throw their lot in with anyone associated in the slightest with that organisation. He couldn't blame them for that either.

Eliza could see in every movement how deeply this revelation had damaged her lover. He had hated his father, suspected he was his mother's murderer even, but this was an entirely different kettle of fish. To find out your father was in league with your sworn enemy . . . Well, she couldn't imagine what that would feel like, and how it would make a person question themselves.

When Eliza placed a hand against his cheek, it was gentle, but her words remained stern. "You know in the army, when it was time to fight, how everyone needed to be a single unit?" He nodded. "Then you must know this is one and the same for us. Promise you won't say anything to our comrades."

Wellington straightened his jacket, and patted his pocket that contained the ring as if to verify it wouldn't slip out. "I promise, Eliza . . . Unless it becomes important to the survival of the Ministry, I will hold my tongue."

She had his agreement just in the nick of time too, because the engines were silent now, and instead footsteps could be heard coming up the stone stairs. Wellington grabbed Eliza, suddenly planting a passionate kiss on her that stole her breath and seemed to slow time. "Might be the last time for a bit," he murmured once they parted in that husky tone of his she'd noticed he reserved for moments such as this. Then he stepped back and flung open the doors to his ancestral home.

"Welcome to Whiterock Manor," he said to the arriving agents, spreading his arms wide as if he were the ringmaster in a grand circus.

Perhaps he had gotten his acting skills from his mother, Eliza mused, before stepping out to help her colleagues with their luggage. Even though it had only been one night since their meeting in the Red Lion, she could not help but count heads, just in case.

It pained Eliza to ask after them all as if they were a group, but she had to. "Where are the rest?"

"Never fear." The director put down his disturbingly small valise by the stairs. "We are arriving in shifts, coming from various directions." His eyes twinkled even in the dim interior of the hall. "It would be, I can only speculate, slightly conspicuous if we all appeared at—where are we again, Books?"

"Whiterock, sir," he replied.

"Ah, yes—Whiterock, all together as one merry party, yes?"

"As long as no one gets shot, I'll count that as a success," Eliza said as an aside to Wellington.

"You mean, as long as another agent doesn't shoot Bruce," the archivist whispered in her ear, before lifting a box Blackwell had deposited on the marble floor right by the door where anyone could trip over it. "Some of you may need to double up on lodging, so feel free to use discretion."

Blackwell and Axelrod appeared to be the only ones with a substantial amount of luggage, hopefully items they had managed to steal away from Miggins Antiquities. Despite the tensions between R&D and Wellington, Eliza was still rather fond of their creations, most especially since she was not afraid of things that went bang.

Everyone else carried remarkably little. Lady Caroline had a single hatbox and a small suitcase that couldn't have held anything more than a pair of bloomers and perhaps a spare corset. Maulik, it turned out, had only a saddlebag and a battered hat to his name. It suddenly dawned on her just how amazing a feat it had been for Wellington and her to have made it to the rendezvous with Alice and children in tow. Possessions were something that agents learned to do without, especially when on the run. Eliza though did have a momentary pang for her own apartment. She hated to think about the state of it, considering how the Department was likely to have treated it while looking for her.

"This?" Doctor Blackwell stood in the middle of the hallway and stared up at all the mullioned windows. "This is your home?" The expression on her face was as if she were looking at some particularly attractive piece of art. *Naturally she likes it,* Eliza thought. *Gothic was always her style.*

"It's very dusty!" Axelrod was not nearly as impressed by either their new headquarters or apparently his associate's reaction to it.

"It's also very safe." Wellington tucked his hands into his

pockets, possibly to avoid knocking Axelrod's block off. "Bedrooms are on the second floor. I believe for what you lot may want to do, the lower kitchens downstairs may suffice."

"The *lower* kitchens?" Axelrod scoffed.

"Speaking of, I shall just go downstairs, check on Alice and the children, see how preparations are proceeding." He stalked away into the shadows of the manor.

"Well, that was awkward," Eliza murmured to herself, but personal issues were going to be the least of their problems.

Barry appeared from the back rooms and embraced the horrified Blackwell as if she were his long-lost sister. "Great to see you! You should see this place!"

"If the rest of this manor is like this foyer, it's stunning!" Blackwell glanced around. "An excellent environment to perform some kind of human experiments."

"Or raze this Gothic monstrosity to the ground and do the world a favour," Axelrod commented with an extremely sour expression on his face.

Barry, for the first time in a very long time since Eliza had known him, looked offended by something. "I think it's grand—actually, quite noble—of Wellington to open up his childhood home to us all, considering the dangers and possible property damage."

The two men glared at each other, and it was Lachlan King who appeared suddenly to diffuse the situation. Placing his firm, barrel-chested frame between the men, he said, "Why don't we continue this discussion elsewhere? Perhaps where our lovely clankertons can set up? Barry, you'll love helping Axelrod and Blackwell out. I am sure they have some wonderful machines."

Barry's face lit up, while the other two inventors' positively collapsed.

Lachlan slapped Axelrod on the back, nearly knocking the scholar over. "After all, we are all part of the same team, eh what?"

They had nothing to say to that—because there wasn't anything *to* say.

"Sounds like a wonderful idea," came a voice from the hallways. The two men looked up to see Wellington, apparently returned from the lower kitchens. From his softer demeanour, he'd seen the exchange between Agent King and the clankertons. He stepped forwards, and for once showed a shrewd grasp of diplomacy. "Allow me to show you where you may set yourself up?"

"In the lower kitchens, Books?" Axelrod scoffed. "Shall we all crowd into a dumbwaiter then?"

"If you would prefer," he said with a shrug, "or . . ."

Wellington placed his hand on a small, carved lion in the sideboard and gave it a gentle push to one side. The whole wall folded in on itself, revealing a spiral staircase going downwards and squeezing a gasp from Barry. When gas lamps in the side of the wall leapt to life, Doctor Blackwell let out a small giggle and clapped her hands together.

"That's just ripping, Books!" Barry actually rubbed his hands together.

"After you are situated, I can show you the armoury." Barry's and Axelrod's eyes both widened with delight as they mouthed in unison, *"Armoury?"*

Wellington motioned to the clankertons and smiled. "For now, if you please?"

Axelrod and Blackwell followed him down, neither saying a word. It didn't matter. As they descended, Barry effortlessly kept up a steady stream of chatter that mostly seemed to be about Eliza's uncle Roger and his tractor.

Eliza let out a sigh. She hadn't even been aware that she was holding it in as she watched them disappear. "I do hope that keeps all three of them out from underfoot."

Lachlan grinned at her. "At least for a while I suppose. I'll go with them . . . just in case. You know, your fellow New Zealander does have far too many ideas, and I think that Blackwell isn't one to dissuade him from anything."

While she had met Lachlan King before, she never had been partnered with the older man; but she could see immediately that his exasperation was somewhat feigned. Partners often became family, Eliza had found. Sometimes more than that.

When she turned around, the director almost made her jump, standing there with his hands in his pockets. Just how much he knew about the new relationship between herself and Books was anyone's guess. Right now, though, he was a pool of silence in the activity of the agents around him. "I was thinking, as there are no servants here at Whiterock, if Cassandra and I could commandeer the third floor, perhaps convert one of the available rooms into a private library?"

"Certainly. If you need books, I believe the library is just down the hall, outside the main dining hall," Eliza replied.

"Oh, is that the main library?" Sound stuck a thumb into one of his waistcoat pockets as he stroked his moustache. "I noticed a few choice volumes missing. I was uncertain if there was another library somewhere."

Her heart sank. She had shoved the remains of Arthur Books' chair into the far corner of the master bedroom's library. Having the director so close was a little unnerving to say the least. Still, she plastered on a smile that she hoped would fool him. "If we come across a second library, we will let you know."

"Very well then, Cassandra and I will begin the move in."

Doctor Sound turned to leave when Eliza suddenly remembered, "Before you begin to settle in, may I have a moment of your time?"

He appeared, for the first time in serving as the omniscient director, surprised. "Of course." She motioned for him to follow her to the main library. "Most uncharacteristic of you, Miss Braun, seeing as it is usually I requesting a private audience." He gave a slight chortle. "Oh dear, I hope I am not due for a reprimand."

"Believe me, sir," Eliza said, lifting aside a small stack of books to reveal the ledger she and Wellington had kept close since their journey across Europe, "you'd rather wish it were. Alice and the children . . ." She bit her bottom lip, then shrugged. ". . . liberated this ledger from a physician's office. There are notes in here pertaining to the Duke of Sussex, the Maestro, and Her Majesty."

The director silently took the ledger. "Evidence."

"Look over the names inside first," she warned. "This doctor has powerful friends."

"Well done," he said, tucking the ledger under his arm, "all of you."

With a final nod of approval, Doctor Sound disappeared in the growing activity of the foyer. Passing the ledger to him felt as if a weight had been lifted. Finally.

Securing the ledger, Eliza discovered, was merely a calm before the storm as her fellow agents claimed bedrooms upstairs, and found throughout the manor their own little nooks and crannies. When the second wave of Ministry agents arrived, even Wellington lost a moment to catch his breath, what with answering questions and helping his fellow operatives settle. Eliza mused on how the archivist had missed his calling and would have made quite a good innkeeper.

It was when he secured arrangements for Khaled, that Eliza noticed the set of his shoulders, the twitch in his neck. She could read him better than most, and saw he was actually rather nervous having the Ministry stomping around his family home. Far too many ghosts resided here for him to be comfortable.

Eliza smiled in suddenly seeing how one particular ghost—Lillian Books—presided over it all. If what Wellington said was true and his mother had been killed by his father, then this collection of cultures, religions, and ideologies within Whiterock might well serve as some kind of revenge for her. The dusty old manor was once more filled with life and vigour, all thanks to her son, Wellington Thornhill Books.

Arthur Books, from what she had learned of him, would have hated that.

"Bless my soul," Wellington said as the fob in his waistcoat chimed, "I forgot about dinner."

"That makes two of us. I'm ravenous," Eliza said. "You settle Khaled here. I'll check and see if Alice has the kitchen crew at work."

Eliza walked to the end of the corridor and called the lift. Christopher and Liam had performed a true yeoman's job in getting the manor's boilers and generators back into full working order. She needed to make sure the boys knew before the end of the night just how proud she was of their assistance in making Whiterock ready for the Ministry.

The lift descended to the main floor where hopefully dinner would be at least in the preparation stages. Just outside the kitchen, Eliza noticed a pair of weathered saddlebags. Bruce Campbell, apparently, had arrived. Her maid, Alice, hardly held Bruce in high regards following the odd times when he would call upon Eliza in London. That was why it was such a surprise finding the Australian cutting vegetables opposite of Alice as if they were old friends.

No one could ever accuse the Australian of being charmless when it came to the ladies.

"—strapping big woman, fists like slabs of meat. Tossed me right over the bar!" Bruce chortled. "Didn't know whether I should get up and fight, or stay down on one knee and propose!"

Alice laughed, and Eliza suddenly wanted to hear the rest of the story. Any tale which involved Bruce getting his comeuppance was worth the hearing.

Brandon suddenly stepped into sight, with the remaining boys of the Seven clustering around him. He was speaking with them with a mighty large ham as the focus of their discussion.

"Lads," he began, "while it may be perceived by popular society that a woman's place is in the kitchen—"

"Best way to keep track of the birds!" Bruce interjected from across the room, earning a bit of laughter from everyone. Including Alice.

Brandon merely waved him off. "If a man can master the kitchen, he will never go hungry. So the Good Lord says in the Bible."

"Where is that, sir?" Christopher asked.

Brandon placed his hand on the ham and emoted, "Give a man a fish and you feed him for a day. Teach a man to fish and you feed him for a lifetime."

"Hold on," Liam interrupted, "that's a Chinese Proverb. Not in the Bible."

"Liam's right," Colin added. "Our Lord and Saviour did say he wanted to make his gang . . ."

"Disciples," interjected Christopher.

". . . fishers of men. And there was the five loaves and fish parable."

Jonathan whispered something to Jeremy. "And that's a ham. Not a fish," Jeremy stated.

Brandon looked lost. "Bright lads, you are."

"Good Lord," Eliza said, attempting to rescue Agent Hill from this losing battle, "I thought you lot went into town earlier to pick up supplies, not Christmas dinner."

Christopher said cheerfully, "Mr. Hill here says an army marches on its stomach."

Brandon shrugged. "That and the balls of its feet."

"Are we an army now, Mum?" Liam asked.

She wanted to tousle his hair and tell him no, they were certainly not, but she wasn't so sure herself. Perhaps they were the last vestiges of the army of Britain, or at least the part that could be counted on to do the right thing.

Doctor Sound popped his head around the kitchen door, just as Brandon returned the boys' attention to preparation of the ham. "Campbell, there you are!"

The Australian who had just finished with the onion chopping actually tensed when the director said his name. Eliza's gaze narrowed. She knew that they really were not in a position to be picky, but she still wanted to keep Bruce at arm's length.

When the director gestured Bruce to follow him, Eliza folded her arms and watched. Wellington paused at the doorway, allowing Bruce and the director to pass. She too left the kitchen, joining her lover in the hallway. For a moment she felt his hand graze her waist. Then he remembered himself and withdrew it.

"I am sure the director has some more stern words for *Mr.* Bruce Campbell," he spoke softly into her ear as they watched the two men disappear around a corner.

"Yes," she replied, more to herself than anyone else. "He is not an agent. He's an outsider, not to be trusted."

"You don't believe in second chances, Eliza?" Wellington slipped his hands into his pockets and stared at her in a rather pointed fashion. "I thought you were the Mistress of the Return to Grace."

"If you are referring," she said with a slight sharpness in her tone, "to my demotion to the Archives, then I hope you are not comparing that to Bruce's failings."

Wellington pushed his hair back. It had grown rather longer than usual in their travels. "I don't like the chap any more than you do, but he might be the one who makes a difference, that we need to get the job done. The Ministry needs all the help they can get."

"Just as long as it doesn't involve us turning our back to him. I won't be taking my eyes off him."

In the corridor, they were alone; so Eliza hazarded pressing her hand against his cheek. Feeling his beard under her palm reminded her of other—far more naked—moments between them.

He nodded, breaking the intimacy of the moment. "Well

then, let's see how Alice, Brandon, and the children are doing in the kitchen."

It turned out rather well. Alice probably had more to do with the success of their evening repast than the Seven, but Brandon—quite the epicurean—was obviously a dab hand as well. The motley crew had resurrected the Whiterock kitchen and made it hum again. The smells of baking ham, pastries, and frying onions soon lured the other Ministry agents to the dining room where the children, under Wellington and Eliza's direction, had set the table.

They would dine very well, if not perhaps as elegantly as the manor might have been used to, as lighting was limited to light no brighter than three-branched candelabras, and windows were blocked by thick heavy curtains. The ham had been bathed in some of Arthur Books' remaining wine reserves, and there were roast potatoes, vegetable pies, braised cabbage—which the children decided to avoid—and cauliflower au gratin.

Still, the gathering of agents in the dining room was almost ridiculously small. Looking around at all their faces, though, Eliza could not help but notice those that were not among them. Too many had been lost. Her mind darted to Miggins Antiquities, and all the staff that had been there. Aside from the workers who knew nothing about the true nature of the building, there were many agents, researchers, and secretaries who at best disappeared underground, and at worst were lost.

Within the warmth and welcomed mirth of Whiterock, the surviving agents assembled. Although bathed and refreshed from their rendezvous at the Red Lion, Eliza could still see bruises, cuts, and signs of a long, hard journey for them all.

The sudden ringing of silverware against glass caught her attention. Doctor Sound, his eyes fixed on her and reading her expression as if it were one of the books of his new library, waited until the din of conversation ceased. He looked over each of them before speaking.

"I am sure as we regroup, we will find more of our fellows. I refuse to believe the Department could best my agents," he said raising his glass to them all. "I have placed messages in the *Railway News* as per protocol. We should expect more arrivals in the coming days."

That seemed to drain some of the tension from the room,

and Eliza passed around the last of the three bottles of wine as the talk turned to the future.

"Perhaps"—Wellington held up his hand—"the children should retire to bed, since we speak of Ministry affairs—"

"Not blimmin likely!" Christopher crossed his arms and glanced at Alice for a second before declaring, "We're as much a part of this as you is, and besides we have to find Callum. We're in the Ministry now."

"Now? I beg to differ, young man," Sound chortled. "After all the service the Ministry Seven has provided Her Majesty in the past? I dare say you all joined our ranks the day you self-lessly rescued Agents Thorne and Braun from certain death."

Eliza blinked. The director knew about the Ministry Seven? How?

"You have lost as much in this whole affair as anyone, and the Department knows of your involvement. You have all shown remarkable prowess in the field, certain to grow into fine agents. You have earned the right to hear what goes on." Sound leaned back in his chair, clearing his throat as he fingered the watch in his pocket. "But as we are now safe, I will not send children out to fight this."

"Then we can be your eyes and ears." Serena sat up very straight at the table, her face awfully mature for one so young. "No one really notices us in the street. You lot . . . you stick out."

He raised an eyebrow at the child's honesty. "I see your mentor has made quite the impression upon you." That earned him a soft rumble of laughter. Sound pressed his lips together, scanned his remaining agents, and nodded. "Very well. And you, Alice"—the maid jumped to hear her name called—"considering how well you served as guardian of the children and of our Agent Braun, may we count on your help in this matter?"

The maid unconsciously tapped the side of her leg where her shotgun resided. "I hope I can, sir."

Sound drained the last wine from his glass and set it on the table. "Well, the very first order of business is to save the Archives."

Wellington sat up straight, as if he'd been electrocuted. "Save? I thought the whole building was locked down."

Bruce, leaning back from the table, took a break from picking at his teeth to let out a short laugh. "Those Department boys aren't the most intelligent folk, but they do have persistence. Given the right tools, even they could break in eventually."

Eliza had never seen Wellington look quite so pale.

"Don't worry, my boy." Sound shot Bruce a significant look. "I have a plan to save everything. What say you and Agent Braun here take a quick trip to London and Miggins Antiquities with me?"

"But, Director . . ." Eliza paused, thought, and then smiled. "You have a secret way in!"

"But of course." He chuckled. "Every lair must have a hidden door or two."

"Big enough to empty the whole Archives out?" The archivist was probably already doing the horrific calculations. "We'll need every one of the Ministry to—"

"As I said before, I have a plan." The director tapped his nose significantly. "Our presence is needed to make certain the Archives is secured. Now the rest of you." The remaining agents and urchins sat up a little straighter. "We could be gone for a significant period of time."

"How much?" Maulik asked, his breathing apparatus leaving some doubt as to the emotion behind the question.

"Some time," the director said as he turned to Miss Shillingworth. "Cassandra will speak with my voice, and you should treat her as your director in my absence. Each of you will find on the desk in the library directions to what you need to do while I am gone. I know you will perform them admirably."

Eliza caught Bruce tensing in the corner. The idea of leaving a woman in charge of their merry little band was bound to rub him the wrong way. A delicious bonus, as far as she was concerned.

Doctor Sound rose from the table. "I think, despite these forty-eight hours, we should head out at first light."

Eliza knew how much this would mean to her lover, so there would be no discussion. Wellington would return to Ministry headquarters, and there was nothing Eliza would not do to help him secure the Archives.

"As for the rest of you, get some sleep. Our security is assured here, is it not, Mr. Books?"

Wellington got to his feet, his face set and resolute. "Chances are the locals believed we were the Whiterock's maintenance staff. As far as Hebden Bridge is concerned, Whiterock is still quiet, still private."

"If you would indulge me, sir," Maulik said, "I will stand watch. I spent most of the day asleep in order to do so."

"Excellent." Sound stepped away from the table. "Good night, everyone. And, Agent Books, thank you."

One by one, the agents raised their glasses. "Thank you, Agent Books," they echoed in unison.

As the table began to clear, Eliza pointed at Bruce. "Behave while we're gone."

Shillingworth was the one who responded. "I'll make sure of it Miss Braun, you can count on that."

Eliza and Wellington assisted Alice and the children in clearing the table. With food put away and what was left of the ham stored in the icebox, they all ascended upstairs to their respective rooms. The quiet falling over Whiterock was reminiscent of when they had first arrived. Their five-branched candelabra being the solitary light in the massive corridor, Eliza and Wellington lingered for a moment, perhaps to make certain everyone had retired for the night.

"I never," Wellington whispered as he closed the master bedroom doors, "expected to find myself here again."

"I am sure," Eliza said, taking the light with her to the side of the master bed. "And I don't doubt you are exhausted with everything that we have done . . ." Her words trailed off.

"And dealt with?" he asked.

Eliza turned to look at him. "Are you all right?"

Wellington crossed the room in wide strides to take Eliza into his arms and kiss her fiercely. The want in his kiss, in the taste of his tongue, in his embrace was all evident. She tugged at his coat and frantically worked the buttons free of his waistcoat.

Her lover, however, was hesitant. He wanted her, but he wasn't undressing her.

"What is it?" she panted between kisses. "Does sound carry in Whiterock?"

"It can," he said, tasting the skin of her neck, evoking a small cry of ecstasy from her. "Oh dear God in Heaven, Eliza, I want you so much."

"I need to feel your skin on mine, Wellington," she demanded, tearing his ascot from his neck.

"I'm just concerned," he confessed before kissing her deeply.

Their lips parted and Eliza gasped for air. "About what?"

A soft knocking came from the door.

"That," he huffed.

Swallowing back a wild desire to scream at the door, Eliza picked up the candelabra and crept over to the door as Wellington ducked behind a folding screen.

"When we finally find that time alone without interruption," Wellington said from behind the blind, "oh, Miss Braun, I will have you dancing amongst the stars."

Eliza gave a soft laugh as she opened the door, then her breath caught in her throat. Little Serena, in the light of a solitary candlestick, looked as pale as the nightgown they had picked up for her the day before.

"I'm sorry, Mum," Serena mumbled. The child was exhausted, pale and wan in the candlelight. "I can't get to sleep."

Wellington emerged from behind the screen, another nightgown in his hand which he handed to Eliza. "Your turn, Eliza," and Wellington led Serena to the large bed as she slipped behind the screen to change.

"Bad dreams then?" she heard Wellington ask. Whatever could upset the street urchin must be truly terrible. She had been through hell and back again on the street, and with the Ministry.

"I keep seeing you and Mum getting grabbed like Callum did." Serena's voice started to crack. "I couldn't do nothin' to save you and Mum. Just like Callum."

"You were back at the doctor's house?" Wellington asked gently. "We're nowhere near there, little Serena, and Miss Braun and I aren't going anywhere."

Once her nightgown was on, Eliza emerged from behind the screen. She found Wellington on his knees, eye level with the child sitting on the bed, his hands gently holding Serena's in his own. The girl didn't say anything, her serious face giving little away. A child of the street, she'd learned, Wellington was sure, not to cry or make a fuss because it simply made no difference. Like a wild animal, any sign of weakness could in fact lead to death or worse.

"We're going to get Callum back," Wellington said slowly and deliberately. "We haven't forgotten him, any more than you have."

Over Serena's head Eliza frowned a little, and mouthed the words he would discern quite clearly. *"No promises."*

This was a slippery slope he now found himself on, but knowing what few certainties Wellington had in his own life with his mother's death, Eliza understood his desire to give Serena hope.

It might have been a foolish pledge, but when she came around to see her face, the child was smiling.

"I haven't forgotten him," she said, in between tiny yawns. "I know he's out there waiting for us. I just wish he was here to see everything. France, Germany, this place . . . we never even seen outside of London before."

"Come along, Serena," Eliza said, motioning to the middle of the master bed. "We should get rest."

"I don't want you to go," she implored.

"We have to," Wellington said gently, "and you need to be strong. For the Ministry."

"The big man said he didn't know when you will come back," Serena said. "You are coming back?"

Eliza looked at Wellington and then curled up next to Serena as Wellington went to change. Both of them curled up next to Wellington after he extinguished the candelabra. Serena was trembling while Wellington gently stroked Eliza's forearm with his fingertips.

"Mum?" Serena asked.

"We're coming back, Serena," Eliza said. "We've made it this far together."

"Promise?" she asked. "Like what Mr. Books did?"

Wellington's fingertips stopped in the comforting touch against Eliza's skin.

"We're coming back, Serena." Eliza kissed the top of the child's head. "We're coming back."

INTERLUDE

❧

Wherein the Queen Reveals
Her New Vision

The *Regina Immortales* stood at her mirror staring at her own reflection with the rapt attention of one utterly consumed by themselves. Lord Sussex, who stood behind her, tried to keep all judgement off his face, and yet every part of him was repelled by the sight.

Victoria had been young once, of course she had, but she had lost the glow of youth, and she most certainly should not have gotten it back. It was against nature, but to say as much would have been the end of his tenure in her Privy Council, and quite possibly his life as well, considering the Maestro and Jekyll's interest in her.

"My eyes," the Queen said, swinging herself from side to side examining her other features, "they are somewhat darker than when I was first young."

"A side effect of the treatment," he replied as tonelessly as possible. "Our good doctor said that not everything would come back exactly as it once was."

She actually pouted a little. It was quite incredible that she was in many ways reverting to her previous girlhood mannerisms; quirks that had been smoothed out by time and experience reared their heads again. That particular side effect, unlike the eyes, could carry serious consequences.

Victoria smoothed back her hair, which was now free of grey, and lightly ran her fingertips over her face, now untouched by care or worry . . . or at least seeming to have forgotten about it.

"Well, it should," she said pertly. She finally gave up the mirror and turned towards the window, where thick fog had moved in to smother the capital. When she pressed her fingers against the glass, her brow furrowed; she appeared to be cross with the weather disobeying her whims.

On the end table beside her, she picked up a small statuette, given as a gift from the people of France. It was a representation of herself, dressed in full regalia, created in commemoration of her Golden Jubilee. Sussex could see Victoria studying the details of the figurine, as if committing the image of her older self to memory.

"I wish the people to see me right now, renewed *Regina Immortales* as God decreed."

Sussex shifted slightly in place. The Queen's belief in her transformation being a miracle from God as opposed to a miracle of science disturbed him as well. She seemed perfectly capable of forgetting all about the doctor's involvement, perhaps because Jekyll had put Sussex in charge of managing her. The doctor had more than enough to do with keeping both of them on their required regimens. Confined to his laboratory, Jekyll remained dedicated in collecting and processing enough formula to make their plans possible.

Sussex would never have envisioned Victoria as quite this much of a handful. Keeping her in her private chambers, or heavily veiled when outside it, was a struggle, and so he knew what was coming after her pronouncement.

Queen Victoria turned from the window and glared up at him. "I want to show my subjects their queen reborn. This week, if not earlier!"

He pressed his lips together, swallowed and tried to think of the right words. "Ma'am, the plans are not yet in place for your grand reveal. Imagine the horror and panic your . . ." Sussex had to pick the right word. *Incurring her wrath,* Jekyll had warned, *could aggravate the nerves, stimulate senses, and evoke another side effect.* It was his imperative to keep the Queen gratified. ". . . *renewal* would give them. It has to be managed and done at the right time. There is no better time than your upcoming Jubilee."

The Victoria he had known, the matron, the mother, the Queen of some experience, would have understood that immediately. She'd become sensitive to the will of her people after several incidents, and a few assassination attempts. This queen who stood before him was something entirely different. His words, from the way she regarded him, had not struck the right note.

Her anger flared bright and hot, instantly transforming her eyes to flickering red flames and her sweet face to one twisted with outrage. For a moment he was looking down at something not human, a contorted hobgoblin of anger with the world at her command.

"Are you suggesting they would not love their queen?" the Queen snapped at him, droplets of saliva striking his face and causing him to actually take a step back. Her eyes were mad, lost in a fury. "Are you saying the common degenerates of my realm would not love their perfect, immortal queen?"

An odd creaking sound tickled his ear. Sussex inclined his head, as if to acknowledge his queen and show his deference, but the gesture merely masked his eyes glancing down at the monarch's hands. Her fists were balled up tight, and the creaking came from the solid gold statuette still in her hands.

He glanced to his right, to the bag the good doctor had left on the sideboard there. Inside were vials that Sussex had been instructed on how to use, but he wondered if he were quite able to restrain the Queen while at the same time dosing her with the liquid. He decided that the best course might first be to see if he could restore her sanity.

"Of course not," he said. "The citizens of the Empire adore their queen, and all she stands for. It is just that many of those in power might well be adverse to your unexpected restoration."

Her eyes fixed on him, but her face remained twisted. "You mean my family?"

He nodded cautiously. "Yes. Your family."

"Too many damn children," Victoria hissed through her teeth. "Too many princes and princesses who will be only too glad to stick a knife in my back when they know I am not giving up the throne by shuffling off to die." Her head jerked in a weird inhuman way. "And Bertie. The worst of the lot. He should have died in San Francisco."

Her eldest son, she had hoped, would have been killed during his visit to San Francisco. This plot against Bertie, apparently hatched between her and the Maestro, had failed on Doctor Sound's proclamation that Bertie was safe and in hiding. Her son's popularity continued to haunt her, not to mention the number of heirs of his own left behind.

"Any word from the Department?" the Queen asked.

"Indian and Egyptian Branches were abandoned, but we managed to confirm five more resolutions." Sussex fought the urge to mock the chosen word for "kill" the Department used in their day-to-day operations. "We have reports of full resolutions in Wales, Ireland, Canada, Australia, and Hong Kong."

"What about Director Sound?"

Sussex took in a deep breath. "No word, Your Majesty. He has not been seen since his audience with you."

The Queen, much to his delight, did not explode. "Whatever they need, whatever it takes, I want Sound before me. I must know where Bertie is hiding. Of all the whelps that would dare take the throne from us, he is the worst of them."

Not for the first time, Sussex bemoaned the fact that his queen had loved her husband so much in her early years. She had birthed a veritable litter of prospective heirs to the throne. If even one of them, in particular Albert Edward, the Prince of Wales, rose up and called her a demon or abomination, then the country and the Empire could be torn apart. Sussex and the good doctor needed Victoria to be accepted as the *immortal* queen. When they controlled her, they would control all she did. It was so much easier than trying to do it themselves. With a shining example of perfect immortal monarchy at their back, their achievements would be limitless.

"Precisely, you are, as always . . . most wise," he crooned to her, and was rewarded as the redness in her face faded. "We have to make sure that your family is contained, and unable to cause you any problems."

"No, we can't just kill them," Victorian said matter-of-factly, with a sweet smile. "That would look most unpleasant, and not set the right tone for my immortal rule. My reign has to be perfect," she said, returning to the mirror. Setting the gold statuette on the end table beside the mirror, Victoria lost herself in its reflection, as if it were the first time. "As I am."

It had taken both Sussex and the good doctor many long hours to wean her away from that particular scenario of maternal filicide. In addition, not all of Victoria's family lived in her Empire. Many of her daughters and sons had married into European royalty, and so she had many grandchildren in power all over the continent, all of who could lay claim to the throne of the British Empire.

"Yes, and it will be," Sussex crooned. "All will be as you wish, Your Majesty."

The duke's eyes jumped to the solid gold statuette she had held in her grasp during her tirade. What had once been a fine likeness of Victoria had been mangled and deformed as if it had been made of soft clay. The distorted lump, he considered, could have not only been the results of another side effect, but an unintentional representation of what his queen had become.

Her voice made him start. In the reflection, her eyes now narrowed on him. "Henry says to trust you in all things, but I have yet to see results. Sound's Ministry must be resolved. *Completely.* There can be none to hinder my plans!"

Sussex inclined his head in a silent acknowledgement, but he reserved the particulars of the Queen's wishes to himself. Though they had managed to scatter and disempower the Ministry of Peculiar Occurrences, Doctor Sound still held influences. There were still many similar organisations in foreign nations, such as OSM in the United States, MOOSE in Canada, and the mysterious OZT answering to the czar, all of whom had worked with the Ministry. After a fashion. It would not do to alert them to what was currently going on in Buckingham Palace.

"All of the colonies are stripped of their branches, any unresolved agents are now fugitives carrying significant bounties on their heads." He kept his voice calm while he spoke, his gaze never leaving hers. "I do not anticipate many of them will survive the week." He preferred not to share just how many agents had escaped the Department. His assurances kept her under control, and since no one else saw the Queen, she would never find out their limitations.

"What of the breaking of the Ministry headquarters?" Victoria pressed.

"The headquarters are locked down, and we will breach the defences tomorrow at the latest," Sussex said, tucking his hands into his jacket pockets, concealing an odd quiver that had begun stealing over him while talking with Victoria. "Our objective will be the Archives. From what I understand, they will yield evidence on where we can find any remaining agents."

"Quite excited about cracking open that particular nut, aren't you?" she taunted from the mirror. A single eyebrow crooked as she added, "This is your business. If you don't take care of it, there will be nothing I can do to help you. I will have to go on without you."

She returned to her desk, opened a drawer, and withdrew from it a small vial of emerald green liquid. Holding it to the light, the Queen spun it in her fingertips. "Such a little thing to rest a whole magnificent empire on." She uncorked it, raised it to her lips, and downed the whole amount. The twisting of her face said it was no treat, and Sussex suddenly remembered Henry's creations were quite bitter. The ones he took to control his outbursts were vile, but necessary.

A common ground for both the Queen and the duke to share.

Victoria wiped her mouth with the back of her hand, staggered back a few steps, righted herself, and stood straight. "So my subjects will wait for the Diamond Jubilee. Do our valiant workers have all they need?"

"They do, Majesty. The grand project proceeds apace and should be indeed ready when planned. The Grey Ghosts will march on the appointed day, and will stand for you."

Her eyes raked over him. "Then the only thing that remains is for you to take command of that dreadful Miggins Antiquities." She flicked her hands in his general direction, as if he were a maid she was sending to fetch her shawl.

Swallowing back his rage took every ounce of control the Duke of Sussex had, but he managed to execute a stiff bow and back out of the room. How could he tell her that the Maestro had stolen that particular joy of breaching the Ministry from him already? It still burned him to think of it.

Unless the Queen was secretly in league with the Maestro. *That bitch,* he seethed. *She would turn on me. After all I have done for her, that whiny, self-centred trollop!*

The idea of this wretch ruling over the Empire on which the sun never set unsettled him. He could only hope that Henry knew what he was doing when he created her.

THIRTEEN

❧❧

Wherein Wellington Thornhill Books
Has His Heart Dismantled

From the boat's solitary smokestack, a thick black cloud suddenly belched into the air. A hard, rhythmic knocking vibrated through the deck, and the captain swore loudly while two crewmen opened the booby hatch to access the engines.

This was Wellington's cue. "Starboard, Cap'n," he grunted. "There's a mooring open."

"I see it!" he barked back. "You tend ta ya' duties, secure that line. We got a schedule ta keep!"

Wellington tipped his cap while he and Doctor Sound, both of them wearing tattered overcoats and caps of watermen, grabbed one of the larger ropes coiled on the side of the modest cargo barge. They limped their way over to the mooring just outside the rear dock accessing Miggins Antiquities. The lasso caught the piling, and as the stern swung about, Wellington and a smaller waterman leapt onto the dock and pulled at the thick rope.

"I said secure that line!" the captain roared. "This ain't some leisurely punting we're havin' today."

"Crotchety old bastard, isn't he?" grumbled Eliza as she and Wellington ran the rope around the thick wooden piling.

"Well, how would you feel if your perfectly operating engine suddenly started sputtering?" he asked her. "Cuts into the profits of the day if the old man is late."

Once the rope served as solid security for the boat, Wellington and Eliza reached out for Doctor Sound, whose fine fashion struggled to remain hidden under the tattered peacoat, and helped him on to dry land.

"Well done," Doctor Sound said, his eyes scanning up and down the dock. "Now quickly, as the crew is currently preoccupied with Miss Braun's speciality."

At a cursory glance, the morning's fog long burned off and revealing the various businesses that made up Industry Row along the Thames, Wellington could not see any sign of watchers, snipers, or flashes of tweed. Miggins Antiquities, or at least its rear façade which usually hosted ships of various sizes, remained intact and—much to the outward relief of Doctor Sound—secure. It was odd seeing their headquarters so still. There were no dockhands busy unloading innocuous trinkets no better than glorified junk while specialists hidden within handled designated crates that were incoming finds of incredible value to the Ministry. Wellington caught no shadows moving in front of windows, no agents recently returned from the field or just about to leave on assignment, no dispatches from field offices being hurried to the director's office. Nothing moved, save for them.

Miggins Antiquities was not dead, though. It was simply secured.

Doctor Sound continued to cast wary glances over his shoulder as he hobbled up to the heavy iron door. He took a deep breath before pressing his thumb into the groove above a numeric keypad. He winced, then sucked at the pinprick point on his thumb while his other hand began punching in a code of some fashion.

"Strange seeing Miggins so quiet like this," Eliza whispered, an echo of Wellington's own thoughts. He'd never had a partner before, but he hoped it was a sign of their growing relationship, not that he was going mad.

"I suppose we should be thankful it isn't crawling with Department agents." Wellington shuddered. "I do hope they haven't helped themselves to the *Ares: Mark One*."

"For once, let us think positive," she said. "They are more concerned over two Ministry agents, one of them a super soldier masquerading as an archivist, as opposed to—"

"Agent Braun," Sound said with a huff, "as this is a rather lengthy sequence of numbers, the light banter between you and Agent Books is a touch distracting, and I would prefer not to prick my thumb again as that needle has, I'm afraid, become quite blunt."

"Sorry, sir," they both replied.

Another five numbers, and then Sound pressed the green button at the bottom of the pad. Seconds later, a bolt softly hissed from the other side of the door, followed by another, and then another. Sound let out a long, slow breath and then turned the large handle downwards.

"Shall we?" he asked, pushing the door forwards.

The iron door groaned lightly, but the echo in the corridor seemed to announce their entrance. When the silence returned, though, Wellington knew without question they were alone.

Eliza threw a switch set in the wall, and the lights set in the ceiling of this access passage flickered to life. "The generator is still operating."

"As it is powered by the Thames, I would think so," Sound returned, closing the door behind them. Once shut, the powerful hissing from the hatch's bolts threatened to deafen them all, but then the sound and the steam settled, and once again all went quiet.

"If you are all armed," Sound said as he let his long peacoat fall at his feet, "I would recommend you remain at the ready."

Eliza drew her pounamu pistols while Wellington drew from an inside holster a Remington-Elliot. On considering the compact weapon, he holstered it and then reached to his side to draw a Wilkinson-Webley.

"A Crackshot?" Eliza asked. "Where did that come from?"

"Whiterock armoury," he said, holding up the larger four-barrelled pistol. "Not quite the stealth of the Remington-Elliot, but a touch more stopping power. Something we will need considering potential close quarter confrontations, wouldn't you agree?"

Eliza sighed. "I love you, Wellington Books." Apparently she had abandoned any attempt to conceal their relationship.

Wellington chuckled, even as he coloured. "How very sweet of you to say, Eliza."

"Would you two care to find a vacant office, or perhaps a spare storeroom to consummate your budding romance," Sound said somewhat sharply, "or would you care to proceed to the Archives which is, may I remind you, the *purpose* of this little outing?"

"Proceed, sir," both replied, shedding themselves of their tattered overcoats.

While the silence served as reassurance they were alone, it also unsettled Wellington. This was not normal, at least not normal for Miggins Antiquities. There should be teletype machines clacking orders and reports, the voices of agents and associates sharing stories of their adventures abroad. There was, however, nothing. Merely the three of them disturbing a void.

They ascended a small staircase, coming to a stop at a modest wooden door. Sound stepped back as Eliza approached the door with her signature pistols held up. She motioned for Wellington, who slipped his hand up to the handle.

"One . . ." he whispered, "two . . ."

On "Three" they swung the door open and Eliza led with her pistols, her eyes taking a quick assessment of the building's main foyer. The interior metal doors, much as it was with the bulletproof blinds that had dropped inside the windows, appeared intact. No signs of fatigue or breach. From the stillness and feel of their surroundings, no one was there. In fact, it appeared nothing had been disturbed since the Phantom Protocol order.

"What do you think?" Eliza asked Director Sound, lowering her pistols.

"It would appear that Miggins Antiquities remains secure," he replied. The man then reached into his waistcoat and produced the clockwork key all agents of the Ministry carried on their person. "Proceed to the Archives, if you would. I have something to retrieve from my office."

"You have—?" Eliza began.

"My dear Miss Braun, you of all people should know and appreciate the value of travelling light, which is what I had to do once Phantom Protocol was initiated. Now, as I have a moment, indulge me."

"But there is over fifty years of history in the Archives, and our time is—"

Sound raised a finger to stop Wellington's words. "As I told you back in Whiterock," he began as he turned the key, calling the lift, "I have initiated a plan. It has been ongoing since the Ministry retreated underground." Once the lift arrived, Sound gave a wink to the two of them. "Now, to the Archives with you both. I will be there momentarily."

Wellington shook his head as they watched the lift ascend up to the director's office. "Curiouser and curiouser."

"Shall we, then?" Eliza asked, referring to the door to the right of the lift.

Once more, they found themselves in an oppressive, heavy silence. It seemed to reflect the job ahead, waiting patiently in the dungeon of Miggins Antiquities. Wellington knew Eliza understood the weight of what they were doing, but it had to be said.

"This is a generation of work we're taking apart."

She looked up from the step she stood on. "This hurts, Welly, I know, but would you rather have those Department pillocks rifling through here? Doctor Sound is right. There are items and artefacts in the Archives far too dangerous for those plonkers to get their hands on."

"Yes, of course."

She ascended a few steps and gently placed a kiss on his lips. "Chin up, Welly. We are doing what needs to be done. Not only what's best for the Ministry, but for the Empire."

He nodded and took a breath. "Very true." Motioning ahead, they both resumed their descent as he added, "With all the surprises we have weathered over the weeks, I admit it will be nice returning—even for a brief time—to a place as familiar as the Archives."

At the base of the stairs, the wooden door opened to the dimly lit entryway where the lift chamber ended. The heavy ship's hatch looked just as Wellington remembered it before he and Eliza caught the last airship out of London bound for America. He gripped the wheel lock and turned it to one side, disengaging its simple mechanism. The door groaned on its hinges as Wellington pulled, eventually opening on its own accord. He motioned for Eliza to enter. She smiled and inclined her head in silent thanks. She stepped through, and he followed suit . . .

. . . and froze on the platform overlooking the Archives.

"What?" he managed to stammer. "What . . . ? *What . . . ?*"

Hovering silently over the rows of shelving units were brightly polished spheres, but *how* they were hovering remained completely and utterly concealed. No props. No steam jets. No thrust of any visible kind. They just *floated*, the faintest of whines only heard when they accelerated from one point to another. Wellington counted four of them, their surfaces so brilliant they caught the gaslight like mirrors.

When a sphere suddenly floated out from underneath the platform, Wellington and Eliza both stepped back. He had never seen his lover—or anyone else for that matter—draw a pistol so fast. A green light appeared in the centre of the odd flying device, and as it hovered before them Wellington had a moment to study its details. The sphere itself was slightly larger than a lady's hatbox, and just underneath its featureless surface, lights flickered on and off as if there were some sort of computation sequence carrying itself out. The light passed across Eliza, then Wellington, and then winked out. With a soft *whoosh* the object flew away, seemingly content with their arrival.

"I think you can put the pistol away, Eliza," Wellington finally said, making his way to the staircase.

Eliza's gun did not lower. "Give me a good reason why."

"They're not attacking."

From behind him, he heard the soft click of a pistol hammer easing back to a safe position. "Damn your logic, Books."

The closer they descended to the Archives, the more the other odd devices came into view. Wellington was certainly acquainted with automatons. Clockwork or steam powered, they were popular devices in most upper- or even middle-class homes. Families had one or two tucked away for either menial tasks, such as sweeping or mail retrieval, or, for the more affluent, acting as guards for their estates.

These automatons, however, were entirely different: featureless and silent with the exception of a soft hum whenever they lifted or moved a crate. It seemed each shelving unit was assigned its own pair; and these mechanical beings had been busy devices as they had already catalogued, packed, and stored someplace the records and artefacts from the higher shelves.

He wondered how they had reached them, when he and

Eliza were given a demonstration. One of the silver automatons let out a low whine, and then the square base on which it rested lifted off the ground. Like their spherical brethren, these automatons had the ability to hover. Also like their flying counterparts, they gleamed in the light of the Archives lamps, as if made of fluid steel, an incredibly high sheen akin to silver.

"Excellent!" came a voice from behind them. "The Staff are making admirable progress!"

Doctor Sound practically glowed with satisfaction as he drew closer to them. He was carrying with him a wide, slender suitcase. If he were to open it, Wellington hazarded a guess, it would easily cover a small dinner table.

A soft whine caught his attention, and he turned to see one of the silver automatons approaching quickly, deftly manoeuvring between Eliza and himself to approach Sound.

"Good afternoon, sir," the automaton spoke, using a purely synthetic voice that sounded as smooth as cream.

Dear Lord, Wellington thought, *it speaks! And it sounds completely human!*

From underneath its bright sheen, lights faded in and out as the device reported, "We have successfully secured forty-two percent of artefacts, prioritizing those identified as hazardous. Shelves between 1840 and 1862 are completed."

"Very good. Make sure to store this by central command," Sound ordered, passing the large suitcase over to the thing. Wellington found it quite unsettling as the doctor, on account of the automaton's reflective surface, appeared to be addressing himself. "Then return to your duties with the Archives. We still have no inkling how much time we have remaining."

"Yes, sir," it replied before quietly floating away with the item Sound had rescued from his office.

Wellington watched in fascination as the hovering device descended the stairs, suitcase clutched in one metallic claw-like hand. It then ducked under the low clearance of the open hatch and disappeared. Moments later, two others emerged from . . .

It was the Restricted Area. That's where these things were coming from.

"Doctor Sound—" Wellington began, wishing his eyes could pierce the metal hatch to discern whatever was behind it.

"I'm over here, Books," he replied drily.

Wellington started, and something about seeing Doctor Sound in front of him dissipated the wonder that had overcome him.

Yet it still made no sense. "Doctor Sound, what—" He stammered out again, "What—" And all he found himself capable of was motioning around him. "What—?!"

"This is the contingency I spoke of back in Whiterock. I can assure you, the Staff are handling the Archives with the utmost care."

"I'm sure that's part of Wellington's concerns," Eliza said gently as if she were translating from another language. "I, for one, would love to know what the hell these things are! The Mechamen Havelock had at his estate were amazing, but these are astounding!"

"Yes!" blurted Wellington. Leave it to Eliza to verbally slap him back to coherency. "What *are* these things?"

"I told you: the Staff," Sound answered. Wellington went to demand more, but the director held his hand up. "Now is not the time. I need you to secure your work area . . ."

"So many secrets!" Wellington turned to see Eliza glaring at the director. He had seen his partner arguing with Sound before, but something about this whole scene in the Archives appeared to have shaken her. He'd been too busy with his own concerns to consider Eliza's emotions. "When are you going to let us in on them?"

"I have no idea what you are talking about," Sound said, blinking at Eliza as if she were some raging schoolchild.

"I am talking about what you said to Prince Edward," Eliza continued, drawing herself up to her full height. "You told him you were going to tell his mother he was dead, and it's obvious you didn't do that."

Wellington was surprised to see the usual kindly expression dissolve from the director's face. His eyes became as still and dark as stones. "I sometimes have to tell people what they need to hear. Bertie wanted to be assured he was safe, and the Queen . . . Well, I needed her to be off balance."

Wellington and Eliza stared at their director as if for the first time, but it was the New Zealander who recovered first. "You're not the jovial fat man everyone thinks you are," she said quietly.

Sound pressed his lips together for a moment before answering. "You have no idea, Miss Braun, you have no idea." Then, just like a switch had been turned, he smiled and clapped his hands together. "Now, if memory serves, there is a small incinerator attached to your analytical engine. I promise you, any remaining mysteries will be explained to you, but at a later date. Now, if you will excuse me . . ." and Sound gave a tip of his cap—which looked a little odd as it was still the tattered headwear of a fisherman—before heading for the Restricted Area.

Wellington felt paralysed from head to foot—even his vocal chords seemed to have been effected. His questions were answered, but only led to more questions. This was his domain. His Archives. What in God's—

"You heard the director," Eliza said with a sigh, seemingly resigned to the menial task ahead. "Despite it all, we have a job to do." She paused, her jaw clenching for a moment. "We'll have to trust that Sound has all this under control."

The Restricted Area was even more tantalising, though. Wellington for the first time could simply walk to the end of his Archives and look to the other side of the hatch. Yet duty called.

Shooting one final, lingering glance in that direction, Wellington joined Eliza at their shared desk.

The logical part of his brain knew that the effrontery and violation of Sound's odd technological wonders removing his work from their particular places was but a trifle compared to how many agents had been killed by the Department. However, the emotional part of him was screaming in horror. Wellington took his glasses out of his pocket, wiped them on his jacket's sleeve, since it was all he currently had to hand, put them on his nose, and stared about one last time, taking it all in: the partners desk that he had been forced to share with Eliza only a year or so ago, the spot where the analytical engine he'd created had rested, the door from which he had first seen the mess that had been left by the last archivist, and the distant storage room where he'd led Eliza to an array of cold cases.

All these details suddenly held extra significance, and he found a strange little knot in the back of his throat. Clearing it, Wellington flipped a switch on the housing of the analytical engine, and the lid to the secondary heating element that doubled as an incinerator slid open. He and Eliza began going through the desk drawers, unlocking them and sifting through any of the papers left behind.

Most of them immediately were fed to the flames. Significant amounts of what he found on his side had already been entered into the analytical engine, but he also found his very first report to the director about the Archives. It contained some rather jaded remarks he had written about his predecessor, Augustus Whitby—the bounder who had abandoned his post without any notice.

Considering the disarray of the Archives, he had written, *Whitby must have been an utter prat.* He gave a tiny snort at that. *I should burn this,* he thought, *in case the Department releases these notes to the public and Whitby comes after me with a solicitor in tow.*

He folded the copy of his report and stuffed it into his coat pocket. A little memento.

"Eight years," he whispered to himself as he dropped the paper into the incinerator. "It was eight years ago, and this place changed me."

"It changed us both," Eliza said, looking up from her side of the desk. It almost sounded as if it were a reluctant admission. "Coming down those stairs, I thought this place would be the end of my career."

"It wasn't?"

"No," she said with a warm smile. "It was the beginning of something better." After keeping her gaze on him for a moment, she opened one of the last drawers and gasped. "There you are." She lifted up a throwing knife that was, apparently, in her side of the desk. "Remember this?"

Honestly, all of Eliza's sidearms, save for her pounamu pistols, were hardly distinguishable. That knife, however, Wellington recognised straightaway. "The knife that forever robbed us of the Lost City of El Dorado."

"Perhaps some things are best left in mystery," Eliza replied with a shrug and a smile.

"Perhaps . . ." Wellington said, his thoughts trailing off as he caught sight of the automatons Doctor Sound referred to as "the Staff" trundle off more crates into the Restricted Area. "What do you suppose is back there?" he asked Eliza, indicating with a slight jerk of his head in that direction.

Eliza shot him a sharp look. "Well, my, my, my . . . look who is all curious now? I thought that was my area of expertise?"

"Whatever do you mean, Miss Braun?" It was easy to fall back into old habits in the middle of the Archives.

She waggled her finger at him. "Think of all the times that I asked you about what could possibly be back there, and you told me in varying ways to mind my own beeswax." He felt a blush steal over his face at that. She blew him a kiss. "I do wonder what you care about more, me or your beloved Archives."

"It depends on the hour of the day or night," he replied with a wink. Being around Eliza was quite beginning to lighten his mood, even in this dark time when everything seemed out of sorts.

She poked out her tongue at him, passing two handfuls of paper to him for the incinerator. "Well, I am sure I cannot guess what we might find there. I thought Blackwell and Axelrod were creating the most dangerous items back there." She glanced at the Restricted Area. "I could have been wrong . . ."

Both of them were interrupted from their musings when Doctor Sound appeared out of the hatch, followed by an automaton and one of the spheres. Eliza shared a glance with Wellington, hastily checking the back of the final drawer of her side of the desk before observing their impending arrival.

Doctor Sound reached them just as Eliza was stretching her back. "So, how go my intrepid archivists?" he asked, patting the spot where his pocket watch rested.

Wellington felt himself straighten ever so slightly, as if Sound were one of his superior officers in the cavalry. "We are almost done here, Director. Most of this paperwork has been previously catalogued in the engine. Except for—" Wellington pulled out the desk's small extension that had his list of codes for the analytical engine. He gave the extension a yank, and it snapped off in his hands. "This. I should have this on hand at Whiterock."

"Well done." Sound looked over to the accompanying automaton and motioned to the desk. "So, Miss Braun, I am in need of your talents."

The automaton gently placed a strange silver box on the desk and pressed a solitary button that opened the crate with a hiss that resembled a steam release, but Wellington was convinced from its odour it was a different sort of gas. A platform from the bottom of the case rose to the top, and Eliza's eyes widened in delight.

Two blocks, similar to the size of bricks, only grey in colour, sat on the platform. Embedded in the blocks were small mechanical devices of a fashion. The third device was some sort of hub with a numeric display and a small numeric keypad.

It was the design that gobsmacked Wellington. He had never seen this sort of aesthetic before. It was so . . . *minimal.*

"Miss Braun, I need these incendiaries placed at crucial points of the Archives wall."

Eliza looked back at the far wall, then went pale. "You're going to submerge the Archives?"

"And, if I have calculated this properly, Miggins Antiquities as well."

Wellington thought his heart was trying to leap into his throat. The Thames River was just on the other side of the brickwork, and powered the whole of the Ministry. Now he suspected it was not for that fact alone that this location had been chosen. The hard expression on the director's face told Wellington this had always been part of the contingency.

The archivist wanted to protest, wanted to say that this place was as precious as the British Library, but he held silent. This was the price of belonging to a clandestine organisation.

Despite the presence of the director, Eliza moved to his side and took Wellington's hand in hers. She said nothing, offered no comforting words, because there were none to give in this situation. He was about to become an archivist with no Archives. The thing that he had pinned his entire being on was being ripped away from him, and the sacred place he had built up from the ashes of incompetency destroyed.

"If this is what must be done," Wellington said, gathering his resignation around him as best he could.

It was then the archivist noticed the strange new echo in the near-empty chamber.

The sound made Wellington deeply sad. He was the last in a line of archivists that had kept the history, the mystery, and the finds incredibly secret and safe. The last person who would have heard this echo was the first archivist of the Ministry of Peculiar Occurrences, Rowan Clayworth, as he was filling the shelves. Wellington despised the thought that he was the omega to Clayworth's alpha.

Eliza looked at him, her lips pressed together, undoubtedly fighting the urge to interrupt.

"This place has been the repository for all number of strange, arcane objects from everywhere on the globe," Sound said, running his eyes over the vast and near-empty space. The melancholy tone in his voice said this was a hard moment for him as well. "Unlike Research and Design which, I have no doubt Blackwell and Axelrod saw to, could be sterilised, we cannot leave anything to chance with the Archives. The Staff has been thorough—"

"Fifty-four percent secured, Agent Books," the automaton offered.

"Thank you," Sound said, his eyebrow crooking at the automaton. His expression softened on returning to Wellington and Eliza. "but any stray notes or wayward item could be catastrophic."

"What do I need to do, sir?" Eliza asked.

"Find the two ideal points that would insure structural failure if explosives were applied."

She looked at the odd explosives. "That entire wall? With only two bombs?"

"Trust me, my dear Eliza D. Braun," he said, with a twinkle in his eyes that unsettled Wellington a bit. "Two will be all that you need. This," he said, referring to the keypad, "is a timer tied to the detonators. Minutes and seconds. Enter your desired time here. Once you press the green key, the timer will begin."

She picked up the hub to inspect it closer. The sphere hovering over them chirped as if an agitated robin trying to ward off Audubons from its nest. "Tamper proof?"

Sound nodded. "If the timer stops prematurely, the detonators trigger."

"Impressive," Eliza said with a nod and glanced at the wall. "I will probably have to pick two high points. Do we have a ladder?"

"Of a fashion," Sound chuckled.

The automaton's square-shaped base extended a small platform, and it offered her a hand. Eliza, giggling like a small child watching an illusionist, stepped onto the platform. With barely a sound, the automaton began to float into the air.

Sound quickly passed to her the two bombs before she floated out of reach. "I recommend thirty minutes."

Eliza's laughter echoed around them as she floated closer to the far wall. At least *she* would enjoy the destruction.

"I am sorry," the director stated. Wellington had never heard him speak so sincerely, save for at Red Lion and White-rock. "Believe me, my boy, this was not an easy decision to come to."

"But necessary," Wellington replied staunchly. Perhaps, if he said it enough, he would believe that. "It's just . . ." He looked at the dock of the analytical engine—his first major triumph. While the brain and heart of the engine remained elsewhere, enough mechanical engineering existed here that, if salvaged, could give the Department an unfortunate advantage. "Forgive me for being so sentimental, sir."

"I expect nothing less. You did more than rescue the Archives, Wellington, you changed it." Sound stroked his moustache. "You, more than any other archivist we've ever known, made this place a functional, important part of the Ministry. All of the others really didn't know quite what to do with all the wonders contained here, and"—he leaned forwards with a grin—"I never liked any of them quite as much as I like you, Wellington."

Wellington tilted his head. The director often said very odd things, but this one he would not let go by. Not at this particular juncture. How would Sound know exactly how the other archivists performed when he'd not been director that long?

Just as the question was about to leave his lips, a dull thud came from above their heads. It was most definitely a sound only produced by explosives, and had come from where the foyer would be.

It appeared the time for questions had passed.

Wellington tucked the blotter containing the engine's codes under his arm. "I'll inform Miss Braun to set the timer for twenty minutes."

INTERLUDE

❧

In Which the Scales Fall
from Sophia's Eyes

The sign above the lintel said "Miggins Antiquities: Finest Imports from the Empire" but the doors felt as if they were reinforced from the inside. Out of character for a simple warehouse on the banks of the Thames. What lay beyond this barrier, however, was not merely artefacts and trinkets from all over the globe, but more invaluable treasures: secrets.

Sophia, standing next to the Maestro in the sanctuary of his battle armour, complete with Gatlings on his arms, surveyed the fortified doors. A subtle, brass sign proclaiming "Closed for Business . . . Until Further Notice" hung from between the handles.

"We're ready, sir," one of his men, an angular consumptive look on his face and a smear of red hair on his head, spoke gently. The way this whelp kept his eyes averted from the Maestro said he was hugely uncomfortable, working for a face of metal and flesh. Perhaps it was because his pale skin seemed ready to blister every time he got too near the Maestro's steam-powered breathing apparatus.

Sophia could see the Maestro was completely unmoved by

the soldier's distress. The Grey Ghosts served a purpose. As she did. And once they failed in their purpose . . .

"Proceed, Commander Benson," he ordered.

The assassin knew what would come next; subterfuge and cunning had failed him. Now he would employ brute force.

"Stand by! Stand by!" the soldier called out.

Sophia and the small regiment of the Maestro's private army slipped protective covers over their ears, as recommended by the gunner. She glanced down either end of the street block, noticing the men and women in the matching tweed keeping the crowds at bay. This Department, Sophia noted, was apparently a gift from the Queen. They granted the Maestro the ability to do what he was about to do with no consequences.

When the order came, Sophia held her breath. *"Fire!"*

The heavy siege howitzer's discharge sounded muffled through her protective earware, but that protection did nothing to save her from the unseen concussive force of the cannon's blast. Such artillery was clumsy in her opinion. No finesse or style whatsoever, but its nature seemed to suit the Maestro's tenor. Much like the monster himself, the howitzer would not be denied. As the smoke lifted like a bride's veil it revealed the doors splintered beyond repair and their metal reinforcement bent and warped. One door defied the Maestro's will, but the right security door was gone.

"Commander Benson, assist the gunmen in storing the howitzer and returning it to the compound," said the Maestro, flicking the ear guards up on his helmet. "The rest of you, accompany me to the Ministry."

Sophia cast her protective gear aside and checked her own pistols. This, along with makes and models of certain rifles, was as much noise as she preferred when in the field. The Maestro's Grey Ghosts, wearing portable Gatling packs Sophia had not seen since her time with the Phoenix Society, flanked them as they crossed the empty street to the Ministry, under the very gaze of the citizenry of London. It still left her unsettled and uncomfortable.

"No need to look so nervous, my dear," the Maestro crooned to her. At one time, Sophia had found a strange, hypnotic quality in the mechanical voice. His attempts at charm were, she now knew, nothing more than part of Jekyll's illusion. They were an insult. "We have ascertained that there is no one inside, just gadgets and paperwork. They hardly offer any danger to us."

Sophia chewed on her lip, her dark eyes flicking only briefly up to meet the ocular, a dull amber light gleaming at its centre today. He must have detected a subtle change in her expression as the ocular's glow intensified. The Maestro no doubt believed himself knowledgeable of her most intimate thoughts. He knew nothing of the mask still carefully kept in place. Behind her own illusion of a love-struck puppy dog following the older, more brutal canine about was her true intention. Was she imagining that he was suddenly wary of her?

"We enter the world of our adversaries," she stated, "in broad daylight. With eyewitnesses. This is all very new to me."

The Maestro laughed. "Consider this privileges of influence. We have the Crown on our side." He laid his armoured hand gently against her cheek. "I will protect you if you are concerned."

Sophia didn't flinch, but her hands balled into tight fists. "Thank you, Maestro," she said, so sweetly that he accepted it with a grin beneath his helmet and a nod. She knew he loved her subservience to him. She could only hope that she retained some control over the Maestro, enough to manipulate him one last time.

"Make speed," he called out to his men, sweeping out his thick brass encased arm "or make your own graves."

As eager as she knew the Maestro was to see the inside of the Miggins Antiquities, Sophia noted he watched his Grey Ghosts scamper inside first, hefting their Gatlings with the help of the hydraulics in their backpacks. Did the Maestro believe the Ministry agents would employ other defence measures beyond armoured blinds and doors? Sophia glanced up at him like a whipped dog, and he bowed at the waist, indicating what a gentleman he was, giving her leave to precede him.

Her beautiful eyes narrowed, but with a grateful smile she followed the breach team, the Maestro himself following in her wake, as she could hear the hissing of pistons that supposedly granted him mobility.

For a brief moment, standing in the foyer, the Maestro looked disappointed. His men made a circle around them both as he looked around their innocuous surroundings.

"The lift," he stated, moving to the gate. "We must go up. Sound's office is there."

Sophia glanced around the Maestro at the small lock. "It appears you may need a key to call the car."

"And thanks to our newest recruit from America," he said, holding up a small brass box no bigger than her fist, "we have one."

Sophia let out the faintest sigh, noting that even in captivity, Edison had the arrogance to inscribe the device with his name and logo. Typical of an American.

The Maestro's hand was only half an inch from the lift's keyhole when it leapt from his hand to attach itself. He pressed the single button on its surface, and he withdrew his hand just before electric bolts danced between cube and lock.

Weights disengaged, cables went taut, a motor spun up to life, and a car rose to their floor.

"Going up, signorina?" he said to Sophia as the lift shuddered to a halt.

"You two, accompany us," Sophia ordered to the Grey Ghosts not weighed down by the Gatling packs. "The rest of you—fan out. Find out what is on this floor. Proceed with caution."

She shut the gate and turned to where a lift's control panel would normally be. In its stead stood a chadburn. *These English seem to revel in their eccentricities*, she thought as she threw the switch forwards to set "Director's Office" as their destination. As their lift rose slowly, she observed through the bars the Maestro's army fanning on the other floors. Four men walked up to the second floor and disappeared into the darkness between floors.

When their upwards ascent was completed, Sophia, the Maestro, and their soldiers were in a similar dark situation. Sophia felt rather than saw the Maestro walk over, open the gate, and continue into the hallway. A soft hissing tickled Sophia's ears, and then gaslight illuminated the top floor.

"Follow," the Maestro commanded.

On the top floor, Miggins Antiquities suddenly turned into any office premises a man would have been proud to call his. Crossing the threshold from the waiting room, the office of Doctor Sound was a seamless union of wood panelling, soft carpeted floors, and grand windows that would have provided a breathtaking view of London and the Thames had it not been for the iron shields covering them. With the exception of a clock on the mantelpiece, still keeping time with its soft *tick-tock-tick-tock*, the office was deathly still

"You," Sophia snapped at a soldier, "check the desk."

Her senses were all on alert. The building was dead and far too empty. The Ministry had disappeared from sight quickly, and it seemed impossible that they would have been able to secure this building like this in such a tiny window of time. Would they have abandoned their headquarters and everything within it, believing no one would try and breach the facility? It did not seem likely.

It would have been an amazing display of arrogance, but she knew these people. In particular, the archivist. She believed the Ministry of Peculiar Occurrences far more clever than this.

"Nothing's here, miss," the soldier reported, an empty drawer in his hand. "Empty."

Tick . . . tock . . . tick . . . tock . . .

"It was here." The voice rose in anger from behind her. "It was here."

Sophia turned to look at the grotesque theatre of man and machine, his ocular casting a haunting golden glow across a large, polished table. Breaching the Ministry should have been his final triumph over the Ministry and its director, but even with its mechanised masking Sophia could hear something in his words: frustration.

"It was here. You showed it to me," he whispered. "Such a work of beauty, and it's gone."

That mad doctor is arrogant as well, Sophia seethed. *The lines are blurring again.*

She watched as the Maestro reached for his right hand with his left, and methodically stripped off the armour. With one hand now free of metal, naked fingers flexing in the cool air, the Maestro placed his palm flat against the table's surface.

Tick . . . tock . . . tick . . . tock . . .

The Maestro's jaw fixed tight, his mouth bending deeper and deeper into a scowl. His hand pressed deeper and deeper into the smooth table surface, and now the scowl bore teeth. A tremble worked across his body, as he methodically encased his right arm back in metal once again. The tremble became a tremor, and suddenly the Maestro exploded into a wild frenzy.

He swung his mechanical arms in wide arcs, splintering the fine mahogany wood of the table. His fury turned on the mantle, and its clock stood no chance against his gauntlets. Sophia and the soldiers scuttled out of the Maestro's way as he stomped over to the director's desk. He threw both arms over his shoulders before smashing them down onto its wide expanse. The desk withstood the first strike, but not the second and third. It appeared as if the Maestro wanted to destroy everything that had ever been touched by the Ministry's director.

Then the fit of rage was done, the Maestro left gasping inside his metal costume. Sophia crossed over to the remains of the ruined mantelpiece and pushed through the cog, gears, and shattered pieces of the once-faithful clock with her boot.

"I think you broke it," Sophia said softly.

Something was spinning up in the Maestro's armour. Sophia returned to her feet as the Gatling guns installed in both of the Maestro's arms locked into place.

"Sound is here," the Maestro seethed. "We must rip open the Archives and devour all its secrets immediately."

This time, the Maestro took the lead, and it was Sophia and his men who followed in his wake.

The assassin kept silent as she gripped the chadburn and yanked on its handle, setting "The Archives" as their next stop. The lift rattled downwards and seemed to descend with a swiftness that was notably absent on their rise to the director's office. They caught a glimpse of the foyer. Empty. Sophia wondered if the other ghosts had found something, or if they had returned outside for new orders from Commander Benson.

Her thoughts scattered when they reached the bottom with a hard lurch. The Maestro tore the iron gate open with such force it let out a scream of tortured metal. They followed him wordlessly into what appeared to be some metal alcove between the lift shaft and a large iron hatch that would have looked more appropriate on a warship than underneath an antiques warehouse.

Without comment the Maestro worked the door lock with the giddiness of a child at Christmas preparing to unwrap their presents. His apparatus mimicked his own hiss of delight as he did so.

When the lock disengaged with a loud, hard *thunk*, the

Maestro stepped back, licking his lips in delight. "My dear Sophia, I insist we announce ourselves to Doctor Basil Sound, Director of the Ministry, properly."

Sophia gave a start at the sound of his Gatlings spinning up.

He looked over to one of their Ghosts. "Open the hatch, if you please."

The man hastily holstered his weapon and pulled hard on the hatch. It opened with a slow, low groan.

"Sophia," the Maestro hissed.

She forced back the urge to glare at the mad monster, channelling her own destructive impulses by locking her arms forwards and leading with her pistols.

She stood on the overhead landing, glancing at the stairs leading down into the Archives. This mysterious Restricted Area she had heard so much of, it suddenly dawned on her, was somewhere down here. She could hear the rest of the Maestro's men fall in behind her, cocking their pistols, perhaps eager for battle after the inspiring power seen behind their leader's tirade.

"The Maestro believes Sound is here," Sophia ordered. "Move carefully."

"I don't understand," she heard from the landing now above her. She could hear a newfound rage flaring in his voice behind her, the Gatlings still spinning, anxious to unleash their death. "The shelves should contain fifty years of investigations. Many of them are empty."

Something managed to cut through the whine of weaponry and the low thrum of unseen generators: the soft chatter of voices. Multiple voices.

"There!" Sophia called out, bringing her pistols around.

Gunfire rang out from shelving units deep in the Archives, but Sophia could tell from muzzle flashes that the gunman was at least ten rows in from where they stood. The Ghosts scattered, one slinking off to the left while another slipped off to the right. Sophia, however, sprinted for the partners desk. Unlike the shelving units, the desk was solid, and she instantly ascertained it was the best cover.

Then she heard the whine of the Maestro's Gatlings turn into a scream as he came down the stairs towards them, and she realised that nowhere was truly safe.

Sophia covered her ears as his cannons roared to life. The shelving units were torn apart, creating debris that became projectiles in their own right. She pressed herself as close to the cool stone floor as she was able, while chunks of wood scattered across and down her back. She was blind, deaf, and pinned down by her lord and master.

The madness of the Maestro's wrath abruptly ended, and Sophia could now hear reinforcements, more of the Maestro's Grey Ghosts, clattering down the stairs. She glanced up to see him motioning to either side of the shelving units. A repeat of the flanking manoeuvre would hopefully yield better results with more men in play.

Two shots rang out and two soldiers fell just in front of her while another two shots quickly followed. Something told Sophia they were now down by four.

"If you value your men," came a familiar voice, "I recommend you call them back."

Wellington Thornhill Books. The archivist. He had returned.

Something inside her went cold. She recognised it as the same dread she felt up in the director's office. They had soldiers, weapons, and the blessing of Her Majesty, and the archivist had dared to return.

This was not madness. There was a stunning logic to this devotion. These Archives belonged to him. This was his domain, and the Maestro was invading it.

"You are hardly in a position of authority at present, Mr. Books, I believe?" the Maestro called, holding up his arms with the still-smoking Gatlings.

"Be that as it may," Books replied, his voice steady and unconcerned, "you will not take the Archives."

Another gunshot thundered in the cavernous Archives. "I would stand down, mate, if it's all the same to you."

The colonial. Suddenly, Sophia felt as if she were trapped in the spider's web with its master and mistress at its centre.

The Gatlings spun up again, and Sophia could have sworn she heard the Maestro scream, *"I will not be denied!"* before he unleashed another maelstrom of bullets. Did he not know she was still here by the desk, pinned down by his gunfire? Or did he know and simply not care?

Sophia knew that she should be firing back, adding her

bullets to those of the Maestro and his army, but something held her back. It wasn't just fear of injury or death. If it had been that, she would never have taken up her mother's profession.

Raising her hand to her cheek, she felt blood there from where a stray piece of shrapnel had cut her. It was a physical representation of his disdain for her life. Once, before all of this, she wouldn't have cared what a client thought of her, but this was different; she had hitched her fate to his. That, she now saw, had been a terrible mistake.

The Archives were now a killing field unless you stood behind the Maestro. She was certain that, along with artefacts that had been lost forever, men who had pledged their loyalty to the Maestro were lying dead or dying among the shelves. None of that mattered to him.

When the Gatlings finally powered down, the Maestro's voice echoed around her. "You are outgunned, so you might as well face your fate standing in defiance of me, not cowering in the darkness."

"I am addressing the Maestro, yes?" A new voice signalled a new piece in this bloody chess game.

"Sound?" the Maestro roared, his voice almost delighted.

"You have me at a disadvantage." Someone was moving through the smoke. "You know of me, but I have not enjoyed the pleasure of being introduced."

"Sir," came Books' panicked voice, "what are you doing?"

"Surrendering, man," came the assured reply. From the haze emerged a kindly looking gentleman, his expression tired and worn. "We are pinned down. I, for one, would rather not be mowed down like wheat under the scythe in a mad dash for escape."

"Wellington?" Eliza asked from her concealment.

"He's right," the archivist spoke up, and then came the clatter of a weapon hitting the stone floor. "We must end this."

As two more silhouettes stepped into the dim light, the remaining men of the Maestro's breach team flanked them on either side. They were, at least on a glance, unarmed but she knew full well the colonial woman would not surrender so willingly.

Sophia slowly got to her feet, taking a moment to look at the desk she had hidden behind. Another attack from the

Maestro's Gatlings and the men standing with him, and she too would have been part of the collateral damage.

"Glad to see you have come to your senses," the Maestro stated, his armour gleaming under the remaining gaslights. "Better an honourable death than a fool's errand."

"Yes," Sound said, slipping what appeared to be a pocket watch into his waistcoat. "Speaking of fools and their errands, exactly what is it you want from us? As your men will no doubt report, our lockdown was more than thorough."

"An impressive feat, but what concerns me is neither upstairs in your fine offices nor even on these meagre shelves." The Maestro dared two steps forwards, allowing more light to spill on him. "My prize today, Doctor Sound, is the Restricted Area, and all of its many secrets."

No, hardly an empty boast. They had won. What seemed to be the last bastion of the Ministry had surrendered to the Maestro, but Sophia felt no cause for celebration. The dread consumed her, and her instincts were all ablaze with alarm.

Why, she asked herself without giving voice to the thought, *was Doctor Sound checking the time?*

Then it all crashed down upon her, threatening to pull the world from underneath her. The madness she had seen after San Francisco. That boy's face as he lay on Jekyll's table. Her own worth to the Maestro.

There are always options, H. H. Holmes had said to her.

The trick was going to be convincing them not to shoot her before she could speak to them.

"Maestro," Sophia called out. From the set of his jaw, he was surprised to find her standing there, alive. Sophia turned her own gaze to the Ministry agents. "The director, you need. What of the archivist and his woman?"

The colonial narrowed her gaze on Sophia. No woman of this age wanted to be considered a mere appendage. Good. She wanted this bitch incensed.

"The archivist still holds value. Agent Braun, while skilled I have no doubt, has a rather rambunctious reputation." His tanks gave a soft hiss, causing Sophia to look over her shoulder to her lord and master. "Kill her."

Sophia gripped both pistols tightly and fixed her eyes on Eliza. If the colonial did have any concealed weapons, they would be in the open in a matter of steps. Braun would be cut down by the Maestro's men without fail, but that would rob Sophia of what would be a most satisfying kill.

Stopping only five paces short of the woman, Sophia sized Eliza up, just as she did at the opera house on their first meeting.

"We are both professionals, yes?" Sophia asked.

"Of course," Eliza replied, her posture relaxed, but the assassin was not fooled—that only meant she was capable of striking in any direction.

Sophia kept her eyes on her target, but said, "Wellington—so you know—I am very sorry."

Her gun came up, mere inches from Eliza's head, but then her hand opened wide, the pistol seeming to float for an instant in front of her adversary. Sophia pivoted and dropped to one knee. She would only have time to aim and open fire on the first thing she would see. The ocular would have made for a lovely target, but the extra second or two she would need to make that shot would cost her.

Thankfully, the Maestro had stepped into the light, and the large, serpentine pipes that worked their way throughout his mechanical arms were practically glowing. Confusion was a situation Sophia favoured, and rupturing the Maestro's hydraulics offered a glimmer of hope as well as an excellent distraction. From behind her, two bullets fired, dispatching the two closest soldiers. No one knew where to look or concentrate attention—the ailing leader surrounded in a cloud of steam and sparks, or the three Ministry agents retreating from where they came.

Over the screams of the Maestro and the gunfire, Sophia heard Doctor Sound shout, "Fall back to the Restricted Area!"

She had no way of escaping her defection now. The die was cast, for the Maestro would never believe her, whatever story she spun. Her fate was now bound with the agents and their director.

From her waist Sophia pulled one of the devices she had inherited from her mother. The small, dull grey, metallic ball was an old clockwork piece but still very useful, easily fitting into her hand.

After giving the clockwork cricket ball a quick, sharp

twist, Sophia rolled it across the floor away from her, making sure the solitary red arrow carved on the top pointed away from her. A space of five seconds followed, which she counted under her breath, until the distraction device began to let out the echoing sound of feet running—away from her in the direction of the arrow.

The effect was immediate, and gunfire from across the Archives focused in that direction. With the Maestro's screams and misdirected munitions as her cover, Sophia slipped into the smoke and shadows behind her.

Through the smoke and debris she followed the three agents, the surrounding shelving units all in various stages of distress. Her eyes caught sight of a crate cracked open by one of the Maestro's attacks. It was leaking some odd, viscous material that cast a scarlet glow at where it pooled. Another item, a mirror of some fashion, was shattered on the ground; but Sophia paused as she caught her reflection in three of the shards. The reflection was silently screaming at her.

She could just make out her unexpected allies disappearing behind a thick iron hatch, and suddenly she recalled what the Prince of Wales had told her in San Francisco. *The beginning and end of all things. Alpha and Omega.*

Had he been right? Was this what she was about to see? For the first time in a very long time Sophia did not have a thought about the Maestro. Instead she was consumed by curiosity.

That curiosity turned into a desire for survival when she heard the sound of a single Gatling gun spinning up.

"Get down!" Sophia screamed as she pumped her legs harder against the stone underfoot.

A hand grabbed Sophia's arm and pulled her behind the open door leading to what appeared to be an airlock. The roar of the Maestro's Gatling was now joined by the metallic patter of bullets slamming into the heavy hatch.

Sophia's eyes darted around her. It looked as if they were in a submersible. A disappointment welled up in her. *This is it, the famed Restricted Area?*

A muscle in Braun's jaw tightened as she stared at Sophia.

"Director, what do you want me to do?" she asked over the assault.

"Nothing." Sound remained absolutely still, the rotund

man taking stock of her much in the same manner that Sophia had of Eliza. "I have a feeling that Miss Sophia del Morte here has something more than surrender on her mind. Amnesty?"

The assassin was shocked. How could he possibly know what was on her mind?

"He does that often," Wellington said. Sophia blinked when she looked at him. "I recognise that look from Eliza's and my own face when he knows what you're thinking."

The attack abruptly ended. From the tenor of the screams she heard, Sophia wagered the Maestro just ran out of bullets. When Sophia turned about, she saw Eliza toss her pistol to Wellington, who, in a motion that was far too fluid to be human, pulled back the hammer and pointed it between her eyes. It was rude enough to see right down the barrel of a pistol, but inexcusable that it was her own weapon. Wellington Books' eyes were steady on her, and she observed nothing in that instant that reminded her of the fumbling archivist she had once seduced. This was a man who would shoot her in the forehead with not a moment's consideration. She admired that in him.

It was apparent that Sophia had to say whatever was needed in the next few moments. "I offer information," she said in a low voice. "The Maestro is mad and I want out."

The archivist and the agent exchanged a look, and she waited for him to pull the trigger, but it was the director who spoke. "Then I suggest we make our escape"—Sound glanced at his pocket watch again—"because, as you know, time is rather limited."

"How much time?" Eliza asked.

"Five minutes."

Eliza drew two pistols from her back and stepped out of the airlock. She peeked around the door, only to jerk back as bullets ricocheted off the iron hatch.

"They're making a push," she grumbled.

"We can't last five minutes?" Wellington asked.

Eliza glanced at Sophia. "You, I don't mind putting in harm's way." The pistols twirled in her hands and extended themselves to Sophia. The balance of the ivory-handled side-arms stole the assassin's breath away. "I've got four shots between them. Make them count."

"Eliza?" Wellington gasped.

"Get ready to close that hatch," she said to Wellington, drawing a throwing knife from her boot. Her eyes shifted to Sophia. "Ready?"

Sophia nodded and then stepped out from the cover, firing as she did. On the fourth and final shot, she heard the sound of a knife cutting through the air. The blade struck what appeared to be a small tin can of some sort secured into the brick wall.

A second later, heat, fire, and stone erupted from above their heads. A heartbeat after the blasts came the water.

Eliza stumbled, but Sophia threw her arms around her and pulled her towards the airlock, stumbling past Wellington and Sound, who pulled both ladies further into the metal alcove.

"Secure the hatch!" Sound cried as from outside, parts of the long brick wall began to collapse.

Now, just audible over the sound of rock grinding against rock and the rushing of water, were cries of alarm. Torrents of water were now rushing into their alcove, spraying in every direction as Wellington pulled the heavy door shut. Sophia had once been on a ship when its hull had been breached. A most unpleasant experience, with screaming, and running combined with getting dreadfully wet. She was back on her feet and next to Books, pulling on the hatch's solitary wheel.

The water continued to force its way in, and now Eliza and Sound joined in the struggle against the forces of nature. A sudden *clang* of metal against metal resounded in the chamber and Sophia felt the wheel jerk in her grip. She let go of the hatch and collapsed with relief along with the others, as it appeared they had held the waters back.

No, she would not die and join her ancestors today.

If Fortune smiled upon them all, then the Thames would be the final resting place of both the Duke of Sussex and the madman known as the Maestro.

FOURTEEN

❧

Wherein Our Intrepid Agents and
Alluring Assassin Drink Deep
from a Fount of Knowledge

Doctor Sound slowly backed away from the heavy iron door, his eyes not leaving the frame surrounding it. His eyes were wide, his skin pale, as he turned his head at every sign of a groan or creak. Perhaps he was thinking what Wellington, Eliza, and Sophia were all thinking at that moment: The Thames was now on the other side of this hatch. Would the door hold?

Then came the rumble which could only be four storeys of architecture giving into the loss of its foundation and sliding into the river.

"The lock will hold," Sound whispered. It remained uncertain if this was for their benefit or his own. As the metal groaned and dull thuds could be heard above their heads, the director nodded slowly. "I designed this structure with our present scenario in mind. The airlock and the roof will hold."

Wellington tightened his grip on Eliza's hand as the metal around them protested this assault, but then the thuds from outside grew less frequent. The hatch's seal continued to resist the forces bearing down on it, and eventually the stress rippling through the iron ceased.

"Everyone all right then?" Sound asked, turning to look at the three of them.

"We all seem to be in one piece," Wellington replied. He glanced at Eliza, who was staring intently at Sophia del Morte as if she were a cat and the assassin a sewer rat. "For the time being."

Eliza looked the assassin over from head to toe. Neither woman revealed anything in their cold stares. Sophia slowly held up Eliza's pistols, flipped them handle out, and then offered them back to their owner.

"Exquisite," Sophia commented.

Eliza took her weapons, glancing at the sidearms before returning them back to their holsters. "Thanks." She ground out the word as if it hurt.

The small alcove seemed to be closing in on the four of them as the silence stretched on. Wellington remembered the odd, awkward atmosphere of the oubliette he had found himself trapped in with del Morte and Lena Munroe during the Culpepper case. This was far worse because, even in that near darkness, there was space and the slimmest possibility of escape.

For all Wellington knew, this alcove led to a private office or a laboratory. This was merely a junction between the Archives and the Restricted Area, and now the Archives was underwater, and undoubtedly buried by the demolished Miggins Antiquities.

"So, do you mind explaining to me what happened back there?" Eliza said pursing her lips.

"Since San Francisco, I have been looking for an opportunity." The assassin motioned to the hatch. "One was presented to me."

"Taking shelter in an airlock is hardly what I would call a good opportunity," Eliza muttered.

Sophia gave a slight shrug. "You should have seen my other options." She then inclined her head towards the other woman. "How did you know I wouldn't kill you on the Maestro's order?"

"You would have never allowed yourself to get that close to

me to make a kill. I could have disarmed you, used a concealed weapon, turned the gun against you. Too many variables." Eliza gave the woman a crooked smile. "Like you said so pointedly, we are professionals."

"That we are," Sophia said with a nod.

"Doctor Sound," Wellington began, stepping in closer to the director. Due to the limited space, it felt as if he were about to become quite familiar with his superior. "Exactly how water tight are these doors?"

"Tight enough, it would seem," he said, his eyes still studying the seal between hatch and frame. "They have been designed in case of catastrophic failure—"

"Let's not tempt fate," sang Eliza.

"—the other door is of a unique design," he said, motioning with his head to the hatch behind them. "It too is watertight."

"Well, at least we won't die from drowning," Wellington noted gloomily.

"That's it, lad," Sound said with a light nod, tapping Wellington on his shoulder. "A positive outlook is essential." He then switched places with him to face the women. "And as I am locked in an airlock with two delightful looking ladies, I cannot think of anywhere else in the Empire I would rather be."

What an incurable flirt he is, Wellington thought.

"So lovely to enjoy close quarters with the formidable Sophia del Morte," he chortled, leaning closer to her to examine her as if she were some exotic butterfly.

One of the assassin's dark eyebrows arched sharply. "Believe me, the pleasure is all mine."

"I have heard so much about you from my colleagues." He then produced from one of the small cubbyholes behind him in their chamber a long box. "In particular, your jewellery has a rather lethal quality about it."

Her brow's angle steepened, but she gave a slow nod and then removed her leather wristbands, along with the three rings she wore across her slender, pale hands.

"It is ridiculous to think I would turn on those taking me in," she stated sharply, placing the accessories in the long box.

"Yes, well, that is my reputation—mad as a hatter, I am," Sound retorted.

Sound snapped shut the box and returned it to its cubby-hole. Free of the stealth weaponry, she offered Sound an invit-ing smile before extending her hand in a polite, mannerly greeting.

"A pleasure to make your acquaintance, Signorina del Morte," Doctor Sound said, taking her hand and kissing her fingertips.

Her smile widened, but then she let out a little gasp when Doctor Sound's other hand clapped lightly around her wrist.

"The pulse point," he said as Sophia collapsed into his arms. "Better introduction of a tranquiliser. Straight into the bloodstream." His brow suddenly shot up as his face twisted in concern. "I say, Books, if you please?"

"Yes, sir," he said, shuffling over to his side. Even with the two of them easing her to the metal grating of the airlock, Sophia was of a considerable weight. "She must be wearing body armour."

"Stands to reason as she was planning a defection to the Ministry." Sound gave a light huff as Sophia came to rest. "A rather charming notion coming from her, if you consider our past. Crossing this Maestro character as she was, she must have prepared for more of a rough-and-tumble than the others in her party." He pressed two fingers against her smooth neck and nodded. "Slow and steady. And more importantly, genu-ine." He then went for his left hand and carefully removed the large ring there. "I won't be needing this, now shall I?"

"Where did that come from?" Eliza asked, motioning to the deadly jewellery he was placing on a small shelf about eye level with him.

"Agent Braun, as a director of a clandestine organisation it would hardly be prudent for me to wander out into the world without some form of protection for myself." He motioned to the ring and added, "An assassin ring is quite subtle, and can be quite handy, if employed properly."

Wellington stared at Sophia. Even with her subdued as she was, he still did not feel entirely safe. "How long before she comes around?"

"Oh, I will wager she will sleep peacefully for a solid four hours. If she was particularly exhausted from undue stress or tension, that may grant us an additional four hours." Sound returned to his feet and pulled out from the wall in front of him a keyboard similar to Wellington's analytical engine. He typed as he spoke. "However, I think the lovely signorina will have to accompany us regardless."

Wellington nodded and went to pick Sophia up again.

"No need, Books." Wellington looked up at Sound, who was still typing, his fingers dancing over the keyboard more deftly than his own. "I'm calling for assistance."

Wellington was about to ask who he was calling and how they were going to reach them now that the Thames was on the other side of the massive hatch when he then took closer note of the screen holding Sound's attention. While the keyboard itself was very familiar, the monitor was nothing like the one on his own analytical engine. For one thing, this one was nearly three times the size, and it was completely flat—the smoothest glass he had ever seen.

There was also the colour of the light coming from the screen. It was a brilliant sapphire blue.

And the words appearing on the screen looked even stranger. It was English he saw appear across the glass, but it was the type itself that was nothing short of odd:

Need stretcher for unexpected excursion member. Subject is approximately 1.7 metres in height, weight 60 kilograms (without corset and armament). Name: Sophia del Morte. Override Apprehension Protocols. Director Authorisation 18950507.

"Right then, just beyond the secondary hatch, assistance should be waiting."

"You mean," Wellington began, his heart pounding in his chest. "There's a way out?"

"Of course there's a way out. Do you really think this"—he motioned to the tight iron alcove all around them—"is the Restricted Area, or that this door leads to nowhere?"

Wellington tried to find a good answer for that. He gave a rather good try. "Well put, sir."

"So if this isn't the Restricted Area," Eliza began, "what exactly is it?"

"I do love your inquisitive mind, Agent Braun," Doctor Sound said cheerily. "One reason of many why I find you one of our top agents here, make no mistake." He squeezed his way around Eliza and progressed to the second door. He went to spin the large wheel at its centre but then turned to face them both. "Before we proceed, I must prepare you for what awaits you beyond this point."

Now Wellington could hear his heart hammering in his ears. The one question in his Archives was finally about to have an answer.

"Only a handful of people know exactly what the Restricted Area holds . . ."

"Yes, sir," Wellington said quickly.

". . . and that secrecy is paramount for us to maintain . . ."

"Understood, sir."

"I would hate to think what would happen if someone of the Maestro's ilk were to have gained access to the Restricted Area." He turned back to Eliza and patted her on the shoulder. "You have no idea the good you have—"

"Sir," she interrupted, "with all due respect—open the bloody hatch."

Wellington felt the flicker of a smile. It was nice to know they both shared the same burning curiosity.

"Oh, yes, very well then," and with a nod to both of them, Sound turned the wheel a quarter of an inch to the left.

The metal rang sharply, its echo lingering in the alcove, even as a small device appearing as a stereoscope lowered in front of the director. He placed his head into the wraparound eyepiece and waited. Wellington could see a blue light rise within the viewer's housing then dim back into nothing. The stereoscope then swung away and retracted back into its hidden compartment above them.

"Agent Books, Agent Braun," Sound began, giving his waistcoat a slight tug, "welcome to the Restricted Area."

Jets of steam shot from each corner of the hatch, but instead of swinging open as other entries of its make would do, this one split in its centre into six sections like a mechanical iris, revealing a massive chamber easily three times the size of the Archives. A metal walkway was suspended above them, and rows upon rows of polished, onyx cubes that Wellington estimated were each the size of a parlour lined the floor. The cubes emitted a soft blue light from the top, and standing alongside each was one of the strange, featureless automatons, the cube's glow reflecting softly across their brushed, metallic skins. Flying only a few feet above the cubes and automatons were the spheres he recognised as having watched over the operations in his Archives. They seemed to be doing something similar here. When he leaned over the gangway, Wellington recognised what he had always known as the signature thrumming of the generators. All this time it had actually been coming from here . . .

The thrumming was louder, though. Much louder.

He half expected to hear himself stammer, but somehow the words came out remarkably clearly. "Doctor Sound, if you don't mind my asking, where are we?"

"Have you not figured that out yet?" Doctor Sound chuckled softly as he motioned around them. "This is the Archives."

Before either one of them could say anything to this remarkable assertion, two automatons quietly approached. Wellington could just make out between them a stretcher, as requested in the airlock by Sound. A breath caught in his throat as he noticed the stretcher was suspended between the automatons by nothing other than air.

Completely accepting this astounding display of the sciences as an everyday occurrence, Doctor Sound approached the lead automaton and spoke to it as if it were another agent of the Ministry. "The signorina is in the airlock. Please escort her to Event Control. While she is wearing body armour, do treat her with utmost care, thank you. Monitor her condition and if she appears to be slipping out of deep REM, return her there. She must not see anything here. Nothing at all. Are we clear on that?"

"Yes, sir," the automaton replied. The Staff began to float forwards but the second one paused on reaching Wellington. "Our apologies, Mr. Books, for not completing full extraction of the Alpha Archives. We did however manage to store approximately fifty-seven percent of Alpha's artefacts, all of which have been secured in climate-controlled environments."

Wellington saw his own distorted reflection in the

automaton's face say, "Er . . . thank you?" He gave a sheepish grin. "Excellent work."

"Thank you, sir," it replied politely, then it turned back in the direction of the airlock with its companion.

"Well then, perhaps I should start at the beginning." Sound's jovial voice jerked Wellington out of the reverie he had momentarily fallen into. He smiled warmly and gave the archivist's shoulder a firm squeeze. "To better understand this place, I think you will need to understand more about your director.

"I once took a journey that changed my life. Quite the feat you must understand as, after half a decade, you would think my course in life would be not only set, but enjoy quite the foundation." He looked around himself and gave a little chuckle. "I suppose you can never be too old to learn, now can you?"

"If you don't mind my asking, sir," Eliza dared in this sudden break of Sound's thoughts, "what did you learn?"

He blinked at the question, and his eyes seemed to twinkle as his smile widened. "I learned, my dear Eliza, that Shakespeare was right. There are, indeed, more things in heaven and earth than are dreamt of in philosophy. One of those philosophies includes the sciences. No matter what we learn, no matter what we prove and reaffirm, there is that which cannot be explained. Those people, places, and objects that challenge the sciences, I believed, needed to be understood. As so, with the blessings of Her Majesty the Queen, I founded the Ministry of Peculiar Occurrences."

Wellington was trying to keep an open mind but that revelation, combined with the image of a slumbering Sophia del Morte *floating* by them all of a sudden, suspended between two automatons, struck him as hard as Eliza slapping him in the face. "I beg a pardon—*you* founded the Ministry? The Ministry was founded nearly half a century ago by Professor Culpepper Source. From Ministry records, he was a man of the sciences and academics."

"Yes, he was. And so he sat as the director for just over a decade, followed by Dr. Galen Phund. He was then followed by . . ."

"Woodruff Spring, a professor of the sciences, yes, but—"

"Bloody hell!" Eliza snapped, startling them both.

It was the New Zealander who was now looking at Sound wide-eyed, her jaw threatening to become completely unhinged.

"Oh, you are clever," she said, wagging her finger at Sound. "I mean, if I'm right . . ."

"I assure you, Eliza, you are," he said with a wink.

"I always thought you were clever, but *this*?!"

"Hello!" Wellington waved at the two of them. "I happen to be here as well. Do you mind enlightening me?"

"You don't know, Welly?" Eliza pointed enthusiastically at Sound. "You haven't figured it out?"

"Figured *what* out?"

Her smile was now almost as bright as the director's. "Really?" She clapped her hands together, giggling ever so softly. "Ooooh, I figured out a riddle before Wellington Thornhill Books. How delightful!"

"Eliza . . ." he warned.

"No no no no, just let me enjoy this moment. It's quite lovely."

"Do you mind?" He couldn't help the rising inflection in his voice; he was becoming rather annoyed.

"It's like beating you in chess. Or in a marksmanship competition."

"Eliza . . ."

"Or more like beating you in chess while beating you in a marksmanship competition."

"Oh for God's sake, please out with it!"

She looked at him with a hard glare. "You really know how to spoil a girl's victory lap, you know that?" Eliza opened her mouth, but then caught herself. "On second thought, I'd rather lead you through this little conclusion."

His skin prickled; the heat underneath it he could swear was at a boiling point.

"Go on," she urged. "Name the directors."

"In chronological order?"

"If that gives you a bit of a thrill, certainly."

Wellington gave a sigh, and recited, "Culpepper Source, Dr. Galen Phund, Woodruff Spring, St. John Fount, Basil Sound."

"And the pattern you see there?"

Pattern? There was a pattern? "Well . . ." He looked upward

as he whispered the names again and again. Then his brow knotted. He could see in his peripheral Eliza bobbing up and down on the balls of her feet. Terribly distracting. "All right . . . Source, Phund, Spring, Fount . . . hold on . . . Sound. Those are all the same thing."

"I know," Eliza said, the excitement in her threatening to explode as one of her sticks of dynamite.

"So then . . . Culpepper, Galen, Woodruff, St. John, Basil . . . herbs." His eyes jumped back to Sound. "Herbert—*Wells*?"

Sound gave a soft chuckle. "A pleasure to make your acquaintance."

"The director of the Ministry of Peculiar Occurrences is H. G. Wells?!" he asked, his voice echoing all around them.

"Since its very founding in 1840"—he gave Wellington a wink—"yes."

"That's so bloody amazing!" Eliza bounced on her toes.

"And this," began their director, again motioning to the seemingly endless number of onyx cubes underneath them, "is the Archives that I—pardon me, Wellington—*we* built. Although Beta Archives covers a bit more of the past."

Wellington went pale. "I see."

"And the future."

Earlier, Wellington would have loved a strong cup of tea. Now, all he wanted was a brandy. Several fingers deep.

"Mr. Wells." Eliza shook her head. "Nope, sorry, mate. It just doesn't work for me."

"You're having trouble accepting who I am. This is underst—"

"No, I can accept you're H. G. Wells. In fact, it explains a lot." Eliza looked him up and down. "But you're . . . Doctor Sound to me, and quite frankly you always will be."

Wellington felt an urge to correct Eliza, to explain that no matter how sentimental she felt, this man who had led them all these years into investigations of the unknown was in fact an accomplished writer of both fact and fiction, an artist, a biologist, and a man of many other talents. This revelation changed everything they knew, everything they accepted as fact.

No matter what we learn, no matter what we prove and reaffirm, Wells had said earlier, *there is that which cannot be explained.*

Doctor Sound was absolutely right. This cannot be explained. Perhaps it was best not to try.

"She does have a point, Doctor Sound," Wellington said.

"Oh, how disappointing, I had hoped after telling you this little secret, I would hear my own name between us." He gave a shrug. "Perhaps I should look on the brighter side. At least this chaos didn't occur when I was Woodruff Spring. I had one agent from Dorset—Smithers was his name. Lyle Smithers—who insisted on calling me 'Woody' all the time. Bloody annoying."

"Doctor Sound, if this," Eliza said, motioning to the array underneath them, "is the Archives, then what exactly were Wellington and I maintaining all this time? It just all feels like a grand lie."

"Not at all. Quite the contrary," Doctor Sound said, nodding to both her and Wellington. "This incredible journey that inspired the Ministry of Peculiar Occurrences needed a central point, as it were, of activity, and it was this time period—a time period I flourished in—that, according to the models I've been following, seems to be where the trouble in the space-time continuum first grew roots. When Ministry agents would unearth or solve various phenomena, I would return to the origins of said case and see if I could go further into the mystery. Sometimes, that would mean travelling to the past. Other times, it would involve the future, although the future can prove rather tricky, as every event of the past carries a cascade of consequences, much like throwing a stone into a millpond."

It was Wellington's turn to interrupt. "If you are doing what you are insinuating—"

"I am not insinuating anything here, my boy. I am doing it. Perhaps just hearing yourself say it may help you accept all this much easier."

Wellington swallowed hard, took in a long breath, and felt a calm wash over him. Doctor Sound's logic, considering all things at present, was absolutely staggering. "Sir, if you are travelling willy-nilly through time—"

"And space." Doctor Sound looked over to Eliza. "I'm particularly proud of that trick."

"Exactly why do you not invite the Ministry in on this little secret of yours? Could you imagine the lives we would have saved in the field had we been able to do what you are doing?"

"Oh, I would agree that we would have saved quite a few lives by allowing agents to take advantage of this incredible technology." Sound leaned against the railing and crossed his arms as he looked at the both of them. "But in light of Agent Campbell's betrayal, a frailty in men and women that is not foreign to this or other agencies under the Queen's rule, I could not risk it."

"So you shouldered the responsibility of time travel all on your own?" Eliza's eyes narrowed. "Aren't we an arrogant pommy bastard?" Her earlier delight looked to have worn off.

Doctor Sound's smile faded. Eliza's bold statement, Wellington admitted, was quite sobering.

"You are not God, nor should you consider yourself the only one able to wield such power," Wellington stated. "I can think of several men and women in our Archives that fell to such seduction."

"An intriguing argument." Sound's voice adopted an unexpected chill that Wellington had never heard from the man, nor ever wished to again. "However, I am shouldering it nevertheless and sharing the burden now with you. If I have made the wrong assumption about the two of you, I will rectify this judgement and do so with a clean conscience."

"Mate," Eliza said, her tone bristling with confidence and a hint of rage, "I'd like to see you try."

"Do keep in mind, Eliza," Wellington said, his eyes motioning around them, "you're not only threatening the man who has led the Ministry for over fifty years, but who has also mastered the ability of traveling through time."

"And space," Sound added once again.

Eliza shook her head. "It's pretentious. It's disgusting. It's—"

"Necessary, Eliza," Sound insisted. "Think for a moment if not one but many people were floating throughout time. Do you think they would be bandying about dimensions benevolently?" He shook his head. "And then there is a matter of balance. One person travelling through time on his or her own volition can effect everything from individuals to empires. Introduce an international government agency to time travel, and you increase the potential for Armageddon exponentially."

"So why exactly did you decide to show us all this?" she asked.

"My chrono-model revealed that the both of you were entrusted with this secret. That is what I rescued from my office—fragile piece of equipment don't you know." He took out the watch from his pocket and his eyebrows popped up. "Now, if you please, follow me. We cannot miss our upcoming window."

Eliza and Wellington shared a glance between themselves before following Sound towards the end of the walkway. Ahead Wellington could make out a large bank of displays and larger versions of the glass monitors that he had seen in the airlock. Floating by a rather impressive door—a most sturdy one, made of a heavy dark cherrywood and sporting a single thick brass handle—was Sophia, still asleep on the floating stretcher. This must be the area of Beta Archives that Sound had referred to earlier as Event Control.

"Window?" Eliza asked. "Why would you be concerned about missing anything? You're travelling through time."

"Time travel is hardly a matter of saying, 'I would love to enjoy a bite with Marie Antoinette on September 23, 1775, just past noon,' but more of calculating intersections between events."

His mind should have shut down the moment they entered this Archives of Sound's making. Wellington knew the mind simply reaches a point, be it in the battlefield or in the confines of a library deep in research, where it can no longer take in any more information. Presently, he could not stop taking it all in. Doctor Sound continued to peel back layer upon layer of this mystery, and all Wellington could do was keep exploring, keep delving into this amazing revelation.

He also just couldn't help himself. He had to know. "Events? Are you saying there are points in time that are fixed?"

"It's a bit of a theory that has proven to explain quite a bit of what I've been doing, but yes, there are these moments in time that are so clearly defined that the array—my Time Machine, if you will—can connect them, and this is how I travel back and forth."

"But the amount of power it would take to power such a

device," Wellington began, looking from one end of the computer banks to the other. "It is—"

"The Thames." Sound rocked back on his heels, crooking an eyebrow. "Are you telling me that you truly believed the generators here were solely for your analytical engine's operation?"

"Well . . ." His voice trailed off as he felt a blush rise on his cheeks. "If this area hadn't been so restricted, as it were, perhaps I would not have been led to believe as such."

"Perhaps," Sound chortled. He then turned to the array's main keyboard and monitor and began to tap into it what Wellington could only assume was a sequence of some kind. "Now then, we have an errand to run for our Whiterock compatriots. There is an ally that I have remained very tight-lipped about within our ranks."

"Another secret? Blimey," Eliza grumbled. "With this much trust, it's a wonder you bothered to let us loose in the field at all."

"I've remained tight-lipped about this ally," Sound repeated, giving Eliza a sharp stare, "on account of this man's rather unique situation. He has provided incredible intelligence in the past . . ."

His words trailed off as he continued to type on the keyboard. Wellington started at what sounded like massive generators spinning to life underneath them. Eliza's hand clasping into his own reassured him that feeling unnerved was proper, if not completely understood.

Words, displayed in their strange typography, materialised on the main screen above them:

Event horizon stable. Connection
established.

"Wellington, Eliza, if you please?" asked Sound as he motioned to an ornate door in front of them.

With a polished brass handle designed as the face of a clock at its centre, the door's shape was reminiscent of an old cathedral hatch, and was incredibly out of place compared to the polished metal and odd wood—if that was what Wellington was indeed feeling under his touch—reaching to either side of the chamber they stood in. It was a wonder he had not noticed the hatch before. The wooden door was stout and heavy, made of a rich, dark cherrywood, polished almost as bright as the sophisticated materials surrounding it; and as it was nearly fifteen feet in height, the portal towered over them. Wellington could not be certain if it was growing taller the closer they drew to it.

Sound placed a hand on the door handle and then turned back around to the two of them. "Ready, are we?"

"For?" he asked.

"A trip 'through the looking-glass'?" he said, the lights around them creating a twinkle in his eyes.

The handle turned quite easily in the director's grasp. From the other side, inviting smells of cinnamon, nutmeg, and burning wood invited them across the threshold.

Feeling Eliza's grip tighten ever so slightly, Wellington looked at her, managed a smile that conveyed a "Why not?" sentiment, and together they followed their director through the open door.

FIFTEEN

❧

In Which Eliza Braun Marvels at a Sunset

A fire crackled in an impressive hearth. There were small incense burners filling the room with scents that reminded Eliza of Christmas. With the amount of books—and there were a lot of them—she would have surmised this was a study at a fine English manor had it not been for two rather odd qualities of this conservatory. There were large glass panes above and around them revealing a landscape reminding her of the Arizona Territories in the United States, only this landscape was far darker. It took her eyes a moment to realise the glass above and around them was tinted. It was a deep golden hue but not such a dark colour as to prevent the dying light from still illuminating the room. The other oddity of this expansive room was how its walls—not the furniture, but the actual walls in which the bookshelves and desks were built—were not wood or brick, but of raw stone. Eliza ran up to the wall and touched the cool rock, confirming her initial thoughts of the wall's slope, its composition, and their relative height based on their breathtaking view.

"We're inside a mountain," she stated.

Turning back in the direction she had come, she could see, just behind Wellington, Sound closing a completely different door, this one weather worn and beaten with a rustic door handle far less ornate than the one they entered through. Just before the door closed, she caught a parting glimpse of Event Control.

"Yes, indeed you are," a voice answered her. From its gravelly baritone and American drawl, it was obviously neither Wellington nor Sound. "My wife and I come here often to entertain dignitaries or friends from far-off places."

Eliza felt her back straighten just a fraction at the sight of the tall man entering the room. The stranger exuded a commanding presence, through a confidence he carried and eyes of a hard, steel-grey colour. All this kept her rooted to the spot. He wore his long raven hair in an intricate braid tied back with a leather thong. While that hair was greying slightly at the temples, his face and trim, muscular frame was that of a man no older than thirty.

The man's eyes softened when he turned to Doctor Sound, his smile warm and inviting as he approached the Ministry director. "Herbert," he said, laughing gently as he embraced him, "you are looking . . ."

His words trailed off as he looked over Sound.

"I look forward to your probing observations, Jonathan," Sound chortled.

"Well, it has been a while," their host offered. "When I last saw you, you were in better physical condition—but also twenty years younger. Now, look at you!"

"It's the perils of time travel, as you know, different selves and all those complications . . ."

"Yes, yes, and please, don't remind me again of how it all works," implored Jonathan. "I doubt if I understand it anymore. It's all too fantastic to grasp, anyway."

Sound motioned around him. "You're one to talk!"

Their laughter subsided as Jonathan glanced over to Eliza, then to Wellington. "I see by the looks on your faces," he began, striding over to a bar, fully stocked with decanters of what Eliza could only hope were the best in spirits, "that Herbert has told you about his fantastic machine, so I will assume you will want a drink immediately. Would you care for scotch? Cognac? Or perhaps something stronger?"

"I could do with a scotch," Wellington said.

Being of a curious nature, Eliza selected, "Stronger."

When his steel-grey eyes looked at her now, Eliza felt her knees weaken slightly. "A girl after my own heart." He poured two fingers deep of scotch into the first glass and handed it to Wellington with a polite nod. Into the second glass, he poured a deep red liquid. Then, as Eliza looked on, Jonathan tapped the rim of the snifter, causing the left portion of the liquid inside to suddenly glow with a dull orange flare. "The locals call this *Ketumsh-ke*. The Sunset. Drink the part that isn't glowing."

Eliza nodded and took a sip of the crimson liquid. What struck her taste buds was an unexpected combination of bourbon and citrus with an overtone of vanilla. It was far stronger than anything she had ever tasted in her travels around the world, and threatened to knock her back a step; but the warmth receded as quickly as it had overcome her.

Whatever this Sunset was, she wanted more of it.

"Where are my manners?" Sound said, clicking his tongue as Jonathan handed him a glass. Of what, Eliza could not be certain. "Wellington, Eliza, may I introduce to you Captain Jonathan Carter."

"Friends and welcomed guests call me John," he said, offering Wellington a hand. "I prefer that."

Wellington returned the handshake. "American? The Carolinas?"

"Virginia actually," John said. "Welcome to my home. Please, have a seat."

Sound took a seat in a luxurious, high-backed chair. "And how is the family, John?"

He sat back in his own grand chair and shook his head. "Healthy and happy, although I am in for a very hard ascension. My daughter. Oh, Herbert . . ." He groaned lightly. "She is growing up to be just like her mother."

"Well, seeing as how well things transpired between you and your wife, you have an inkling as to what lies ahead."

John toasted his drink to Sound. "You have a point there, Herbert." He took a quick sip, then set his drink to one side. "However, I believe this visit is hardly social in nature."

"Not entirely, no," he admitted.

"When I received your message—"

"Excuse me a moment." Eliza took a deep sip of her drink; the glowing portion of it felt warm against her face. Her courage somehow returned to her, and so she turned to Sound. "Did we just time travel?"

"Well, we did not go so far back in time," Doctor Sound said with a shrug, "but yes, Eliza, we did travel."

She looked over to John. "When did you receive this message from Sound?"

The man took a sip of his own drink, and she had the distinct impression he was studying her closely. "This is their first trip, isn't it, Herbert?"

It could have been an effect of the drink or the lighting of the room, but Eliza thought she could see Sound blush. "Yes," he admitted.

John's mouth bent into a smirk. "When did you plan to explain the principles of how you travel?" He pointed to Sound with an accusatory finger. "I am speaking from experience. Nothing is more unnerving than finding yourself unexpectedly somewhere other than where you plan to be."

"Things have been moving rather quickly," Sound replied, a tone of sudden regret in his words. "Sometimes I get a bit—"

"Caught up in things, yes, that happens with you often." John motioned to Eliza and Wellington. "Why don't you take a moment? Get your agents here caught up?"

Sound blinked. "I know your time is most valuable . . ."

"Knowing how they must feel, I insist." He raised his glass to the agents. Eliza returned the gesture with an awkward and slightly uncertain smile.

"Very well." Sound took another sip of his scotch before setting it down and clapping his hands together lightly. "So, while I did explain in brief how we travel between two fixed points in space and time—I should have explained exactly how Event Control accomplishes this." Sound reached for the table between him and John, and took from the small memo desk a simple slip of paper. "The central analytical device searches for the closest fixed point and narrows down either previously visited points or stable coordinates in which to establish a connection." He quickly drew two X marks at the top and at the bottom of the paper before holding the paper up for Eliza and Wellington to see. "A brilliant physicist will hypothesise"—he cleared his throat before adding—"fifty years or so from now—that the most efficient way to travel either through space, time, or both, is to connect a departure and an arrival point," Sound explained as he bent the slip of paper, making the two *X* points touch.

Eliza inclined her head to one side. "So it is a bit like æthergate travel? Only instead of just going from point *A* to point *B* as you do there, you're going from year *A* to year *B*."

"A simplified analogy," Sound chortled, "but yes, yes indeed."

"And so the technology we've seen—the automatons, the Restricted Area, and so on—this is all from a distant future."

"Or perhaps," Wellington ventured, "distant worlds, as you are no longer restricted to planetary boundaries as æthergate travel seems to be?"

"Exactly," confirmed Sound, his satisfaction tinged with a hint of pride. "Well done, both of you!"

"So why not have us jump forwards into time, grab what we need, and then return to Old Blighty?" Eliza asked. "That makes far more sense than having a small band of disavowed agents dive into the belly of the beast, as it were."

Sound nodded. "A compelling notion, but the fabric of the universe is delicate, to be certain. Every time technology is brought from the future to the past, infinite possibilities arise of where future technology impacts history, bringing about what can only be described as a chronological chain reaction. This is why I carefully monitor my travels and how it effects my timeline."

Wellington snapped his fingers, pointing at Sound suddenly. "That odd clockwork model in your office," he stated. "I had seen it so many times in your office but never asked you what it was. That was how you tracked the outcome of your visits."

"Correct, Wellington. That was what I retrieved from my office. My chrono-model will be coming back to Whiterock. Every time I returned from a journey, either past or future, I would consult my model to see exactly what outcome came with it." He leaned closer to Eliza. "Yet another reason I chose to shoulder the burden of this technology alone."

"So for all we know," she began, her tone growing colder

than the study they were meeting in currently, "one of your trips through time could have sparked this whole mess."

"On the contrary, I have been journeying back and forth into the future, attempting to manage any fallout from this approaching point."

"What approaching point?" Wellington asked.

"Event Control has been effectively tracking various points in past, present, and future; but those points have been growing fewer in numbers the closer we grew to 1895. There is an 'age' for the lack of a better word between 1897 and 1915 that is simply hidden."

"Hidden?" Eliza asked. "You mean, as if it is blacked out?"

"Yes," Sound replied, "and ever since this blackout first appeared within my model, Event Control has adjusted and re-adjusted future events to compensate. It was so unpredictable that just before I activated Phantom Protocol, I had to visit my younger self to protect my very existence. Each time Event Control's calculations are concluded, the outcome either falls back into the future that I know, or other futures of various outcomes, most of which are most unpleasant."

"So even with travelling through time . . ." Eliza began.

"Even with fixed events in the cosmos, time is still fluid and always changing," finished Sound. "This strange period of lost time, hidden to both Event Control and my model, has but only one constant."

"What?" Wellington asked.

Sound polished off his own drink, took a deep breath, and then stated, "The two of you."

Eliza felt Wellington's warm hand gently take hers. It seemed as if the madness of everything unfolding around her knew no limits. She was suddenly reminded of the death spiral she briefly struggled against when undercover at the Phoenix Society, but then she felt weighted down with Wellington along for the ride. This time, she felt stronger.

"With each calculation and projected outcomes," Doctor Sound revealed, "both your names continue to appear as important and influential—in what way remains a mystery. It could be in your victory over insurmountable odds or your death for the greater good of the Empire that sets things right or tips the scales deeper into darkness. I cannot say for certain."

"Lovely," Eliza stated flatly.

"Bringing more technology from the future presents risks that are just too great," Sound said.

"So we have to make do with the technology at hand?" Eliza asked. "Technology of the present day."

"Yes." Sound then turned to John. "Which brings me to you."

"I was wondering when I came into play within this delightful drama," the other man said, setting his drink down.

Sound's face darkened. "You know what I need."

"How many?"

"Just one."

"One?" He chuckled softly, and then motioned to Eliza. "I would side with this lovely lady here. It is Eliza, yes?" She nodded, tightening her own hold on Wellington's hand. He inclined his head in a silent reply, then returned his attention to Sound. "I would imagine a fleet is what you need, if I understood your message."

"I don't need an army." Sound winked, his smile oddly comforting to Eliza. "I just need one. It will suffice."

John arched an eyebrow at Sound's request. "Now, Herbert, you know my head for strategy. What are you playing at?"

"It's an endgame I'm laying out," he replied, "and I'm playing to win."

He nodded, his grey eyes catching the warm glow of the room, seeming to dampen the intermittent chill Eliza felt.

"Very well then. When and where would you like it? The door certainly won't give you enough room."

Sound reached into his waistcoat and produced a small piece of paper. "This should provide both a desired time and coordinates for the landing site."

"This won't be easy to keep secret."

"I am well aware of that," Sound assured him, "but by the time anyone attempts to investigate, we will be under way."

John took the coordinates from Sound, nodding silently as he read the information there.

"Doctor Sound?" the New Zealander asked.

"Yes, Miss Braun?"

"Exactly why have you brought us here?" She did not know what Sound was about, but she recalled how he admitted telling people what they needed to hear.

"Because you and Wellington play heavily in this endgame, and it is my intent to keep you both alive throughout all this." His face was expressionless.

"Well, that's reassuring," she muttered.

"No, Eliza, this is more about following the unchanging factor," Wellington said. "Whatever it is about that blackout of seventeen years, we play into the outcome of it. So Doctor Sound wants to keep an eye on us, see just how important our part in all this is."

"That's just brilliant, that is," Eliza said with a slight frown, disliking being some kind of pawn in Sound's games spanning decades.

"Eliza," Wellington began, leading her over to the conservatory's panoramic window, "I know that what is happening around here is nothing short of—"

"Overwhelming?" she whispered tersely.

"That's a start," Wellington said. "The sole reason I have not run in the opposite direction screaming is that the only other way out was flooded. That, and my own curiosity." He motioned to Sound with his head. "The technology, not to mention the knowledge Sound—Wells—whatever you wish to call him—has amassed under our very noses is enough to keep me invested."

"You don't think it a little dangerous that Sound is the only one with access to this technology?" She looked into his hazel eyes. "Think of how many deaths could have been prevented—"

He stared back at her just as steadily. "No, Eliza, no, you cannot contemplate the 'What Ifs' with all this. You just can't."

"You know as well as anyone how much I do not like being told what I can and cannot do." She could feel her jaw tightening and her dander starting to get up.

"That I do, but please heed my words on this," Wellington implored. "Your way lies madness."

She let out a long breath, folded her arms in front of her, and tapped her fingers against the sleeves of her blouse. Eliza hated feeling cornered, but this was a situation she could have never planned for. "I trusted that man. He's a lie. Everything we've ever believed about him has been a lie, and you're asking me to blindly trust him again?"

She hated it when he was this calm. "I'm asking that you look at this from a different perspective. Doctor Sound has entrusted us with this secret, and he has confided in us our part in all this. Consider all these things his signs of trust in us."

Eliza turned away to look at the sunset now under way. The sun seemed smaller for some reason, but that still did not rob the surrounding valley nor the steel-grey sky stretching above them of any grandeur. There was no rhyme or reason to accepting what was happening around them, even with actually seeing for herself, as she crossed from the Restricted Area into this man Carter's conservatory. She should have demanded more from Doctor Sound once she had deduced his true identity.

"You're asking a lot, Wellington," she said, rubbing the back of her neck, trying to find her own calm.

"Yes, he is," came the voice from behind them.

Both Eliza and Wellington turned to see John approaching. "I still remember when I was first introduced to Herbert's marvels of technology."

"How did you accept it?" asked Eliza.

It was a strange answer to her query. He laughed. "Asking me something like that isn't really fair, considering my own experiences."

Wellington's brow furrowed. "Did you have a rough go in America?"

John's smile faded ever so slightly. "Just a moment. Sound didn't tell you where he was taking you?"

"It bears repeating," Eliza begrudgingly offered. "Things were moving somewhat rapidly."

John turned his eyes to the sunset as he took a sip of his drink. "So, how did I accept this brave new world, you ask? It was hardly easy, but I continued to discover such amazing sights, sounds, and smells . . ." His voice trailed off, and then he shook his head. "Well, all right, I'll give you that the smells were a bit hard to take, but you build up a tolerance over time." He took another drink before continuing. "What I learned over the years, even when adjusting from Virginia to Arizona, is that you need to rely on your instincts when it comes to change you accept and change you can't. It's a lot to take in at times, I won't begin to question that; but consider who guides you."

"Doctor Sound, you mean?" Eliza asked.

"Yes. Regardless of whatever name he's travelling under these days, Herbert should be held accountable based on his actions of past as well as present. I know his work from the Ministry of Peculiar Occurrences, and he prefers missions where his agents come home unscathed. The amount of concern he gives those in his service is not only admirable, but the trait of a leader worth following." John paused for a moment, the corners of his mouth tugging back in a contented smile. "If he kept his Restricted Area restricted, he had good reason. And if he is sharing its secrets with you, then that means he not only trusts you, but he believes you have the ability to accept the fantastic."

"That's our job," Eliza stated, thinking to the vows she had made when she joined the Ministry.

"No, your job is to explain the unexplained. Not accept it. You two, however, have something Herbert believes is extraordinary."

"No, we're a constant in an apparently ever-changing mystery," she said.

"And you don't think that is absolutely extraordinary?"

She let out a frustrated sigh. "I'm not sure what I am thinking at present. What about you, Wellington?"

The silence made her turn to look at the archivist who did not appear to have been paying attention to their conversation. His eyes were turned upwards, taking in the sight overhead.

What he said told her he had in fact been paying attention. "Actually, I find this view extraordinary."

Eliza followed his gaze. Overhead, two moons were emerging from the glare of the dying sun, casting a dull illumination over their valley.

"I've been here for many years. Many more based on the Terran clock. This view is quite lovely." John then said over his shoulder, "I'll issue an order for your lander, Herbert. If we give it enough kick, I should have it at your desired coordinates within two years."

"That may be cutting it close."

"Oh now, cheer up, Herbert," John said with a sly grin. "It's more than enough time to reach you. It's what? February, at the time?"

"January, actually," the director replied, joining them at the massive window. "As a matter of fact, I believe at this very moment I am chatting with the two of you on a train platform concerning some rather amazing events on the Edinburgh Express."

Eliza whipped her head around to Sound. "You mean, we travelled into the past?"

"It's a time machine," Doctor Sound replied. "It can go in both directions."

She nodded. "Of course. Silly me. And as it can also travel through space, it can bring us here."

"To Mars," Wellington added. Eliza wondered if she should have been shocked at someone stating the obvious, but it was actually comforting.

"See?" John said with a wink. "You're doing just fine." He motioned to Sound with his drink. "May I offer you a place to stay? Along with prep time for launch, I will have to train one of your agents here how to operate the lander."

"That would be splendid." Doctor Sound finished off his drink. "If my memory serves, Cassandra will be entering my office reminding me I have a ten o'clock appointment with Sir William Christie. A few days from now, so we have time."

"A few days, sir?" Eliza asked. "Don't we have all the time in the world, literally?"

Doctor Sound mulled her words over for a moment, then checked his pocket watch. "Only a few days until the next event, then back to Whiterock. Until then, we look forward to your hospitality."

"Thank you, Herbert," John said. He then leaned closer to Eliza. "If you find this sunset amazing, just wait until you see our stars. Quite impossibly beautiful."

INTERLUDE

❦

Wherein Brandon Hill Touches a
Piece of Bruce Campbell's Past

"**I**'m telling you, mate, they're dead. Pushin' up the daisies, they are," Bruce whispered to Brandon as they waited in the October chill of a London night.

That the Australian felt the need to *yet again* state his mind on the ongoing matter of Doctor Sound's disappearance, along with their hosts Wellington Books and Eliza Braun, at this particular moment of their mission was largely because he believed it was beneath him.

It had been five months since Sound had left Whiterock to return to Miggins Antiquities and not a word had come since then. Not a single note, communiqué, or æthermemo. While he knew the director had made clear he, Braun, and that tosser Books could be gone for a prolonged period of time, it really did not bode well. This was the Department, after all. They had made a mess of the Ministry. Even with those lucky few that had managed to find their way to Avebury Circle and then, eventually, to Whiterock, the Ministry he knew was now reduced to a mockery of what it once had been.

Brandon crouched in the shadows next to him, did not make any gesture to show he'd heard his partner's complaint.

The Australian let out another annoyed huff. It was little relief to Bruce that, in the director's absence, Miss Shillingworth was in charge. He liked the director's clerk better when she was the mousy, silent bird that Bruce *thought* she was. The last time anyone barked orders at him like that was during his basic training in the Australian Defence Force. At that time, Master Sergeant Burgess towered over him, could have easily bested him in a fight, and never had to worry about freezing to death on account of the gorilla-like body hair he sported. Shillingworth possessed none of those characteristics, but when she managed to send him to the floor with a lightning-quick aikido takedown and screamed into his face to perform the obstacle course "with a purpose" he knew her authority would never be brought to question. Again. Ever. Full stop.

Bruce still never found out exactly what Sound was up to in the Archives, let alone that Restricted Area.

And now, five months without a word? Chances were he would never find out.

"Dead as damn doornails," Bruce muttered, glancing up the street to the right.

"Agent Campbell," Brandon whispered tersely, reverting to angry formality, "now is not the time to tread this ground again. We are following orders."

The Australian was finding this newfound bravado from his partner in the field less and less charming. "Yeah. Orders from the afterlife."

Brandon held up a cautionary finger. "Orders from the man who gave you a second chance. Or did you conveniently forget that?"

The Canadian, during their salad days, would never have questioned Bruce's judgement or instincts. The two of them complemented one another, and managed to solve cases deemed too impossible or improbable by the director himself. Bruce knew that, and was always anxious to head out on assignment with him. They were a well-oiled machine. Unstoppable. Uncompromising.

And it made Bruce look even better on paper as a field agent. Something else that he enjoyed the benefits of.

Everything was different now, and now Brandon was less the devil-may-care partner and more of a conscience-in-the-field that was working on the Australian's few remaining nerves. Bruce longed for that trust, that sense of reckless adventure; and yet that desire for the old days, he found, continued to war with this new side of him, stalwart in that the Ministry needed him, not the other way around. He preferred self-reliance. The idea of "brotherhood" and "camaraderie" were quaint notions to say the least, but that was a dependence Bruce preferred not to encourage. However, something continued to drive him ever since Rockhampton. Whatever spurned this need for acceptance, Bruce had no inkling.

It was this bizarre sense of duty that had nagged at him when, following another hard day of training—training for what, still a mystery—Shillingworth approached him with the envelope bearing the seal of the Ministry.

Orders. From Sound. Bearing that day's date.

The words he had read could have been penned only moments before Bruce had received them:

Agent Campbell:

You and Agent Hill must infiltrate Central London Aeroport's warehouse and retrieve Wellington Books' motorcar. It should be kept with other unclaimed luggage (their airship docked back in April 1896) and, I imagine, will be unguarded considering the amount of time it has been there. Do keep in mind that "unguarded" may not equate to "unwatched" so therefore exercise the highest of cautionary tactics. Avoid Department interaction at all costs, and return with the motorcar to Whiterock. I know what I am asking of you is of the highest risk, but I also know what the two of you can accomplish together.

Good Luck,
Doctor Sound

Now, here they were on a fool's errand into the darkness of London, where the unclaimed luggage depot's warehouse stood. The night watch casually walking about seemed hardly the kind of opposition Bruce was accustomed to dealing with.

"So now we are chauffeurs, are we?" Bruce grumbled. "Fetching the car for the lord of the manor, eh?"

Brandon looked over his shoulder. He appeared to be shocked about something or other. "Did you bother to *read* the report accompanying the orders?"

It hadn't been that long since he and Brandon were in the field together, watching one another's back. "When, in all the time we have worked together, have you ever known me to read a report from beginning to end?"

"Books modified the car. It's a bloody armoury."

"Wait—*Books* weaponised a motorcar?"

Brandon shrugged. "According to the report. And we need it."

From the satchel hanging at his side, Brandon produced a monocular and pressed it against his eye. From the details he imparted to Bruce, the device must have possessed some Starlight technology.

"A single door to the east and then we have two barn doors on the west side. I would imagine they would have the car there, close to the doors."

"If they didn't receive any other motorcars or contraptions similar over the past four months."

Brandon nodded. "Closer to five. Bloody thing is probably buried in there."

"What about the Department? Any sign of them blokes?"

He swept the monocular to either side of the warehouse. "Just the night watch. I think once this man's turned the corner, we can make for the door."

Bruce removed from his back the long rectangular suitcase and set it at his feet. "Give me a bit of light, will ya, mate?"

Glancing to either side of them, Brandon produced an *illuminati*, cracked it against the street underfoot, and held the glowing stick over Bruce and his case. Bruce gently flipped the latches back and revealed six dismantled components of a Lee-Metford-Tesla rifle.

"That's a Mark II," Brandon whispered, his eyes appearing larger in the glow of the illuminati.

"That it is, mate," Bruce said as he assembled the rifle. "Not many of these were made, but with those street urchins working an assembly line, and a little bit of love, we got this one working." As much as he disliked the drills and training of the past few months, there was the begrudging fact that his "rusty" skills were perhaps sharper than ever. With a final *click* of the transformer sliding into its housing and the reassuring feel of the rifle's full magazine locking in tight, Bruce hefted the rifle, getting a feel for its weight. "Our toffy archivist was sporting quite the arsenal back at Whiterock. It was as if he had been preparing for something."

Just before he buried the illuminati, Bruce caught Brandon's quizzical, concerned look. "Preparing for something? What do you mean by that?"

Much as he liked Brandon, sometimes the Canadian could be a bit thick. "Oh, come off it, mate, a complete and utter tosser like Books, and he's stockpiling enough firepower to supply both the Ministry and the Department? You don't think that's a bit strange?"

Brandon looked him over. "Honestly, there have been a lot of things I have seen of late I'd describe as particularly strange."

He opened his mouth, ready to fire back a retort, but thought better of it. He closed his mouth with a soft *snap*, puckered his lips, and nodded. "Fair enough, mate."

"We're right as rain with you getting me out of South America, but Doctor Sound reinstating you as a field agent; I am still not sure what to think of that. Bit of a kick to the bullocks, if you ask me, but it is what the doctor ordered, now isn't it?" Brandon dropped the monocular back into his satchel. "Get ready to move. We should have an opportunity coming up."

Bruce's stomach growled softly. "You wouldn't happen to have a steak pie in there perchance?"

Brandon held up the saddlebag's flap and peered in. "I have illuminati sticks, a few sticks of dynamite—must make sure not to mix the two up—an '87 with a small box of ammunition . . . no. Not a meat pie of any kind here."

"Maybe my luck isn't what it used to be in the field," Bruce grumbled, his stomach echoing the sentiment in its own way.

"Think positive, and your luck will change," his partner urged. "Are you ready?"

Bruce's thumb flipped the switch on the mini-generator atop the Mark II. He wasn't sure where the sentiment came from, but it had to be said. "Don't worry, Brandon. I'm not gonna let you down."

Once the guard disappeared from view, Bruce took point in a sprint across the landing field to where the warehouses stood. Brandon crouched behind him and started to work on the lock.

"Taking your sweet time, Hill?" Bruce whispered over the various clicks and scrapes coming from the door.

"Never you mind," Brandon returned. "I have this well under—*Oh bugger!*"

Bruce could see a form materializing through the evening fog. "Care to get it a bit more under control there?"

"Al—most—" The sharp *clack* of a lock sounded in Bruce's ears. "We're in."

"Celebrate inside," Bruce growled as he pushed Brandon into the warehouse.

When the door shut, both men flanked either side of the hatch. Brandon, now armed with one of his long knives, positioned himself across from Bruce. As they waited, Bruce dared to look around him. There were plenty of suitcases, glimpses into the various lives of people who either forgot about their personal belongings, or simply couldn't be bothered to collect their things after a transcontinental or transatlantic voyage. Then there were those people who would simply choose to disappear, either during the voyage or afterwards, not always to end a life but in some circumstances to start a new one.

His attention flicked back to the door. The footsteps were just audible from the other side. Considering the girth of the night watchman, Bruce was surprised he had not heard the man sooner. They both waited as the steps came up to the door. For a moment, there was no movement. Bruce's grip tightened on the Mark II as the doorknob jiggled. Once. Twice. Then after a moment, the footsteps resumed and eventually disappeared in the distance.

"All right then," Brandon said, sheathing his knife, "let's hope luck is on our side."

"Start on the opposite end," Bruce said, taking an illuminati from Brandon and cracking it to life. "I'll work my way down here."

Suitcases. Towers of wooden crates, some marked "FRAG-ILE." The pale light of the illuminati threw shadows in all directions, making it hard for Bruce to keep an eye out for any movement. He paused by one suitcase and checked the tag:

Rabarts, Daniel
Flight 5, RMS *Olympia*
Destination: London, England
17 April 1896

At least he was in the right warehouse, if things were sorted by the year and time of travel. He had not gone far before he came up to a long pallet with what appeared to be a carriage concealed underneath a long tarp. He followed the edge of the tarp along its length until his hand found a baggage tag, at what he assumed to be the front of the vehicle.

Seemed as if Campbell's luck was also on a path of redemption:

Lawrence, Wellington Reginald
Flight 11, USAA *Atlantic Angel*
Destination: London, England
15 April 1896

Bruce whistled twice for Brandon. He watched the glare from his partner's illuminati bob and weave through the makeshift labyrinth of luggage until he emerged from behind a pillar of crates.

"Looks like this is it, mate. Help me throw back the tarp."

Dust and debris scratched and blinded him as the sheet snapped and furled. When it finally slipped away, both men turned their illuminati on the automobile.

"That," Brandon began, his eyes moving from beginning to end point of the vehicle, "is a thing of beauty."

"And it belongs to Wellington Books," Bruce grumbled. "What a bloody waste!"

Brandon rounded on him, finally demanding, "What is your issue with our archivist?"

Bruce went to answer but as he had done before with his partner, his mouth closed with no words. He took in a deep breath and shrugged his massive shoulders. "You know how sometimes you meet someone and you just don't like them?"

"No," Brandon answered, "I don't know that feeling. I need a good reason to not like someone."

Bruce gave a quick shrug. "He got the better of me in a scuffle once."

That appeared to catch him by surprise. "Really? When?"

Bruce was about to tell him about the incident at Ministry headquarters when his throat seized. It had been during his brief time as assistant director, during his time in the back of the Duke of Sussex's pocket. It had been right before Brandon informed the Ministry of Agent Pujari's death.

"Look," Bruce said, shaking his head. Now Brandon's opposition was just grating. Why couldn't he just go back to the way he had been before all this? "The man just ain't right. I got a suspicion about him."

"So you have insinuated. Are you sure it is nothing to do with Agent Braun at all?" By the glimmer of the illuminati Brandon looked an awful lot like he was grinning.

"No bloody chance! I just don't trust him. It's always the quiet ones that we have to watch that much closer, eh what?"

"Then, keeping that in mind"—Brandon turned on his heel and looked over the car—"I'll drive. I would hate for you to bring upon his wrath if you were to scratch the car."

"Funny, mate," Bruce said, looking around them. "Funny." He could just see the barn doors ahead, several stacks of luggage between them and the door. "Before you settle in behind the wheel, maybe you'll want to help me clear the way?"

With a grunt, Bruce and Brandon began the arduous and somewhat tedious effort ahead of them, filling their hands with either a set of luggage or a crate. The path would have taken less time to clear had it not been for the occasional check for the night watch.

"I have known cricket matches that have taken less time than this," Bruce grumbled, picking up two suitcases.

"This would be less of a chore," Brandon said, lifting two bags of his own and hefting them off to one side, "if you did a considerable less amount of bellyaching."

"I like bellyaching," he quipped, pushing a large—but thankfully, light—crate further into the shadows. "Ladies find it endearing."

"Perhaps that is why," his partner said, returning to the remaining few bags, "I'm finding it working on my last nerve."

Bruce dusted off his hands and nodded as he went over to another crate. He gave it a slight push, and it moved with ease. "Good to know you are all man under that gentlemanly exterior."

A laugh came from his partner. First one from him since they had set off. "Well, I don't know about gentlemanly. There was this one woman, I remember in Colombia—my Scheherazade. She was anything but proper for a gentleman's company."

Bruce managed to slide the crate—the application of one hand more than enough effort—out of the way when he stopped in mid-step. "That isn't right."

"Oh, she was a lovely lady, even considering her profession . . ."

"No, Brandon, that's not what I mean," he said, still staring at the crate. "We've been lucky on missions before, right?"

Another laugh. It would have made Bruce feel hopeful about their relationship on the mend if it were not for the sudden tightness in his stomach growing.

"We have seen some close scrapes together, my friend." Brandon was now beside him, giving the Australian's shoulder a playful punch. "I remember that time in the Americas with that lunatic and his flying covered wag—"

"And we were lucky. We've always been lucky. It felt like we were riding with the angels."

Brandon's head inclined slightly. "I suppose so, yes."

"I'm not feeling that right now," Bruce said, shouldering the Mark II. "Are you?"

Bruce stepped back and took aim on the crate he had just moved. Two shots thundered throughout the warehouse.

"Dammit, Bruce!" Brandon shouted before the echo ceased around them. "Have you lost your mind? The watch—"

"Are not here. And not because we're lucky," he said, slipping the rifle over his shoulder while getting a good grip on the crate.

With two of its corners now blown free, opening the crate was simply a matter of a few hard tugs from Bruce. When its panel finally tore away, Brandon could now get a full view of what had been bothering his partner.

"Because all this has been arranged," Bruce said, motioning to the empty space within the crate.

Brandon scrambled over to the barn doors while Bruce worked his way deeper into the warehouse. As he had dared to consider, the cargo located in the back of the warehouse was far sturdier. Even with his shoulder and back into it, moving any of this luggage was not going to happen. It would be easier moving Ayers Rock.

"We've got what looks like a line of Department agents," Brandon said as he peeked through the split between the barn doors, "and two armoured vehicles taking position in front of the doors."

"So we have a number of choices, I'm seeing," Bruce began, returning to the car. "The first one: we surrender."

"Rather not, cheers very much," Brandon stated, joining Bruce.

"Second choice: we barge through those doors and give them a right reminder of why the Ministry is not to be tangled with."

Brandon wagged a finger at Bruce. "That would be against the doctor's orders. Avoid Department interaction at all costs."

"Which brings me to our third option." Bruce held out a hand. "Give me the dynamite you got there, Brandon."

There was a sense of relief on seeing the Canadian's smile. His smile widened with each nod of his head. "Are we giving these ruffians a Vancouver?"

"That would be too nice," Bruce scoffed, taking the five sticks and heading back into the darkness. "I was thinking more of a Bruges."

"Bruges?" he asked. "Are you sure?"

"Just start the car, and be ready."

Roughly four rows of crates and luggage would be between them and what he hoped would be an exit. Based on how much time he would need to position himself for the blast, Bruce measured the fuse, gave himself and extra inch for luck, and then cut. The fuse, designed by Axelrod and Blackwell, immediately lit itself once it was trimmed to Bruce's desired time. He placed the bundle at the spot he believed would give maximum power in the direction he wanted, and then walked back to the car. Books' treasure was now shuddering gently as

Brandon picked up the front half of the tarp and Bruce the latter. Both of them covered themselves and the car and waited. As the seconds seemed to creep by, Bruce took the Mark II and released the safety on the generator.

"Now just a moment," Brandon chided. "I don't remember a Lee-Metford-Tesla of any kind being within reach when we were in Bruges."

"Just a variation on a theme, mate," Bruce said over the building whine of the rifle's generator.

Brandon let out a little sigh, then asked, "How long did you make the fuse for?"

"I thought I made it for five minutes."

"Well"—he shrugged—"you know how hard it is to guess these things accurately, and how time feels when you're waiting for something."

"Oh yeah," Bruce said, his mouth bending into a wry grin. He glanced in the backseat. "Looks like their luggage is back there too."

"Oh, I'm sure they'll appreciate that."

"Yeah." Bruce nodded. "I remember once having my luggage lost. Spent five days in Hong Kong in the same suit. I swear, my undergarments could have probably found their way back to Sydney by themselves by the time my luggage was found!"

Brandon chuckled. He gave a slow nod, then let out a long breath as he checked his pocket watch. The nod turned into a shake of his head. "Bruce, are you certain you made that fuse for five—"

The concussive force rocked the car up and forwards slightly. Bruce pushed back the tarp and shouldered the Mark II. A wave of blue-white erupted from the bell of the rifle, ripping through a teetering wall of wooden boxes and unclaimed luggage. He worked the bolt action once just as the barn doors pulled back to reveal a line of men and women backlit by two massive armoured vehicles.

"Drive," Bruce called as he pulled the trigger.

Department agents scattered, but not before Bruce's second shot claimed another agent. Bruce felt himself thrown forwards as Brandon opened the throttle and Wellington's motorcar lurched backwards, ran through the gaping hole that had once been unclaimed baggage, and out into the night. Bruce fired off one more round before the car launched forwards, speeding past the disoriented Department and across the London Aeroport.

"Love the variations there, Bruce," Brandon called back to him.

"Thanks, mate." He looked at the Mark II in his hands. "Pretty proud of them too."

A second rumble brought Bruce's attention back to the receding aeroport. From between a pair of warehouses, another motorcar appeared. Just visible in the cab were at least three bodies.

"Either hold her steady," Bruce shouted to Brandon with a wild grin, "or give her all she's got. We've got unwelcome company on our back door."

Bruce glanced down at the rifle's generator and that second's distraction cost him. He looked up at the moment something leapt from the pursuing cab and into him. The rifle flipped out of his grip while their motorcar swerved dangerously, nearly slamming into the other.

"Oye! Bruce!" he heard Brandon shout. "I think we've picked up a passenger."

Through the twinkling lights that danced before his eyes, a face took form. A face framed by a head of bright blonde hair whipping in the night wind. She had a good grip on him and seemed thrilled to lay eyes on him.

"Hello, sweetie."

Bruce blinked and hoped to manage an equally pleasant greeting. "Good to see y—"

His words were cut short by a quick jab to his mouth. Apparently, Beatrice Muldoon wanted to pick up where they had left off in Rockhampton months ago.

Considering she had tackled him and scored the first punch, Bruce was trying to gather his wits but just at the point of clarity, he felt a hammer rattle his skull. It was, in fact, Beatrice's meaty fist keeping him down. Bruce never liked throwing blind punches. He always found those who did it against him looked foolish, so in turn he particularly did not care to look ridiculous himself.

However, in this circumstance, necessity willed out.

Bruce felt nothing but air as he brought his own hook around. When he countered with a backhand, there was also nothing. As his right hand made its return voyage through space, he brought his left fist forwards. He just needed to connect with something. *Anything.*

Then his left fist found a reinforced corset.

Beatrice Muldoon's fight for balance gave Bruce enough time to get some fresh air and get a sense of footing in the front seat. When he finally got a focus on the Department operative, he could make out a rather intimidating knife that only Brandon could truly appreciate free of a sheath inside her tweed.

The car lurched suddenly sending Beatrice backwards, but also sending Bruce into her. The knife, still in her grasp, cut dangerously close to his face as he found himself plunging deep into the woman's cleavage.

"Sorry!" he heard Brandon call out.

Why, mate, Bruce thought quickly, *are you apologising?*

He felt talons dig deep into his shoulder and spin him around. Those instincts he had worried had dulled to a point of uselessness brought his arms up in an X pattern, catching the blade bearing down on him, suspending it inches from his eye.

If he lived through this, he would have to make sure to thank Cassandra Shillingworth for a job well done.

"This could have been so much easier," Beatrice chided as she struggled to bring the knife closer, its tip wavering closer at him, "if you had just said yes in Rockhampton."

Then the motorcar came to a sudden stop, and Beatrice soared over the front of the car and slammed against the runway. Despite her initial impact against the concrete, she rolled and then propped herself up to one knee.

"Excellent braking system Books has got here," Brandon said conversationally.

"Nice one, mate," Bruce said to Brandon as he opened his door. "Now be a good chap, and point this car in the direction of headquarters."

"Where are you going?" he asked.

"I'm tending to Miss Muldoon, if you please," he replied, stepping out of the car.

Beatrice was chucking, as she dabbed her bloody lip on her shirt cuff. "That's going to cost you, darling," she called.

"If I gave a toss, I would be concerned." Bruce stood over her. She must still be winded from that impact. At least the corset kept her ribs intact. "Don't read into this, love, but I really don't want this to get messy."

From behind him, he heard Wellington's motorcar rumble back to life.

"Sweetie," Beatrice said, looking up at him, "it can't get any messier."

"It always can, love."

"Bruce!" Brandon barked from behind him. "I really cannot stress how imperative it is we get a move along."

"Sorry, love," and Bruce delivered his favoured "Thunder from Down Under" that snapped her head back and returned her to the runway, flat against her back. "Got to run, and I'm not going to leave you at my back." He hoped she appreciated that he'd proven her wrong about not being able to learn from his mistakes.

Bruce had just secured the passenger's door when a bright glare suddenly flooded across their escape. The armoured transport that had been waiting for them outside the warehouse was now bearing down the runway, heading straight for them.

"Anytime now, Brandon," Bruce said, pulling what he hoped was a lap belt across himself.

Brandon looked across the dash, leaned over and flipped a few switches in front of Bruce. Two red lights flickered on. "Damn."

"Brandon?" Bruce asked quietly, the lights of the vehicles growing brighter.

"What about . . ." He flipped another switch and another light appeared. This one was green, and released what looked like a control stick that landed by Bruce's right hand.

"Brandon!"

The Canadian reached across Bruce and grabbed the control stick. Headlamps flipped upwards, and then the darkness between them and the Department's armoured transport was suddenly interrupted by wild flashes and streaks of fire erupting from the front of the motorcar. The vehicle bearing down on them began to swerve, but then burst into flame as bullets tore into it.

Brandon released the trigger, then flipped the switches on the dash which returned the headlamps to their proper place.

"Next time, Bruce," Brandon spoke frankly, "read the accompanying field report. It can prove useful."

The automobile launched into the creeping sunrise, Department agents scattering in their wake and lost in too much chaos to stop their escape. Brandon and Bruce were soon out in the streets of London, seen by no one other than the odd Blue Bottle or those who served an office during twilight hours. Even with their substantial lead, Bruce continued to watch for pursuit from hidden places now emerging in the early light of dawn; but the Department, it seemed, had counted on taking them at the warehouse. He didn't allow himself to relax until they were outside of the grips of the city proper and in greener surroundings of simple country homes on the outskirts.

"I do hope Wellington remembered to top the boilers before leaving the Americas," Brandon spoke as they followed the growing light of morning towards Yorkshire.

Bruce knew deep in his bones Books was the kind of bloke who saw to little details like that.

SIXTEEN

❦

In Which a Colonial Pepperpot
Keeps Her Enemies Closer

Stepping through the doorway, with Sophia draped over one shoulder, Eliza was entirely unprepared for what she would find. Wellington and Sound went through first, and she followed on their heels, wondering not for the first time how she had managed to end up hauling the sleeping Italian; it was a little too enlightened of her male companions she thought. Eliza dropped the faintly snoring Sophia into a chaise longue, and looked around.

The office was not lavish by any means. In fact, it looked as if the office had been once a classroom large enough for a variety of lessons and subjects. When she saw the papers on the desk bearing the Ministry crest, she knew their connection had been a success. They were back at Whiterock.

Sound had already pulled his pocket watch out and, having located a nearby grandfather clock, was adjusting it accordingly. It was hard to imagine that they had lost so much time, and she shuddered to think what might have happened to her compatriots while they were away. Outside the many windows, rain was falling steadily, a usual summer event in

Yorkshire, so it made it hard to see the condition of the estate or to judge what season they had arrived at.

When she turned around, Sound was locking the doorway they had just stepped through. He then placed his chrono-model on a table, making himself—and the humour was not lost on her—right at home. She then noticed a desk that looked as if it had been occupied recently. Reports. Maps. Agendas for Research and Design and Mission Training. The gamble on the other side of the door had been a rousing success. They were not only back at Whiterock, but they had established a connection in Sound's temporary office.

Checking her remaining stock of bullets, Eliza leaned up against the window searching the grounds for any sign of activity, be it Ministry agents on survival training or Department agents intending to catch them by surprise. She didn't have much ammunition left after the firefight in the Archives, but hopefully it wouldn't be needed. Peering through the crack between the doors, Eliza heard softly filtered music coming from down one of the darkened corridors. It seemed as if Whiterock was just waking up, but that hardly meant the estate was secure.

Eliza ground her teeth together in frustration. Just when she thought she could accept time travel as a feasible innovation, variables she could have never trained for surfaced. Between their departure and present time—whatever that was—Whiterock could have changed from haven to trap.

"Any idea what time it is?" she finally asked. "Or the date, for that matter."

Sound flipped up the latches of the chrono-model's case, and the silver case began to open on its own accord. With a satisfied glance over the clockwork device now unfolding across the table, he strode over to the desk and perused the papers there. "From the looks of things, business as usual. No unexpected turn of events." His eyes flicked up to the end of the desk. "And a desk calendar. Oh, Cassandra, you are a dear."

"Doctor Sound?" Eliza insisted.

"Oh, yes—the twenty-third of May, 1897," he replied. "As close to that blackout I told you about as Event Control can manage."

The floor felt as if it teetered underneath her. She suddenly had no idea where to look. Her world felt as if it were to spin out of control . . .

. . . but then a set of hands caught her as she felt her knees buckle from underneath her. Eliza was not one for fainting fits, but taking a breath was proving quite the challenge.

"Eliza?" Wellington said her name, and for a moment she didn't answer. It had all been wonderful fiction inside Sound's marvellous device, but he had actually done it. Somehow the sands of Mars had seemed more acceptable than this.

Looking into Wellington's hazel eyes gave her a focus point, and then the ground underfoot steadied. She took a breath, and Whiterock suddenly took on a strange, vivid clarity.

"Time travel," she managed with a nervous giggle. "We have just returned from time travelling, did you know that?"

The archivist patted her hand. "Welcome to where I was back in Sound's Event Control. It is quite incredible when you think about it, yes?"

Eliza wanted to laugh as, after having just taken in a sunset on Mars, everything seemed up for grabs. At that particular moment, Sophia del Morte stirred on the chaise longue.

Like everything that damned woman did, it attracted male attention. Wellington and Doctor Sound immediately went to where the assassin now propped herself up. With some satisfaction she saw Wellington draw a Remington-Elliot. Eliza heard the soft click of the safety, the high-pitched whine of its compressors priming, and it brought a smile to her lips.

Sophia looked around her, her gaze flickering over the details of the office. "How did I . . ." Eliza did take in some delight seeing the Italian at a complete loss. Sophia had no idea what she had slept through. "Where are we?"

"My home, signorina," Wellington replied, his fingers splaying around the handle of his three-barrelled pistol.

Her eyes went to each corner of the room. Perhaps this was her habit—find any and all potential exits, look for any clear indicators as to geography and location.

When her eyes landed on Sound, kneeling in front of her, Sophia looked as if something came to her. Then her gaze darkened as she pointed at him. "You drugged me!" Considering her past, the accusation being delivered in such a tone was laughable.

"Forgive me, signorina," the director said, opening his hands wide before her. "Precautions had to be taken."

"We were trapped underwater," she began, motioning around them. "How did we—"

"The Ministry has many contingency plans in place. Your presence in the midst of one, however, was not taken into account so we had to improvise." Doctor Sound's expression became somewhat sombre. *An amazing ability that Sound must have mastered through years of time travelling,* Eliza thought. *He should have sought a career on the stage.* "You suffered some rather unfortunate side effects, Miss del Morte, to the tranquiliser I administered. It is just after eight o'clock in the morning, on May twenty-third. 1897. You have lost nearly a year to slumber."

"*Mio Dio!* May twenty-third?" Her eyes filled with tears, but any sobs were muffled by her hands. Blinking her eyes tightly, she covered her face for a moment and, on taking a deep breath, said, "You may be too late. The Maestro's plan nears completion."

"The Maestro's plan?" asked Sound with such a chill in his voice it was hard to believe he even knew how to be jovial. "I suspected we would need to move against the Queen after discovering her secret, but you're saying this Maestro persona has an agenda of his own?"

"In a manner of speaking, yes," she answered.

"In a manner of speaking?" Eliza barked out a laugh. She knew Sophia del Morte to be as reliable as a poisonous snake, and Wellington's discomfort in her presence only served as validation. Their history together had begun with her kidnapping him for the House of Usher, and progressed downhill from there. "Can we accept any words out of her mouth as anything other than a deception?"

"What is happening, it is not entirely the Maestro's doing," Sophia insisted, opening a small pouch at her side.

Eliza's hand went for one of her pistols, but it was Wellington's that pressed against the assassin's head. In his eyes was none of his trademark affability. He was now the stone-cold killer his father had created here at Whiterock. "Very. Small. Moves."

Sophia stared at Wellington, moving deliberately and

evenly, as if she were a clockwork figure. Her hand dug into the belt pouch and came out as a closed fist. Keeping her eyes on Wellington, she slowly opened her palm to show two small vials, one pale emerald, the other blue.

"What, pray tell, would these be?" Doctor Sound asked on taking them from her hand and holding each up to the light.

"A doctor named Jekyll has been feeding them to not only the Duke of Sussex, but also to your queen. This is what keeps them under the man's sway."

"Jekyll?" Wellington asked. "Eliza, isn't that the name in the ledger?"

"Check there, Books," the director said, motioning to the grand desk across the room. Wellington pushed aside several stacks of papers and files until finally finding the ledger. "As you can see, Miss Braun, I was planning to tend to this acquisition of yours upon my return."

"Considering everything happening on that first night here, Director," Eliza said, "I'm just thankful you hadn't lost the bloody thing."

Wellington opened the book to the two pages featuring notes on Peter Lawson, and schematics on the Maestro's apparatus. Eliza caught Sophia flinching at the sight of Jekyll's sketches.

"He must truly be a monster," Eliza said to her, "to get a reaction like that from the likes of you."

"At first I thought the Maestro was the one to be feared. I was mistaken." Sophia slowly shook her head. "When I found Jekyll looming over that young boy, strapped to his table, I knew this particular madness was not for me. He had caught the child in his office."

"Callum!" Eliza felt her skin run cold. "This Jekyll was the children's mark. He was the doctor that took him!" Her eyes welled with angry, frustrated tears as she turned to Wellington.

"You know this child?" Sophia's already pale skin grew paler. "I am sorry, signorina. I do not know exactly what Jekyll did to him, but I saw him administer the green liquid to this Callum of yours."

Eliza sank down onto a chair opposite of everyone, any sort of earlier desire to deal out bodily harm to Sophia stolen in an instant. It didn't matter. Nothing mattered. She'd failed the Seven. She had promised to get Callum back, and because of Sound's time machine, they had lost approximately a year. What could this foul Doctor Jekyll have done to Callum in that time? What would he be now?

Wellington advanced on Sophia, his whole body rigid with fury as he grabbed the assassin by the arm. "You stood by while this child was experimented on?"

She wrenched herself free. "I wouldn't have stood a chance against the Maestro and his men—"

"Agent Books, have a care," Sound ordered gently. "Stand down."

"I beg your pardon, Director?" he snapped.

"I said," Sound repeated, his tenor never changing, making it all the more menacing, "have a care. Stand. Down." He was flipping through Jekyll's ledger. "When you find true evil, you must stand against it. Someone must or all will be lost."

"Pardon my frankness, sir," Wellington began, "but what are you on about?!"

"Think about all this. The manipulation of the Duke of Sussex. The Queen. That ledger." Eliza felt detached from the conversation, but she knew she was talking somehow. It was the last side she would ever expect to take, but Sophia could not be maligned. At least, at this particular point. "Jekyll is a man of detail. He would notice those missing vials. He would know who took them. Sophia risked her life. For us."

For a moment Eliza thought she might have observed guilt in the assassin's eyes, but then it was gone. "Touching sentiment, but I think of my own safety first, as we all do."

"Not all of us," Eliza broke in.

A creak from behind the door snapped Eliza out of her melancholy. She slapped the Remington-Elliot out of Wellington's hand and into her own, and crossed the room in wide, silent strides as she held the pistol out towards the office's double doors.

She felt one of her pistols leave its holster, and Wellington flanked her. "Just wait. In case we are wrong."

Eliza nodded and watched the door as Wellington crept up to it. Bracing himself against the wall, he stretched his hand out to the middle of the right door. He gave two knocks in close succession, a pause, two quick knocks again, another pause, and then one solid knock.

From the other side of the door, the pattern of knocks repeated.

"Ready, Welly?" she whispered.

Wellington rapped his knuckles against his own bullet-proof corset. "Be prepared. Be vigilant."

He opened the door, revealing a Lee-Metford-Tesla and two Rickies pointing back at them, but only for a moment.

"Books? Braun?" came the gravelly baritone of Lachlan King. The two hand cannons he brandished returned to their holders before he stretched his arms out wide. "Lovely to see you back, my friends."

Even after their embrace ended, Wellington felt the need to shake Lachlan's hand with great vigour. "It is a very great relief to be back, sir."

The older man greeted Eliza with a flourish, a delighted laugh, and a friendly embrace for her as well. Ever the charmer. "Mavericks? You?" she asked, motioning to the combination pistol and hand cannon holstered at his side. "I always thought of you brandishing something more elegant."

Lachlan tapped the lapels of his velvet coat. "How do you think I have lived this long in the Queen's service?" he asked her with a rakish wink.

"Doctor Sound," Cassandra Shillingworth said, resting the rifle over her shoulder. "Glad to have you back, sir."

"Ah, Cassandra," the director said, placing a light kiss on her cheek, "considering the looks of things, may I assume all is well here at the manor?"

She smiled just a fraction. "Our operatives are shipshape and Bristol-fashion, and have been taking real care to follow your orders. There have been a few"—she paused for a moment—"naysayers on that count, but nothing I couldn't handle."

"Bloody Bruce," Eliza said, crossing her arms over her chest. "Never could take orders from a woman."

"Pardon me for asking, sir," Cassandra said, looking at the new arrivals, "but we have patrols on the perimeter, guards at each entry point, and the estate wired with alarms. How did you—?"

"Our escape plan if conditions called for it," Sound said. "Æthergate travel. Courtesy of the R&D office."

"And that's why he's director," Lachlan chuckled. "Shall I go ahead and gather everyone up?"

"Probably best," Sound replied. "Well done, Cassandra. I'll meet you downstairs."

"Very good, sir," she replied, then excused herself from the room.

Alone once again in Sound's Whiterock office, the director shared a glance at the three of them. "So, are we ready to speak with the troops?"

Out of the corner of her eye Eliza saw Sophia tense just a little. "Yes," she and Wellington replied.

"Good." The director smoothed his moustache a little as he turned to Sophia. "I will serve as your champion, signorina. Have no fear."

"Sir," Eliza said, "what about our"—she was about to say "time travel" but caught Sophia crooking her eyebrows—"escape from the Restricted Area?"

"Æthergate technology is hardly alien to our people, Miss Braun," the director said, loosing a wink only she and Wellington could see.

Descending down the stairs, they could hear a commotion from the grand hall that lifted her spirits. Apparently, more agents had found their way to Whiterock. When the four of them came around the corner, they were greeted by elation and applause.

"I don't think this ballroom has seen a crowd like this since one of my mother's parties," Wellington remarked. "She would be thrilled at this turnout."

Eliza thought that the outfits were not quite as splendid as they would have been for a grand social occasion, but the number of them present certainly lightened her heart. The operatives who had first arrived at Whiterock were all in attendance. She was able to see that immediately, but the crowd had more than doubled since then. Eliza recognised many of the faces all beaming back at her: Commander Constance McGee of the Ministry Shock troops, Robert Smith from the India branch, and Matthew Flowerdew, who'd been in deep cover in Brazil, were the ones she was able to pick out immediately.

"Eliza!" a strong female voice boomed out. *"Kia ora!"*

Eliza blinked, hearing the familiar greeting of her home. She turned to see the Maori woman, who had always served as an inspiration for Eliza, pushing her way through the press towards her. She could scarce believe it. "Director Murphy?"

Aroha Murphy, head of the New Zealand office, embraced her with what Eliza believed to be all the love from her homeland. Then in one smooth gesture she pressed her nose and forehead to Eliza's, causing their breaths to mingle. Eliza felt a lump in her throat; the *hongi* brought back a flood of memories from New Zealand.

"So glad to see you safe," her mentor said, her smile bright and just as Eliza remembered.

"Likewise." She smiled. She took a good look at her, chuckling lightly as she touched the woman's feather cloak. "Still wearing a *kahu huruhuru* against the clothes of a *pakeha*, I see."

"Some things in the world remain constant, Eliza," Aroha said, running her fingers through her salt-and-pepper hair. "Aotearoa misses you. We have saved a place for you there, when you are able to come home."

Eliza took a breath at the sentiment. New Zealand seemed even further away than it had before. Quickly, before she became lost in memories, she turned to introduce Wellington to Aroha. Instead, she was delightfully taken aback at seeing Lady Caroline grabbing him for a very uncharacteristic squeeze. The outpouring of emotion was entirely informal, and rather un-British, but she found herself enjoying it. When they had left, the group at Whiterock had been demoralised, kicked about, and just lucky to be alive. This larger gathering had the air of an army, a well-trained, tight-knit unit of talented specialists ready to serve for the betterment of the Empire.

"Eliza Doo!" Barry Ferguson grabbed hold of her. *Soditall,* Eliza thought, returning the hug of her childhood friend. "Great to see you," the young agent practically shouted in her ear. "I had a few bob on the fact you were still alive." He glanced around. "Won't tell you who bet the other way."

"Please, everyone," she heard Sound call out over the throng, "agents, please, come to order."

The din had settled by the time Eliza joined Wellington at

the end of the ballroom. Staying very close to Sound was Sophia del Morte. Undoubtedly, that was the safest place for her to be at present.

"I must say it is very good to see you all," Sound began, "though I am sad to find some faces missing from this crowd."

A soft murmuring arose but no one interrupted as he continued.

"Cassandra here tells me that you have all been hard at work, fulfilling the instructions I left with her . . . at least mostly." His gaze drifted to Bruce, who at least had the good sense to look ashamed. "So, where to begin? We set out to secure the Archives. We managed to secure more than half of the finds you and your predecessors returned from the field. Sadly, we were besieged and Miggins Antiquities was lost."

A long silence followed as that ill news sank in. It was Agent Flowerdew that broke it.

"The bloody Department," he swore, tugging angrily on his beard.

"One would assume," Sound said, his face set in a dispassionate mask, "but at least now, we have discovered our true enemy, and this is where things get particularly peculiar. Even for a merry band like ours." Perhaps that should have brought a round of questions, but the remnants of the Ministry were hanging on every word by now. "He calls himself the Maestro, a manifestation of the Duke of Sussex come to life."

"Sussex?" barked Bruce. "That wanker?"

"That *wanker* as you so elegantly put it has ensnared the Queen in his nefarious plot. Dark times threaten us, my friends, but Fortune has smiled upon us. One of the Maestro's hirelings has defected to our side." He held out his hand and gestured to the assassin. "I will now turn this address to Sophia del Morte."

Eliza gave a start at the collected flash of metal. Remington-Elliots. Rickies. Crackshots. Shanghai Surprises. It was a wild collection of armaments that, seconds ago, were not there.

"That was impressive," Wellington whispered in her ear.

"Much better response time than at the Red Lion," she added.

Sound was already in front of her, his hands up in front of him as if he could fend off bullets. "Now I know many of you know her dossier, and yes, some of you might have even tangled with this lady, but she brings us valuable inside information. She also comes to us at significant risk."

"As significant as the risk we've shared with her in the past?" Lady Caroline asked, the Egyptian-made "Ra-gun" still and steady in her grasp.

Eliza had always liked Lady Caroline, and this moment just affirmed that.

"She brings to us secrets that could very well tip the scales in our favour." Sound continued with a slightly sinister smile on his face, "So, to offer a variation on an Arabic proverb, our enemy's friend . . . is now our friend."

"Acquaintance," Eliza grumbled, "never friend."

Her sentiment must have carried as a ripple of laughter crept through the ranks. It was enough of a relief of tension that agents holstered their weapons. Eliza enjoyed her kick into touch, but a cold glare from Doctor Sound robbed her of her grin.

"Tell us what you know, Signorina del Morte," Sound urged.

To her credit, though, pale as she looked at knowing those collected before her would happily send her to her grave, she stood straighter and replied, "Your duke and queen are not in their proper minds," Sophia began. "They are under the influence of a mad doctor. A man named Henry Jekyll."

"Jekyll?" a mechanical voice called out.

The masked figure, Agent Maulik Smith, worked his way through the ranks of agents. Anyone else under Maulik's "stare" would be unsettled, but Sophia was as a statue.

"You are certain it is Doctor Henry Jekyll?" he asked again, the rasp of his respirator underscoring his words.

"You know this doctor?" Sound asked, with a tilt of his head.

Maulik looked over to the director. "I made his acquaintance at the Water Palace in Rajasthan. A young man of considerable talent, but he had a reputation of testing ethical boundaries. Safe to say, when I caught up with the good doctor, he was"—he tapped his fingertips together, then continued—"not himself."

Now Maulik had Sound's rapt attention. "How so?"

"My Queensbury Rules emptied a full clip into him. He

should have been cleft in two." Maulik shook his head. "Barely left a rash on Jekyll."

"He accomplishes what you describe through serums he is still attempting to perfect," Sophia broke in. "These formulas, while making their subjects susceptible to suggestion, also increase strength, senses, and—in the case of your queen—restore youth."

"Youth?" Eliza glanced at Sound, who did not appear at all surprised by this development. "Our queen has her youth back?"

"After all we have witnessed in recent days," the director said to Eliza, "you would dare to doubt such a thing?" He silenced the other sceptical agent by holding up his hand. "I have seen Victoria myself, as young and vibrant as she was the day she took the throne, but considerably different in temperament I am afraid."

"Your queen mentioned rallying the Empire, something she says is desperately needed," Sophia continued. "Her and the Maestro's plans will unite all the corners of the Empire during her Jubilee celebration."

"Where is the Jubilee going to be held?" asked Eliza.

"St. Paul's Cathedral," Shillingworth offered. "It's been in all the papers for months."

"Right then, so the Jubilee is where the Maestro and Her Majesty intend to carry out their mad plan." Eliza tried to remain calm, but the idea of the Queen of England being in league with the Maestro had temporarily disturbed her focus. "What is in sight of St. Paul's?"

"The river, the financial district . . ." Wellington's voice trailed off. "She's unlikely to want to destroy any of those and bring down the Empire with it."

"The East End," came a small voice from behind them.

All heads turned back to the great hall's doorway. Eliza craned her neck to see who had spoken, and her breath caught in her throat.

Quickly, Eliza shoved her way through the agents. When she broke out of the crowd, Serena in her turn leapt away from the Ministry Seven standing by the door, and wrapped her arms around Eliza's neck. The New Zealander held the child close, making no effort to stop her tears from falling.

292 Pip Ballantine and Tee Morris

"You came back, Miss Eliza," Serena whispered in her ear, sounding very vulnerable.

"Of course I did," the agent said. "I promised you I would, and I keep my promises."

It had only been a few days for Eliza, but for the children it had been far longer. Over Serena's shoulder, Eliza looked up at the Seven. They were clean, but their eyes were shadowed. No one mentioned the name "Callum" but it hung between them nonetheless.

"The Queen hasn't made her dislike of that end of the city a secret, now has she?" Christopher's soft tone was full of sadness, keeping everyone to silence.

Eliza looked up to the eldest of the Ministry Seven. What a difference one year had made with this young man. The resolve in his eyes had only grown stronger over all those months.

"No, she has not," Doctor Sound replied, glancing down at his shoes as if embarrassed to mention his once-friend's attitude. "She told me to cut back on the investigation into the Rag and Bone Murders, and she may have muttered something about the poor deserving it."

Eliza knew that Victoria would not be the first monarch to massacre her own people, and if she was mad and controlled by this Jekyll, then she was not herself. It made sense too; in her early days Victoria had struggled fruitlessly against the rule of Parliament. The people had turned against her once, so in her mind, warped by Jekyll's serum, they could do it again.

"Perhaps," Eliza broke in, wiping any sign of tears from her face, "she means to kill two birds with one stone; unite the people, and get rid of a London eyesore. When I was a little girl, there was a large earthquake in Canterbury."

"Everyone, Maori and white man alike, pulled together to help those displaced," Aroha said. "Nothing knits a nation together like a calamity."

"And there is surely no better time," Sound said in a low, serious tone, "to have a crisis than on the happiest day for the Empire."

"She will never need Parliament ever again," Wellington whispered in horror. "Like her ancestors she can be absolute monarch."

For a moment there was silence as they all contemplated what the Empire would look like if that happened.

"We still have time." Barry stood up near the back and broke the spine of the chilling silence. "The Jubilee is still a month away."

"I believe Ferguson here is right," the director said, causing the energetic agent to sit back down hurriedly. "I had you all training for a reason and now we have the details. Now the time has come to apprehend this Henry Jekyll and return order to the Empire."

"Before you rally your troops," Sophia interrupted, her smile slightly crooked, "you should know I delivered certain plans I stole from the Phoenix Society to the Maestro."

"Doctor Havelock's Mechamen?" Wellington blurted out. "I thought they had been lost in the destruction of his estate!"

The assassin's smile was chilling. "They most certainly were not. I saw to that. The Mark II and Mark III Mechamen the Maestro has built are magnificent and deadly."

"I see," said the director, showing no sign of deflation. He then produced his pocket watch. "Fortunately for us, a weapon from one of our allies we will need in the coming fight should arrive . . . any minute . . ."

An explosion, louder and sharper than thunder, echoed through the valley, causing the windows in the ballroom and the chandelier to shudder. The tinkling of glass and crystal overhead had barely ceased before agents lost all formality, and dashed to Whiterock's windows to see what had arrived.

"Now," Sound chortled, slipping his watch back in his vest pocket. "A little decorum if you please, agents . . ."

Wellington walked over to Eliza and Serena who apparently had no intention of releasing her grip on her. He held out his arm to her. "Shall we?"

They joined their fellow agents, who were all at the windows scanning the skies. Then a dark spec appeared in the sky, falling fast from the high cloud cover. Then parachutes emerged from either end of the object. What was at one moment nothing more than a falling machine now became an object possessing a modest amount of control and intent. In a matter of seconds, the object now revealed itself as a gigantic cylinder, looking to land somewhere on Whiterock's estate.

Eliza felt Serena's grip tighten on her hand. She looked down at the child, but Serena was not looking outside or at her; she was looking at Sophia, who was standing next to Wellington.

"Not tempted to run for the hills?" Eliza found herself asking the assassin. "Hide out on the Continent perhaps?"

Sophia gave her a withering look, but did not reply.

Serena glanced between the three of them, and a slow smile spread on her face. "The director promises what could be an absolutely wonderful adventure! Let's give that nasty doctor a bloody nose!"

Eliza looked over at Wellington, locking eyes with him, and smiled slowly. "As they say, from the mouth of babes."

He grinned back at her, and for this moment that was quite enough for her.

SEVENTEEN

❦

Wherein Mr. Books and Miss Braun
Take in a Parade

"Well, she certainly has a crowd." Eliza lay flat on her front, binoculars to her eyes, on the top of the Carlington building looking towards St. Paul's Cathedral, the wind blowing her hair back and forth. Wellington was a comforting presence to her right, scanning the crowd as she did. The woman on her left, however much she was doing the same thing as the Ministry agents, continued to unsettle her.

Fortunately, or unfortunately, Sophia del Morte did serve a purpose, though. "Do you see him?" Eliza asked.

"I find it highly unlikely Doctor Jekyll would be mingling amongst the crowd," Sophia returned briskly, as if this whole thing was an annoyance to her.

"A large crowd of nameless, faceless citizens, all gathered in one place; and in the chaos both now and what will come, how many people could suddenly go missing?" Wellington let out a huff. "Yes. Highly unlikely."

Eliza smiled at her lover's gallant tendencies—it was quite endearing really.

Their initial objective to tag the Queen of England with Blackwell's tracking isotope, just in case they lost her in the pending madness, and then snatch her right in front of her adoring public had all seemed simple enough . . . back at Whiterock. They had planned for this event, put all their best minds and strategists to work, and their distraction was as good as it was going to get. Wellington had his bag of tools at his side, and she had hers.

Now, even with the one person in their ranks who could identify the mad scientist while not in his monster form, the secondary objective—capturing or eliminating Doctor Jekyll—looked to be a lofty goal.

Through the binoculars, Eliza could see the crowd below, and it was a vast one. Such a collection of people introduced variables. The chaos of a crowd remained the one variable difficult to predict. It was why the Ministry operated covertly and in the shadows. Even the best laid plans could easily go awry in this situation.

Citizens of London poured out of every building and draped themselves off lampposts, ledges, and balconies. Then there were the soldiers, and it was not the thousands of soldiers all serving the Queen and showing up to pay honourable deference who looked to be the main problem. It was several divisions of men and women dressed in grey uniforms bearing a Union Jack on one shoulder, and on the other a strange insignia she did not recognise.

"Sophia," Eliza spoke softly, "those people in the grey uniforms. Are those the Maestro's private army?"

"The Grey Ghosts." Sophia lowered her specs. "I take it you recognise those Gatling packs they wear?"

"I remember Havelock's men having those." Eliza looked over at her with a scowl. "Your design, as well?"

"He was a man of many faults, but Devereux Havelock respected my work." Sophia returned her eyes to the binoculars. "Do have a care around the Grey Ghosts. I remember finding my schematics in Jekyll's laboratory one day. Who knows what changes he has made."

"How many do you think are out there?" she asked.

"Five thousand," Sophia replied, as if she were merely conveying the number of apples in a barrel.

"Lovely," Wellington grumbled. "Add one more to the many variables . . ."

Eliza cast a glance over to the collection of haversacks they had borne with them to this isolated rooftop. Even with the supplies her fellow operatives carried, and the preparations Axelrod, Blackwell, and the Seven had carried out the night before, there was no way the Ministry would be able to stop the Maestro's army, especially armed with mini-Gatlings on each forearm. *Add one more to the many variables,* as Wellington observed.

What they would have to their advantage: the chaos Wellington mentioned earlier. Once their madcap plan was under way, it would be bedlam in the streets. They would move swiftly and unseen within the madness.

The steps leading up the cathedral were swathed in deep purple, and lining the carpet were gigantic bells, painted to resemble brilliant daylilies of orange, red, and yellow. The bells pointed outwards, their "stalks" leading back to a huge metallic podium positioned at the centre of a raised dais. With flowers, flags, and draperies of every colour hanging from balconies and windows, today promised to be a gala of highest pageantry and spectacle.

"I see a lot of familiar tweed," Wellington muttered in an undertone. "The Department's down among the crowd, and they seem to have a lot of bags with them."

"It's bound to get very ugly, very quickly." Eliza pointed to the device on the stairs, and rubbed her eyes. She feared a headache of epic proportions was on its way. "What do you make of those bells?"

Wellington leaned in closer to her. "Some sort of aural amplification system, probably working with that podium. I would hazard our queen is about to make a grand speech that she doesn't want anyone to miss." He gestured back along the street. "If you look, there are smaller ones down all the roads."

Eliza would have made some quip about the vanity of monarchs, but from street level, music, specially created by Elgar for the occasion, blared into the morning, drowned out by a groundswell of approval from the Queen's subjects. Eliza could see Sophia turn her attention farther up the street, in the direction of cheers and ovations that were considerably louder than the music.

"Movement," Sophia uttered. "The Queen is en route."

"We have more than a few minutes yet," Wellington said as horses and carriages suddenly appeared from around the corner below them, the crowd waving their flags furiously, sending warm wishes and welcome. "These are the dignitaries. Her Majesty will be the last carriage."

It would have been far easier to take Victoria from the procession further away, say when she was touring the streets, but Eliza understood the reasoning: they had to wait until the Queen was in public and made her intentions clear. Otherwise, the Ministry would appear as nothing more than a treasonous splinter of radicals bent on overthrowing the throne. As Tower Hill had not seen anyone's head cut off for a good few years, Eliza preferred not to start up any old traditions.

Leaning across, she planted a quick kiss on Wellington's cheek. In turn he grabbed her hand and squeezed it. None of them wanted to say the words, but she understood completely. If she had to die in an attempt to save the Empire, then there was no one else she wanted to do it with.

She would just have to pretend Sophia wasn't there if it came to that.

The streams of guards on prancing horses and rattling carriages just seemed to whip the crowd into a greater frenzy, and for a moment it was hard to hear or see anything in the flapping of flags and the cheers of the masses.

"I think we're getting closer to Victoria's arrival," Wellington called over the roar of the crowd. "I'm beginning to see family."

And then she appeared.

Voices as if descended from heaven sang out "Te Deum" from the steps of St. Paul's as the Warders of the Tower of London snapped to attention. Eliza felt her heart begin to race harder, sucking in a deep breath when she caught a glance through the coach window of the unmistakable profile of Queen Victoria, backlit underneath her mourning veil. The closed carriage that bore her was a spectacle worthy of a grand monarch, all gilded and painted, shining bright under the breathtaking summer's day. Quite different from the previous sombre appearances she'd made, which had been all black against black, a mourning with no end in sight. Through Eliza's binoculars, she could see Victoria's subjects craning their necks, swaying from side to side to catch a glimpse of their queen, who had not been seen in public for many, many years. A hand from inside the carriage rose, drawing a mad elation from the crowd.

"Any sign of Jekyll?" Eliza asked, tightening her hand on the edge of the building.

"None," Sophia replied in a cool tone.

He was down there. Eliza felt it. God would not miss the grand unveiling of his creation for an experiment in the lab.

The carriage pulled to a stop, its horses stamping and chafing at their bits. As the door swung open a hush descended on the crowd, even as they waved their banners back and forth like clockwork automatons. After the carriage jostled sharply back and forth, two figures emerged into the sunlight, both swathed in black, making them pop against the brilliance of the day. They were also bedecked in the mourning fashion of Victoria's youth, so heavily petticoated and bulky that it was impossible to tell age or sex. They ascended St. Paul's stairs at a quick, healthy pace, taking a place before the double pillars, the podium just within reach, and framed by the magnificence of the cathedral.

Eliza kept her voice low even though their rooftop was not exactly covered with people. "The Queen, last I heard, was not the most spry of the monarchy. Climbing those steps would have been impossible."

"Still doubting?" Sophia asked, crooking an eyebrow.

With nothing more than a silent look exchanged, Eliza crawled over to the centre of the rooftop and unfurled her satchel. Along with her rifle, there were several pistols, rounds of ammunition, a few select Experimentals that she knew might actually work, an assortment of quaint incendiary devices, and a small blanket.

As she began assembling the Mark IV on loan from Shillingworth, Eliza noticed Wellington's eyebrows rose.

"Is that all for you?" he asked.

"Yes," she replied, feeling her defences rise. "You have your devices from Captain Carter, so this is all mine."

"And I see," Wellington said, tapping his fingers on the *plures ornamentum*, "you managed to get your favourite toy back from R&D."

"With a few new surprises, I'm told," Eliza returned cheerily. "Never hurts to be prepared."

"The more time we share," Sophia cooed, "the more I like you, Signorina Braun."

"If this goes pear-shaped," Eliza scoffed, locking the barrel in place, "perhaps the del Morte clan would consider adopting me?"

Eliza returned back to the overlook point, loaded the modified projectile—a dart carrying Blackwell's creation of both tranquiliser and radioisotope—and covered the rifle with the blanket. With a final look at the sun, just to assure herself no brass fixture or lens would catch the light, she opened the scope.

Now, for the waiting game. The Queen had to implicate herself.

The front-most figure leaned forwards towards the device and began to speak. "Welcome, people of the Empire." The voice was soft, even with the help of the loudspeaker, and contained a tremulous shake to it.

Eliza *hated* waiting.

Down on the street, the soldiers' attention was straight ahead, even as the crowd swayed backwards and forwards like a restless animal.

Eliza disengaged the Mark IV's safety. Alongside the electric generator, the rifle's compressor hissed to life.

"On the occasion of Our Diamond Jubilee, We thank you for coming to celebrate the grandness of Our dominion." Victoria sounded so breathy that Eliza was surprised she had managed to make it up the stairs at all. It had to be oppressively hot under all that mourning lace too. "When We were nothing more than a young girl, We dreamed of becoming Queen and bringing this nation and all its outposts to glory. So much responsibility to shoulder, so much to undertake, but We bore the Empire with love, and with duty, and with honour, for We love its subjects as if it were Our own children . . ."

As the Queen rambled on, Eliza could feel herself becoming angry. This frail woman hardly acted like the threat that they had been told she was. Maybe the plan they were about to put into action to rescue her from a manipulative scientist was all a game. She looked over her shoulder to Sophia. Even with seeing the ledger, knowing of the Maestro's madness, could this plan be nothing more than an elaborate ruse to bring both Ministry and Department agents to an untimely end? Maybe the Queen's quick step up the stairs was due to nothing more than an extra strong pot of tea this morning?

"Then when We married We hoped Our dear Albert would help Us make that sweet dream a reality." As if someone had thrown a switch, her voice hardened even as she swayed on her feet. "But he was brutally taken from Us." Victoria composed herself, and with the help of her veiled supporter stood up again. When she did, her voice now suggested she was on the verge of tears, though it was impossible to tell under the veil. "We prayed to God on Our knees to give Us the strength to go on, and do Albert's work, but unfortunately the government of the nation had already turned its back on Us."

A wave of astonished whispers, peppered with discontent, wormed its way throughout the collected crowd. That was, assuredly, the first hint that suggested Sophia had not led them astray.

"Any sighting of Jekyll?" Eliza asked, daring to sweep the collected dignitaries through the rifle's scope.

"No," Sophia said, and her voice now contained a hint of fear.

Dammit, Jekyll, Eliza seethed inwardly. *Show yourself.*

Eliza felt Wellington shift at her side. "Movement. Out on the Thames."

"Yes, Welly, they're called boats," she hissed in reply. "People celebrating Vic's Jubilee and all that."

"Last time I checked, boats don't walk," Wellington snapped.

Eliza looked away from the scope and felt a chill creep under her skin. Five Mechamen were emerging from the Thames; river water poured from their sides, raining down on the crowds gathered along the banks. She sometimes saw them in her nightmares, but there they were: Doctor Havelock's unholy creations.

Yet there was something very different about these Mechamen.

"My God, Wellington!" She grabbed his binoculars and focused on the Mechamen's chests. "They're painted with the Stars and Stripes. What the hell is that about?"

"As you said, to galvanise a country you need a calamity."

Wellington now crawled over to the collection of haversacks as the screaming from further away began to reach them as if it were the Thames slowly coming in for high tide. "You also need a villain, don't you think?"

"The Maestro did not share this with me," Sophia stated, tilting her head as her jaw tightened. "This will be seen as an act of war."

"Your powers of perception are boundless to be sure, Sophia. *Now find Jekyll!*" Eliza barked, returning her attention to the rifle. "Wellington, time for that surprise of Captain Carter's."

"Already ahead of you," he replied from behind her.

In the scope, it appeared that Victoria was still droning on about her time on the throne, despite the mechanical wheezing of the approaching doom. As it had been with the earlier discontent the Queen voiced about Parliament, a new emotion was now infesting the masses: fear. The more she rattled on, the more nervous the crowd got.

Still the Queen continued, "Our Empire is a glorious Empire, not without its losses, not without its failures, but with this Diamond Jubilee, the Empire shows the world its majesty, its fortitude, and its resolution—"

Her words were cut off by powerful explosions from the Thames. Eliza shot a glance over her shoulder. The "American" Mechamen were in sight, a trio marching past the ruins of what had been Southwalk Bridge. Their massive legs reached up and dug into the dry land of London's East End, their massive arm cannons spinning up as they continued inland. Surprisingly, initially there was no wild panic, no mad scramble for shelter. The people of the East End merely stood under the shadow of the steel giants, stunned into a deathly silence.

That silence vanished under the firestorm that tore across the East End. Bullets blasted through a modest row house until its middle sagged and then surrendered to the swift, terrifying damage dealt to it. Even from where the Queen held court at St. Paul's, people could be seen falling from windows, plummeting to their deaths while smoke and debris expelled into the clear morning's sky, a grotesque scar marring the wonder and majesty of the celebration.

Eliza brought the crosshairs of the scope back upon the

Queen. Nothing to implicate the throne in any wrongdoing, save for a backhand against Parliament. Still at the podium, her black fashion made her a more-than-easy target, but no provocation had been given. In fact, she appeared to be cowering in the moment . . .

That moment turned quickly however, as she placed her hand on an attendant's arm, and he grabbed her shoulder. Her body went rigid, her back arching as if it were an archer's bow, and then she turned to the direction of the Mechamen. Something about her posture and stride made her appear taller than her usual, diminutive size.

"Sophia," Eliza called, her heart racing, "the attendant currently flanking the Queen, is that . . ."

"That's him!" Sophia cried out, losing all of her cool assassin demeanour. "That's Jekyll!"

"My people!" They must have pushed the loudspeaker to its absolute limit, because the Queen's voice rose over the screams, the firing of guns in the distance, and even the racket of the mechanical legs getting closer. Perhaps it was the informality of the Queen that wrenched their attention from the Mechamen. The people of London stopped and turned to their queen. It was truly a demonstration of the power of monarchy.

"I don't believe it," Eliza whispered. As she watched through her rifle scope, the Queen pulled aside heavy lace shrouds to reveal herself. The satisfaction in Victoria's face was frighteningly overwhelming as the black fabric gathered at her feet in folds like a bride's dress on her wedding night.

It was the Queen of England—but as no one had seen her for decades. The Victoria known to be a plump, old woman with an almost erotic fixation with the colour black was stricken from memory now, reduced to nothing more than a lie or propaganda. The monarch standing before her people was the Victoria that had ascended the throne, her smooth milky complexion of youth casting an angelic glow in harmony with her new raiment. She was clad in some kind of highly polished battle armour that threatened to blind Eliza in its brilliance. From its colour, Eliza guessed the steel had been mixed or at least decorated with gold plating as well. Victoria held aloft a sword and a shield as her ancestors might have worn on the field of battle.

"My people!" she called again. "I prayed, and God has seen fit to make me young and strong again, to repel our enemies and take back what was ours." Victoria held out her arms in their gleaming armour, the sword's tip catching the sunlight. "I am now *Regina Victoria in aeternum*. Queen Victoria the Eternal!"

The crowds were torn as to where to look—from the Thames loomed imminent death while before them was a queen known only from portraits.

Stepping free of similar black fabric was the Queen's second, the Maestro. Also clad in his steam-armour with helm firmly locked down, he stood beside the Queen for all the world like some mechanised knight answering the call of his monarch.

"God save the Queen!" his grating, artificial voice cried, amplified by the Queen's podium.

"God save the Queen!" thundered the East End.

It was quite the statement and Eliza, despite everything, was impressed. She'd not seen a show like it in her life—far outstripping the ringmaster in the circus she'd been so gobsmacked with when she was eight. The unfortunate truth was, the masses who rallied with their queen had no idea they were lamb for the slaughter. Jekyll's circus promised only death and destruction . . .

"I've got the doctor in my crosshairs," Eliza stated, her finger around the trigger.

"He is a secondary target," Sophia reminded her, not that the reminder was needed. "The Queen is our primary."

Wellington chimed in. "Eliza, the window of opportunity is closing."

Eliza's jaw twitched. Both of them were right. She returned to the scope. "Target acquired. I'm taking the shot."

The two Mechamen closest to the East End extended their Gatling guns forwards once more, but before they unleashed their special brand of hell on their own countrymen, a single, solitary shot cut through the chaos.

Jekyll doubled over in Eliza's scope. Now mass panic erupted in and around the dais, both the Queen and Sussex looking for any sign of who would dare strike down Doctor Henry Jekyll. Screams of horror filled the air for only scant heartbeats before the thunder returned from the iron giants, laying to waste the darker corners of London. Jets of flame arced against the brilliance of the blue sky while from the ground, pieces of the street and surrounding buildings were tossed high into the air.

"*Secondary* target is down," Sophia stated flatly.

"Snap decision. We had nothing to hold against the Queen, and I had to make the shot count," Eliza returned, feeling her hackles rise. "Now it's your turn. Assemble the grapplers." She then began breaking down the Mark IV. "Wellington, you're up."

"Very well, Miss Braun." The excitement in his voice was absolutely endearing. A child on Christmas morning, he was. "Time to fight the Maestro's monsters with one of our very own."

EIGHTEEN

❦

In Which a Clash of Titans Occurs

Wellington could still recall when he first saw the Mark II Mechamen; he had been horrified by them. Yet when he'd had a chance to inspect them more closely, he'd thought they were machines of incredible design and ingenuity. They were still machines serving only one purpose, but the skill in their creation had to be admired.

These newborn Mark IIs emerging from the Thames bearing the stars and stripes of the United States achieved the unimaginable for him: doubt. Wellington had applied many of the engineering advancements—albeit, on a smaller scale—to the development of the *Ares*, so he knew the designs of the Mark II intimately. At a glance, though, he could tell the Maestro had made modifications of his own. He could only guess what that would mean in battle.

"Right then," Wellington said, lowering the dark-lensed goggles over his eyes, "it's time."

He felt Eliza's lips touch his, her kiss lingering for a length of time he deemed inappropriate for such a public place. Even more so as they were on a mission at present. "I'll be right here. Don't worry," she whispered to him.

When you are close, I never worry, he thought. *I love you, Eliza.*

Cold metal pressed against his temples and then, moments later, the pulse points of his wrists assured him that Eliza had made the connections as per his instructions. Soon, according to what Captain Carter had told him, he would no longer "be" on the rooftop with Eliza.

"Ready, Welly?"

"Onwards into the great abyss." He let out a long breath.

He heard Eliza flip the switch—a switch he remembered was a bright shade of red—and then his vision filled with a blinding light. If he did not know any better, he would have thought he had been snatched up by the electroporter; but even with finding himself comfortably settled in the modified pilot's seat, Wellington knew that somehow he hadn't moved one inch. Surrounded by all this amazing technology from another world, Wellington could not forget the fact he was still on the rooftop with Eliza watching over him—just as she had always done in their time together, whether officially or unofficially for the Ministry. What he now saw all around him was merely a projection.

Granted, a very *vivid* projection—but a projection nevertheless.

Wellington looked out through the viewport stretching all around him, and saw only a murky darkness, but then light flickered from above and below his field of view, illuminating the blue-green waters of the Thames a few feet ahead of him. The controls, their gauges, and various indicator lights flickered to life, and Wellington understood each component's use, each readout's meaning. *Just relax and do what you do best: accept the fantastic,* Captain Carter had told him. *The rest will come naturally.*

But of course it will, Wellington thought, trying to ignore the insane pounding of his heart.

When he wrapped his hand around the knob he knew was the main power coupling, it struck him as fascinating how cool to the touch it was.

"Flourish," Wellington heard himself say out loud. "Enter Henry." He turned the knob to the right. "An entrance that would make Shakespeare envious."

He felt the machine around him lurch. The deep blue-green haze outside the viewport grew lighter and lighter in colour, until finally he saw the sun through thin curtains of water running down the front of his machine. Higher and higher he rose in the air until he felt his ascent stop.

Wellington felt that as a lurch, and yet he was still, in reality, next to Eliza, wearing the intricate goggles and bizarre gauntlets. Absolutely fascinating.

The sounds of distant screams and rapid gunfire interrupted his reverie.

Beneath his Martian Lander, water rushed around and between its legs as he closed in on the Mechamen. They were moving inland, tearing into the East End, so Wellington's advance went unnoticed. At least, for a time. The two lumbering leviathans still in the Thames came to a halt; and within the span of time it would have taken to send a wireless of some fashion, the lead Mark IIs quieted their Gatlings and slowly came around to face him.

Five Mechamen. One Martian Lander.

"Once more unto the breach," he muttered to himself as he brought levers up to a neutral position and pulled back a pressure regulator overhead.

Wellington flipped three switches on his tactical control panel, and in the centre of his window, a single crosshair appeared. *Look at the lead Mechaman,* he thought to himself, *and decide where you want to target.* It unsettled him how he suddenly knew what he needed to do, but Wellington merely took a deep breath, put his faith in God and Martian technology, and focused on the lead enemy's lower torso. The crosshair on his display blinked, then split to a second crosshair that remained connected to the first by—what he knew in that moment to be—a firing solution continuing to the second Mechaman. This crosshair blinked at a connection between the second Mechaman's waist and right leg, then split off to connect another crosshair at the third lead Mechaman's knee joint.

Odd symbols he recognised as the Martian language flared across the top of his viewpoint. Wellington read the letters as fluently as his native tongue and switched his attention to the controls in his grasp. His thumb flipped up a single amber switch on the top of the lever in his right hand, and from above his head he could hear generators spin up, their soft whine joined by a second low, thrumming cadence that resembled a heartbeat. Like his own, the heartbeat was running faster and faster until Wellington saw another Martian notification flash in the top of his viewport. Wellington squeezed the trigger in his hand, and heard a hard, sharp crack of thunder followed by an angry crackle of electricity, although what he saw leap from the top of his lander was nothing like electricity. This was death from another world.

The firestorm, a concentrated plume of heat and power, shot out from above Wellington's Lander and struck at the point of the first crosshair. The Mechaman lurched back, struggling to remain upright as the beam worked like a welder's torch. The beam sliced into the Mark II's central hull, and continuing downwards, liquefied the joint in the second Mechaman and the knee of the third. Targets two and three collapsed into waterfront warehouses, a great plume of flame and debris blossoming there as a grotesque flower threatening to consume anything in its path. The lead refused to fall, its drive to move, though, tore and strained at the now-weakened metal. With a metallic moan Wellington suspected came from somewhere deep within the inner workings, the Mechaman's torso sagged against itself, then swayed forwards and back. Something inside the monster—possibly a boiler—exploded, opening the tear further and throwing its balance completely off. As it fell, the remaining pair of Mechamen fired their weapons. Wellington's eyes jumped from one side of the control panel to the other. Lights flickered between green and yellow, while two gauges showed their respective needles drop slightly. The Lander's invisible shields would keep the Mechamen's bullets at bay, although he was far from indestructible. With enough bullets, this alien armour would be weakened, leaving only the Lander's external hull for protection.

The strange language flickered in the viewport's lower right corner, granting him a touch of hope. He targeted both Mechamen's heads, and waited for the signal to fire.

Without any warning, a blinding light filled his viewport. This sudden attack had to be one of the Maestro's modifications, courtesy of Thomas Edison.

Shields were now flickering between green, yellow, and red, but Wellington shoved the controller in his left hand forwards while his right reached for a small crank wheel above his head. He turned this crank clockwise purely on instinct. This was the "trust" Carter told him to never question that told Wellington to lean the Lander directly into the Mechaman's death ray's blast. The craft shuddered while needles bounced madly underneath their lenses. Wellington pushed hard against the left handle that protested against his effort. He glanced up at the blinding white viewport and read the notification blinking there.

So long as his shields could withstand . . .

Everything went still in the Lander suddenly. Wellington righted the Lander with one hand while flipping a row of switches above his head and turning a knob to "Full" with the other. The bouncing needles steadied but only for a moment as pressure gauges and power distribution bobbed in the red when the Lander stepped back to the left of the remaining Mechamen. His stomach lurched as he dipped low out of the lead Mark II's aim, its electric death ray crackling over his Lander and striking what Wellington could only guess was somewhere in or around the Old Bailey.

At least he possessed better mobility than the Mechamen. Caught by their death ray again, though, neither the shields nor he would last long. *Just a few more seconds,* he thought quickly.

The Martian language blinked back across the top of the viewport. The analytical engine, it seemed, was compensating for his new altitude and angle, and his heat ray remained primed. Wellington pulled back on the lever next to Attitude Control, and the Lander stood upright once more. The crosshairs ceased blinking. Indicator lights flipped from yellow to green. Wellington fired.

Both heads of the Mechamen incinerated on impact, leaving the metallic monsters without a central command. They were now decapitated statues standing within the Thames.

Easing back into the chair, Wellington let out a long, slow sigh. He could only imagine what the multitudes of people, some of whom had come from the farthest reaches of the Empire, were thinking on seeing a three-legged metallic spider downing five iron monsters bearing the colours of the United States. It was something they all had wondered about before they had returned to Whiterock.

That was exactly why this gift from Captain Carter came with a feature uncharacteristic of his Martian Landers.

His eyes turned to the single blue switch in his armrest. Wellington flipped the switch to the middle position, illuminating a small amber light alongside it. Lowering a microphone suspended from above his head, Wellington remembered Eliza's advice from the night before: *Keep it simple. Keep it brief.*

And make sure to send the Queen into a fit.

Another deep breath, and then Wellington flipped the switch to a "Transmit" position, turning the light from amber to red.

"God save the Empire," Wellington spoke into the microphone, then he returned the switch to standby.

And waited.

He could not tell if he was hearing the rumble of the crowd's approval from where he remained with Eliza or from within his Lander, but the support from the people was clear.

"NO!" roared a voice over the Jubilee's loudspeakers that would not go ignored or questioned. The Queen, still amplified by the device meant to carry her words of encouragement to all corners of London, silenced her people's rejoicing with words of wild fury. *"NO! THIS IS NOT WHAT I WANTED!"*

It looks as if his words evoked the reaction Eliza, Doctor Sound, and the Ministry had desired.

"Too long have I remained complacent while within the heart of the Empire a wound festers. Too long have I served those who believe we are doing 'well enough.' And for too long I have been silenced by politicians! It is your queen that should lead. I have been *chosen by God, bred to rule*, not like the simpletons who divide the monarchy amongst themselves. Those that *you* place in power in my stead. You, who continue to drag us to their depths, to their depravity. I will tolerate this no more!" Victoria spat.

"KILL THEM!" Victoria demanded, pointing in the direction of the East End. *"KILL THEM ALL!!!"*

Alerts blared in Wellington's cabin and the viewport flickered up a warning of something new closing on his position.

These new targets, however, were not in the Thames but above it.

Wellington remembered only glancing at the schematics of the Mark III when rejecting Doctor Havelock's offer for employment. They were the next step in the evolution of Mechamen. The Mark I would serve as ground forces. The Mark II would serve both on the land and sea. The Mark III, at least on paper, would conquer the air.

Through his viewport, Wellington could now see three of the V-shaped machines, their wings moving up and down in rhythm, flying between the spires of Tower Bridge and now heading for him.

Wellington fired the Martian heat ray completely on instinct, connecting with one of the oncoming Mark IIIs, while the other two easily avoided the attack. Their evasion tactics were nothing less than exquisite, an aerial ballet that he would have loved to watch from the banks of the Thames as opposed to the cockpit of their target. He would have so loved to observe more of these technological terrors, but Wellington flinched as his viewport filled with repetitive flashes of light.

This time, his Lander listed dangerously. He turned valves, threw levers forwards, and flipped switches, but could not adjust altitude or attitude quick enough. Against the Mark IIIs, he could only delay the inevitable.

Something rushed past the Lander, circled around him, and then came another hard impact, this time from the left. Indicators around him flipped to scarlet; gauges were showing one system after another failing. It would all be over soon.

As his last act of defiance, Wellington fired the heat ray. Something exploded. Whether it was the Lander or a Mark III, Wellington could not be certain as he felt the world teeter around him . . .

Darkness.

It was so quiet.

Sadly, the silence didn't last for long.

"Wellington?!"

The breath he took tasted so good, at first. He was just thrilled he could breathe. The breath, however, must have been too sudden as his throat felt tight, and the second felt less pleasurable, more painful. He was struggling now against a hacking cough, one that racked his entire body. The third breath was when he tasted the smoke, an acrid, unpleasant taste that reminded him of the destruction he had just wrought on the Thames, and that he had just left abruptly only a few heartbeats ago.

"How did I do?" he wheezed as he looked up into Eliza's blue eyes.

"You took down two of the Mark IIIs," Sophia said, removing the interface from his arms. "Well done." It was hard to tell how seriously the compliment was given.

"That still leaves one," Eliza said, her eyes following the last Mark III.

"Aim for the wings," Sophia stated. "Not a suggestion. I remember how vulnerable they are compared to the body."

Eliza walked out to the middle of the rooftop as the Mark III screamed through the air, coming around for what looked like another strafing run on the East End. The pilot must have seen her as the craft banked harder and set a trajectory that put her right in its path.

She shouldered the rifle, switched to electric, and waited for the moment. The moment they both knew from America. The moment when the Mark III's death ray made that preliminary flash just before firing.

The blast from Eliza's weapon cut through the craft's right wing, sending the Mark III spinning wildly out of control. Over the Thames, the craft exploded.

"Cheers," she said to Sophia.

His eyes burned and he was having trouble focusing, but breathing was coming easier now. "How are we faring on the ground?" he asked, his arm over Sophia as she lifted him to his feet.

"Remains to be seen," Eliza said, dismantling the ocular and neural headset. "One thing's for certain—the Queen is most definitely not amused."

INTERLUDE

❧

In Which an Achilles' Heel Is Exploited

"**N**O! THIS IS NOT WHAT I WANTED!" roared the Queen over the Jubilee's loudspeakers. Bruce had heard some women angry in his day, but they all paled in comparison to Ol' Queen Vic. "KILL THEM! KILL THEM ALL!!!"

Doctor Sound had counted on this moment. Why the Fat Man actually wanted Her Majesty to go completely off her nut escaped him. Maybe it was to show her true intention for these poor sods in the East End, and that was fine; but there was a flaw in this plan of the director's: when monarchs lose their minds, people wind up dead.

These clods in the grey uniforms, the Grey Ghosts, weren't going to make his job any easier. Unlike those steel monsters that were appearing above the buildings, these flesh-and-blood soldiers were brandishing Gatlings powered by small boilers and fed munitions from gears strapped to their backs, and they looked like the kind of blokes that could take care of themselves in a fistfight. Hauling around the gear as they were, they would have to be brawlers of some sort; but nothing that Bruce couldn't handle.

That was before the Queen lost her mind.

Normally, Bruce was not the one for noticing the details;

but somewhere between Eliza's shot—and how she shot *an attendant* when the Queen was sticking out like a bloody sore thumb, he could not understand—and the Queen's tantrum, something odd happened. The Maestro's soldiers stopped where they were, right on the spot. They all started screaming, and . . . *growing.* That was when he noticed just underneath the right arm of their arm cannons a vial of green goo, its contents appearing to be pumped into the soldiers. He watched as a small group of the Grey Ghosts got pumped with this serum—*probably the serum that Italian bint's been on about for the past month*—but two of the soldiers started bleeding out of their ears, eyes, and noses. They dropped like stones, a bloody froth dripping out of their mouths as their mates began popping buttons on their shirts.

Once their transformation ended, these soldiers with bulging muscles and crazed stares released the safeties on their Gatlings and started cutting down men, women, and children as if they were ready for harvest and their weapons the threshers. Usually Bruce could handle the plots and crimes of madmen, but the lack of discrimination or consideration struck the Australian deeply. These Grey Ghosts didn't care if it was soldier, street urchin, or visiting dignitary that got in the way of their rounds. Their orders were simple: if it was moving in the East End, kill it. This was a slaughter masquerading as a great purge for the betterment of the Empire. Hopefully, Books' standoff with those Mark II contraptions—which, much to Bruce's chagrin, had been a spectacular battle—had revealed that to the masses, and would spur an uprising against the Crown.

Now it was up to the Ministry to help that resistance along.

"So right now," Bruce muttered to Brandon, hefting the weight of the long bag in his hands, "the fate of the East End is restin' on who we get these to, and whether or not those little contraptions from Axelrod and Blackwell work?"

Brandon looked at the simple control device in his hand and at a bag similar to Bruce's slung over his own shoulder. One button, it seemed, carried the lives of the innocent, the destitute, and the visiting dignitaries from all parts of the Empire. "Looks like it."

His eyes turned back to the shotgun in his own hands.

"Dear Lord," he prayed, motioning for Brandon to remove his hat and hold it over his heart, "please—of all the days for us to do so—keep us on the straight and narrow, and keep the cock-up's at bay."

"A-men. Eloquent as always Bruce," Brandon said, replacing his hat. "Shall we give this a go?"

Bruce gave a curt nod, watching a full unit of mutated Grey Ghosts running down the street. "When this is all done, Mr. Hill, the first round is on me."

Brandon gave a tiny laugh. "Really? You really are trying to get back in my good graces." He gave Bruce a playful punch in the arm. "Good hunting."

Bruce went left towards the charging soldiers while Brandon ducked out to the right. He had only gone a few steps before he pulled out the small box with its single button and pushed it. Science always worked for him when it was kept simple. The button underneath his thumb gave a hard, sharp *click* as he pressed it. Bruce always knew the shlockworks in R&D straddled that razor's edge between genius and utter crackpot, but what he saw unfold on New Park Street could only be described in one word: elegant.

On being briefed by the assassin del Morte, R&D designed and implemented in the field an invention inspired by Books and Braun's recent mission in the States. They called these rocks they created *cobblefaux*. At a glance they would have appeared as replacement cobblestones for any that had been damaged or worn out from wear; but the clankertons had created powerful magnets, designed specifically for these Grey Ghost blokes and the packs they bore. The cobblefaux flared blue for a moment before flying free from the street and attaching themselves to various soldiers. The *CLANG* from the cobblefaux striking the Grey Ghosts was followed by a loud crackle of electricity, causing many of the Ghosts to tremble and jerk uncontrollably before dropping to the ground.

Now that the Maestro's men were thinned out considerably, it was Bruce's turn.

A beautiful thing about the boilers granting the Grey Ghosts superior firepower against his conventional rifle could also turn on them, provided you knew the right place to shoot. Bruce, it so happened, knew exactly where that was. Wherever

Bruce aimed and fired his rifle, the target at the other end would either explode in a super-heated cloud of vapour or send the soldier careening into a number of fellow Grey Ghosts. He continued down New Park Street, firing and then spinning back behind cover. It was impossible to tell whether or not this second phase of the plan was working. There were so damn many of them, and on this side of the Thames they numbered thirty. Not that Bruce wasn't enjoying himself. Things had most assuredly improved since Rockhampton. Hopefully, Good Lord willing, he would have to make good that wager with Brandon and pick up the first round at the George.

He slapped in his third clip and spun out of his hiding place to fire, but three Gatlings roared in protest to the agent's sharpened skills. Bruce ducked back behind cover and looked to one side. Dead end. Across the street, a sturdy looking pub.

Thank you, Lord, Bruce prayed silently.

Two shots managed to leave his rifle before a hell storm of bullets dogged his every step. Bruce ploughed his way into the dim house . . .

. . . and saw himself staring at his past.

"You mad, boy?" the gruff man shouted. "Get down!"

Bloody. Hell. "Sergeant Burgess?"

The burly man looked him over from head to toe. "We know each other, mate?"

It was hard to believe this man, practically pissing in his pants from fear, ever intimidated him. Then again, fresh from the riding crop of Cassandra Shillingworth, the sergeant had a high bar to clear now.

Bruce looked around the pub to find himself surrounded by countrymen, all of them hiding behind tables. "What the hell is all this about?"

"Pommy bastards disarmed all the colonial forces once we arrived," Burgess barked. "Not just us, but all the visiting colonials!"

"That's right," one of the soldiers offered. "Boys from India and Egypt lost their swords too."

It made perfect sense. When the Ghosts started to fire on citizens of the Empire without provocation, it would stand to reason that some British subjects—possibly those command- ing regiments of armed soldiers—would take a stand.

Bruce placed his rifle to one side and removed the long bag from across his back. "You're representing Australia, boys. Time to show these Poms how we do things in the Southern Hemisphere."

The Australians gathered around the table where Bruce ripped the bag open. Rifles and pistols of all makes and models scattered across the long table. Some soldiers immediately reached out and took up a weapon striking their fancy.

"These may be older than what you're used to firing out on the range, but trust me—they'll work." He glanced out of the pub window and saw the Grey Ghosts closing in on the pub. "How about you all give those a try right now?"

Bruce took up his rifle as his fellow Australians fortified themselves in the pub. The Grey Ghosts turned to open fire; but before a single Gatling could spin up, Australia made their presence known. When the last Ghost fell, Bruce stuck his head out of the door. He looked down either side. He could hear gunfire beginning to rise in the streets. Looked like Brandon and a few other Ministry agents had also made some new friends.

"Gotta run, boys," Bruce said to them all. "If it's wearing grey, shoot for the head."

He was nearly out of the door when he heard, "Mate!"

It was Sergeant Burgess. "We never did catch your name or unit, boy."

Bruce gave the man a proud grin. "Agent Bruce Campbell, Ministry of Peculiar Occurrences."

Those words had never felt so good to utter, and that elation followed Bruce out in the street—back into the fray, which was not hard to find. Bearing around a corner, the Ghosts were pushing a number of British citizens down the street, their Gatlings refusing to show mercy of any kind. Bruce began picking off the lumbering monsters from behind as if they were targets in a shooting gallery. Their assault came to a halt when Ghosts noticed their soldiers either disappearing in a cloud of steam, or wildly flying off into another direction. Bruce's aim refused to fail . . .

. . . until he ran out of ammunition.

Bruce patted his coat pocket and they were as his rifle. Empty. He had to move, and move now as the transformed

Ghosts were facing him, their Gatlings spinning faster and faster.

Then the Ghost closest to Bruce, his head exploding in a spray of blood, stumbled back. Four other soldiers also rocked and teetered on suffering the same fatal wound.

Spinning around, Bruce was now eye to eye with the formidable Beatrice Muldoon, flanked by a small team from the Department of Imperial Inconveniences. For the first time, and Bruce was a big believer in trying new things at least once, Bruce Campbell had never been more thrilled to see that signature brown, burnt orange, and amber tweed.

He was not so happy with Beatrice saving his hide.

"Hello, sw—"

"Blimey, you took your time comin' round, didn't ya, Bea?" he snapped. He really didn't feel all that comfortable with her calling him "sweetie" as that was usually a prelude to her trying to kill him.

"Cheers, Bruce," she returned, tossing him a fresh clip for his rifle. "And perhaps you should consider straight-and-to-the-point head shots instead of the melodramatic disabling of the boilers. Cut the snake at the head, and all that maybe?"

Bruce guffawed. "Now, Beatrice, you know my style better than anyone."

That earned him a sharp, crooked eyebrow. "Before you think this is some sudden change of heart from me, let's get something crystal clear, Campbell." Bruce could hear more and more pops of gunfire. Maybe this harebrained scheme of Doctor Sound's had a snowball's chance in hell after all. "Our director was watching the Jubilee, on orders from the Queen. Once the Queen ordered the purging, he made an executive decision and deemed Her Majesty an inconvenience." She gave a gruff laugh. "To the Empire."

"Makes sense," Bruce said, loading the clip into his weapon and shouldering it. "Lean left."

Beatrice spun down to one knee, drawing a pistol and firing just as Bruce did the same.

"Now we're even," he stated with a smug smile.

"Bullocks!" Beatrice replied. "That was *my* bullet."

"Do you really want to take a look at the ballistics?" Bruce brought up his rifle again, scoring a head shot on another

Gatling soldier while Beatrice felled another one a few yards further behind. "Nah," he said, his next bullet piercing a charging Ghost's tank to send her flying into three others. "My way is more fun."

Beatrice rolled her eyes and drew aim on an oncoming Ghost, paused, then adjusted her shot. The unsuspecting sod spun like a top at the sudden propulsion and stopped only when slamming hard into a heavy brick façade of a boarding house.

"Fair enough, Bruce," Beatrice chuckled. "I'll give you that one. Got any other clever Ministry tricks you want to impart?"

Bruce looked around at where he was and smiled brightly at the sight of the Man at Arms public house. Good thing these watering holes were so frequent in this part of London Town. Man at Arms, however, was the agreed-upon spot where he would signal the Ministry as a secured checkpoint. He ducked into the seedy pub to retrieve from above the door—logic dictating that if there was to be heavy gunfire in the East End, anyone taking shelter would stay *low*—a heavy disk just larger than his palm. He held it up for Beatrice to see and handed it to her.

"Just this," he said, firing off a wink to Beatrice as he pulled out a box of matches. "One way of letting the lads know this part of the East End is right as rain." He gave a slight guffaw as he lit the disc's sole fuse. "Well, right as the East End can be, at any rate."

As the fuse ignited, Bruce dropped it to the ground then pushed Beatrice back against the wall of a nearby building. A wide spray of sparks spewed in all directions behind him. He dared a look over his shoulder to see the disc spinning faster and faster in place, until it lifted off the ground and rocketed straight up into the smoke-filled sky overhead. It disappeared from sight just before it exploded in a brilliant burst of red, violet, and blue.

"Nicely done, Bruce," Beatrice said with a nod.

Bruce looked at the woman he had been shielding from the ground fireworks. She was the same height as he was, a broad-shouldered woman, and not to be underestimated when it came to bare knuckles. Perhaps she intimidated weaker men, but Beatrice Muldoon was an equal in so many ways. The fact she wouldn't give up until the very end, and then watch his back after hunting his hide around the world—the woman was cast from a very different mould than others of the Empire.

Again, she lifted a single eyebrow at the Australian, her head shaking ever so slightly as she looked him over from head to toe.

She went to say something, but Bruce stopped her words with the kind of kiss that he knew Beatrice liked. The woman liked the unexpected, the spontaneous, and the passionate; and that was exactly what this kiss conveyed. It had been a few years since he had enjoyed any sort of intimacy with Beatrice Muldoon, but this kiss and her reaction to it was as if not a day had passed between them. He felt her hands on his shoulders as their kiss continued with gunfire and explosives echoing across the East End. When he finally pulled back, Beatrice took a deep breath, her eyelids fluttering like the wings of a Monarch caught in a light summer breeze. She could be quite the lovely bird, when she wanted to be.

Maybe that was why he didn't expect the beautiful Beatrice Muldoon to suddenly clock him soundly in the nose with her forehead. Bruce stumbled back, giving her plenty of room to cock her fist back and land a hard hook against his massive jaw. This time he landed on his back on the ground.

His nose still worked but it was stinging something fierce. He also felt his jaw swelling from the punch. Bruce propped himself up on his elbows and looked up at Beatrice, demanding an answer to what she was on about.

"Always reading into things, aren't ya, Bruce?" Beatrice chided, shaking her head.

INTERLUDE

❦

Wherein the Mighty Fall and
a Child Shall Lead Them

Seeing the giant robots was a sight. Truly.

It had also been the distraction that was needed for the Ministry Seven to slip beyond the gawking throngs of onlookers, including the various soldiers in Her Majesty's service, to slip inside a building opposite St. Paul's Cathedral, opposite where Miss Eliza and Mr. Wellington were watching the Queen and her reaction to their lurk.

Christopher glanced to either side of the door as Liam worked the lock. On hearing the telltale sound of the release giving way, he ducked into the building, turned in a complete circle, and then leaned outside to beckon the rest of the Ministry Seven into the apartments. He was not certain of exactly what this place was all on about, but he could not be distracted by potential marks. Today, he was helping Miss Eliza and Mr. Wellington. Today, he was saving the Empire.

That was a hell of a score in itself.

He shifted the long haversack across his back and met the rest of the Seven at the stairs. "We're all set with the lay?"

"Why are you worried about this, Christopher?" Eric hissed. "We've been doin' what Miss Eliza and Mr. Books been wanting us to do. We did the practisin' at the manor with the grown-ups."

"Yeah, Christopher," Liam said, "what are you suddenly on about?"

Christopher tightened his grip on the shoulder strap while his other hand brushed the holster of his sidearm. The lads were right. Now was not the time to catch the chills. He had to look at this as just another job.

"We're down a man," the voice beside him spoke, his tone a little hollow, daring to wrap up everything eating at Christopher's gut. Colin looked at each of them and added, "Or did you all forget about Callum?"

The roar from outside—no one could tell if it was the Queen on a tear or the shock of the crowd at what was happening—seemed oddly out of place. In their gathering at the foot of this stairwell, no one really wanted to say anything, even though they knew it was a truth that Colin had just forced into the open. This was their first job without Callum.

"He didn't forget about Callum," said Serena, the shared silence now broken. "And while it would be nice and all to have eight as what we know, we can't, now can we?"

Jeremy leaned over to his redheaded twin and whispered something in his ear. Jonathan nodded and said, "Jeremy and I are all set, Christopher. On your word, mate."

"So am I, Christopher," Serena echoed.

The oldest of the Ministry Seven looked at the twins and at Serena for a moment. He then took in a deep breath and gave a curt nod to Eric and Liam. "Colin's spot-on. I don't want to lose anyone on this job, ya follow? I'm just wantin' ta make sure we are all ready for this."

"Right now ain't th' time to be looking over your shoulder," Liam replied. "We're already burning candles, ain't we?"

Christopher looked at everyone, then looked at the stairs leading up. "Then let's do this job. No cock-up's. We got Miss Eliza and Mr. Wellington counting on us."

With another quick heft of the haversack, Christopher led the rest of the Seven up flight after flight. On reaching the top of the building, Christopher opened the bag provided by those odd clankertons back at Whiterock, removing the gear within as he spoke. "Liam, Colin, find the closest window to St. Paul's.

Jonathan, Jeremy, check the rest of the floor. Don't want no interruptions. Serena, you're the crow." At the bottom of the bag, he saw components for what he knew would be two rifles once he and Eric were done. "Eric, start building."

They all moved silent as air. Tenants here could enjoy a view of the Diamond Jubilee from such a great vantage point. Christopher remembered asking Miss Eliza about that possibility when planning this job, but Miss Eliza had made a good point: anyone this close to St. Paul's would rather get close than prefer a bird's-eye view. There would be a good possibility that the building around St. Paul's would be vacant. There was a possibility of crossing paths with the Department punishers, just wanting to make sure there were no blokes attempting a Work Capitol. There were so many possibilities, and Christopher not only had to keep them all in mind but also had to set them aside. Hesitation, he knew from life in the street, was the fastest path to wearing the broad arrow. Now the Ministry had taught him hesitation kills.

"All clear," Jeremy said. Jonathan leaned over to his brother, whispered something in his ear, and Jeremy nodded. "All clear," he said again.

"Serena?" Christopher asked, locking the heavy coil of rope in place.

"She's a deadlurk," the little girl responded.

"Watch for peelers." He checked what that bloke Axelrod told him was a "high pressure something-or-other" that would make sure the grappling hooks would make the distance between buildings. "It only takes one to notice us, and then Miss Eliza and Mr. Books are in lavender on account of us."

"Right," she said, scampering away to the edge of the open stairwell.

The rifle appeared ready. Something behind him snapped hard and sharp, its echo lingering all around him. "How are we looking, Eric?"

"Second rifle, all set," the younger lad confirmed. "And that was the last of the pulleys."

Christopher looked down the sight of what Eric had constructed. Everything felt right in the rifle's build. He looked at the indicators along the top of the stock. All was in the green.

"It's this window," Liam said, pointing to a window

sporting a grand arch atop it, the length nearly reaching from floor to ceiling.

"Good work," Christopher replied, handing Eric the rifle. There remained only one more gun. This one resembled Miss Alice's Samson-Enfield Mark III, only the shells he loaded into it were not like any shells he had ever seen. "You and Colin, get to work on that anchor those clankertons built for us. Eric, it's time." He opened the window looming over him to feel cool air caress his face. In the streets below, the posh and the hoity-toity mixed with simple blokes like himself, all of them scurrying around like ants escaping a destroyed nest, their mingle borne from madness and chaos of a queen right off her rocker.

As Christopher shouldered the weapon, Eric asked him, "How many o' them fancy shells they give you?"

"Five." Christopher looked over at the banners far below flapping in the wind. Just as the agents taught him at Mr. Books' fine manor, he adjusted his shot. "I don't want to use 'em all. It's gonna make quite the noise."

"Go on then."

Christopher took in a deep breath, pulled the trigger, the dull, heavy *thwump!* from the shotgun still pounding in his head when he pulled the trigger a second time. He watched as something dark and thick slapped hard into the panes of glass across from them.

The gun cracked open, sending the spent shell casings bouncing across the floor. "Two minutes and it's Guy Fawkes Night," he called out as Liam handed him the longer rifle. "Jonathan, Jeremy, you're up." Christopher felt one of the twins wrap around his right leg. Next to him, he knew the same thing was happening with Eric. After shifting back and forth in his stance, feeling extra security from the twin anchoring him to the floor, he shouldered the rifle and lined up the sight with his target across the distance. "One shot, Eric. That's all we got."

"I've been practicing. Had a good teacher." Eric gave a gruff laugh and added, "Who would have guessed that toff Books was a crack shot?"

"You got the window?"

"Yeah, I got it."

The windows across at St. Paul's exploded, the ironwork and glass shattered and now falling to the streets and panicked citizens below.

"On three," Christopher said, slipping his finger around the trigger.

He knew he had said "Three" but he just barely heard himself over the discharge of both rifles. He tightened his grasp on the stock of the rifle as the coil continued to unwind. Underneath him, the twin tightened his own hold on Christopher's leg. The grappling hook sailed through the decimated window, and then he felt a tiny jolt in the rifle as the rope slackened ever so slightly.

"Eric?"

"I hit something," he replied, though Christopher caught a hint of fear in his mate's voice.

They both gave a start when a small explosion sounded from behind them. Colin and Liam were now testing the odd apparatus that was built for the rifles once everything was secured. The two boys shoved and tugged at the metallic tree, but its struts were now bolted to the floor.

Still no peelers, and the bedlam in the streets was only getting worse. Right now, Christopher was about to piss himself. "Eric, give it a tug."

Both ropes tightened and then snapped on their second yank. Their lines were solid.

"Lucky sons-a-bitches, ain't we?" Eric nodded as he secured his rifle within the branches of the anchor. He flipped a switch located next to where the rope originated from. A small winch continued to pull at the rope until the line was good and taut.

"I'll believe that when we're back at Whiterock, enjoying a pint with Campbell and Hill," Christopher grumbled as he locked his own rifle into the anchor and tightened his own line. "Serena, anyone in the stairwell?"

"Not a soul," she replied, now rolling up the shotgun and its remaining shells into the haversack. Even without the other equipment, the bag looked ridiculously long across the little girl's back.

"All right then," he said, checking the gun Miss Braun had

called an "Experimental," before picking up a pulley. "Time to fly."

He looked over to the second line to see Eric, Colin, and the twins hook themselves onto the cable overhead. Over his shoulder, he saw Liam lift the diminutive Serena up to the line just before he hefted himself into place behind her.

"Eric, remember to—"

"Lift at the knees, lead with the feet," he said impatiently. "I know what to do."

Christopher took one last look at Eric before giving his pulley a quick tug. The rope was still solid. According to the clankerton, all he had to do now was let gravity do its work.

It was the drop five storeys down that made his last bit of advice something hard to swallow.

"Go!" he called out, pushing off from the stone windowsill.

He was fighting an urge to kick or to swing his legs. That would only add stress to the line and hamper his ability to hang onto the pulley. *Just let gravity do its work,* he told himself as he continued to slide faster down the line above him. *Just let gravity do it—don't look down, you git!—just let gravity . . .*

Then another thought screamed in his head: *Open your eyes!*

Christopher's eyes popped open, and St. Paul's was just within striking distance.

His knees instantly came up to his stomach and he stretched his legs forwards, his boot soles ready to make quick work of what remained of the window. He heard a shattering of glass and a tearing of metal, and then he was inside a grand library of some description. He let go and dropped only a few feet to the floor, a second level that overlooked tables where bookish types probably met and talked a lot about what they had just read. This was a place he thought Mr. Books would appreciate. Christopher turned and caught Serena in his arms. Seconds later, he helped Liam down from the cable.

The cry from behind them instantly quashed any sort of elation he was feeling.

"What happened?" Christopher asked, kneeling where the twins and Colin were gathered.

"Eric got the lifting of the knees part right," Colin said,

motioning to the boy's leg, "but he waited too long to lift up his feet."

"Bloody hell," Eric cursed through clenched teeth, "that hurts!"

His thigh now sported two deep gashes, sliced by either the iron windowpane or the window glass itself; Christopher couldn't be sure. Fortunately, nothing was sticking out of Eric, so there was some comfort in that. From the looks of the cuts, though, walking on that leg was going to take nothing short of a miracle.

"Right, I want the twins to stay here with you, Eric," Christopher began, handing him the odd gun. His only defence.

"Are you daft?" Eric scoffed. "Just go on. I'll deal with the peelers on me own."

"We got a queen downstairs wot's partnered up with a mad scientist," the Seven's leader barked back, "and you think *peelers* are your worries?"

"Don't worry about me, Christopher! Make sure Miss Eliza and Mr. Books are square!"

"I am, but I won't be losing you whilst doin' what we set out to do!" Christopher turned to Jeremy and Jonathan. "You watch that leg, and listen for trouble. I don't care if you hear something what sounds like a mouse in the walls, first sign of something not right, you blow a hole in these walls and scamper. *With Eric.* You follow?"

Both boys nodded as Christopher pulled off his coat and shoved it into their hands.

"Stop that bleeding and find something that could work as a crutch." Christopher then faced the remaining three. "Work just got a bit more difficult for us, but nothin' we can't handle, right? We gots to give Miss Eliza and Mr. Books a way out of here."

The two boys nodded.

"Just stay close, and we'll make it through," Christopher assured them. "Good then?"

"Stick close," Liam repeated.

"We'll make it through," Colin said.

Serena nodded in silence.

Christopher looked around their balcony and found a break in it. Motioning to the ornate ladder of dark wood and brass fixtures, the four of them slipped silently down to the main floor, their footsteps hardly making a sound save for the odd creak or groan from the ladder itself.

All they needed to do now was get to ground level. Their escape would also ensure the escape of Miss Eliza and Mr. Wellington.

"Hello, Christopher," spoke a voice from behind them.

Christopher spun on his heels, then felt his blood chill as it would when he was in need of a gin. "Callum?"

He looked good, and that was what terrified Christopher deep to his soul. Callum was cleaned up, dressed smart in what looked like a suit from Savile Row, his hair neatly combed and styled with a clean part to one side, his shoes polished. It was as if he had come to the Rothchild, but this wasn't a flimflam of any sort. At least, not in the way Callum was carrying himself. In fact, the longer Callum looked at Christopher, the more Christopher's instincts urged him to run.

"So," the young boy said, walking towards the four of them, "you all look as if you are doing well."

"We should say the same, ain't that right?" Christopher returned. He felt something tug at his sleeve and he dared to look at what was causing it. Serena was pale, and looked as if on the verge of screaming. Colin and Liam were not faring any better. "We thought you were done in, we did."

"Did you now?" Callum nodded. "Is that why you told everyone to run?"

His throat was tingling. Christopher was in desperate need of a drink. "I had to do that, Callum. Was always a rule when on a job, right? We'd come back for ya, if we could."

"But you didn't," he stated. "You watched as that thing cornered me. You ran, you told the others to run"—Callum paused, his eyes sparkling with some sort of light Christopher could only describe as Greek fire—"and you never came for me."

"Lots been happening, Callum." Christopher now felt himself backing up, countering each step of Callum's. His mate looked like he had been well looked after, but there was something unnatural about him now. "We couldn't come for ya, not that we didn't want ta."

The boy shrugged, motioning to the other three of his comrades. "Busy, were we?"

"Mate, the stories we could tell you . . ."

Christopher's voice died away as Callum came to a halt. "Tell me your stories then."

The boy disappeared in a blur, then Christopher felt the floor disappear from underfoot. He couldn't breathe, and there was an uncomfortably tight cinching at his waist. Was Serena finally letting loose that scream she was bottling up? Where were Colin and Liam? Nothing was making any sense, save for the pain at his throat and at his stomach.

Then Callum came into focus underneath him, his smile impossibly wide, threatening to touch his ears; his eyes two pools of flickering red light staring blankly at him. Christopher couldn't take in a breath as Callum's hand was around his throat, and his other hand had hold of his pants.

"Tell me all your stories, Chrissy. We have time," Callum growled. "No one is coming for you."

Christopher's hands scrambled for anything to use as a weapon. He felt something thick, and when he tried to lift it with one hand, he found he couldn't. His other hand swung over him to grab the rest of the massive book he had found, and with a little grunt he brought it around like a giant club.

He hit . . . something.

The book came around again, and again Christopher felt purchase. He looked up, but the Callum-monster stood there with his impossible smile.

Callum inclined his head to one side, waggled his finger as if to say silently *"Now, now, Christopher . . ."* and then he kicked, sending Christopher through the air and over another table of books.

When he took a breath, Christopher was certain by the stinging in his chest that something was either bruised or cracked. It wasn't like Callum to hold back . . .

. . . unless Callum wanted to.

The table Callum walked up to was easily four times his size and it looked sturdy, but he lifted it as if it were a lady's purse. He held its polished surface over his head for a moment before bringing it down on Christopher, apparently determined to squash him with one blow. The older boy rolled to one side, the pain in his chest exploding. The agony only drove him to move faster, and he was thankful for that sudden rush as the grand table snapped in two.

"Doctor Jekyll was right," Callum tittered, tossing his half of the makeshift weapon aside. "This *is* fun."

"Oye, Callum!" barked a voice from above them.

The flash consumed the library for a moment, and through grey spots Christopher saw Callum stumble back several steps. He managed a weak smile of relief but it soon disappeared as his former compatriot caught his breath and stood to his full height.

No. *Grow.* Callum was getting larger.

"Ouch," Callum grunted over the sound of tearing clothes and popping bones.

"Oh, bugger me!" swore Eric.

"My turn!" came a high-pitched voice.

Serena?

Christopher forced himself up to a sitting position to see both Liam and Colin bracing themselves against the girl, providing her sure footing and posture against what was to come. Serena worked the lever action of the Samson and fired. The round sailed past Callum, striking the base of a massive bust of some bloke with long wavy hair. Definitely a toff.

Two minutes, Christopher thought quickly.

A gruff laugh cut through the silence. "You missed," Callum growled.

"No, I didn't," she said, chambering another shell.

The Samson came up again, and this second shot slammed Callum in the chest. She fired again, sending him back towards the only visible exit. With each shot, he continued to grow, his muscles bursting the seams of his fine shirt and coat while the hems of his trousers continued to lift away from fine, polished shoes.

"Serena," Christopher called out to her. "What the blazes are you doing?"

"Making him angry," Serena shouted over Callum's frenzied howl, his fangs borne in full as his mouth opened wide.

"Why?"

The monster that was once Callum now struggled to stay upright, the black sludge from the Samson stretching across his expanding chest.

"To throw off his balance!" she shouted, just before ducking for cover with the boys.

The first round that had hit the bust exploded, launching the stone statue at Callum. He staggered through the archway, and his scream was abruptly cut off by a more massive explosion and a tearing of wood and metal.

The silence that followed seconds after made Christopher ill.

He was on his feet just as he heard the echo of heavy objects striking a hard surface far away from their library. Christopher braced himself against tables as he hobbled over to where Serena and the two boys were. Liam slipped underneath him as they now dared to cross through the library's threshold.

The four of them stood at the edge of a grand spiral, a staircase continuing straight down several storeys. Before them, the banister rail running down its winding length had splintered and snapped at the point where Callum and the bust had continued on into space. At the bottom of this pit lay Callum, the bust of the curly haired toff resting against his shoulder. From the unnatural bends in Callum's body, his neck or his back, or both, had been broken on plummeting from this height. He no longer had the frightening smile, the massive shoulders, or the lumbering countenance of a monster. His chest and parts of his face were covered with burns, and that was all. It was Callum. The Callum they had once known, dressed in the singed tatters of a fine suit from Savile Row.

"It wasn't Callum," Liam spoke sombrely, his words echoing all around them. "Not the Callum wot we knew."

"The mad doctor did this to him, didn't he?" Colin asked.

Christopher winced as he relieved himself from Liam's assistance. "Right then, it's up to you three, and I think you'll have to go by Callum to get there." He pointed to the base of the spiral staircase, continuing, "Make sure Mr. Books and Miss Eliza have an escape then, and maybe they will catch us a mad scientist."

"Stick close," Liam said.

"We'll make it through," Colin muttered.

Serena looked up at Christopher, her gaze hard, especially for a child so young. "Give the bastards wot for."

The Seven were set, but time was fleeting. They had to get moving. Now.

NINETEEN

❦

In Which the Queen Has a
Disagreement with Her Subjects

With the fall of his last target, Wellington was able to slip off the control gloves. Eliza saw his wide eyes and pale skin, but she knew they had little time to relax. Below on the street events were unravelling at a rapid pace, even as the smoke from the downed Mechamen blew across London.

Victoria, for one thing, looked very unimpressed. When Eliza looked through the binoculars again, the sweet calm face was twisted with outrage that transformed it into something else.

"Commoners, worms!" The monarch of the Empire was throwing an impressive temper tantrum. Eliza might have found it amusing were it not for the battle armour and the control of terrible forces the woman wielded. The monarch's battle armour glinted so brightly in the sun that it was almost impossible to see her, gleaming like a bright mote on the steps of the cathedral. Yet she wasn't a bright beacon that would lead the Empire to greatness. Eliza knew that. Victoria was a dark maw that would suck the Empire into even more war and chaos.

Eliza felt her breath catch when the Queen yelled into the

loudspeaker, "Take it down. The city must be cleansed. *The Empire must be cleansed!*"

At first it seemed like she was just ranting, but then Wellington tugged at Eliza and pointed back to the Thames. The river was rocking wildly in its banks, as more Mechamen emerged from its depths. They must have been waiting in the ocean, and steamed their way towards London in a straight line.

These ones were not painted in mimicry of the American flag. They were a flat, iron grey, and their heads turned towards the East End.

"She needs to be taken down," Eliza said, tightening the straps on the *plures ornamentum*, now encasing her right arm. Flexing her fingers within the weaponised gauntlet, she felt a jolt of delight. She then reached for Blackwell's tranquiliser pistol. It was a "close quarters" option they were hoping to employ on Jekyll or the Maestro, but only if the opportunity presented itself.

"A shame you did not take down your *primary* target then," Sophia said with a savage smirk.

Slinging the bag over her shoulder and getting to her feet, Eliza rounded on the assassin. "Let's understand one another, dearie—you are here because you serve a purpose. That snap decision I just made about Jekyll, I could just as easily make about you."

"As intoxicating as some would find two highly skilled women indulging in close-quarters combat," Wellington grumbled, strapping on weapons as he did so, "might we focus on the task at hand? The grapplers, if you please."

They had no time to think, no time to become melancholy, and certainly no time to delve into grudges. This was what Sound had told them might be required and they had to do it.

Eliza looked Sophia over from head to toe. "How's that corset of mine?"

"Finely crafted," she replied, running her hand along its curve.

"Turn around," Eliza said. "Let me double-check the lacings."

"They are fine," she insisted.

Eliza pinched the back edges and seams of the corset. "So

long as the back remains closed, you'll be fine." With a nod, she rapped Sophia on the side. "Let's get to ground."

The grapplers had been Sophia's responsibility, and within moments they were assembled and bolted into their rooftop. Sophia then handed over to Eliza a rifle loaded and primed with a large amount of cable coiled underneath it. They shared a glance with each other, but this time the Italian's gaze was softer. Sophia nodded and shouldered her own rifle, its grappling hook pointing down to St. Paul's.

Eliza glanced at her partner, her lover, and her archivist. "Ready?"

He gave a short nod, nothing more, and she saw again the soldier.

"On my mark." She raised the grappler to her shoulder. "Fire."

The grappling hook shot its way across the now-heaving street of people and imbedded itself in the masonry of St. Paul's. Once the rifle was secured to its scaffolding, Eliza cranked its rope taut and then grabbed her own pulley from Sophia. Wellington locked into place his pulley behind her as she secured hers overhead. Eliza went first, leaping into the unknown. A moment later she heard Wellington and Sophia doing the very same, all three of them plummeting into the mouth of madness. The crowd below them was surging in a tide of anger and confusion towards the dais where Victoria had called for a cleansing. They were pushing their way up the stairs, and even the Grey Ghosts, as Sophia had pointed out, were unable to contain them.

On her descent, Eliza spotted the Maestro's dark bulk amongst the crowd, and he also looked to be having trouble contending with the London citizens driven quite mad by this day of celebration run amok. He was slipping back towards the cathedral doors, his Gatling arm raining death on the citizens while shielded underneath the other arm was Dr. Henry Jekyll. Grey Ghosts were struggling to hold a circle around the monarch while she screamed to the sky, striding backwards and forwards in her insanity. Getting closer to the end of the line, Eliza could see the monarch's face red and twisted, a far cry from the serenity she'd displayed in the portraits of her younger days. Whatever Jekyll had done to Victoria, it was not without a price.

Eliza dropped to her feet and rolled back up as smoothly as if she were a circus performer, but that was the only thing that would be smooth. Wellington and Sophia landed almost as elegantly next to her, but the Queen rounded on them just as quickly. Her eyes were darting left and right as though she couldn't focus, but the hiss of her armour as she swung at them seemed precise enough.

Subduing this mad Queen was going to be the tricky bit.

Eliza split off to the right, while Wellington and Sophia darted left. The New Zealander had Blackwell's Experimental drawn, but no one had quite anticipated the Queen in battle armour. This little surprise now made the diminutive Victoria a tough nut to crack.

Wellington ducked a metallic left hook, but nearly found himself caught by Victoria's sword swinging in her right. Sophia attempted to get in close as well but the Italian was knocked clear by a well-placed foot to the midsection. Perhaps it was the concoction created by Jekyll, the madness induced by his treatments, or a bit of both, but the Queen fought with a ferocity that would make rugby players envious. The armour also sported a ridge that protected the Queen's neck from Eliza's angle. She needed a higher vantage point or to get closer, both options impossible at present.

With Victoria turning back towards Wellington once more and Sophia pulling herself back to her feet, Eliza saw her chance, mad as it was.

"Sophia!" she shouted, tossing the tranquiliser gun to her.

Flipping three new switches on the *plures ornamentum*, Eliza thrust her hand forwards, fingers splayed out wide, just as Axelrod had instructed. She saw the space between her palm and Victoria's shield ripple and warp, the distortion throwing Victoria off-balance. The shield ripped free from her left arm as the monarch twirled like a top before clattering to the ground.

Eliza flipped a blue switch on the *plures ornamentum* and reached in the direction of the shield. The metal trembled for a moment and then flew into Eliza's grasp.

"Sweet as," she cooed to herself.

The Queen's gaze locked on her, but Eliza turned her attention to Sophia, crouched down with the shield, and tapped its edge. It was their one shot, and when Sophia's eyes lit up, Eliza knew the assassin recognised it as well. Sophia sprinted for the grounded shield; and when Eliza felt her foot press against it, Eliza flipped on a small motor within the *plures ornamentum* and thrust the shield upward.

Sophia, propelled by Eliza's shield, soared high above the fight. At the top of her arc, she fired. The dart found the Queen's neck without fail or doubt.

It was when Eliza turned to face Victoria that she heard the Queen release an ungodly scream. When she crashed to the ground, her battle armour making a dull *clang*, the enraged mob pushed forwards again.

Both British citizens and Grey Ghosts parted at the report of a Gatling gun. This roar of munitions Eliza could distinguish over the chaos on account of a whine crying from high-pressured steam engines.

Emerging from the melee came the dark, hooded figure of Agent Maulik Smith, his "Queensbury Rules" angled upwards, away from any bystanders. His cannon dealt more damage to St. Paul's exterior, but its terrifying sound was enough to push the crowd in several directions, all away from the dias.

A wild scream made Eliza jump. A Grey Ghost materialised from the haze and smoke, his face twisted and malformed as if his body were a wax statue left out in the noonday sun. He bore a similar Gatling to Maulik's; but in his maddened state, he looked to Eliza as if he had forgotten how the gun worked. The Maestro's man was now wielding it like a club.

Something cut the air in front of her with a loud *whoosh*, and a flash of metal accompanied by brilliant blue feathers caught her eye. Eliza watched as the *taiaha* cracked into the the bridge of the man's nose and then engulfed his face in white-hot steam. The Ghost stumbled back, giving Office Director Aroha Murphy enough time to step between him and Eliza.

"Kia ora, Eliza," Aroha called over shoulder as she twirled the metallic staff in her hand. "Stubborn buggers, these *pak-eha* in grey."

Her taiaha sliced through space again, slamming into the Ghost. Aroha flipped a switch just under her thumb and a crooked, blue bolt of lightening arched between the Maori weapon and the soldier. He was still collapsing to the ground by the time Aroha returned the staff to her side.

"That's new," Eliza said.

"An exciting age of science we live in. Best to keep up," Aroha returned, casting her gaze left to right. "Maulik and I saw something happen to these Grey Ghosts in the streets. We think Jekyll's loaded their gun-packs with something other than bullets. We thought you could use the help."

"We've got to get the Queen out of here!" Eliza shouted over the roar of the crowd.

"Working on it," Wellington replied, struggling against a howling Victoria, appearing to be fighting against her own armour.

"Grab her and get inside!" Sophia insisted, grabbing her other side.

"But the Maestro and Jekyll are in there, as well!" Eliza said.

"Really?" Maulik asked. He glanced at the pressure gauges on his Gatling and nodded. "We should pop in and give our regards then, shouldn't we?"

"You all go on," Aroha said. "I should be able to hold off any scrappers if they try to follow."

Eliza placed the *plures ornamentum* on the Queen's chest and felt the hard connection between her open palm and the monarch's armour. Moments after picking her up with assistance from Wellington and Sophia, she felt the heat. Eliza's gaze went to the Queen. Her skin was scarlet red and almost bubbling, as though demons were stretching to get out from it.

The din of the outside crush diminished as they managed their way into St. Paul's Cathedral, but soon came the echoes of Grey Ghosts charging through the sacred church. They were not as tortured as the one who'd attacked Eliza, but they appeared just as mad. Maulik rounded his Queensbury Rules on them and the steam-powered cannon filled the cathedral with such volume that Eliza believed the stained glass around them would shatter.

Eliza released her magnetic grip on the Queen and went to secure the doors behind them.

"She's having a reaction to that tranquiliser," she said as her gauntlet ripped away the doorknobs on their side. Provided anyone got past Director Murphy—highly unlikely—it wouldn't keep the mob out completely; but by that time, they would be gone, provided the Seven had followed their orders.

"Could it be warring with Jekyll's serum?" Sophia offered, attempting to pry Victoria out of her armour.

"Finally!" Wellington managed access to what appeared to be a small release lever. The suit suddenly disgorged its contents, sending the Queen sprawling across the cathedral floor, writhing, furious, and spitting.

"You wretched traitors," she slurred, her skin still scarlet while beads of sweat ran from her temples. "I will have you all executed."

"Well, something is happening. She doesn't even appear winded," Wellington said. "We have to calm her somehow."

"Your Majesty," Eliza began, offering her free left hand to her. "We are your humb—"

"Foul, ignorant colonial!" Victoria snapped as if she were a rabid dog. "Get your hands off me!"

The woman's defiance seemed to echo in St. Paul's for a moment, driving home to Eliza D. Braun just how difficult Victoria was going to make this extraction. So with the hand rejected by her sovereign, Eliza did the next best thing that came to mind.

Eliza punched the Queen hard in the jaw with an impressive left hook.

When she slumped backwards, Eliza caught Wellington's gaze, and shot out before he could complain. "Calm enough?"

His eyes widened. "You just punched the leader of the British Empire!"

"I'm certain the del Morte family could find a place for you, Miss Braun," Sophia offered with an arched eyebrow.

At least *someone* appreciated her efforts.

The scream, a strange marriage of malice and mechanation, echoed through St. Paul's. Kicking aside the dead as if they were wayward autumn leaves was the Maestro, his scarlet ocular so bright that wisps of smoke trailed from it as he lumbered towards them.

"Get moving," Maulik said evenly, motioning to the now-prone Queen with his head. "If Her Majesty is having a reaction to the tranquiliser, she needs a physician straightaway."

"No, Maulik," Eliza began. This was Bombay all over again, but on that mission she and Maulik had had far better ground support. "You cannot—"

"I'm fighting Queensbury Rules," he said, hefting his cannon. "While we can't say who will walk away, we can rest assured it will buy you time." He then shouted, *"Go!"* just before charging at the Maestro.

Wellington hefted Victoria across his shoulders as Eliza and Sophia took point, crossing through the sanctuary to the doors leading to the various offices and libraries of St. Paul's while Maulik's gun and the Maestro's curses erupted in the cathedral.

Doorways led to corridors, the maze of offices and hallways all appearing as some surreal dream as what should have been a serene place of peace now reverberated with combat in God's House. They did not stop in their escape until Maulik's Gatling went silent.

"Maulik?" Eliza asked, her voice destroying the false serenity as if it were a stone hurled at a pane of glass.

"We must move on," Sophia urged.

With a quick glance to the assassin, Eliza pushed on, leading the four of them deeper into St. Paul's.

"I will give the mad doctor one praise," Wellington said, huffing ever so slightly at the royal burden he now bore. "Returning Victoria to her youth did make her much easier to carry."

"Little blessings," Eliza said, drawing one of her pounamu pistols. "Through this door and we should be in the alcove where the children were supposed to gain us access to—"

Eliza stopped on seeing the broken body. His face and chest appeared singed by powder burns. Explosives? Where had he gotten this suit from? From the unnatural way his head and neck were bent, the fall had assuredly killed him; but his body also showed signs of deformity. Areas just visible around his waist had skin which had been stretched far and beyond what nature would have allowed.

She had failed him.

"Callum?" she whispered, falling to her knees, the pistol clattering out of her hand.

"He did it," Sophia whispered. "That devil of a man actually did it."

Eliza wanted to cradle the boy—for even though he was twelve, he was still just a boy. Crumpled in a heap at the bottom of this spiral stairwell, he seemed so very fragile. If she attempted to pick him up, Eliza feared he would crumble in her embrace.

"I am so sorry," the woman behind her whispered gently.

The *plures ornamentum* shot outward, knocking Sophia back to the wall. Eliza was on her feet, her pounamu pistol in her grasp, the hammer pulled back.

"You could have gotten him out of there," Eliza insisted. "Goddammit, he was just a child!"

"I was a prisoner, just as he was," Sophia snapped in return.

Even in the depth of her rage, a small part of Eliza admired the assassin's bravery. Right to the end. "You could come and go as you please, you bitch. Don't try and gain any sympathy from me."

"I could do nothing for the boy."

"His name was Callum!"

"Agent Braun!" echoed Wellington's voice. *"Stand down!"*

Eliza's gun wavered in her hand. "I'll be along, Welly. Just one last detail to sort."

"Agent Braun," he insisted, "we are on a mission."

Eliza briefly turned the gun on Wellington. "Stuff the mission, Books! He was just a boy, and she could have saved him from that monster."

"Agent Braun," Wellington said, his hazel eyes hard and cold, "I carry on my back the Queen of the Empire. This mission is our priority, and we will lose more of our friends and comrades if you do not pull yourself together and stand down."

The mission. As if she cared anymore. Eliza returned to Sophia, her pistol still ready to bring justice for Callum, a boy who'd had a life ahead of him, or at least a better chance at one under her protection.

What about the other children? They had done it. And Callum? He was in league with Jekyll. Were any of the children up there hurt, or worse—dead? Had Callum tried to hurt them?

She returned the hammer gently to its safe position, then

holstered her pistol; only then did she hold her hand out to Sophia.

"Lead the way," Eliza managed, her voice trembling.

"We will mourn our dead later," Wellington offered.

"Just—" Eliza began. "Please, just be quiet. Focus on the mission."

The sky outside was decorated with dark clouds, but in their alleyway all appeared clear for the moment. She and Sophia unfurled the tarp to reveal the other objective of the Ministry Seven's orders: delivery of the *Ares*. Having seen her lover's motorcar in action in San Francisco, Eliza was more than happy to throw the Queen of England into it. They just had to get Victoria away from here, and hopefully she could be brought back to her senses to help sort this whole sorry mess out.

Wellington leapt into the driver's seat and started the engine.

"Going somewhere?" The amplified voice was chillingly familiar, and Eliza felt her heart begin to race even faster than it was already when the tall shape of the Maestro appeared at the end of the alleyway. His armour had been dented, no doubt by numerous rounds from Maulik's Queensbury Rules. However, Eliza could not tell how much of the blood splattered across the armour belonged to the Maestro, or to Maulik.

Then Eliza's gaze narrowed on the man-machine blocking their escape. "Does he look—"

"Bigger?" Wellington's hand clenched on the steering wheel. "I am afraid so."

As the Maestro stood there, saliva dripping slowly from his mouth, a small man limped from behind their armoured foe and disappeared around the corner.

"That was Jekyll," hissed Sophia. "He must have administered to the Maestro more of his formula."

"Should we run him down?" Eliza knew that if they didn't get the Queen free of the area there was no hope of anything being normal ever again.

The engine let out excited puffs of steam, but Wellington made no effort to open the throttle. "Eliza, the man has a Gatling gun for an arm."

"Well put, Welly. Well put."

"I think," the Maestro said, walking towards them as his cannon arm began to spin, "that we need a little discussion about your interference in my Jubilee celebrations. It really has to stop."

The venting of his breathing apparatus suggested he was really rather angry. The moans of the Queen in the tumble seat became louder, and Eliza realised there was no getting away from it. They were going to have to deal with the Privy Councillor under all that technology.

TWENTY

❧

Wherein Sussex and the
Maestro Make a Point

Wellington knew a tight spot when he saw one. Just outside this alleyway the world was going mad, he had a queen in the backseat who might or might not die unless a proper physician saw to her immediately, and the behemoth of a man striding towards them was intending to make life very messy.

Their primary objective: keep the Queen alive. The Empire would fall to chaos if they lost their sovereign. Wellington wrung his hands against the steering wheel of his car. He was determined to see this mission through.

But how?

Eliza stood in the passenger seat and drew both her signature pistols, firing each one in succession. Wellington saw some of her bullets hitting the Maestro's elaborate costume. A few struck flesh, the sickening sound barely discernible over the hullabaloo of the crowd in the streets beyond. Also barely discernible—the effect of Eliza's attack on the Maestro. He took a great breath and flexed grotesquely muscular arms. If the bullets had done anything, they had merely agitated the man.

"I'm going to smear you all over London." The Maestro's

gun had now spun up to speed. "Then I am going to kill the Queen."

"Not if we kill you first," Sophia shouted, shouldering the Lee-Metford-Tesla.

The electroblast blinded Wellington for a second, but when his vision returned, the Maestro was pulling himself back to his feet as bright blue tendrils of energy danced along his metallic arms and mask. Whatever Jekyll had fed him with before absconding made him immune to pain it seemed.

"All right then," Wellington said as the Maestro seemed to inflate like a terrifying balloon, "any recommendations?"

"Yes," Sophia said flatly, "anything more powerful than this rifle."

Eliza flipped a few switches on the dashboard. "Like this?" she asked, pressing the yellow buttons.

A pair of rockets soared out from underneath the grill of their motorcar, exploding against the monster of metal and muscle. Wellington held himself upright against the car as a wave of heat swept past him. Over the thunder of the explosion, he heard a wail that turned into a wild growl. When the Maestro stepped out of the flames and smoke, his clothes were torn and tattered while soot stained his once pristine armour.

"Damn," Sophia swore.

"Quite the understatement," Eliza said to her.

The Maestro took a few more steps forwards. The smile on his face was one too macabre, too hellish to find any mirth within its nature. The corners of his mouth stretched from ear to ear, his eyepieces flaring angrily as he looked at them.

"I thank you, all, for joining me on this merry escapade, but I fear that our time together has come to an end." The Maestro thrust his great Gatling arm forwards. "Signorina, our arrangement is at an end. For your service, you have my eternal gratitude."

The cannon began to spin, faster and faster, until the whir turned into a grating grind. The grind then became a loud screaming of metal against metal until the cannon jammed and locked tight, its sudden stop throwing the Maestro's arm away from his body.

His body began to tremble the longer he stared at the Gatling. First, it was as if he could not fathom why his cannon no longer functioned. The nightmarish smile was now replaced by a dark scowl that only deepened as he pointed the gun at the three of them.

"No," the monster whimpered. "No, I . . . I need this. This must work . . ."

The Maestro's head looked to the other arm, to another Gatling that ran along the underside of it. It was far smaller than his suit's primary Gatling, but it could still kill them all.

That was when Sophia thrust her hand outward. A pair of steel cogs shot out from her concealed gauntlet and lodged deep in the mechanism of the gun. The scream of machinery was silenced with a grinding howl.

"Never say Sophia del Morte doesn't contribute," she said with an arched eyebrow.

The howl that the Maestro let out was almost a sob, as he slumped forwards on his knees. He was certainly having a rather bad day, but Wellington was happy to make it a little worse.

He took the Lee-Metford-Tesla from Eliza. She frowned. "Welly, I've burned through the battery."

He held up his hand. "It's just what I need to get the job done," he said before getting out of the car.

Over San Francisco he recalled the Maestro's reaction to losing his helmet. At this stage it almost seemed a mercy. The closer Wellington came to the Maestro, the larger he seemed; but he would not be denied. He would not fail the Ministry, or the Crown. The archivist leaned back and swung the butt of the rifle like a cricket bat. He repeated the swing again, and again, the Maestro's wails sounding as if Wellington were pre-forming some terrible surgery on him.

When finally the mask came free, and the tormented face of Peter Lawson, Duke of Sussex, was revealed, he went silent. His grotesquely swollen fingertips touched his own face. Wellington stumbled back when the Maestro howled, lurched to his feet, and ran from the alleyway.

Wellington felt his shoulders slump as he looked back to the ladies in the motorcar. "Really?" he said with a sigh. "A foot chase?"

Sophia smiled at him. "It's not a foot chase when you know where they are going."

Eliza looked askance at their unexpected ally. "You've got us this far; if you have any idea where Lawson is going . . ."

It turned out the assassin did indeed. With the Queen of England tied up next to her, Sophia gave Wellington directions as their motorcar rumbled through the deserted streets of London, the bulk of the city still huddled around St. Paul's Cathedral, still trying to understand what had happened on what was to be the happiest day the Empire would have ever known.

She led them to the leafy streets where bedlam had never dared to venture. This was where the wealthy and aristocratic lived, and the silence was absolute.

The contrast to what they had left behind on the East End should have soothed Wellington, but the goose flesh rose in his skin. His senses had never felt more heightened. This stillness was born of a malice he did not know and had never encountered.

Each white stone building was as perfect and serene as the next. Except for one, which had its door smashed in. The Maestro as always was leaving a trail of destruction.

Carefully, Sophia, Eliza, and Wellington picked their way over it. He hadn't made it far. The battle armour was strewn across the fine marble floor of this fine town house, scattered before a door that had been torn free of its hinges.

The weak mortal flesh that had once been within it hadn't gotten much farther. Wellington started to feel the first real twinges of sadness for the duke, when they found him propped up in what had once been the front parlour for this home.

"So dusty," Sophia complained, waving her hand before her, and she was right. This room appeared to have been locked up for years.

Sussex was leaning against a mahogany cupboard door. His skin was grey, his eyes bloodshot.

"Everything's gone," he murmured. His hand trembled up to fix the remains of his mask, as if it were a bowler in need of a milliner's attention. "My sweet Ivy is gone."

"Eliza," Wellington spoke softly, "check the house."

Sophia clicked her tongue. "That will not be necessary."

He fixed the assassin with a hard look, and then said to Eliza, "See if we are alone."

The Duke of Sussex did not notice Eliza leaving the

neglected parlour. His other hand continued to clutch the pho-
tograph close to his breast, the memory seeming to wear
heavy on him. His breaths were deep and ragged. Whatever
the serum had granted him, Wellington ventured, was now
determined to collect a due from the duke.

"My lord?" Wellington asked. "My lord, is this a picture of
your family?"

The duke looked at Wellington and gave a dry, cold laugh
as he nodded. "Oh yes, yes, my beautiful family. Ivy, and my
boys. We were visiting Europe last spring."

"Were you now?" Wellington asked, smiling warmly.

"Such a lovely time," the duke said, adjusting the mask
once again. Wellington dared not remove the remnants of his
alter ego, in case it were to spark a resurrection of the Maestro.
"But Ivy . . . she's gone. My sweet Ivy has left me."

Behind him, Wellington heard the footsteps of Eliza
returning from her search of the rooms. "Welly, there were
signs of someone being here, but whoever they were, they are
long gone now." She leaned in closer and added, "Along with
any valuables not nailed down."

"My Ivy." The duke smiled, holding the picture up to the
two of them.

Eliza's brow furrowed. "Welly, I went into the lady's room.
That's *not* the same woman."

"That is what I was trying to tell you." Sophia glanced
warily at the duke, and then beckoned Wellington and Eliza to
a corner of the room far from the duke. "The woman posing
as Ivy was one of Jekyll's patients. She received treatments in
exchange for her charade as the duke's woman."

"Where is the real Ivy Lawson then?" Eliza asked.

"That I do not know," Sophia said.

"My Ivy is gone . . ." Sussex then looked over to a cupboard
under what would have been the main staircase. ". . . but my
boys are still here."

Wellington followed the duke's gaze to the cupboard.
Swallowing back the knot growing in his throat, he flipped the
latch and opened the small door.

The smell threatened to knock him over. Sophia's posture
straightened ever so slightly as Eliza's hands went to her
mouth, the small gasp echoing in the confined cupboard.

"My boys, John and George," Sussex wheezed, a tone of pride still present in his voice. "They had been bad boys so I had to punish them, but they learned their lesson. I'm so proud of them."

The two corpses were in a process of natural mummification and were holding on to one another. Considering the comforts of the duke's home, it was more out of security. Had he forgotten about the children, or had something happened? Something so traumatic that it had pushed him over the precipice, into the "care" of Jekyll?

"My boys," Sussex gasped. His breaths were laboured even more now. "How proud you both have made me."

He drew in another shuddering breath. Then one more again.

The duke's body sagged, his eyes full of pride now emptying as his breath softly, gently joined the stillness of the parlour.

Slowly Wellington leaned over and touched his fingertips to the duke's neck. Nothing moved under them. Peter Lawson was dead, and so was the Maestro.

"And with that," Sophia said suddenly, causing them both to jump, "I believe our business is concluded."

Eliza stiffened. "You really are a charmer, aren't you?"

"If you endured what I had when he was the Maestro, believe me"—she scowled—"you would hardly feel pity for him."

Wellington touched Eliza's arm gently. "Ladies, please," he whispered, motioning with a nod to Sussex. Silently they stepped out of the old parlour and continued out to the front of the house. "Sophia is correct, Eliza," he said, the fresh air seeming to clear his mind already. "Our business is done here."

"And don't you have a queen to deliver?" Sophia smiled sweetly.

"We do." Eliza went to interrupt but Wellington held up a solitary finger, keeping her thoughts at bay for the time being. "And I'm sure Doctor Sound would have offered you some sort of compensation for your sterling service to Her Majesty."

"I have no doubt," she agreed.

"But," Wellington said, "he is not here."

Sophia's smile faded. "What do you mean?"

He turned to Eliza, shrugged, and said, "Snap decision in the field. We decide what must be done with you, and if you believe one good deed—"

"*One* good deed?!" Sophia protested.

"So, Miss del Morte, our business is concluded," Wellington said. "Best be on your way."

Sophia looked at them both. Wellington could just see Eliza in the corner of his eye. She seemed to understand what he was offering her.

"May I—?" and Sophia motioned to his motorcar.

"Don't even finish that ridiculous notion," Wellington interjected.

"We're giving you a head start," Eliza stated, "because considering all that has happened, we owe you something."

"A day's head start?" Sophia asked, tilting her chin up.

"We don't owe you that much," Eliza stated. "Try two hours' head start. You might be able to get pretty far in that time."

Once again, the assassin considered the pair of them and then nodded. "Two hours to choose my fate? I accept." She walked to the gate of the Sussex manor and paused. "I must say, working with you was hardly a pleasure, but it was most worthwhile." She kissed her fingertips in Wellington's direction. "Arrivederci!"

With that, she turned on her heel and proceeded down the city block. Her pace was hardly frantic or even hurried. If she had been dressed as a proper woman, she would have appeared to be enjoying the streets of London's upper-class district.

Wellington flipped the cover of his pocket watch open. "Two hours? You really do like her."

"We get the Queen to a physician and then we get on her trail." Eliza looked up at him. She really did have the loveliest blue eyes he had ever known. "Thirty minutes tops."

"Pick up her trail? Just like that?"

"Provided she doesn't find the tracking device in that corset I gave her, yes, just like that." Wellington looked at her. "On the rooftop." She gave a tiny snort. "You really didn't think I was checking that corset for her safety, did you?"

They walked back to the car in silence. Victoria was quiet in the backseat, her face still twitching and ruddy, her youth slipping away as they looked on her.

"You better remind me how fast this automobile can go," Eliza said on clambering into the passenger seat, "otherwise all of this will be in vain."

He leapt in beside her. "Utter chaos on the street, massive automatons fallen all over London, and a rapidly aging queen in our backseat? Just another day at the office, Miss Braun."

And with that, he opened up the boiler and accelerated away to set things to rights with the Empire.

TWENTY-ONE

❧

In Which Our Agents Hope
to Vanquish Old Ghosts

"Well, the cover-up is under way." Eliza folded the newspaper and tucked it into the console of the *Ares: Mark I*. How she had managed to read it while bouncing along through the Yorkshire countryside was quite the mystery to Wellington.

"What are they saying?"

She shrugged. "The Jubilee was an elaborate hoax devised by radicals to put a fake queen on the throne."

"Well-financed radicals, considering the Mechamen," he said with a grin.

"They don't speculate too deeply—that would destroy the mystery, sell less papers."

"Journalists do enjoy the fantastic." Wellington sighed, not entirely sure how he felt about being part of this cover-up. "How did Sound explain the Queen's appearance?"

"Yes, that." Eliza let out a chuckle. "Apparently the woman that had stood before her subjects, claiming her right to rule the British Empire, was nothing more than a young shop girl, snatched up for nefarious purposes purely based on her resemblance to the young Queen Victoria. As for the true queen—"

"Let me guess," Wellington interrupted. "The rightful and

elderly monarch was rescued by the fine agents of her government."

"Looks like the director's outrageous story took hold without a problem."

He shot his partner a look. "I don't like it any more than you do, my love, but Doctor Sound is unfortunately right. The public would lose everything if they lost faith in the Queen. Besides, how many more years can she possibly have?"

Eliza rolled her eyes, her gaze eventually falling on the pretty countryside passing by them. They were close now, and Wellington could feel his body tense in response. They passed through the charming village of Hebden Bridge, and headed out the other side, to the road that led to Whiterock. It should have been comforting to think that his estate was now serving the Queen. His grip tightened on the wheel. Instead it did not put his mind at ease.

Gravel crunching under the tyres of the *Ares* pushed memories to the back of his mind. Perhaps what he had planned today would alleviate some of these fears. For good.

"Remind me what we are doing here," Eliza said as they bounced along the driveway back to Whiterock. "Oh yes, that's right, you haven't told me why we have to be here. We could be back helping the rest of our fellow agents mop up the mess in London, or"—she slid her hand onto his thigh—"something even more fun."

"Or you could be reading, once again, that *æthermissive* you received after we sent word to intelligence agencies around the world their visiting delegations were all safe and sound. Rather fortuitous the Queen granted the Department so many technological wonders."

"Wonder if she will show similar appreciation to the Ministry?"

"Time will tell." He glanced over at her as his family estate appeared over the rise, far preferring the view of her than it. "So what was in that æthermissive?"

Eliza just smiled. "Good news."

He could see the strain around her eyes, the stress their journey over the Atlantic and across Europe had caused her. The children were safe. The Empire was safe for the time being. That responsibility had been lifted from her shoulders, and now she could enjoy a moment's peace. No one else would have been able to see it through, and that realisation made him rather happy. For Eliza, the Ministry meant as much as the Archives did to him, and she wanted to celebrate their success.

Raising her naked hand to his lips, he kissed it. "Trust me, darling, I want nothing more than to take advantage of some alone time with you as soon as I can, but there is something I need to do at Whiterock first." He gave her a rakish wink. "We may even find an empty room in the East Wing."

Her blue eyes traced his face, but she did not pry. As the Gothic face of the estate loomed before them, though, she asked suddenly, "Do you plan to move back here, Welly?"

The very idea made his throat dry up. He shook his head. "No, I couldn't abide that. If the Ministry needs a base of operations until Miggins is rebuilt, I think the manor serves Doctor Sound most admirably."

"The Old Man has no idea how good he's got it at White-rock," she offered.

"When Miggins is restored, perhaps it could serve as head-quarters for Research and Design."

She patted his leg and smiled at him. "I think that's a wonderful idea. I imagine that would annoy your father no end, if he could see it."

They pulled up before the main stairs. "I hope he can."

Eliza looked up at the grand estate's empty windows. "I don't care for it, truth be told. It was all right when the rest of the agents and the Seven were here." She jumped from the motorcar and went around to open Wellington's door, bending down and giving him a low bow as if she were a footman.

He stepped down and pulled her close for just an instant. "So, no lady of the manor for you?"

Her long, loud laugh told him all he needed to know. Miss Eliza D. Braun harboured no aspirations to be mistress of Whiterock.

Taking her by the hand, he led her back into the gloomy halls, the house's corridors, parlours, and floors eerily quiet as all hands, save for the two of them, were restoring London's East End. Wellington looked neither left nor right as he led her into the kitchen. She let out a slight *"Oh"* as he snatched up a small hatchet from the woodpile by the stove, but she didn't ask any questions. Adventure was one thing Eliza never denied, and he did love that about her.

Together they went up the main stairs to the bedroom that had once been his father's. Eliza kept pace with him, a slight smile on her face. Most women would have demanded answers about being led into a bedchamber with an axe. Wellington was not sure if that was just another endearing trait of hers, or something that should concern him greatly.

Wellington passed through the bedroom to the personal library. Letting go of Eliza's hand he yanked open the cupboard where they had shoved his father's chair. He glanced back at her, standing in the sun, her hands folded before her, watching with an arched eyebrow.

The chair sat before him, and suddenly Wellington found himself empowered by the sight of it. He wanted to clear the decks, make things anew, and that meant he had to get rid of his nightmares. He slipped out of his jacket and waistcoat, and passed both to Eliza.

"Tallyho, mate," Eliza said, draping his clothes across her arms and stepping back to give him more than enough room.

The first swing felt like freedom. The axe crashed into the chair, making Whiterock echo with each strike. Splinters bounced off his arms, cheeks, and even the lenses of his glasses as his hatchet made quick work of the chair's arms. Wellington gripped the axe handle tighter as he unleashed decades of emotions on the chair. Each blow was for his mother, and for him.

Wellington didn't stop until all that remained of Arthur Books' life-preserving chair were shards of wood, torn scraps of metal, and tangles of wire scattered across the floor.

"Welly . . ." Eliza's voice broke through his fugue.

He found himself slightly winded, a bead of sweat running down his forehead; but through the oncoming fatigue, he could feel the smile on his face. "If you are not too alarmed by my behaviour, Eliza, I think I can find—"

"No," she managed, tossing Wellington's jacket and coat to the floor.

Wellington followed her stare and felt his stomach tighten. She had not been admonishing him for his behaviour. It was the far wall of the master bedroom which had, at some time during his destruction of the chair, slid away. He had thought he knew all the secret passages and rooms in Whiterock, but the chamber before him apparently reduced that confidence to a bold assumption. His father, it seemed, had one last secret to share.

He glanced down at the remains of the chair. "Something must have triggered . . . "

Eliza's gaze locked with his, and for a moment Wellington considered grabbing her, locking up Whiterock once more, and telling Doctor Sound the Ministry was no longer welcome in his boyhood home. He didn't need or want any more surprises, nor did he wish to hear the voice of his father in his head anymore.

Yet, he was above all an archivist. He could no more walk away from secrets than Eliza could abandon explosives. He held out his hand. Eliza took it, and with a long, deep breath, Wellington led the way inside the final secret of Arthur Books.

Illuminated by light connected to the house's main lighting, the hidden chamber was not large, but roughly the size of a classroom or workshop. Pinned across the farthest wall were a number of charts and calendars. At the centre of the notes and pages was a horizontal line that ran the length of the wall. A timeline. For a moment, Wellington found it hard to focus on the various points along it, until his analytical talents took hold.

His fingers traced back to the beginning. Impulse made him read aloud, regardless of the grating texture evident in his voice. "Eighteen sixty-four, subject born. Weight seven pounds three ounces. Apparently healthy." He followed his fingertips only a few inches before he read again. "Fourteen months, subject takes first steps." All the milestones that parents celebrated were here. First word. (Kitty.) First sentence. ("I love you, Mummy.") First book read. (*A Study of Astronomical Theories.*) However, these cherished memories had with them accompanying notes with Wellington referred to as "subject" instead of his name.

Then came an event that turned his blood cold.

"Eighteen seventy-four, subject's maternal bond must be severed in order to progress development to full potential."

Wellington felt his throat tighten, and he had to steady himself against the table central to the room. He had always suspected, but never been able to prove, his father's involvement in his mother's death. Now here it was, right in front of him.

All part of a grand experiment.

He forced himself to continue reading. Various missions from his days in the military. The notes reflecting his acts of bravery, his accomplishments, and his distinctions. Honours that he believed won of his decisions, his actions. According to his father, these achievements were planned, if not expected. The timeline, however, ended abruptly. Wellington's gaze narrowed on the date of when his father's subject went awry.

"Eighteen eighty-eight," he read, his voice trembling through ragged breaths, "subject has taken an unexpected initiative. Project faces imminent failure if not corrected." Wellington swallowed, speaking to Eliza over his shoulder. "Eighty-eight. That was the year I joined the Ministry."

She didn't respond.

"Eliza?" *Please, Eliza, don't leave me here. Alone.*

He turned away from the timeline to find her lost in the pages of a ledger. In the dim light of the room, she was reading more detailed notes connected with the timeline across the wall.

It appeared some of his bad habits were influencing Eliza. "Subject's regimens with serums are complete," she read aloud. "Small doses may need to be given at annual intervals as required." She covered her mouth as her eyes darted from one page to another. Then she flipped the pages forwards in a flurry, then back towards the beginning.

Wellington looked around him, at moments of his life, fully embracing Arthur Books' final nightmare, his last poison. The discovery of the House of Usher ring he'd believed to be the worst thing he could learn about his father, but once again, he had underestimated the monster that had raised him.

No. Not raised. Engineered.

"Wellington," Eliza said, pressing her fingertips against one of the pages of the book in her hand, "this handwriting isn't your father's—but I recognise whose it is." She pinned him with her bright blue eyes, her lips trembling slightly as if she didn't want to say the words that would identify them. "It's Jekyll's. This handwriting belongs to Henry Jekyll."